MW01708713

TOMORROW'S EMPIRE

TOMORROW'S EMPIRE

SANDRA ARNOLD

ISBN 0 9582126 4 3

Design and pre-press by J. Elliott Freelance

Printed by Hutcheson, Bowman & Stewart, Wellington

Published by

HORIZON PRESS

Horizon Press
PO Box 5520
Lambton Quay
Wellington
New Zealand

Phone: 04 479 7337
Fax: 04 479 8589 or 04 233 8204
Email: horizon.press@xtra.co.nz

For Chris, Susannah, Benjamin and Rebecca

The author thanks Creative New Zealand for awarding her a
Major Project Grant to complete this novel

ABOUT THE AUTHOR

Sandra Arnold lives in North Canterbury with her husband and youngest daughter. She has also lived in England, Turkey, the USA and Brazil. She currently teaches English as a Foreign Language at Christchurch Polytechnic.

Sandra is a founding editor of the literary magazine *Takahe.* Her short stories have been widely published and broadcast and in 1992 she published her first novel *A Distraction of Opposites.*

What critics said about *A Distraction of Opposites*

"In this most competent first novel Arnold skilfully moves between dream and reality. Her writing is clean and taut, her characters convincing, her denouement satisfying. The book is no cosy duvet of a novel – rather it disturbs and extends the frontiers of New Zealand writing." *Daily Telegraph.*

"In this venturesome novel... her stories are about discovery, they are graceful, rainbow-coloured, often funny. The scenes are at once satirical and poignant." *New Zealand Herald.*

"Sandra Arnold's well-constructed and very impressive first novel... the tension is maintained throughout, the rhythms of speech and narrative are beguiling. This is a remarkably assured piece of work." *Christchurch Press.*

CHAPTER ONE

When I came out of prison, I asked my mother why she hadn't ever held me when I was a child. She said that she had been advised not to as no one expected me to live. She had given birth to four sons before I was born but none had survived infancy. My grandmother fed me from a bottle and washed and dressed me, but mostly I had been left lying alone in my cot. To everyone's surprise, I was still alive a year later. But by then Osman was born, followed a year later by Mehmed, and a year after that by Ahmet.

My brothers were noisy, boisterous children who liked nothing better than to kick a ball round our back garden, screaming at the top of their lungs. The only time I tried to join in ended with an asthma attack that almost closed off my air passages and my mother would not let me attempt it again. I used to watch them from the window of my bedroom, aching with a feeling I had no name for.

On my fifth birthday my mother asked our neighbour's son, who was visiting his family, to take a photograph of us with his new camera. He told Osman, Mehmed and Ahmet to stand together, 'The big ones at the back and the youngest in front,' and gestured to me to come forward. My cheeks flooded with shame and I stood still, unable to move or speak. My father stepped forward, pulling a chair with him and set it behind my brothers. He lifted me up and set me upon the chair, saying, 'Celik is our eldest.' The neighbour's son laughed. 'You'd better start eating more, little mignon, if you want to catch up with your brothers.'

I faced the camera pressing my lips together to stop them trembling and narrowed my eyes to contain the tears. When my mother showed the photograph to my relatives I heard my grandmother say with a sigh. 'What big, handsome boys, Ayesha. They are like Ismael when he was young. What a pity Celik had to spoil the photo with that sour expression of his.' I bent my head over my jigsaw puzzle on the floor, pretending I hadn't heard.

The summer was especially hot and golden with breakfasts in the garden after Ramadan and my mother bringing us pastirma, olives, cheese, cold meats, tomatoes, fresh bread and rose-petal jam. We had picnics on the city walls with my father after he finished work at the tanneries at the end of the day. And we spent hours in the Bosphorus learning to swim and fish. In all these activities I saw my younger brothers run faster, jump higher and swim further than I.

When the scent of wood-smoke filled the air and the leaves fell from the great plane trees my father took us to gather chestnuts. My brothers ran off whooping to see what was lying on the ground. I surveyed the trees. The nuts I could reach easily were too small. The best ones were on the highest branches but I didn't know if I could climb that far. And then, at the very top of a tree I saw the biggest chestnut I had ever seen in my life. A giant. I bit my lip in excitement and began to climb. I pushed my legs harder and higher, ignoring the scratches and stopping only to take breath. Finally, unbelievably, I reached it and pulled it off the branch. My heart sank a little. It was slightly mis-shapen, not as perfectly round as it had looked from the ground. But still it was as big as an apple and shining like dark honey. And it was mine. I rubbed it against my cheek enjoying the cool smoothness of the silky skin. Slowly, painfully, I climbed back down, my heart beating fast at the thought of showing off my prize to my father. I had to rest against the foot of the tree to steady my breathing before I could run over to my family who were still searching amongst the chestnuts on the ground. I saw Ahmet bend to pick something up and toddle over to my father with his hand outstretched. And in his open palm lay an enormous, perfectly round chestnut glowing with red-gold perfection. My father clapped Ahmet on the shoulder and told him how clever he was. I closed my eyes, sick with disappointment and dropped my chestnut on the ground.

'Find any good ones?' asked my father. I shook my head.

Ahmet took my clenched hand from behind my back, opened it up and put his wonderful chestnut inside, closing my fingers over it.

'For Celik,' he beamed and skipped away to find more. I wandered behind some trees as if I were searching for chestnuts, and dropped his gift on the grass, grinding it to pulp beneath the heel of my shoe.

From time to time I asked my mother to measure us against the wall. I saw the marks for my brothers go higher each time she did it but mine stayed the same.

'Why are they bigger than me even though they are younger? Why do they grow and I don't?'

'Don't worry,' she always replied. 'All this sunshine and fresh air will make you as tall and strong as your brothers.'

When the first icy blasts of winter blew in from the north, leaving lacy patterns on the windows but freezing the water in the pipes, my mother made Ahmet a new coat out of beautiful blue wool. She gave me the coat that Ahmet had worn last year. I fought back the tears of humiliation and asked her to measure us against the wall. Only my brothers' marks had changed. Every centimetre she added to their heights made my heart shrink a little more and now I knew my mother had lied.

As the dark, sleeting nights of winter kept us all indoors by the stove, my brothers pressed their faces against the window, willing the return of the sun. But now I felt a kind of relief, for they were forced to join in an activity that only I enjoyed. This was listening to my father reading stories of the Prophets from the Kasas-i Enbia and passages from the Masnawi. When my brothers squirmed with boredom he stilled them with a sharp command. I loved the deep, resonant tones of his voice. I closed my eyes and repeated words out loud even though I didn't understand their meaning, just for the pleasure of rolling the rhythm around my tongue. My father stopped reading, and when I opened my eyes I saw him looking at me with a smile. In all those freezing months in the prison I recalled that smile to bring me some warmth. He explained the meanings of the words to me in language I could understand and took me on his knee so I could follow the print as he read. He wrote out the letters of the alphabet and taught me how to put them together to make these beautiful sounds. I studied hard for I wanted to see the smiles of pleasure light his face when I read haltingly from the books he brought me. For my sixth birthday he gave me my own dictionary.

It was my job to help my mother serve coffee and sweet cakes to the women who visited her. I began to entertain them by singing songs and reciting passages from the Masnawi that my father had taught me. This had the astonishing effect of turning their attention away from the physique of my brothers and onto me. I listened to their praise with growing disbelief.

'He's a bright boy, that Celik of yours, Ayesha.'

'I've never heard a child that age speak like that. He sounds like a little adult.'

'That is why Ismael has decided he will go to school next term.'

'But he doesn't need to go for another year yet.'

'I know, but already he can read.'

This was the first time I had heard such plans but when I questioned my mother she said I must wait until my father told me himself. A few days later my father told me I was going to school.

'But I want to work in the tanneries like you, Baba,' I complained.

My father had worked in the tanneries since he was twelve, along with all his brothers. He had told us that, in the old days, criminals on the run used to escape into the tanneries and the police did not pursue them there. The tanners made them work in exchange for food and shelter and in some cases they became master tanners themselves. He also said that a tanner's wage was the most honestly earned money that existed and it was an honour for a pilgrim going to Mecca to be able to take with him money that came from a tanner. He put his hands on my shoulders.

'When you grow up you will be a strong man. Your strength will come from your knowledge. And the key to that knowledge will be your education.'

I did not understand what he was talking about but I knew that if he said this was so then it must be true. I had no idea what school was like but I thought it must be a wonderful place full of stories like my father's and I longed for the adventure to begin.

Large iron gates and grey concrete; our footsteps echo in the empty halls; rows of staring children in black smocks and white collars; a tall woman takes my hand and speaks to my mother – a gentle voice, with smoother tones than I am used to hearing, and she has soft eyes that look at me with pity.

I sit on my own in a huge chair and my feet can not touch the ground. In front of me the desk is too high to reach. I look around and see that mine is the smallest desk in the room. The other children know it too and titter and whisper behind their hands. On the dirty cream walls there is only one picture, an enormous portrait of a glowering man with blue eyes and bushy eyebrows. I sound out the letters under his name A..T..A..T..U..R..K. The children burst out laughing. I am determined they will not see my humiliation, so I laugh with them.

Soon after I started school a beautiful little blonde girl came to live in our street. She was paralysed and always stayed indoors, sitting at her window. I had never seen hair this colour before so whenever my mother let me out I visited her and stood under her window entertaining her by talking and singing. She enjoyed this and rewarded me with clapping and cheering. I liked to watch her blue eyes light up and the dimples appear in her round, pink cheeks when she smiled. I asked my mother why she was this colour.

'Because her father is German.'

This was the first time I had heard that another country outside Turkey existed and when I asked my teacher where Germany was she took out a large globe from a cupboard and showed me. I liked the shapes and colours on the globe and sounded out the names of the countries as she pointed them out. The teacher smiled with approval and gave me an atlas to take home. I lay on the floor on my stomach and traced the oceans and continents with my finger and said their names over and over so I would remember.

Within three months of starting school I caught ringworm and all my hair had to be shaved off. This was not particularly unusual so my bald head attracted little comment from my classmates. A few days later I passed by the German girl's house on the way home from school. She stared at me without any greeting. This puzzled me but I began singing a children's song, which we had learned that day, turning around the trunk of a young acacia tree that grew by the window as I did so.

'Don Baba Donelim,
Hacilara Gidelim.'

('Turn father turn, Let's go on the pilgrimage.')

I sang with great joy and happiness and as I finished I waited for her applause. She pointed at me, laughing, and threw a glass at my head. Blood splashed into my eyes. Crying with pain and shock, I ran home to my mother. When she asked me what had happened I told her I'd fallen and cut my head on a stone. When I could escape from my mother's clucking I ran to my room, hid under the bed and sobbed into my pillow so no one could hear.

My mother's voice soon called me from my hiding place. I must go to buy bread from the baker at Kocamustaphapasha. I wiped my eyes, my injured feelings at the girl's treatment now overshadowed by the fear of encountering the gang. On the street there was a gang of four boys, older and bigger than me, who ran after other small children and beat us up whenever they got the chance. I was afraid to walk alone around there so I always tried to stick by some elderly people to cross those dangerous parts of the street. On this day there were no other people around. The boys sat on a wall, smoking, and yelling insults to people passing by. They saw me and began to point and laugh. I walked quicker, pretending I hadn't heard them, but they began to follow me, shouting.

'Hey, baldy, what's the hurry? Stay and have a smoke. Or are you too good for us? Perhaps we need to teach you some manners.'

They surrounded me and closed in. My mouth went dry and my heart started pounding against my ribs. How could I save myself? I felt in my pocket for the little lead hen that I always carried. I held it out in the palm of my hand.

'You can have it if you let me go!'

Their leader snatched the hen then shoved me to the ground. Another one kicked me in the balls. An old man across the road waved his stick and shouted something and they ran away, laughing. I got to my feet, trying not to cry.

Not daring to let my mother see me bloodied a second time on the same day I washed my face and knees in a roadside fountain. As I splashed cold water in my eyes, rage welled up in my heart. Why did this always happen to me? Was my life always going to be like this? How could I stop it? I decided there and then to make a plan to protect myself, because nobody else was going to do it for me. When I returned home I went up to my room and wrote a note, twenty times, calling all the children in our street to a meeting at my house that evening to work out a plan for dealing with the gang. Then I delivered all the notes.

When the last child arrived at seven o'clock we crowded into the kitchen. I began by showing them the cuts on my nose and bruises on my legs. I added the cut on my head from the blonde girl for dramatic effect. There was a collective gasp at that one because the tissue had swollen around it and was turning violet and navy blue.

I said, 'If anyone else has been beaten by that gang, show us your bruises.'

Nearly everyone turned up his trousers or opened his shirt.

'Are we going to let this happen every time we go out on the street, or are we going to work out a strategy?' I asked.

There was silence, then a short, fat boy with glasses, called Yashar, murmured, 'What's a sta..stra.. that word what you said, Celik?'

I explained. 'If we all walk to school and back home again together they won't dare touch us. If we go to the shops for our mothers we can ask others to go with us. If we all stick together our safety will be guaranteed.'

Twenty pairs of brown eyes stared at me solemnly and twenty heads nodded.

As I showed them out the door Yashar hung back and said, 'What does guaran...you know, mean?'

I explained.

'How do you know all them big words?'

'I have a dictionary,' I said.

His eyes widened. 'All your own? To keep?'

I nodded.

'Wow! he said, as he slipped out into the night.

When I closed the door I went up to my mother's room and stood looking at myself in her mirror. Not only was I head and shoulders smaller than all my classmates, I was exceedingly skinny. If I were to lead an army against the street gang I must look like a general. I remembered the portrait of Ataturk in my classroom and the stories the teacher told of his bravery in leading Turkey through the war. I asked my mother to make me an army coat. She made it out of a khaki coloured rough fabric just as it was worn in the army, with epaulettes. When her eldest brother, also called Celik, came to visit us, he watched me try on the coat and admired it. He told me he would bring me something to go with it, on his next visit.

A few weeks later he handed me a parcel. I unwrapped it with great excitement and took out a white captain's hat. It was so beautiful and perfect, with a golden badge on the front, that I could only gaze at it in astonishment.

'It must be from Paradise,' I whispered.

He laughed. 'No! It's from Europe.'

'Does God live in Europe?' I asked.

My uncle burst out laughing and replied that Europeans had more science and technology, that was why they were so advanced. My father looked at me and smiled.

'As a Moslem you will gain even more knowledge. What we believe is the latest, purest truth in religion. And the source of this religion and the knowledge and the science is the same – God. He it is who created for you all that is in the earth – Koran 2:29. It is your Lord, the Most Bounteous, who taught by the pen, taught man that which he knew not – Koran 96:2-5. We shall show them Our Signs on the horizons and within themselves until it will be manifest unto them that it is the truth – Koran 41:53.'

My uncle laughed again. 'Ismael! The boy is not even seven!'

'That's old enough. What he doesn't yet understand he will learn,' my father said.

My uncle, who had a small leather shop in the city, said, 'Is that a requirement for the tanneries these days?'

'You can mock all you like,' said my father, 'but this boy is not going to the tanneries. He is going to the university.'

'What's university?' I asked.

'It's a place for scholars where you will go when you finish school at eighteen,' said my father. 'You will be there for three years.'

My heart sank. I had not realised I had to go to school for so many years. And now, according to this new information, even longer. I calculated how old I would be when I had acquired all this learning. Twenty one. My God! I would be an old man. My father couldn't be serious. I looked at his face, desperately trying to find a hint that he was joking. But no. I knew then that this was my future.

The next day I put on my army coat and the white captain's hat and waited till all the children in my street had gathered outside my door as we'd arranged. They gasped in astonishment at my uniform and stood back respectfully to let me take my place in front of them. The epaulettes made me look broader than any of them and with my hat, taller. We marched silently up the street on our way to school. Halfway there we met the gang, hanging round the fountain, smoking. My tongue stuck to my mouth and my breathing became shallow but I marched on and the children followed me. The gang stood up and stared at us with open mouths as we passed but they did not make a move towards us.

When we got to school we crowed like cocks at our success. And this success was repeated every day over the following weeks. The plan I had worked out now seemed so obvious to me I couldn't understand why I hadn't thought about it before. An unexpected and immensely gratifying bonus was that the pity I was used to seeing in the eyes of people who looked at me turned to an expression I had only seen when they looked at my brothers. My fame spread throughout our quarter. Children from neighbouring streets asked us if they could join us on our marches to and from school. Occasionally, to show generosity, I let someone touch my hat, but no one was allowed to wear it, though they eyed it hungrily.

Yashar said, 'It's not the hat what protects us, it's you, Celik. You saved us.' He stood looking at me beaming. I smiled back. This was the beginning of a friendship that lasted through a crisis worse than neighbourhood bullies in the years to come.

Halfway through my first year I took a test in mathematics and reading. The teachers decided to promote me to the next grade. I was disappointed to be leaving my nice, pretty teacher and my classmates, but what really worried me was that I had recently been almost able to touch the ground with my feet from my chair and I knew that the desks and chairs in the next grade were much bigger.

On the first morning in my new class I looked around anxiously. Not only were the desks and chairs and children even bigger than I'd feared but the teacher was a large, fat woman with a ferocious red face. Without any welcome she pointed me in the direction of an empty desk. I climbed into my seat. My feet swung ignominiously above the ground and the blood rushed to my face. The teacher opened her own desk to take out the register. She gave a hoarse scream. Terrified, I jumped out of my seat. Her already flushed face had deepened to the colour of beetroot and she was holding up a dead mouse by the tail.

'Who is responsible for this?' she bellowed in a voice that almost separated my skin from my bones.

The class fell silent. She stood up and towered over the front row of desks. Two girls squealed as the mouse was swung in front of their faces.

'If the person responsible for this does not own up immediately I will thrash the lot of you.' No one moved. She dropped the mouse into the rubbish bin and turned to unlock a cupboard. She took out a long, thin stick.

'You! Out here!' she yelled at the first row and a line of shivering children stood in front of her with their hands outstretched. She raised the stick above her head and swished it down across each palm. She continued in this way, showing no decrease in energy as she caned row after row.

I watched this performance with mounting horror and disbelief. My mouth filled with sick. I swallowed it down determined that no one would see my fear. When it was my turn to go to the front I pretended I was wearing my captain's hat. Even so, it took all my willpower to remain standing while the stick cut across my flesh, but the pain was nothing compared to my outrage at being punished for something I had not done. I made my way back to my desk, struggling to hide an even greater humiliation. I had wet my pants.

My hatred for school grew day by day. It was like a camp for training slaves. Whenever my teacher passed by the children had to bow from the waist or be beaten. To avoid being beaten for not bowing I avoided the routes taken by her. I was no longer interested in the lessons but I made sure I passed my tests with high enough grades to avoid feeling the sting of her cane again.

One by one, my brothers started school. Osman and Mehmed were popular with the teachers because they were polite and studied hard. Ahmet was loved by everyone because he was tall and strong and handsome and could play football. I began to hear the familiar remarks.

'It's hard to believe they're from the same family.'

'That young one is destined for great things in sport.'

Then one remark made me break out in a cold sweat.

'The eldest showed promise but actually his test results are very mediocre. I'll recommend that he goes back a grade next year.'

The thought of my shame in having to return to a lower class and study with children I gave protection to each day was enough to spur me into poring over my books at night in preparation for the end-of-year tests.

I finished the tests in half the time it took my classmates to do them. Three weeks later the teacher announced the results and with surprise in her voice said, 'And the top of the class in every subject is Celik.' She added that because of my high grades I could start learning a foreign language the following year, English or German. I thought of my treatment at the hands of the German girl and shuddered. I would choose English. When Ahmet told my father, sorrowfully, that he was bottom of his class I had to turn my face away to hide my smile.

When Ahmet was eight, my father decided to send him to the Military School. My mother did not want him to go as it meant he would have to board there, but my father said that the education there would be the best for him. My mother took him for the entry examination, praying for him to fail and be rejected, but, to everyone's surprise, he passed.

Before Ahmet left for the Military School, my father said it was time we were all circumcised. I had attended my cousins' circumcision ceremonies and listened horrified to their description of the process. I thought of the glint of razor-sharp steel with my blood on it and asked in a trembling voice why it had to be done.

'Do you want to stay a child all your life? You won't be a man until you're circumcised,' my father replied.

When the day arrived, we accompanied him to the mosque dressed in white satin suits and white hats. We each wore a red sash across our chest, with the good-luck word, Masallah, written in white. Everyone we passed smiled at us. I tried to smile back but waves of nausea left me feeling faint.

At home again we waited in the kitchen together, until my father summoned me to the living room first, because I was the eldest. Before we went in he said, 'You must bear this with courage and set a good example to your brothers.'

I nodded and straightened my shoulders, trying to look as tall as possible as I walked through the door. I looked straight ahead while I was being prepared, to avoid seeing what waited gleaming on the table. To stop any sound escaping from my mouth I bit my lip so hard I tasted blood.

My father lifted me and carried me to my bed. He patted me on the shoulder before he left and nodded his approval, but when he closed the door behind him I sobbed into my hands.

I had dried my tears before he brought Osman in, then Mehmed, both howling, and lastly Ahmet, who was white-faced, but dry-eyed. Relatives and friends came into the room to congratulate us, to give us presents and sweets and pin little bags of money to our bed. I heard someone say, 'Ahmet is so brave. Look, not even the trace of a tear.' The words cut into my heart as sharply as the blade which had made me a coward for all to see.

My father had arranged a Karagoz shadow show as a treat. My brothers forgot their tears as they laughed at the antics of Karagoz and Hacivat and Beberuhi and Celebi. I had been looking forward to this but now all I wanted to do was curl up in a dark corner on my own. I saw my grandmother's short, tank-like frame fill the door. I quickly re-arranged my face in a smile. One of the neighbours joked, 'Ismail! What kind of a circumcision party is this! You have forgotten the belly dancers!'

My father silenced him with a frown. At that, my false smile widened to a genuine grin, which had the added bonus of convincing my grandmother I was having the time of my life.

The tables groaned under the weight of all the food prepared by my mother and her sisters. Salads, pilavs, dolmas, chicken and lamb, bowls of yoghurt, candies, lokum, baklava and helva, all arranged on her best china tea set – a wedding present from her brother Celik, after whom I was named and who had given me the white captain's hat with the golden badge. This uncle came to me now and shook my hand.

'Well, Celik, how does it feel to be a man?'

I didn't know what to say but he was looking at me waiting for an answer so I murmured, 'May it please God that I will grow up to make my father proud of me.' I don't know where those words came from, but as I uttered them I knew that was what I wanted more than anything else in the world.

The day ended with storytelling. Everyone coaxed my mother to tell tales of her village childhood:

'Tell us about the time you were driving home in your father's oxcart and you passed a cemetery and you saw lights floating over the graves...'

'And about when you were driving the goats home at night and everyone was frightened to go past the fountain because it was haunted by a Jinn...'

'And when your sister was kidnapped because the man could not pay the Bride Price and his family kept her locked up in their house till she agreed to marry him and how your father...'

Six months after our circumcision my father woke me up early one morning. The grey light of dawn seeped into my bedroom through the cracks where the curtains didn't quite meet. I was puzzled because it was Sunday so I didn't have to go to school. He was smiling widely and told me to come to my mother's room. My mother was lying in bed smiling at me too and in her arms she was holding a white bundle. As I drew nearer I saw a tiny face with a yawning rosebud mouth. My own mouth opened in astonishment. 'How?...what?...who...?'

'She's your new sister,' said my father, 'and she is a gift from God. Her name is Hulya. You are the eldest so you must whisper her name into her ear and tell her you will be her protector for as long as you live.'

I took her from my mother's arms and held her carefully while I followed my father's instructions. When I looked up I saw my brothers standing in the doorway, their sleepy, amazed faces making me burst out laughing. Hulya's eyes opened at this sound and rolled around and crossed before shutting again. Something I had never felt before began to seed in my heart at that moment and flowered over the coming months as I watched this tiny new creature grow. I hurried home from school each day so I could feed her and sing her to sleep. Her first footsteps and her first attempts to talk gave me more pleasure than anything else in my life up till then.

Ahmet came home from the military school every weekend. He was now even taller than our father. Our kitchen was filled to bursting with neighbours and relatives who gathered to see him and hear his stories and admire the medals he had won for running and jumping.

'He's so handsome, Ayesha! And so tall.'

'He looks like Ismail when he was young.'

'His manners are so gentlemanly.'

'Ismael was right in sending him to Military School.'

'He will be a Colonel one day.'

'Whatever God wills.'

Even though asthma had stunted my growth and made me smaller and weaker than all my brothers I privately considered that I was the most handsome. My hair was darker, thicker and curlier than my brothers'; my eyes were bigger and brighter and my nose more beautifully formed. I leaned across and whispered this information to my Auntie Lale.

She grinned. 'Yes, you're right.'

As luck would have it, my grandmother heard and swatted me across the ear. 'You bad boy! You will put the evil eye on Ahmet with your jealousy! May God forgive you if anything happens to him.'

Auntie Lale saw my stricken face and whispered, 'Ignore the silly old cow. It's just superstition.'

Even so I watched Ahmet anxiously over the next few months until I forgot about my grandmother's warning.

One winter weekend he came home with a cough. It seemed to be worse with each visit and everyone was surprised because Ahmet was never sick. Then one weekend he didn't come home. We had a letter to say he was in the Military Hospital and the doctors had diagnosed TB. The neighbours flocked round to comfort my mother.

'Don't worry so Ayesha. He's young and strong. He'll get over it. My cousin did.'

The doctors sent Ahmet home the following spring. Auntie Lale found me brooding in the kitchen when she came over to visit him. She was only nineteen but her husband had died of TB in a sanatorium last year and she had returned to live with my grandmother.

'What's this long face for?' she smiled.

I swallowed. 'This is my fault, isn't it? Like grandmother said?'

She stroked my hair. 'Don't you believe any of that nonsense. TB is common in the military.'

'Will he get better?'

She paused. 'Some people do.'

I kick the first drift of falling leaves around the corner into our street, hoping that my mother has made saffron rice for dessert tonight. I will feed Hulya while my mother cooks and then I'll read Ahmet a story, even though he sleeps most of the time now. My mother has moved his bed into the living room by the stove where it is warm and she says he is getting stronger every day. But he has stopped eating and sometimes I see blood on his pillow.

Halfway up the street I hear a shrill keening. It sounds like the pig when my uncle cut its throat. I press my hands over my ears but I can't block out that sound. My mouth is dry. I can't swallow. My heart is going to burst. I see our neighbours poke their heads out of their windows and doors. They see me standing there and clap their hands to their mouths.

Then I am running, flying through our front door. Ahmet is on his bed by the stove. My mother and three of her sisters are bending over him. The noise begins again and I do not want to believe it is coming from my mother. I stare at my father who is standing apart from the group. He is as white as a statue and so still I can't be sure if he is breathing. I crouch down beside the door, covering the front of my trousers with my hands to hide the spreading stain.

My father stays in the room reading passages from the Koran and praying, until the arrival of the man who is going to wash Ahmet's body. I am sent across the road to my grandmother's house. She is sitting in her chair opposite my Auntie Lale, sobbing into her hands. I hear her say. 'Why him? The wrong one died!'

Auntie Lale looks up and sees my shocked face. She reaches out her arms to me but I turn and flee from the house.

Osman, Mehmed and I help my father and uncles carry the coffin to the mosque. As we walk away I turn and see my mother standing by the window, held upright by her sisters. This is just a nightmare and I will wake up because I can't believe it is really happening. When I wake up I will tell Ahmet how much I love him. I make a promise to God that I will never think a bad thought about my brother again. But now please let me wake up. Please.

We lay the coffin down on the stone table in the courtyard and go inside the mosque for afternoon prayer. Then we come out and stand beside the coffin to offer prayers for Ahmet's soul. I stand next to my father and the Imam begins, 'How do you know this person? Can you witness if he was good?' I see Ahmet in my mind when he was two years old, taking my hand and giving me his wonderful chestnut. I see myself, sick with jealousy, crushing his gift under the heel of my shoe. I do not want to hear the Imam's words. I do not want to look at the coffin. I want to run away and hide in a place where no one can ever find me.

After the prayers we carry the coffin to the part of the cemetery where all my father's family are buried. My father and uncle open the lid and lift Ahmet out of the coffin. They lower him into the newly dug grave, lying him on the ground, facing Mecca. Then my uncle loosens the white wrapping sheet so that his body will mingle more easily with the earth. It slips off his face. I don't want to look at him but I can't avoid it. When I see that grey face and blue unsmiling lips I understand with all my mind and all my heart that Ahmet has gone. No breath moves in that dead chest, nor ever will, while I continue to live and breathe though I have no right. No right at all. The wrong one died, said my grandmother. Pain fills my stomach, squeezes my chest, my throat, fills my ears.

Dimly I hear the Hodja put the questions to Ahmet that he will have to answer before he is admitted to Paradise. He calls his name. 'Ahmet, son of Ayesha...'

My father reads from the Koran, 'My God forgive his sins and exalt his place in your presence. I send this to the soul of my son. Praise be to Allah, Lord of the world, the Beneficent, the Merciful, Owner of the Day of Judgement. Thee alone we worship. Thee alone we ask for help. Show us the straight path. The path of those whom thou hast favoured. Not the path of those who earn thine anger nor of those who go astray. He is Allah the One, Allah the eternally besought of all. He begetteth not nor was begotten. And there is none comparable unto him.'

Everyone turns to leave the cemetery, reading passages from the Koran and sending them as presents to Ahmet's soul. As we walk away leaves fall from the plane trees, wood-smoke drifts on the wind. A chestnut falls through the air towards me. I reach out my hand and catch it. Hot tears burn my cheeks. When we get home, my father is very angry with me.

'He is with the Prophet himself now. Is that something to cry about?'

'No father,' I weep, my fingers closing around the chestnut in my pocket, 'but it says in the Koran that even Mohammed cried at his mother's grave.'

He stares at me for a moment then turns abruptly and leaves the house.

My mother no longer laughs. Sometimes she sets a knife and fork at Ahmet's place on the table at weekends. We pretend not to notice. My father spends more of his time in the mosque. When he is home he is always reading the Koran and his green leather-backed Masnawi. So that my father will not see me cry I stay in my room as much as possible. One day I am lying on my bed staring at the ceiling. He opens the door and comes into my room, holding the Masnawi in his hand. He sits on the side of my bed and hands it to me, already open at a marked passage. I barely glance at it.

'I don't understand it,' I tell him sullenly. He takes the book from me.

'Mevlana says we must celebrate death like a wedding, for death is the soul's return to God. You must learn to understand the language. Then you can read the whole book for yourself and understand why you must not cry for your brother.'

My eyes begin to fill. He stands up and leaves the room, closing the door quietly behind him, whereupon I turn my face into my pillow to stifle my tears.

At school people look at me with pity and stop talking when I approach. I hate their pity and their uncomfortable silences. To stop this I begin to mimic the teachers' voices and mannerisms and develop to perfection the art of playing the clown. In the playground I am usually surrounded by a crowd of children and I pick up the swear words used by the older boys. I discover that I can make people laugh. Occasionally I hear adults whisper how well I am coping, but sometimes their lips tighten. Once I hear a neighbour say the word 'callous'. I look it up in the dictionary. My face flushes red with anger when I read the definition. 'Those bastards know nothing!' I cry.

I decide not to go to school that day and join my new friends behind the fountain, smoking and shouting rude remarks to people passing by: 'Hey, baldy, is that a head or a light bulb on your neck?' This makes my friends roar with laughter. Encouraged, I get bolder and when a young girl of about sixteen saunters past I slip behind her, swaying my hips and tossing back my hair. My friends collapse. Tears pour down their cheeks and they can scarcely breathe. They beg me not to return to school and I join them as often as I dare. We spend our days roaming the streets, stealing bread, fruit and cigarettes from the market.

Lale smells cigarette smoke on my clothes. 'You stupid boy!'

'I don't care,' I say.

After I fail all my end-of-year exams my teachers take the unusual step of writing to my father. When he reads their report he gives no sign of emotion. Next day he goes to my school. When he returns he does not tell me what has taken place at the interview and I know better than to ask. To my amazement, however, he says, 'It seems that you won't be going to university now, Celik, but I may be able to get you a job in the tanneries.'

We ride a short distance in the train and walk past some run-down wooden houses. Here, even though snow is on the ground, several women, dressed in the baggy floral pants and headscarves of Anatolian peasants, are dying wool in tubs on the pavement. Hanging over the fences are old carpets they are going to repair.

Then the air turns sour, at first like a hot room full of boots after a football match. As we approach the tanneries the smell becomes a thick, permeating stench that coats my throat and stings my nostrils. The factories are huddled together in a maze of filthy, wet, narrow streets. Men move in and out of doorways shouting to each other above the screaming machinery. Some are standing in groups eating meatballs from kofta stalls or washing their hands in roadside fountains.

We go into a building where I see some apprentices, boys my own age, working with skins in big tanks of water and the water slops about on the floor, ankle deep. I remember my father's hands each winter, red and swollen because he has to break the ice in the tanks before he can start work. The stink is so bad I can't breathe.

My father explains. 'Here they use dog shit to soften the hides and it is the task of the apprentices to gather it.'

I stumble outside, appalled that I am losing the struggle to subdue my heaving guts. My father follows, not noticing my plight, and buys some meatballs from a kofta stall. He hands me one. I look at the greasy grey lump, feeling the blood drain from my head and lean against a wall for support.

'Eat,' he commands. 'We have a long day ahead of us.'

I put it in the back of my mouth and gulp it down quickly so I do not have to taste it. It sticks in my throat and I begin to choke. Someone comes out of a doorway in front of us and throws down a steaming pile of animal fat and hair and tails. I slowly slide down the wall. As I crumple to the ground the last thing I see is my father's face. He is watching me, smiling.

CHAPTER TWO

Three months after Ahmet died my grandmother died too – of a broken heart, people said. I asked Auntie Lale if this was true, ready to add another sin to my overburdened conscience.

'Rubbish,' she said, 'No one dies of a broken heart. She was so fat her heart could no longer take the strain of keeping her alive, that's all.'

I gasped, then burst out laughing. Lale smiled.

My grandmother's death meant that Auntie Lale had to come and live with us because she was my father's youngest sister. Her name means tulip. When she was sixteen her marriage had been arranged to a man twenty years her senior. They had lived in Germany for a year then he got sick and they had to return home. He went to a sanatorium and Lale went back to her mother.

A month after grandmother died Lale came downstairs one morning wearing a light blue cotton dress and matching high-heeled shoes just like the pictures in foreign magazines that I sometimes saw on the news-stands. Her long, black hair was tied back off her face with a blue ribbon. Her lips were bright red. At the sound of my mother's gasp my father looked up from his newspaper.

My mother said in a trembling voice, 'Go and take those... things... off at once. Your mother...'

Lale laughed, 'I'm not a child, Ayesha. I shall dress as I please. And why should my mother's feelings worry you now she's dead?'

'That's enough!' My father stood up, scraping his chair back along the wooden floor.

'If I upset you then I can go and live in a flat,' said Lale in a quiet, cold voice that I had never heard from her before, 'but you are not going to tell me what to do, how to dress, or how to live my life.' And she turned and left the room.

No one moved. We all stared at the door. Lale's footsteps clattered along the wooden floor in the hall. The front door opened and shut. In one movement my mother gathered up the breakfast dishes and slammed them into the sink. My father sat down again and buried himself in his newspaper. Apart from the speed of my mother's dish-washing, nothing had changed in the room and I couldn't believe what I had just heard.

For the rest of the day I couldn't concentrate on my lessons. I kept seeing Lale in her lovely dress, my mother's blanched face, my father's inability to stop Lale doing what she wanted. When I got back home in the afternoon there she was, sitting in the kitchen reading a magazine about Germany. I asked her what the reactions of the neighbours had been when she walked down the street in those clothes.

She shrugged. 'How should I know? I pay no attention to that kind of thing. If they have nothing better to do with their time than gossip about me then at least I'll have given them something interesting to think about. Here, come and look at these pictures.' But I was too disturbed to sit beside her and made an excuse about homework.

A week later I accidentally burst into the bathroom after she had just stepped out of the shower. She was wrapped in a large towel and was sprinkling her arms with a white powder. It smelled very sweet.

'What is it?' I asked.

'Talcum powder,' she said, 'here, try some.' And before I could stop her she threw some on my neck and hair and rubbed it in with her hand while I wriggled to escape her grasp, choking with laughter. That night as I tossed and turned in bed I could still smell it. I woke up next morning feeling exhausted.

My mother tried to insist that Lale keep to the women's part of the house when my father had visitors, but Lale only laughed at her. She laughed a lot and that seemed to upset my mother even more than the way she dressed. But whenever she walked into a room where my father was his face softened, and his voice took on a lighter tone. I mentioned this to my mother.

Her lips tightened in the way they did every time she looked at Lale and she said, 'Her father was killed before she was born. Her mother was very ill for a year or so after the birth and couldn't look after her, so your father and his sisters cared for her. They all spoilt her and she grew up assuming the world existed just for her pleasure. Her husband was just as bad. All she had to do was smile at him and she got exactly what she wanted. And, as you see, she can wrap your father around her little finger.' She beat the batter in the mixing bowl with more vigour. 'What she needs is a good whipping. The way she behaves how on earth will we ever be able to find her another husband?'

I already knew that Lale did not want to get married again. She had told me that her husband had left her some money so she had no need to depend on another husband. I was thinking about this while I was eating my breakfast in the kitchen with Lale. I wanted to ask her what she would do with her life if she didn't get married, but it was a very personal question and while I was struggling to form it my father walked in holding the newspaper open in front of him.

He said in an excited voice, 'Listen to this: *American archaeologists have completed their excavations of the tumuli around Gordion. One of the larger mounds contained the skeleton of a boy aged about five. The body had been placed on a bed in one corner of the chamber and on the floor were bowls of food and toys in the shape of small wooden animals. In the other large tumulus they found two elaborately decorated screens and ten tables loaded with beautifully worked bronze grave offerings. There was also a skeleton of a man aged about sixty which they believe to be that of King Midas.*'

My spoon stopped halfway to my mouth.

Lale said, 'He was a real man?'

My father said, 'It says here: *According to Phrygian tradition an oracle had predicted that one day a man would come in a wagon to rule over them. As the elders were discussing the oracle, a peasant appeared with his donkey and cart. His name was Gordius and he was proclaimed king. To show his gratitude he dedicated his wagon to the Goddess Cybele and tied the yoke and shaft together saying that whoever undid the knot would rule over all Asia. It stayed there for centuries until the arrival of Alexander the Great. The next king of Gordion was Gordius's son, Midas. Under his rule the kingdom achieved vast wealth.*'

I was infected by my father's enthusiasm over this news. I tried to recall the stories I had read about Midas. 'Everything he touched turned to gold. Was that true?'

'There was gold in the Pactolus River,' my father said. 'That was probably the origin of the story where Midas accidentally turned his daughter into a gold statue and he was so grief-stricken that Bacchus told him to go and bathe in the river and be freed of the curse. When he did the power left Midas and passed into the sands of the river bed.'

Lale said, 'My favourite used to be the one about Midas hiding his ass's ears under a hat. When his barber found out and couldn't keep the information to himself he dug a hole in the ground by the river and whispered the secret into it. But when the wind blew, the rushes released the secret.'

My eyes grew wide as my imagination played with the picture of the barber whispering secrets into a hole in the ground. Lale laughed at me and teased, 'We'll go there one day and whisper our secrets into the ground just like Midas did. But we'll do it on a day when there is no breeze blowing. We don't want the whole world to know our secrets, do we?'

I had no idea what she meant but I blushed crimson and, for once, was glad when my mother came into the kitchen and told me to hurry up or I'd be late for school, so that I had an excuse to bolt.

When I got to school the teacher also read out the news about the discovery of Midas's tomb. She told us we would do a school play about the arrival of Alexander the Great in Gordion and the untying of the knot. She asked for volunteers to audition for the parts of the characters. I immediately volunteered to audition for the part of Alexander. I thought it would be wonderful to play the part of such a conqueror.

After the auditions were completed she read out the names of the children who were successful. No one paid much attention to what she was saying and carried on with their conversations as if they couldn't care less whether they got the parts or not. I pretended to rummage for something in my school bag to hide my concentration as I waited for her to call my name. But she folded up her list and started to give instructions about rehearsal times. I straightened up and assumed a bored expression to disguise my disappointment, though my stomach was hurting because I had clenched my muscles so hard. The boy who had been chosen was head and shoulders taller than I, and very broad and handsome. I heard him complaining to his friends about having to give up his free time for a dumb play.

Then the teacher said, 'Of course Alexander didn't actually untie the knot, he sliced through it with his sword. There was an eclipse of the sun at the same time and the local people took this as a sign that the predicted ruler had arrived.'

Now, my disappointment turned to amusement. Cut the knot with his sword? What a trickster! I was glad I was not playing the character of such a person. I decided I would tell this to Lale later but then thought of the way she would laugh and tease me, so in the end I decided to keep it to myself.

My mother didn't like the way Lale treated me as an equal. The truth was Lale had no friends of her own age. She said that after her husband died she had to spend all her time taking care of my grandmother.

'She was a domineering old woman and now I'm free of her. It bores me to tears listening to all this talk of cooking and children and husbands. Look at all these women round here. They're like dried prunes. In Germany I had a job typing in a lawyer's office. I bought my clothes with my own money... oh... let's go out and feel the sun, Celik.'

I too disliked staying indoors in fine weather but I had never before realised that women could feel the same. My mother, and all the women I knew spent their whole time cleaning and cooking and looking after children. It had never occurred to me to wonder whether they enjoyed it or not. I simply thought that's what women did. This new revelation startled me. The secret about Lale's job was shocking. I tried to imagine her going out to work in her European clothes. As I thought of my mother's horror if she knew, I felt a delicious thrill of complicity run up my spine.

Now, for the first time I started noticing how hard my mother worked. I wanted to ask her if she ever felt like spending a day just watching the ships in the Golden Horn and enjoying the warm sea breeze. But I didn't ask because I knew she would realise Lale had put those questions in my head, and I knew by now not to give her any more ammunition to fire at my beautiful aunt.

The summer was so hot. We spent our time walking all over the city. When the days were humid we walked by the Bosphorus to watch the fishing boats. Lale let me go swimming and sometimes, even if there were people about, she swam herself. I never told my mother that.

We walked to the Old City and explored the mosques and museums and palaces and she told me tales of the Ottoman Sultans that she had learned from her husband, who had been a teacher.

'I didn't love him,' she told me, 'but I respected him for his intelligence and kindness.' This confidence sent a thrill like an electric charge through my body.

I loved the story about Mehmet the Conqueror. Lale said, 'He was undersized, Celik, but because of his military brilliance he was able to capture Constantinople from the Christians and make it part of the Turkish Empire.' And she looked at me with big, round eyes that reminded me of the day I overheard my grandmother telling her it should have been I, not Ahmet, who had died. I didn't say anything but I knew Lale remembered that moment too and I didn't mind because I wanted her to go on looking at me like that.

When we went to see the Byzantine mosaics in Santa Sophia, she whispered, 'It was only because of Mehmet's tolerance of other religions that they have been preserved.'

Once, we went to the Covered Bazaar. There were so many people and the sunlight shone through the glass roof and onto the brass plates and jugs in the dusty little shops, making them sparkle like gold. Each shop smelt old and full of treasures. But the heat was intense and my feet must have been dragging at last because she said, 'Just around the corner, then – a surprise.'

One minute we were part of the surging crowd and the next we were in a tiny courtyard with a big shady tree growing in the centre. An oasis of peace and quiet. I couldn't believe it and stared at her. Her eyes were shining.

When we walked past the fancy European shops of Istiklal Cad, and the restaurants, theatres and hotels of Taksim, she said, 'One day, Celik, you'll be rich enough to go in those places.' And because she said it, I believed her.

The leaves turned crimson and gold and gusts of wind tore them off the trees, scattering them through the grey streets. Lale and I ran into the leaves, crunching them under our feet and throwing them high in the air and laughing. She noticed my ears were blue with the cold so she took my scarf and wound it around my head like a turban, letting one end dangle over my ears. I protested that I looked ridiculous.

She said, 'No! You look like a Pasha!'

So I assumed the role. We were approaching a soldier on guard at Topkapi Palace and I saw him stare at me with a slight smile. Lale saw it too and she took my arm and as we passed by she stared back at him, as bold as a gypsy. His smile disappeared and he looked straight ahead. As soon as we were out of sight I laughed so much the tears were pouring down my cheeks.

When I recovered I said, 'Lale, you are amazing!'

I was so proud to be seen in her company with her hand on my arm that

I felt as tall and strong and broad-shouldered as that guard.

We went inside the palace, which had been a museum since the Republic was founded in 1923, and stared at the jewelled thrones of the Sultans and the gold cradles of their princes. At rubies and emeralds as big as ostrich eggs and diamond encrusted swords. At the tiled rooms in the harem, which had once been the most mysterious and carefully guarded place on earth. We stood in the gateway where the sultans had departed on their campaigns to bring victory and glory to the Empire. As we emerged from the palace and walked to Sultan Ahmed Square I was lost in daydreams. I was Mehmet, or Bayazid, or Selim or Sulieman about to set forth to put things in order in barbarous Europe.

A group of tourists stopped in front of us to take photographs of the mosque. They were English girls about the same age as Lale. She touched my elbow and pointed to their shoes. They had very high heels. I had not seen such shoes before.

One of the girls said, 'That mosque looks as though it's floating in the air.'

I looked at it and saw she was right. I had not noticed that before.

Then another girl replied, 'It amazes me that in such a barbarous country they were able to produce this architecture. All those bath houses, schools and hospitals built around the mosques. Incredible town planning.'

'All the more incredible when you see the crap they've produced since the Republic was formed.'

Lale asked me if I understood what they were saying and as I started translating for her they turned round and walked past us. One of them, a tall girl with blue eyes and blonde hair looked at me and smiled. In her smile I thought I could see that she was looking at a tall, handsome boy. I smiled back.

Lale saw my expression and laughed, 'She likes you, Celik!'

I felt sweat break out on my back and chest and I was appalled to feel my cock swell till it seemed as if there was a cucumber stuffed down the front of my jeans. I tore my jacket off and held it in front of me, my face burning. We watched the English girls till they hailed a taxi and were driven away.

When the days grew colder we bought salep from street stalls and sprinkled cinnamon on top, sniffing the spicy aroma before we let our frozen lips taste the delicious hot liquid. At home, on the evenings when my father was at the mosque and my mother out visiting relatives, my brothers and I pulled the mangal into the middle of the living room and filled it with charcoal from the stove. Lale roasted chestnuts on top and we all ate and talked until we were hot and full and sleepy. We curled up on cushions on the floor like fat lazy cats and gazed at the glowing charcoal in the darkening room, enjoying the heat on our faces and the comfortable silence. I watched the shadows dance on Lale's face and saw so much sweetness and softness there that I longed to reach out and touch her cheek with my finger tips.

In the winter, Lale developed a cough. At first it was not particularly noticeable but it was persistent. By the following spring, I had become aware, in the way that I was able to put things into separate categories, that she stayed in her room a lot. Nobody mentioned it and I ignored it too. We still walked everywhere together but she had to keep stopping for rests. Gradually our walks became shorter and fewer. And she sometimes seemed to be preoccupied because when I spoke to her she just looked at me without replying.

One evening we walked over Galata Bridge because Lale wanted to watch the sun set over the mosques. I sat on the wall and Lale leaned over it, staring at the water. The sounds of the city surrounded us. Home-going crowds jostled for space with honking traffic and shouting street pedlars. The constant booming of ships echoed in the Golden Horn with the sirens of the packed ferry boats crossing to the Asian side. Fishing boats unloaded their catches on the dock side watched by waiting shoppers. And the smell of fish and exhaust fumes soaked the evening air.

After a long silence, Lale turned to me. 'Celik, what are you afraid of most?'

I was surprised and didn't know how to answer. Then I said, 'I'm afraid of not making it to university.'

She looked at me, smiling, 'The tanneries?'

I shook my head. 'If I don't go to university, I won't be an officer when I do my military service. My worst nightmare is that I find myself in the army as a private. Then I wake up covered in sweat and crying.' I looked away, embarrassed by my revelation. I had told it to no one before.

She touched my cheek. 'Your worst nightmare? Poor Celik.' Her fingers were cool and I wanted her to go on looking at me for ever with that expression in her eyes, but she turned away, coughing.

Her coughing got worse and she spent most of her time in her room. My father grew silent. When he heard Lale coughing he would glance at my mother but she always looked away.

I was walking back from school one day when an American tourist asked me to direct him to the Castle of the Seven Towers. It was near our house and therefore easier for me to take him than to try and explain where it was in my halting English. He was very pleased and gave me one hundred lira. I did not want to accept it but he insisted.

On the way home I passed a flower shop with jugs of tulips crowded together on the pavement. I stopped to admire them, such a splash of red and yellow on the drab grey stone. Then, with the American's money, I bought a big bunch to give to Lale.

I hurried home but when I got there, I felt awkward and stood in the kitchen not knowing what to do next. Then I heard her coming slowly down the stairs. She walked into the room and immediately saw me standing there, holding the flowers. Her eyes opened wide and she smiled when she realised my confusion. She took the tulips from me saying quietly, 'Thank you, Celik. No one has ever given me flowers before.' Then she leaned forward and kissed me on the cheek. I smelt her soft skin and felt the warmth of her lips. I closed my eyes.

When I opened them, I saw my mother standing in the doorway, watching us. She didn't say a word. She turned and went out of the room before Lale even realised she was there.

After that, my mother kept trying to occupy me with jobs away from the house. One day, she gave me a picnic lunch and told me to take my brothers to the city walls and not return before evening because she wanted to clean the house. I trailed reluctantly behind them as they ran off to look for cannon ball marks. For a long time I sat on my own while they rushed about exploring, but then they were bored and begged me to play with them. So I was Sultan Mehmet riding on his white horse, telling the Byzantines (my brothers) not to fear, for although I had captured their city, they would find me a kind and just ruler.

And so the day passed. And strangely, I enjoyed myself. Then the gradual awareness of hunger reminded us it was time to go home.

Osman and Mehmed took the quickest way back, through the thistle fields. But I wanted to be alone so I chose a longer route.

I reached the end of our street. Dinner smells drifted on the air. Not many people were about, a few men digging in their allotments, the occasional horse and cart hurrying homeward, mothers calling their children in from the streets. Lost in daydreams, I almost fell down a hole in the road. I looked around for something to cover it and saw stones and rubble from a nearby demolished house. As I dragged these over, a man stepped from the shadows and said, 'May Allah be pleased with you. I covered it myself this morning but someone kicked away the stones.'

Pleased by his praise, I ran the rest of the way home, arriving at the door just as the call to prayer filled the evening quiet.

There was no one in the kitchen, but the smell of dinner cooking made me realise how hungry I was, so I took a dolma from a plate on the table. I heard raised voices from the living room so I went out into the garden and glanced in the window. My mother and Lale. I couldn't hear what they were saying but their faces were red. Lale turned and strode out of the room, slamming the door behind her. My mother stood staring at the door for a moment, then covering her face with her hands, she began to cry.

I returned to the kitchen and crept quietly upstairs. Lale was coughing very badly in her room. I slid into my own room, wondering what to do. Then I began moving things about noisily so she would hear me and know I was there. After a minute, her door opened and she called, 'Celik, come here, I have something to give you.'

I jumped up and ran into her room. She was standing with her back to the window so I couldn't see her face clearly. Then I noticed she was holding a dish of something in her hands. Something red and yellow. Sweets? Fruit? My mouth watered in anticipation.

'Take this to your mother.'

Disappointment.

'Show it to your mother.'

I took the dish and glanced at the contents. For a moment – utter disbelief. Then the bile rose from my gut and the blood drained from my head.

I turned and went downstairs to the living room, pausing outside the door. My mother had stopped crying so I opened it slightly. She was kneeling on the floor and I couldn't see her face as it was covered with the white veil she wore during prayer. Closing the door I went out into the garden and buried the dish in the soil.

Then I ran back to my room and after locking the door, threw myself into bed, curling up into a tight ball with the blankets over my head.

Next day, Lale called me to her room again. Her face was white though her cheeks were flushed. 'You didn't give that dish to your mother, did you?'

I looked at my feet.

'What did you do with it?'

Silence.

'Get it and bring it to me.'

I dug it up and returned it to her without speaking. She snatched the dish from my hands, muttering, 'Idiot child!'

I stared at her but she turned away.

After that I didn't see her again because she was taken to the sanatorium. A short time later, she died there. Everyone said I took the news very bravely. They kept watching me to catch me off guard.

CHAPTER ♦ THREE

A month after Lale's funeral I walked across Galata Bridge to the spot where she had asked me to tell her my greatest fear. In the driving rain and bitter wind I stood still and tried to remember the warmth of her fingers as they brushed my cheek, but I could not. My hands and face, numb with cold, were not as chilled as my heart.

I don't know how long I stayed there. When I straightened up I was stiff, and frozen with misery. Then, without any warning, I saw her. She was about three metres in front of me, hurrying in that way she had with quick, little steps, head held high, tossing her curly black hair over her shoulders. I couldn't move until she was almost out of sight then I forced my legs to function. Her face, her smell, her voice were so vividly in my senses as I ran after her. I had almost caught her up and I yelled, 'Lale! Wait!' She turned round, startled. And it wasn't Lale. Of course it wasn't Lale. I ran on past her, pretending I was calling for someone else. I kept on running till I got home and I locked my door and fell on my bed. This pain was as hard as bone, with edges that stopped my breath.

I recalled the face of the girl I had followed and her look of surprise when she saw me running after her. To my astonishment my cock stood up hot and hard against my hand and a warm sticky jet spurted over my fingers. The pain in my chest softened.

I played that game on and off over the next few years. I learned to develop a polite, impassive mask so that no one could possibly suspect me of such behaviour. At the same time I applied myself vigorously to my studies so that I finished each year with the highest grades in the class. My grades made me popular with the teachers and I took care to keep on the right side of my classmates by dismissing my achievements with a casual, 'I was just lucky!'

In the darkness of my room I recalled the faces of the girls I followed. Until one day I got careless and the girl turned round and yelled at me in a coarse voice, 'What? Are you some sort of pervert or something?' Her mouth was screwed up and she jabbed her finger at me as if she would stick it in my eye.

A crowd gathered round her and stared at me, jeering and laughing. 'Look at the little mignon-steak! Go home to your mother's tit!'

A split second before I fled in horror I saw a friend of my father standing at the edge of the crowd. He was looking straight at me.

Each time my father came home during the following week I glanced nervously at his face. Nothing in it betrayed that he had learned of my activities. I began to relax. When I handed him my mid-year report I was confident he would be pleased, but as he read he didn't comment on my high grades. He just said, 'Woman's attraction comes from her physical appearance, while man's from his use of language. So said the Prophet. May God be pleased with Him and may God's peace be with Him.'

He didn't look at me as he said this but I felt my face and neck burn. I coughed and said awkwardly, 'How can I discover the source of this power of attraction?'

'You'll need to read the classics of literature from east to west,' he said.

Feeling weak with relief I muttered, 'Then I had better enrol in the Advanced English class.'

He nodded.

At the end of that year, which was my final year, my father told me to enrol at the University of Istanbul to study economics and business administration.

'You will be able to work in a bank when you graduate and become a bank director eventually,' he said.

I had not actually thought about what courses I should study or what I would do when I graduated and although economics did not seem particularly interesting if that was what my father thought was best it did not occur to me to argue. Osman was in his last year at school and was planning – at my father's urging – to go to university the following year to study political science. Mehmed, at my father's insistence, had gone to military school.

At the end of my first year at university my father told me to find work in the summer vacation to earn my pocket money. I found one at Pershembe Pazari near the Golden Horn, where the trade and industry of Istanbul was based. The job was boring, consisting of debit credit balance mathematics and waiting in queues to pay taxes at gloomy government offices. I hated being stuck indoors and kept gazing out of the windows at the blue sky and golden sunshine, though whenever my father asked how I was doing I said, 'It's good experience for me.'

A couple of weeks after I started work, another boy about my age joined the office. He came straight over to my desk and said, 'Hi, I'm Omer.' I was very flattered for he was tall and handsome. He asked me to go out with him to have lunch. All the girls stared at him as we walked along the street and into the café, though he seemed not to notice. I tried to pretend it was me they were looking at.

Over the next few days, the scene was replayed. Every girl looked at him, wherever we went. I said to him, jokingly, 'What does it feel like to be the centre of all this attention?'

'What attention?' he asked.

'Oh come on,' I laughed, 'You can hardly have failed to notice how the girls look at you.'

He looked around. 'What girls?'

I tried to imagine how it must feel to be so handsome and at the same time not to know it. 'If I were in your skin I should think I were the luckiest man alive.'

Omer looked puzzled. 'Would you? Why? I'm nothing special. Just an ordinary boy from a poor family. Now, if I were rich, then I would think I was lucky. I would buy a yacht and sail around the world.'

I burst out laughing. I had never heard anyone express such a strange ambition. Then he told me he had joined an international pen-friend organisation and was corresponding with girls from Germany, France and England to practise his skill in those languages, presenting himself as the son of a rich merchant who had yachts and cars and mansions on the Bosphorus.

Again I laughed. 'But that's ridiculous to cheat like that. Would it not be more enjoyable to establish contact with others as one's plain self?'

He grinned. 'But the point is, one day it *will* be true. I'm just practising. Anyway, you're studying English, aren't you? Why don't you choose an English girl to write to?' He pulled out his address book and handed it to me.

I flipped over the pages. 'Well, it's not a bad idea.' I chose one at random. Sarah Weston. 'I shall show all my charm to this Sarah Weston writing nothing but the truth.'

Omer slapped me across the back, roaring with laughter.

That evening, in the quiet of my room I began drafting out a letter. I wondered whether to include details of my height. I did so, then crumpled the letter up and wrote another draft leaving that information out. I agonised over this and changed my mind a dozen times. In the end I decided to stick to my vow to tell the whole truth and if this girl decided to write to me it would be because she was charmed by my truth. Surely that was better than living a fantasy like Omer? On the other hand, if she decided not to write to me I would not have to suffer the humiliation of meeting her. She was just an unknown girl in a foreign country. No one knew what I was doing. There was no danger in this game at all. By the end of the week I had written the letter several times until I felt satisfied with it enough to post it. I enclosed a head and shoulders photograph of myself. I studied this photograph and thought my eyes looked very dark and striking. I sealed the letter.

Over the next few weeks while I wondered if she would bother to reply, I tried to imagine how this English girl would look. Blonde hair? Blue eyes? I loved the rhythm of the English language and the way the words were pronounced lightly from the front of the mouth. What sort of house did she live in? I knew from seeing pictures in foreign magazines that English people lived in big country houses with servants and Rolls Royce cars. Would such a girl be interested in writing to a poor Turkish boy? For a second I regretted being so honest in my letter and wished I had taken Omer's advice and concocted a better history for myself, but then I dismissed the thought with a shrug. If this Sarah Weston wanted to start up a correspondence with me she may as well know the truth from the start, then if she wanted to come and visit me I would not have to hide.

A few weeks after I had sent my letter, I came home one evening and my mother told me there was a letter for me from England on the kitchen table. My heart skipped a beat, but I casually squeezed myself a glass of orange juice, then picked up the envelope. The writing was in purple ink and the handwriting was large and flowing.

My mother said, 'Well why don't you open it instead of just staring at it? And how is it you've got a letter from England?'

I opened the letter. Out fell a photograph of a very pretty, slim girl with long blonde hair. Wonderful! Just as I'd imagined. She was wearing blue jeans and a T-shirt and was sitting against a tree in a garden with her arms around a black labrador. I stared at her thinking how pretty she was, then my mother said, 'You're spilling your juice!'

I jumped because I had forgotten she was there and I dropped the glass I was holding. Feeling myself going red I grabbed a cloth from the sink and started mopping up the mess. My mother picked up the photograph and laughed. 'Oh, I see.'

I turned my back to hide my glowing face and rinsed the cloth out in cold water, folding it neatly on the bench and saying in a bored voice, 'No you don't see. It's just a pen-friend I got from Omer. To practise my English. I'll read it later when I have time. I have to go out to meet Yashar to get some books from him.' I stuffed the letter and photograph back in the envelope, pushed it in my pocket and bolted out the door.

Yashar and I were taking the same courses at university and shared the same tastes in music and books. When I arrived at his house, his father greeted me at the door. 'Celik! It's good to see you. What's new and what isn't new eh? Come in and wait, Yashar won't be long. You'll have a glass of tea?'

I took off my shoes and put on the house-slippers he handed me. Then we went into the living room and I sat by the window while he disappeared into the kitchen. I always felt welcome here. Yashar's mother had died several years ago and his father enjoyed the company of Yashar's friends. He quickly reappeared with the tea and a plate of helva and we talked for over an hour before Yashar and his younger brother Ali arrived. Then there was more tea and cakes and talk. I was there for three hours and all the time I felt that letter burning a hole in my pocket till I thought I would die of curiosity.

Finally I escaped and hurried home. When I opened the front door I heard music and laughter from the living room. I pushed open the door and saw my mother and Hulya and a neighbour sitting in a circle clapping their hands. In the centre of the room was the neighbour's daughter, Rukiye, a very pretty girl about sixteen. She was demonstrating a dance and I stared in astonishment. Everyone laughed and cried, 'Come in, Celik, this is a good dance, you may watch it too!'

I withdrew quickly, to a great deal of laughter. Closing my hand over the letter in my pocket I ran upstairs to the safety of my room.

After I'd locked the door I took out the photograph and settled back on my bed to look at it. I touched the golden hair with my finger-tip, wondering how it would feel in reality. Soft? Like silk? Finally I opened the letter and scanned the text.

Dear Celik,

I was very pleased and surprised to get your letter. I have penfriends in France, Italy, Spain and Germany because I studied those languages at school and I've travelled all over Europe with my mother. I don't know the Turkish language and know very little about Turkish culture, so it would be really interesting to correspond with you.

I am eighteen years old and about to start my first year at Reading University, doing a double major in ancient history and classics. When I graduate I want to do a diploma in journalism then travel all over the world then get a job as a foreign correspondent on a national newspaper.

I was born and grew up in New Zealand on a sheep farm in the South Island, near a town called Timaru, but my parents divorced when I was twelve and my mother and I returned to England. Since then we've lived in a small Northumbrian village called Warkworth, which is where my mother was born. The landscape reminds me of New Zealand and it is also sparsely populated. The main difference is that it reeks with history. Are you interested in history? If you are let me know and I'll tell you some of the stories of this area.

What are your hobbies? Mine are riding my horse, walking my dogs and reading. My favourite authors are the Brontes. This summer I visited Haworth, where they lived, with my mother who was involved in a symposium there. (When we returned to England my mother went back to university to do her Ph.D in English literature. Now she lectures at the University of Newcastle.)While she was busy with the other boffins, intellectualising about the effect their social isolation had on the development of the Brontes' imagination, I walked on the moors where they played as children. I lay in the heather beside the ruins of Top Withens which was the setting for Wuthering Heights and listened to the skylarks singing, trying to imagine a happier ending for the book.

Do Turks have more than one wife? Are marriages arranged? How do you feel about that? I can't imagine someone presenting me with their choice of husband. Are women still veiled and secluded? I suppose you don't have divorce in your country?

People say I am very shy because I don't talk much. But actually I find it more interesting to watch people's faces while they are talking and their expressions and behaviour show far more than their words. Also I can never think of anything to say that sounds funny or silly, which is how most people talk. Sooner or later if I am in a group of people someone will look at me and say, 'Gosh, you're so shy, aren't you?' So generally I try to avoid social gatherings.

I had a teacher at school last year who used to tell us about his travels all over the world and I found that really interesting and asked him lots of questions. The other people in my class looked at me really surprised because they had never heard me talk so much. But the things most people talk about are so pointless. I find I can express my thoughts better in writing. I think that's why I like to write to pen-friends. And also, they are more interesting than the people I meet here. I like to learn about different ways of living and thinking.

You didn't give much information about yourself but your English was very good.

I'm looking forward to hearing from you.

Yours sincerely,

Sarah Weston.

I read the letter over and over. I held the paper to my lips and breathed in the faint perfume. She had not made any comment about my height, but instead had revealed personal information about herself. I hugged myself in relief. And she wanted me to write again! I immediately began a reply.

Whenever I wrote to Sarah over the following months, I composed several drafts of each letter before I was satisfied with the results. She bombarded me with questions about my life and about Turkish history. In order to answer them I had to think carefully about things I'd always taken for granted. I began to see myself as she seemed to see me. What I had always thought of as an ordinary, boring existence looked exotic in her eyes.

When Omer asked how my correspondence was going, I said, 'I was right! I don't have to tell lies. She thinks I am interesting enough just the way I am.' He laughed and shook his head in disbelief.

She sent me more photographs of herself. At home with her animals, on the beach, dressed for a university ball. I arranged the best ones in my album. In turn I sent her pictures of my family and scenes of the city. After I'd sent her some close-up pictures of myself, she said she had passed them around her friends at university and they'd all said I was very handsome. Handsome? I was so excited when I read that I wanted to tell someone but I didn't because I knew they would just laugh at me. Occasionally though I looked at myself in the mirror from different angles and said aloud, 'Not bad'.

We wrote about pop songs, films we had seen, parties we had been to, although mine were just wedding parties. She was very amused when I told her that the girls danced with girls and the boys with boys and that Mehmed taught me the latest dances when he came home from military school. I sent her a record of Turkish folk music, a book of poetry by Yahya Kemal, one of my favourite poets, and a book of stories and sayings of Nasreddin Hodja.

The scenes of the Northumbrian countryside and their historical associations that she described in her letters fired my imagination. I could almost see the desolate moors and hear the wind howling and the rain beating on the walls of ruined castles along the Northumbrian coast. I could feel the loneliness of the Roman soldier as he stood on guard on Hadrian's Wall, in an alien, barbarous land. I could imagine the terror of the local population when the Vikings attacked and the hazardous seven-year journey of the monks of Lindisfarne when they carried the body of St. Cuthbert to safety. Sarah painted a vivid word picture of a world I had not known existed and my imagination was captivated by it.

I wrote to her all the time. While I was waiting for lectures to begin I composed letters to her in my head. In the streets I looked for faces that resembled hers and I peered in shop windows for the kind of clothes that I thought she would wear. I began to spend more time alone in my room looking out of the window at the moon shining on the old city walls.

At night, my dreams were full of the scenes of our meeting. But they always ended with her walking away without my being able to make contact. Then she sent me a letter which set in motion the processes which were to change my life.

Dear Celik,

We've had the Christmas holidays. I've been very busy because I was working as a 'postie' to get some extra money for presents! There've been the usual parties and visits to relatives and a couple of pantomimes. I got lots of book tokens and money as presents and I had a great time going to the bookshops and stocking up on books to read over the holidays. I'm presently reading T.S. Eliot and Robert Frost.

On Christmas Eve I went around the village singing Christmas carols with a group from church. The sky was so black and full of stars and the frost sparkled under the street lamps. All the trees in the village were draped with fairy lights. Sometimes people gave us cups of hot punch and Christmas cake when we sang for them. Then at eleven o'clock we went to the midnight service at church. When we came out it was snowing! We went home and my mother brought out hot mince pies and sausage rolls.

As usual we had all the relatives, piles of cousins and people over for Christmas dinner. In New Zealand my grandfather used to kill a lamb and we ate that with a salad, raspberries and cream on a swelteringly hot summer's day! Here we have roast turkey and pork and apple sauce, roast potatoes, carrots, cauliflower, peas, cabbage, cranberry jelly, and plum pudding with white sauce. Loads of chocolates, nuts and dried fruits. I gathered holly, thick with red berries from the trees in our garden and decorated the table with that and hung mistletoe in the hall. I thought about my father bringing in armfuls of bottlebrush and Christmas lilies and I remembered how the smell filled the room and mixed with my father's smell of hay and earth and I found tears running down my cheeks. If he were still alive I would go back to New Zealand to live with him. If my mother knew that I think she would die.

After we returned to England I wrote to my father a few times and I couldn't understand why he never replied. Then one day I found the remains of a letter from him in the fire. When I confronted my mother about it she began crying and said I would understand one day. I was very shocked because I had never seen my mother cry before. All the fury and frustration I felt at that moment was compressed into a hard little ball that rolled somewhere behind my ribs and got stuck there. I made up my mind that one day I would cause her as much pain as she had caused me. But I also now knew that my father hadn't forgotten me. So I continued to write letters to him telling him how much I loved him and how I would go back to New Zealand one day and find him again, but instead of posting them I kept them in a suitcase in my wardrobe. I did that until he died.

I went into the kitchen to help with the washing up. As I walked through the door I heard two of my mother's sisters say, 'It's hard to believe she's Deirdre's daughter, isn't it, she's so quiet.' I just couldn't be bothered going through all that again and at that moment I hated them, hated being in England where everyone I knew played a part like an actor on a stage, always conscious of who was watching and the impression their acting was making on the audience. Then the other aunt said, 'She's like her father. I never did understand what Deirdre saw in him. And you know what they say about still waters!'

I froze to the spot. First of all I didn't know I was like my father, but he was a kind, gentle man, so what was so bad about that? Secondly, who were they to judge my or my father's personality being right or wrong? Against what standards? As for not knowing what my mother saw in him I remember how they used to kiss and walk arm-in-arm everywhere. I never heard them shout at each other. In the months before they separated they were even more polite to each other than they normally were. Anyway, I turned and grabbed my coat and scarf and ran out the door. My mother called, 'Sarah, where are you going, we're playing charades in a minute!' I told her the dogs needed a walk and escaped for a couple of hours.

In the village there were a few kids about, riding their new sledges and playing with torches in the dark, but in the fields there was no one. Not even a single footprint in the snow. Even after walking quickly and throwing sticks for the dogs I was freezing, but I felt better being out there alone and cold than going back to the party.

When I returned I stood in the garden for a minute watching the party through the window. The room was full of light, coloured streamers and balloons. Everyone was playing charades. My mother was miming something in the centre of the room and I could hear the hoots of laughter. She looked so beautiful and so at ease. I felt such an ache in my stomach because I realised I could never be like her, no matter how much I tried, so there was no point in trying, because people like my aunts would always keep comparing me with her and find me deficient.

I was going to go up to bed without going back in the room but as I was taking my coat off in the hall an old man who lives in the village came over to me and said, 'Sarah, do you realise you are standing under the mistletoe?' I looked up to see where the mistletoe was and he grabbed me and tried to kiss me. I couldn't believe it. He must be at least forty! His mouth looked all pink and slobbery. I managed to twist away and escape into the living room. He followed me and every time I turned round he was standing just behind me, winking and nodding. What makes it even worse is that he is a sidesman at the local church. To avoid him I made sure I was always in a group and talking ninety to the dozen so that people wouldn't drift away from me the way they usually do. I even thought of some jokes and people laughed! I saw my aunts watching me with narrowed eyes, and I knew they thought I must have been drinking the rum punch because they came over and stood very close to see if I had alcohol on my breath.

That night, when it was all over and everyone was in bed, I stood at my window and thought that all those people at the party were really so pathetic, the way they responded to my silly talk, as if suddenly I was a person worth listening to. And that old man who actually thought I would want to kiss him will feel very embarrassed next time he sees me in church, assuming he isn't still drunk then! I started to laugh but the laughter twisted into a kind of spiral that got smaller and smaller and disappeared like a wisp of smoke and I was left feeling even more alone than ever. I just stood there watching the snow turn yellow in the reflection of the street light, then dropping in great silent lumps onto the trees and bushes, changing the shape of everything in the garden.

Sarah.

When I read this letter I felt Sarah's sadness and aloneness like a heavy ache in my chest. Also I realised, for the first time, how vulnerable she was. The thought of that old man taking advantage of her sweetness disgusted me so much the bile rose from my stomach and left a sour taste in my mouth. I knew, of course, that life in the west was in decay because they had no religious principles. Even the way Sarah had written about Christmas showed that it was an empty ritual which was just an excuse for drinking and fornication. Actually, that did not surprise me because it was a religion based on myths. In fact it was beyond my understanding how anyone could believe in such things as a virgin birth and a resurrection.

I thought about my feelings when my brother was buried and I could understand something of Sarah's sense of loss over her father. But at least I had the comfort and beauty of the Imam's words at my brother's funeral and the guidance of my father. Sarah had nothing.

She had trusted me with some very personal revelations about her life and feelings. I would guard them in my heart like the most precious possessions on earth. I spent days wondering how I could reply to this letter in a way that would express my understanding of her pain and also offer her some constructive help for her life. Then the idea came to me that the way to do this would be to teach her about my religion – better still, if she could come to Istanbul and see for herself the way we lived according to the principles of Islam – then she would see the way to a richer, more purposeful life and she would know that even in her darkest moments she would never be alone. I immediately wrote to her to extend an invitation to visit my family.

She replied saying she would love to come but her mother wouldn't allow her to travel so far on her own. My heart sank when I read this. Okay, if she could not come to Istanbul, then somehow I would have to get to England. There was a student exchange scheme that would have enabled me to go but I was too late to apply for it that year so I made an application for the following year. After several months of interviews and filling in forms the application was approved and in great excitement I wrote to tell her and waited for her reaction.

When her letter came she said she was delighted that we would be able to meet at last though she was disappointed she couldn't come to Istanbul as she was so curious to see for herself what I had told her about Islamic culture.

I was happy to have aroused her curiosity. Over the following weeks I spent a lot of time consulting books and talking at length with my father who was knowledgeable in the rituals. This process felt like putting together the fragments of images. It escalated into joy and excitement. It was something like creating the movements of an orchestra in imagination and then there comes the music, in existence, in reality.

This convinced me that if I could arrange this information in perfect order and harmony in my imagination then it might happen that I had described a fact. I began to understand better Jesus, son of Mary, saying, 'Lo, I fashion for you out of clay the likeness of a bird and I breathe into it and it is a bird, by Allah's leave.' (Koran 3/49).

CHAPTER FOUR

I wrote six drafts before I was satisfied with the composition of my letter. Then I sent it to Sarah.

My dear friend,

Your letter moved me to tears. To lose a member of one's own family is one of the worst calamities of life. When my brother died I would have gladly given my own life in exchange for his. Only my father was able to help me endure the suffering. He is the wisest person I have ever known and I wish you could meet him. I would like to share with you some of the things he has taught me, though my language is inadequate to do justice to this. Please accept these words from me as a gift, to do with as you wish.

Islam is an Arabic word which means 'surrender to the will of God'. It also means peace and purity. A Moslem accepts the supreme power of God and lives his life to reflect the revealed teachings.

Moslems, as taught by Mohammed, have five duties to perform which are known as the Five Pillars of Islam.

1. To believe there is only one God and Mohammed is his prophet.
2. To pray to Allah five times a day, and particularly on Friday which is the holy day for Moslems.
3. To give money to the poor.
4. To fast from sunrise to sunset for thirty days during the holy month of Ramadan.
5. To make a pilgrimage to Mecca.

Islam is more than a religion. It is a way of life. It is very simple to become a Moslem. All you have to do is to declare that you are one and live according to the laws.

Say, 'We believe in Allah and that which was revealed to us and that which was revealed to Abraham and Ismail and Jacob and the tribes and that which was given to Moses and Jesus and to the prophets from their Lord, we make no distinction between any of them and to Him we submit.' (Koran 3:83)

Unless Allah wills, one can not will. Everyone's concept of Will is reflected in his/her way of life and holds it together like a soul. If you wish to understand the differences between two ways of life, compare the workings of the concept Will in them. I have made a research about the concept Will. Or rather, I can say that all my investigation is triggered by and related to the concept Will. For a given way of life, unless I understand the working of the concept Will in it, I can not say that I understand it (the working of that way of life.) But, of course, my remark, 'Unless Allah wills, one can not will,' is meaningless and to practise it, to use it, leads to fatalism. But what I can say, meaningful here is, in the Koran it reads, 'Unless Allah wills one can not will,' and I believe it is revealed by God. And that is why it is meaningful. My talking like God doesn't make me God, or as powerful as God or gives meaning to what I am talking about. To talk the language of God, and be meaningful, one needs to be God.

Peace and love.

Celik

I had gone to great lengths to construct this letter perfectly, using grammar books and my best language to convey the depth of my feelings for her. I hoped and prayed she would sense all of this through the beauty of my language in its description of the most beautiful religion on earth, and I waited impatiently for her reply.

After several weeks it came. She thanked me for my letter and said she was touched by the way I had written it. The same day she had received my letter she had also read an article in the newspaper by a French woman who'd been born and brought up in Algiers and had been forced to flee when the Arabs took over the country. The article was in direct opposition to what I had written about Islam, she said, and she would like me to read and comment on it.

As soon as I started reading the article I realised it was just an expression of the bitterness and hatred this woman felt towards Arabs and the danger she saw for the world in the 'insidious spread of Islam.' If Sarah had not asked me for my reaction I would have screwed it up and thrown it in the rubbish bin. However, I carefully composed a reply which I felt combined originality with wit and I told Sarah she should send it to the newspaper as a reply to that vulgar article by the Frenchwoman.

Dear Mrs Treadgold,

Your use of language helps to spread enmity, hatred and confusion among human beings. Moslems believe that nations are created just to recognise each other and interact in harmony to prove that humans are created higher than Satan. If we start with your arguments we would easily end up with absurdities like the following:

Well, actually, nuclear club members are all disguised Moslems. You know all the nuclear war head producers are financed by the Arabs (call them Moslems as well if you like.) If they didn't have the oil we wouldn't have the nuclear threat. You know those minarets are deadlier than missiles. Just imagine them circling around the earth used for calling to prayer five times a day, can you imagine that? Thousands of minarets aimed to your heart, calling you to peace and prayer, praising God, five times a day. Wouldn't that be more dreadful than a silent nuclear umbrella? But comrades, don't worry, we will know how to deal with them. We will have astronauts with little hammers, hammering minarets around space. Also, today, if people are dying of hunger around the world it is all because of minarets. My Gosh, they are already everywhere, calling people to unemployment, idleness and laziness. Comrades, do whatever you choose but beware the minaret.

As you see, my dear Treadgold, when you start confusing minarets with missiles then you definitely end up in a black hole in space, without knowing what to do and how you arrived there. But, I'll tell you what, in fact, what you are missing is a proper vehicle which you would know how to use and be in command in the space of your language. A functional and useful concept which would save your race and my precious time. My dear Treadgold, you are looking for Satan himself while you confuse Islam with Satan. However my dear, Satan is the open and common enemy of humankind and he loves to spread hatred and hostility among humans like you and me, to make them enemies to each other to keep them busy with vanity and pride, to be able to run his sovereignty.

God calls human beings to unity and peace, but Satan to mischief and nuclear war with their little hammers separating a single atom. Then comes the DARK AGES WITH A BIG SMILE ON HIS DEVIL'S FACE.

Therefore, my sister, let us beware of the devil himself while we have time and means to communicate and unite, not to let him LAUGH behind our ASHES!

Peace to your agitated heart.

Celik Ertas.

I was lying on my bed reading when my mother brought Sarah's letter to my room. I ignored her knowing smile and tossed the letter casually on the table till she went out of the room and I heard her go downstairs. Then I leapt off the bed and tore the letter open.

Dear Celik,

Judging by your response I think maybe I shouldn't have sent you that article. I tried to imagine how I would have reacted if I'd been a Christian and you'd sent me an article from a Moslem criticising his treatment by Christians. Anyway, as I'm not religious it isn't a realistic comparison. But I feel that the article, in a very personal, subjective way, of course, expressed, very graphically, one person's suffering at the hands of Moslems. If that is how she felt then she had every right to say so, don't you think? She was turned out of her home by the Arabs. Of course she feels bitter about them. No religion on earth is better than another when it comes to committing atrocities. Surely you must know that? I'm not saying it's the religion that's at fault, it's the people who practise it and the way they distort it for their own ends.

When we left New Zealand we went to live with my mother's parents in the house that generations of her family had lived in. My grandmother told me that when she married my grandfather, who was a Catholic, she had to get married in the Catholic Church, but got only a hurried, inferior version of the ceremony, because she was a Protestant. After her first son was born the priest hounded her to get him baptised a Catholic otherwise if the child died he would go straight to hell. My grandfather arrived home one day to find her in tears and the priest standing over her haranguing her. Grandpa threw him out of the house and told him if he ever returned he'd hit him. The end result of that was that grandpa was excommunicated. My grandmother told me that story because at school we were studying the Spanish Inquisition and she was trying to get me to see that religious intolerance wasn't something that only happened in faraway countries.

She went on to say that our village green had once been a pond which was very popular with the local children, although most parents strictly forbade their children to play anywhere near it because so many people had drowned there. She almost drowned herself when she was fifteen because she'd been climbing along an overhanging branch which stretched right over the middle of the pond and it snapped. None of her friends could swim so nobody could help her. She said she heard them all screaming and then her ears filled with a loud buzzing and everything went black. Then someone grabbed her as she was going under for the last time and got her to the bank. When she'd spewed up all the pond water and opened her eyes she recognised the boy who'd saved her. He was one of a small group of Catholics who lived in the same village. Sometimes she'd gone to his school with her friends to yell, 'Catholic dogs stink like frogs...' but other than that she'd had no contact with him before. He took her back home and stayed at the garden gate till he saw her mother open the door and let her in and then he left. Unfortunately her father was home and he demanded to know what the hell she was doing with that damned Catholic and why she was soaking wet. When she explained he beat her with a leather strap for being near the pond in the first place and told her to stay away from that boy.

The next day she went to find him so she could thank him for saving her life and to apologise for her past behaviour. Then they started meeting on Saturday nights at the Methodist Church dance but someone told her father and he beat her again and forbade her to see him any more. So she continued meeting him in secret and then she got pregnant so her father had no choice but to let her marry him.

The last child to drown in that pond was a girl who used to bully my mother at school and had actually been trying to push my mother in but she slipped and fell in herself. Her father was someone important on the local council, which, presumably, was why it got filled in after that though the villagers had been trying for years to persuade the council to do just that. At first the idea was to make it into a little park full of flowers, but everything they planted withered and died. Even the grass was patchy and brown. My grandmother said that according to folklore the pond had been used to duck witches in the seventeenth century and some people believed the area was cursed, which was why no flowers ever grew there. I was so fascinated with that story I asked my teacher if I could change my project from the Inquisition to a study of the persecution of witches in our village. She helped me find information in the local library and the librarian sent away for more.

I found out that one of my ancestors, a girl called Ellen-Mary, had been accused of being a witch by a woman named Elizabeth Carter, because she had seduced her husband, borne his child and made Elizabeth miscarry. Ellen-Mary was taken to the pond and tied in a chair which was lowered into the water three times. She was told that if she was still alive after the third ducking that would prove she was a witch and she would then be taken to a fire and burned alive. If, however, she drowned, she would be proved innocent. Before she went under for the third time she cursed the woman who'd accused her and all the people who'd had a hand in her death, and all their loved ones for generations to come. When they brought her up again she was dead. Now the really weird thing was that the girl who drowned because she'd tried to push my mother in the pond was called Liza Carter. I wrote all that in my project, saying that with the death of Liza the curse had run its course. The teacher was so thrilled with this story she contacted a friend of hers who was a reporter and he wrote a piece about it in the local paper. He took a photograph of me and when it was printed next to his article the caption underneath said I was a descendant of Ellen-Mary, the witch, which infuriated my mother but made my grandmother roar with laughter. He also told me I had the right kind of nose if I ever wanted a career in journalism!

This is a very long explanation for why I sent you the article. Please accept my apologies for upsetting you. Put it down to my nose!

This term I have a new classics tutor called Simon whose mother is from Saudi Arabia and his father is English. His parents met at Oxford University. He lived in Jeddha until he was ten then they came to England. When I showed him the Treadgold article he said he once saw a woman stoned to death for adultery in Jeddah. She was buried up to her neck in the ground. I felt absolutely ill when he described it. How can anyone justify such violation of human rights in the name of religion? It was after that incident that his father moved the family to England.

Simon is in his thirties and has travelled all over the world. He met his wife Alexandra when they were both working as park rangers in Canada. Her job was to take photographs of all the aircraft that flew over the park because there was such a big problem with poachers shooting the bears. Simon was her nearest neighbour, fifteen miles away. One day he appeared at her hut, absolutely distraught, and told her he'd been asleep when this huge black bear tore the side off his hut and reared up at him. He'd had to shoot it or it would have killed him. He was really upset to shoot the bear, she said. That's what appealed to her. This big, gorgeous man in tears because he'd had to shoot the bear.

They sometimes have parties for the students in their house. It's so beautiful, full of pictures and books and things they've collected from their travels. Alexandra is really exquisite. Very tall with long, black hair and blue eyes. She's a photographer and the last time I was there she showed me photographs she'd taken for Time magazine of a monastery she had stayed in, in the Andes. She also showed me photographs of the hut with the side torn off where Simon had shot the bear, and lots of others on icebergs, in forests, on the tops of mountains, under the sea. She often goes away on assignments for months at a time. She's leaving for the Antarctic next week for three months. She's exactly the kind of person I would like to be. Free to travel, confident, financially independent. The amazing thing is she told me that when she was my age she was also very shy. Travelling helped her to overcome it because whenever she went to a different place she could re-invent herself. No one knew her so she could be whoever she chose to be. Simon and Alexandra also seem to have the perfect marriage. When I told my mother that she said there's no such thing, but I prefer to believe the evidence of my own eyes.

Sarah.

When I finished reading this my knees would not support me and I sank back on my pillow, feeling sick to my stomach. With cold, shaking hands I reached for my pen and paper and began my response.

Dear Sarah,

Like you, I also found the story of the witch pond interesting, and you have no need to explain or apologise for your 'nosiness'.

But I think you are implying that I am intolerant and this hurts me. I read Mrs Treadgold's article just because you sent it to me, otherwise her kind of writing has no place on my list of literature. In contrast to her disgusting hatred, my reply still keeps its charm and humour in invitation to the unity of humankind. Can you find the slightest evidence of intolerance in my reply?

If you are so much in favour of freedom of thought you should be able to tolerate my criticism. I have been recommended in Koran 3/200, 'Oh ye who believe, endure. Outdo all others in endurance, be ready and observe your duty to Allah in order that ye may succeed.'

I won't return to the subject of the argument again. My pattern of behaviour in similar situations is part of my character, it isn't a product of a temporary impulse so try to understand if you can, rather than ignoring it as an error.

Imran 36 (Koran)... Oh Adam! Inform them of their names. And when he had informed them of their names, the Lord said, Did I not tell you that I know the secret of the heavens and the earth. Genesis 2 (the Bible) And the Lord said, Behold, they are all one people and they have one language and this is only the beginning of what they will do and nothing they proposed to do will be impossible from them. Come, let us go down and there confuse their language that they may not understand one another's speech.

So the Lord caused them to deflect therefrom and expelled them from the happy state in which they were and he said: Fall down one of you a foe upon the other! There should be for you on earth a habitation and provision for a time. So the Lord scattered them abroad from there and over the face of all the earth.

All I will say on the subject of your lecturer's story about the stoning of an adulteress is this: It's the kind of sensationalism that the gutter press in the west likes to report about Moslems.

Satan! Our common enemy number one. Clarity dismantles your mask.
Selams,
Celik.

Her letter, when it came after a long delay, did not address the topic at all. In fact, to my amazement, she introduced another, completely irrelevant, subject.

... Simon has been helping me a lot with my Greek history papers so I've got to know him and Alexandra really well. I spent an evening with them just before Alexandra left for the Antarctic and they showed me their photographs of Athens. They'd spent a couple of years there. I could have listened to them all night. I can't believe how ordinary my life has been compared to theirs, but, as Simon pointed out, I'm fifteen years younger!

Last week I went with Simon to London to see Waiting for Godot. It is an amazing play. Afterwards we went to a pub and stayed talking about the play for hours. Now that Alexandra is in the Antarctic I miss her a lot but at least I still have Simon to talk to.

Soon it will be summer and I'm looking forward to some long lazy days on the beach. I've been studying so hard for my exams and now all I want is sunshine!!! I'll probably take a waitressing job again, for a short while anyway. It'll be a pleasant change from swotting, spilling soup on people!

Sarah.

At first I was puzzled by her lack of response to my letter, then I realised it was probably because she wished to avoid upsetting me again so she was steering clear of any kind of comment. Now it was up to me to make her see this was not necessary because I was quite prepared to engage in intellectual debate with her. Despite the fact that most people would have given up at this stage, I was proud of the way I persisted with patience, for I am not a patient person by nature.

Dear Sarah,

Islam is based on logic. Christianity on a myth. I am only trying to help you see the truth for yourself. So at least keep your mind open. Compare the two religions side by side and then tell me truthfully which is the most logical.

See for yourself that family life in western countries is in decay. The family system of Islam brings the rights of each individual into an equilibrium. Racism is a problem in all western countries. Islam shows how racism can be ended. Freedom, equality and justice are protected in Islam. 'Whosoever kills a human being for other than manslaughter or corruption in the earth, it shall be as if he had killed all mankind. And whosoever saves the life of one, it shall be as if he had saved the life of all mankind.' (Koran 5:32.)

Don't give up Sarah.

With love and peace.

Celik.

After three or four months she sent me a reply.

Dear Celik,

I love the way you write and the way you present your feelings and opinions in a language that isn't even your own. I don't agree with what you say about religion, but at least you have a point of view and you can express it with conviction and passion. Simon does that too. Maybe it's a cultural thing. Simon is only half English and not at all English in his behaviour, which is what I found so attractive about him.

I went to Simon and Alexandra's goodbye party a month ago. At the party he told me I'd come top in my whole year. They were delighted but all I could think of was that I was losing two of the best friends I've ever had. Actually, the *only* friends I've ever had. I don't know why but I can't seem to relate to people my own age. It's always been like that. My mother says it's because I grew up so isolated on my father's farm so I never learned to socialise. It's not altogether true though. I just don't feel interested in talking about fashion, boyfriends, magazines, television, which is what people my age talk about. And whenever I try to bring up an interesting topic people's eyes glaze over and they drift away.

With Simon and Alexandra it was never like that. We never ran out of things to say to each other. Now they have gone to live in Italy. I could hardly bear to go to the party, I felt so sad. I've never been so in tune with anyone in my whole life as I was with Simon and Alexandra. I could talk to them about things that really mattered. He gave me books to read and we talked about them for hours in the coffee shop after lectures. Alexandra took me to art galleries and photographic exhibitions. Sometimes the three of us went to concerts and plays. When Alexandra got the job in Italy I taught her some basic Italian. Alexandra cried when she said goodbye to me and Simon gave me his copy of Omar Khayam and said there were words in there he couldn't say to me. After they left I felt so empty and lonely. The other students in my hostel kept trying to drag me out to parties. They kept asking which one I was in love with, Simon or Alexandra. I kept saying their names over and over when I was alone. It's like a kind of music, but it also makes me cry.

Last week, at a party I finally went to, I met an agricultural student called Dave. To stop everybody going on about Simon all the time I agreed to go out with him a couple of times. It turned out to be much better than I expected. He's not deep, like Simon, but I actually found that quite refreshing because he's really easy to talk to. Well, actually he does all the talking, so I never have to think of anything to say. He's also very funny and makes me laugh. He spent a year travelling in India before he went to university and he told me that when he has finished his degree he wants to travel again. Going out with him is helping me cope with the loss of Simon and Alexandra. I was going to tell him that then I realised how stupid it would sound, so you're the only one I've told. Maybe it's because it's easier for me to write it than to say it.

Sarah.

I read this letter several times, feeling more and more confused. Had she written all this to provoke me? If so, why? Did she want to make me jealous? She must have wanted some opinion from me about these people she had spent so much time with or she wouldn't have written about them. I re-read the comment she had made about me being the only one she had told about her feelings for those people. That made my heart beat a little faster because it was the first time she had indicated we had a special relationship. Did this mean that in fact she had sensed my feelings for her in the letter about Islam but was too shy to openly acknowledge them? Or perhaps my words had been too oblique for her to be sure of what I was trying to communicate?

When this thought occurred to me I was so filled with emotion I closed my eyes and wrapped my arms around my shoulders, trying to pretend they were Sarah's arms. I lay on my bed looking at her photographs, her sweet face, her slender body, and whispered her name over and over. I tried to imagine what she would look like naked, lying next to me on the bed. My face burned with shame then that I should sully her purity with such base thoughts.

Over the following weeks I read poetry so I could absorb the language into my soul and produce words that were the finest distillations of the purest forms of love. After writing more than twenty drafts I was reduced to tears of frustration by the inadequacy of my language. For three months I struggled and the contents of my rubbish basket grew as high as a mountain. Before I was able to complete my task, another letter arrived from Sarah.

... and when I took Dave home to meet my mother she was so awful to him I couldn't believe it. Afterwards she said I should drop him. He's one of the sweetest, kindest people I've ever met so there's absolutely no reason why she should have taken such a dislike to him. I wondered if she had found my packet of pills in my drawer but it couldn't have been that or she would have exploded. Anyway, it's none of her business. I've decided to go on holiday with him to...

I wrote two more letters to her.

Sarah,

Always I have felt lonely and sad. I think this is my natural condition with just occasional moments of happiness.

Celik.

Sarah,

I had a terrible dream last night. You were running away from me in a line, like this______________. And then you disappeared leaving only three pebbles, with a message, 'Say goodbye by phone.' I caught them in the air.

Celik.

Then, when everyone was asleep and the world outside was as black and silent as a tomb I stripped off all my clothes and set fire to these two letters with a match. When they were reduced to curls of grey ash in my hand I smeared them over my face and arms. Then I opened my bedroom window, leaned out and spent the night there, welcoming the freezing rain as it numbed the blood in my veins and turned my tears to ice.

The psychiatrist said, 'Did you ever meet this girl?'

'No.'

'Well, you're young. You'll meet lots of girls. Better stick to those from your own background. But to clear up your immediate worry, I can find no physical reason for your headaches. And you are definitely not insane. You'll get over this and in a few months you will wonder why it seemed so important.'

CHAPTER FIVE

On the 7th July 1967 I was standing on the platform of Sirkeci Gari waiting for the train that would begin my journey to London. My parents, brothers and sister gathered round me, besieging me with requests and advice and Yashar kept hugging me and grinning from ear to ear.

'Celik don't forget to write. Tell me about everything you see, all the museums and art galleries you go to, all the books you read.'

'Don't forget to wear your scarf, I've heard about how cold and foggy it is in England, they have no summer.'

'...and if you go to a Beatles concert get me their autograph.'

'Remember the words of the Prophet...'

As I stepped onto the train they still kept hugging and patting me and heaping their good wishes on my head. The train started slowly and the last thing I saw was my mother's anxious face and my brothers waving and cheering. I leaned back against the seat and blew out a long deep breath. I felt in my pocket for the photograph and pulled it out in front of me. Sarah. The beginning of a headache nagged at my temples. Would I contact her or not? I still didn't know. Anyway, it didn't matter. I was going to a country full of beautiful English girls. And I would make the most of this adventure, not waste it by grieving.

The door slid open and a boy of my own age entered the compartment.

'My name is Feridun, may I sit here?'

'Please do.' I smiled, pleased to have company.

It was noon when we arrived in Sofra Station. Feridun and I mopped our sweating brows with our handkerchiefs as we hopped off the train to find refreshments.

'Thank God! An ice-cream cart!' We rushed to buy some, but the ice-cream seller shook his head. 'Sorry, you can't pay in foreign currency.'

We ran to the bank to change money but it was closed for the lunch break. Feridan said he would change it on the black market and after ten minutes he came back grinning. We found the ice-cream man again. This time he said, 'Sorry, it's too late. It's the government's order not to sell ice-cream during the lunch time.'

'Oh, I see, you need the government's permission to sell ice-creams? When is the next session then?"

'Sorry, this is how it is.'

I thought, 'Well fuck your government!' and turned away before I was tempted to create a scene and we clambered back on the train.

The train started going faster and faster as we travelled further west. Our next long stop was in Munich and I got off the train again with Feridun. I orientated myself to the city easily and made investigations about tourist places nearby. I bought a map and took the street car to an art gallery near Bahnoff St. Both sides of the street were under construction. I thought perhaps they had been damaged in the war. My friend was amazed by my quick orientation and asked, 'Have you been here before?'

'No,' I replied.

'Have you ever been out of Turkey before?'

'No, why?'

He laughed and shook his head.

We parted at the door of the gallery for he said he was more interested in girls and bars.

After I had visited the gallery, I went to the Ancient Greek Art Museum. I spent my time there looking at the white softness of Venus.

In the evening I was on the train again making new friends, this time all girls, one Australian, one Austrian, one Greek. They introduced themselves and asked me where I was from. I answered, 'You guess.'

The Greek said, 'Italy?'

The Australian, 'Spain?'

The Austrian, 'Give us more clues.'

I told them, 'I am from the centre of the universe.'

Everyone laughed and the Austrian said, 'I know where you are from. You are from Istanbul.'

I was amazed, 'How did you know?'

I enjoyed the journey very much in their company and the hours passed quickly. The Greek girl was attracted to me but I was able to keep the right distance to protect my independence.

Late at night, we arrived at Victoria Station in London. We exchanged addresses and said goodbye. Then I had to direct myself towards Birmingham, managing somehow to change money and get tickets in that rushing crowd of people to Euston.

At the station in Birmingham, I asked an English lady to dial a number for me for I didn't know how to operate the phone and the area code. She did it with courtesy and I thanked her gratefully. I was amazed with my English doing work for me. By the time my contact arrived to pick me up, I was feeling completely exhausted.

Accommodation had been arranged by AIESEC student organisation. An English student met me at the station and took me to the house where a crowd of people were living. Two Americans, one Spaniard, one Greek, two Englishmen. Everyone took it in turns to wash and cook. After suffering one week with those people, two or three sleeping in the same room, I decided to move into another place. By looking in the newspaper advertisements section I found myself lodgings with a very pleasant English family. They charged about the same rent but I didn't have to cook or wash my clothes. Besides, when I travelled out of town at weekends, they gave me a refund. For that I was surprised as I didn't expect such generosity.

I couldn't believe I was really in England. It was even better than I had imagined, with neat houses in orderly rows and beautiful, green, tidy gardens. Red letter-boxes on street corners, big red double-decker buses and courteous policemen. I was amazed at the systematic flow of the traffic with hardly anyone honking horns even in the rush hour. And the patient queues of people at bus stops and post offices. People were always polite and helpful when I asked for directions and my first impression of the country was of civilised efficiency. I loved wandering around the city shops, beautifully decorated with the latest fashionable clothes and crowded with the loveliest girls I had ever seen, all wearing mini-skirts. Whereas high-class Turkish girls walked with a slow, swaying motion, these English girls hurried along with a spring in their step. The music of the Beatles was everywhere, reminding me of those lovely, sad days, 'Eleanor Rigby, died in the church... I look at all the lonely people...' 'We all live in a yellow submarine...'

After spending a couple of days in the selling and purchasing department of Stoppards Ltd headquarters, opposite the fire station, I made a few friends from all levels of the organisation, from the secretaries to the assistant manager. Then I found I had been transferred to the traffic department. There, I was working hard all day long, but I didn't have much company. I complained about this to the manager.

'You're an excellent worker,' he said. 'We were very pleased with your help here, but I understand your problem. I'll recommend that you are transferred to the Accounting Department. I hope you'll enjoy yourself there.'

So then I was sitting opposite the manager of the accounting department. He explained about the rules and welcomed me and hoped I would spend a nice time with them and remarked on the beauty of the girls working for the department. 'They're all pin-ups aren't they?'

I mumbled a shy response.

Actually, the department was full of beautiful young girls from fifteen to eighteen, with one old spinster in charge. I was the focus of attention all of a sudden and after a few days I was friends with everyone. I hadn't seen so many beautiful girls all together in one room, even in pictures. Everyone invited me to social functions, ice-skating, a wedding, bowling, cinema, swimming. I don't know how the days passed.

Later on, I asked to work in the computer department to learn something about the automation of the company stock and distribution system. The department was situated on the same floor where the chairman of the company had his office. This increased my popularity and status. I was attending meetings with the top level people and they explained to me how they would be upgrading their system from ICT500 to another modern system which would work faster. The existing system was based on punch card input using second generation equipment and semi-mechanical tabulators, sorters and duplicators.

I worked with enthusiasm in that department for it was my ambition to become a programmer or systems analyst in the computer business. After learning more about the company, I discovered the more artistic face of it in a model window setting and advertising department. And later on I spent two weeks at a branch office getting more contact with people from all levels of English society.

I learned the worst of the language from an Irish shop assistant whom I called 'shop-nuisance.' She was a lovely, lively character. One day, when we were having our lunch together, the girls started calling me 'Turkish Delight.'

'Well then,' I said, 'I'd better go before you all eat me.'

And they all rushed towards me with outstretched arms, laughing and shouting. I couldn't believe it and felt my face burn with embarrassment and I escaped out the door, pretending to scream, before they could see for themselves how affected I was.

I visited London during the weekends and holidays. I went there first to visit the Australian nurse whom I'd met during my train trip from Munich to London. She was a plump blonde girl, very friendly and uncomplicated. She was sharing a flat with an English girl. Their flat was near Putney Bridge. On the Friday evening they prepared a dinner for me, something like kofte and potato puree. I asked them if it contained any ham and they said no. After dinner they took me to a pub. It was a very famous one. While they were drinking, I got engaged in a semi-political, philosophical discussion with an engineer. After eleven o'clock we went back to their flat. They made me a bed in the living room in a sleeping bag and then both retired to their rooms.

Next morning the Australian nurse was on duty so her friend looked after me. First we went to a tennis court. After we finished playing tennis, we went to the National Gallery, had lunch and returned to the flat late in the afternoon. We had dinner together and in the evening we went to the Fun Fair. After spending a lovely time with them I said goodbye on Sunday evening, crossing the bridge under the rain to take the bus back to Birmingham.

Another weekend I travelled to Edinburgh with a couple of Turkish students and spent my time looking around the museums and art galleries. In the evening we met up again and discussed where to go. The other two wanted to go looking for girls.

'Are you crazy?' I said, 'This is a foreign country, you don't know the language or the customs that well. You're looking for trouble!'

But they insisted, so I stayed in the car we had hired and went to sleep. About half an hour later I looked up to see them walking slowly along the road towards the car. They were cut and bleeding about the face and they looked utterly miserable. When I saw them, I couldn't help laughing and asked, 'What happened to you? Did you run into their boy-friends?'

But they wouldn't tell me. Just then a couple of men about our age appeared and started questioning us. I was alarmed and thought we were in for more trouble but as soon as they realised those two idiots had been beaten up they asked us to accompany them to their house. I didn't want to go because I had no way of knowing whether they would rob and kill us when they got us to their place, but the other two were in a sorry state so we agreed to go with them. We were met at the door of their house by a short middle-aged woman whom they introduced as their mother. When they had explained the situation to her, she was very sympathetic and insisted on us staying there for the night. She made us beds on the floor of her sitting room. Next morning she packed sandwiches, cakes and fruit for us and indignantly refused all our attempts to give her some payment.

We drove back to Birmingham in silence and I wondered about the strange, conflicting, characteristics of these British. For the first time since arriving in this country I allowed myself to think of Sarah. 'So this is your land, these are your people.'

After I had been in England for two months I decided to send a card to Sarah. I had been determined not to contact her but as the date of my departure drew nearer I knew I couldn't leave without at least letting her know I was there. I did not include my address and wrote simply:

Dear Sarah,

I am in your beautiful country. It is the country of my dreams. I shall pass through this lovely green land like a pale ghost.

Celik.

A week later I sent another card, this time including my address for I couldn't help it.

...I am having a wonderful time here. I am surrounded by beautiful girls all day long, but I just talk to them. You know I am a Moslem so I can not do anything with any woman outside marriage. We may meet if you wish, if God wills. If you would like to meet me come to Birmingham.

Celik.

A few days later a letter arrived from Sarah. I stared at the familiar writing on the envelope. I wanted to tear it open but I was afraid to and before I could change my mind, I tore it up and threw it in the fire. Then I wrote a brief note.

> Sarah,
> Please send me your phone number.
> Celik.

A postcard arrived by return with a phone number on it. The card simply said,

> Celik,
> Phone me at nine o'clock on Tuesday evening.
> Sarah.

I felt sick when I read this, not joyful at all. This was nothing like the way I used to imagine our first meeting would be. I didn't know whether I could bear hearing the sound of her voice. My head began to ache and my eyes felt dry and tired. I could not understand why I was feeling like this. I thought about my easy friendships with the girls in my office. I was popular. People enjoyed my company. I could make them laugh. Why then was I so terrified at the prospect of talking to a girl I had merely corresponded with for a while? These thoughts spun round in my head in circles but I could not answer them and there was nobody here I could talk to on such an intimate subject.

On Tuesday evening, I lay on the bed in my room trying to read and as the time drew nearer I felt myself trembling. Then the clock in the hall downstairs struck nine. I went into the hall and picked up the phone, taking several deep breaths to calm myself, then dialled. It was engaged. I waited, tried twice more and still it was engaged. By then I had almost lost my nerve. On the fourth try someone answered.

'May I please speak to Miss Weston,' I said, slowly and clearly.

'Who? Oh, Sarah. Just a sec please.'

A long pause. Then the phone was picked up again and... 'Hello, Sarah speaking.'

Her voice. Soft and warm. Sarah's voice. My own voice locked in my throat.

'Hello Sarah. This is Celik.'

A slight hesitation. Then a quick intake of breath.

'Oh Gosh! Celik! How are you?'

'I'm very well thank you. How are you.'

'Fine thanks. What a surprise it was to hear from you! How long have you been in England?'

'About two months.'

'How much longer have you got?'

'A few more weeks.'

'Oh?' She sounded disappointed. 'Why on earth didn't you let me know you were coming? I haven't had any letters from you for ages. What happened? Did you stop writing or did they get lost in the post?'

'Well, I was very busy with exams,' I lied. 'There was no time left over to write letters. I was going to surprise you when I got to England but since I've been here I've been working very hard.' I had not intended to say anything like this and involuntarily I pressed my hand to my hot face. It sounded highly implausible, even to my ears, but she didn't seem to think so.

'Oh, what a pity! I could have shown you around and introduced you to people.'

My mouth was so dry it was difficult to form the words, but I said, 'Yes, I'm sorry. But I still have a few weeks. Can you come to Birmingham.'

She said something in reply but I could not understand as she talked quietly and quickly. I asked her to repeat it slowly.

'It would be more interesting for you to come here. Dave and I will meet you at the station.'

'Dave?'

'Yes. We got engaged last month.'

I squeezed my eyes shut as if I could pretend I had not heard these words.

'Are you happy?'

'Yes... of course. And I'd love you to meet him.'

To my horror I felt tears well up in my eyes and my breath choke in my throat. If I continued this conversation a moment longer she would hear this. Before I humiliated myself further I put down the phone.

I stood staring at the phone for a long time, unable to believe that I had actually been talking to Sarah. My forehead felt clammy with sweat though I was shivering and my hands were ice-cold. I had an overwhelming urge to escape. A door opened somewhere and then there were footsteps on the stairs. Someone called from the kitchen. I could not face any of the family just then so I took my coat off the hook in the hall and rushed out into the dark, rainy night. I walked and walked and would have spent the whole night walking if I had not been afraid that my landlady would be anxious about my disappearance. When I returned, I went straight to my room because the muscles in my throat and chest were squeezing tight and my breathing was very hoarse. I did not want anyone to see me like this. I lay on my bed struggling for breath but it was like trying to breathe through a straw. I lay like that for half the night, not sure if my next breath would be my last.

Next morning, feeling as if I had no blood left in my body I wrote Sarah a letter.

My darling,

Why do you not come? Do you think I will put you in a cage and take you back to Istanbul? If so, you are a little bit foolish as well! I do not believe that you intend to marry someone else. Who else can understand your personality the way I do? Who else understands me the way you do? I will wait for you here every weekend but I do not have many weeks left. You must come. There are so many things we have to discuss. I know it is not going to be easy for us, we are from two different cultures but I do not like the things which are easy anyway. Always I have run away from easy things. I believe that every problem can be solved with discussion and compromise. I will have faith that you will come to meet me, even up to the moment that the train leaves the station.

Then I burned the letter in my hand.

There were two letters from Sarah after that which I threw straight on the fire. The rest of my days in Birmingham went with preparing myself to return to Turkey. I could have stayed in England if I had finished university, but I had to go back to take my final exams. However, the news about Sarah's engagement was a definite push out of England for me.

On my last day I was walking back into the office after completing an errand when I noticed all the desks were covered with tablecloths and plates of food and drink. I blinked, puzzled. No one had said anything to me about a party. Before I realised what was happening, everyone jumped out from behind filing cabinets, desks and doorways, shouting, 'Surprise! Surprise!'

Then they all surrounded me, singing, 'For he's a jolly good fellow...' and patted me on the back and said how much they had enjoyed having me with them. 'Oh Celik, it'll be so boring here after you go.'

My eyes filled with tears and I had to pretend I had a coughing fit so I could blow my nose. I was so moved that I didn't know what to say.

'A toast to a really fab bloke, fill up your glasses everyone.'

For the rest of the afternoon we ate and drank and laughed and joked. They had even remembered I didn't drink and had supplied bottles of coca cola. Somebody had brought a record player and played pop music so we could dance. All the girls wanted a turn at dancing with me. It was a wonderful climax to my happy days in that place. Before I left they gave me presents and farewell cards and we exchanged addresses and promised to write. Some of the girls were crying and all of them put their arms around me and kissed me on the mouth. Someone shouted, 'Speech! Speech!' They cleared a circle round me and I was standing alone, looking at their kind, smiling faces.

I forced myself to raise my glass of coke.

'Thank you for the best days of my life in your wonderful country. I will never forget you or these months.' It sounded so banal to my ears but they cheered and clapped and I thought how easy my life would be if I were really the person they were looking at.

Early next morning it was cold and rainy. I sat on the train searching the grey faces of the milling crowd on the platform. Doors opened and slammed and lovers embraced while others pushed passed them to scramble onto the train. A man in a grey business suit, clutching a brief-case sprinted across the platform at the last minute, gasping and puffing as he looked up and down the carriages for a vacant seat. Some noisy young boys in grey uniforms were leaning out of windows shouting goodbyes. Bags and cases and coats were heaved into racks as more people squeezed past along the aisle. A fat, harassed-looking woman with frizzy grey hair settled a crying child in the seat beside me. Groups of schoolgirls pressed their faces against the steamed-up windows. Outside the train, knots of people formed and changed shape. Craning necks, waving hands. Colours merged and blurred. Babbling voices and high-pitched shrieks and laughter mingled with far-away echoes.

A whistle blew – a long, mournful wail. The chaos subsided. The train pulled out of the station and the crowds melted away leaving only an empty space on the platform.

CHAPTER ◆ SIX

After my return to Turkey I spent sleepless nights alone in my room. Each day there was a steady stream of neighbours and relatives who came to welcome me back and hear my stories. I distributed the gifts I had brought and showed them the photographs I had taken. My father had arranged the letters and postcards I had sent him in a separate album and he enjoyed bringing this out to show me so I could explain whatever was not clear to him. Osman and Mehmed asked endless questions and were fascinated with my accounts of English life and customs. Although Mehmed could not speak English, he was fluent in German and was expecting to go to Germany in about a year. Whenever I started talking about my experiences, Hulya would come into the room and listen quietly with wide open eyes. To all of them it was as though I were describing a strange, distant planet.

Yashar came over to see me a few days after my return. He was standing in the hall taking off his shoes when he looked up and saw me. He dropped the slippers he was putting on and threw his arms around my neck and kissed me repeatedly on both cheeks.

'Celik! Celik my friend! How good it is to see you. Let me look at you! What's new and what isn't new? May God be praised for bringing you safely back to us. Let me look at you! Oh my God you look wonderful. Doesn't he look wonderful?'

His welcome brought tears to my eyes and I hugged him, this dear, dear friend, but at the same time I knew that this scene belonged to the past and was not connected with the present or future. While I was struggling to accommodate this new idea, Yashar was punctuating his remarks by slapping my back and squeezing my cheeks between his hands till at last my father burst out laughing and said, 'You'll kill him before the day's out.

He's been gone only three months, not three years.'

My mother stood by smiling at my tears. She loved Yashar as if he were one of her own sons and I saw the happiness in her face at this scene of my reintegration into the family and community. The tears I brushed away from my eyes were not for my return home but for the sudden awareness that from this day on I would have no concept of home. I would spend my life alone, roaming the earth like a stranger. I have no idea how I knew this, only that it would be so. I did not want anyone to suspect the cause of my tears so it was easy to pretend I was overwhelmed with joy at this reunion.

After we had been fortified with tea and cakes and I had shown Yashar my photographs, he suggested we take the ferryboat to Çanlica to have a quiet, leisurely day together, rediscovering our old haunts.

We waited for a dolmus to take us to the ferry and in a short while one screeched to a halt beside us, scattering mud on our clothes. Though it was bursting at the seams with people already, hands reached out to help us on and a space was made for us by the other passengers who simply moulded themselves around our bodies. The dolmus accelerated off again at top speed, weaving in and out of the tangle of traffic and pedestrians, the driver slowing only to shake his fist at a peasant who was driving a donkey and cart in the middle of the road. The vehicle careered across to the other side of the road, accompanied by a cacophony of horns, whenever our driver saw more passengers waiting. Only by the sheer volume of people were we prevented from falling flat on our faces as the driver slammed on his brakes. We passed our fare over the heads of the other passengers who handed it down to the ticket officer.

When we stated our destination there was a chorus of concern: 'They may be too late to catch the ferry...' 'You should drive faster or they'll miss the ferry...' 'You can't let these poor boys miss their connection...' The driver nodded vigorously in agreement and tried to ignore a traffic policeman in his anxiety to get us to the ferry on time. However, a shrill whistle from the furious policeman brought him to a shuddering stop. He shrugged his shoulders and muttered under his breath. I observed this scene – one that I had seen times beyond counting and had never thought remarkable – as if I were a visitor to this city and I couldn't help laughing.

Yashar looked at me inquiringly. 'What's funny?' – which made me laugh even more.

Incredibly, we got to the ferry just as the gangway was being lifted so we scrambled to buy our tickets and dashed on board almost colliding with a tea-server who was balancing glasses of tea on a tray, calling, 'Cay, cay,' in a raucous voice.

We bought a glass each and then a ragged shoe-shine boy with an artificial eye appeared. I asked him to polish my shoes and he set to work with enthusiasm. A waiter strode up to him and ordered him off the boat. The boy protested. 'But I've been working here for months.'

'No matter, you have no right to be here. It is against the rules.' The waiter strode away again and the boy grinned at us and commented, 'That idiot! Some people don't know how to behave.'

Back came the waiter. 'I heard that! You had better leave now or I will call the police.'

At this I intervened and said to the waiter, 'Please. Let me not remain half-polished!'

He glowered once more at the boy and then hurried below deck. The boy winked his one eye at me and finished his work, cocked his head on one side to check that it was done to his satisfaction then gave my shoes a final leisurely flick with his cloth. After I paid him he looked for work amongst the other passengers with a determination that, if it were up to him, not one should leave the boat without a shine on their shoes. After that, the waiter pretended not to see him. The other passengers watched this game with appreciation, grinning and nodding and commenting to each other, and I recalled the way the English travelled on buses and trains as if all other passengers were invisible; the way they whispered when they talked in public and ignored other people's conversations. I wondered how Sarah would react to this scene of public enjoyment of a little power game. This thought slid into my mind through an unguarded crack and settled there despite my annoyance at own weakness. I resolved to be more vigilant about what I allowed to creep uninvited into my head.

I settled back to enjoy the trip across the Bosphorus, watching the parade of pedlars on the boat selling everything from plastic bags to expensive-looking wallets. The air was cool, salty, fishy. A watery sun shone out of a high white sky specked with migratory birds.

Disembarking on the Asian side, we walked hand in hand for some time without speaking, half of me watching the boats and listening to the familiar sounds and savouring the pleasure of Yashar's company. The other half watched from a distance as though observing the inhabitants of a strange city. This half also saw Yashar looking at his companion with a slightly puzzled air and quickly said, 'I have to admit it, it is pleasant to re-acquaint myself with all this.'

Yashar's laughter sounded relieved and he said, 'What do you say to stopping at a café to eat some yoghurt?'

We sat at a table outside a café overlooking the Bosphorus, for although the streets were shiny with rain, the air was soft and warm. After ordering a pot each I said, 'In England they sell it in little cartons, mixed with fruit, as a dessert. They've just discovered it as a health food. It's very fashionable.'

Yashar wrinkled his nose and I laughed. 'Ah, but still, you have never tasted anything like their chocolate cake! I went with some friends to a little coffee-house in Hampstead and ate the most delicious chocolate cake in the world!' I closed my eyes in ecstasy.

'Celik,' he grinned, 'Do you not think of anything other than your belly?'

'I judge how civilised a nation is by its food,' I protested. 'I admit to some doubtful moments in England when I was served boiled meat and watery cabbage and potatoes, but I found a landlady who could cook like an angel. Her shepherd's pies and steak and kidney puddings were even worth being deprived of this yoghurt for a few months.'

We both laughed and to cover up my feeling of dislocation I concentrated on making Yashar happy. We spent the afternoon walking in the streets and bringing each other up to date with our news, stopping occasionally to buy an orange from a stall, some roasted chestnuts, a glass of pickle juice. Yashar was very interested in finding out which books I had read in England and I had to confess I had had very little time for reading.

'Oh, you spent all your spare time sight-seeing then?'

'I did quite a bit of sight-seeing, but really I was in such demand socially that my free time was limited! Especially by the girls I worked with. Every evening I was out somewhere. It was, "Celik come roller-skating with us." "Celik I'm having a party tonight and I want you to come." "Celik are you busy tomorrow? We are all going dancing." "Come on a picnic with us Celik." I tell you, I was worn out!'

He stared at me in disbelief. 'Girls asked you to go out with them?'

'Of course. I was a novelty. They felt very privileged to have an exotic

Turk in their office.'

'I don't believe you!'

'It's true. Those English men didn't stand a chance while I was there. They don't know how to behave with girls.'

Shutting Sarah's voice out of my mind I started to mimic some of the girls in the office. '"Celik, you are so courteous, what a pity you have to go back to Turkey." "Celik, Turks are so much more romantic than Englishmen. It's that Middle Eastern charm isn't it?" "Oh Celik, you really are a Turkish delight aren't you!"'

By now Yashar was doubled up with laughter and our antics had begun to attract the attention of passers-by. We leaned against a wall helplessly, trying to recover ourselves. My play-acting was so effective that I could almost believe in it until, at last, arms around each other's shoulders, we walked back towards the ferry.

The boat was crowded but we managed to find standing space on the top deck because I wanted to watch the sun set over the mosques. Seagulls screeched and dipped around the returning fishing boats and as the sky darkened, lights winked on the water like jewels in a sultan's treasury.

A girl of about eighteen came and stood next to Yashar and stared at the flickering lights on the opposite shore. I noticed Yashar glance at her and look quickly away again. The girl also noticed him for he was very handsome and a little taller than I.

I thought of the morning one of the typists in the Birmingham office walked into the room where I was working and commented loudly to her companion. 'He's a bit of all right, eh?' I smiled at the memory of my face reddening with surprise and pleasure and the giggling of the girls. I said to Yashar, in English so the girl wouldn't understand, 'She's very beautiful, don't you think?'

He looked at me in surprise, but said nothing.

I continued, 'She looks like a film star. I tell you, I have never seen such a beauty. Look at the way her hair falls in thick, black waves over her shoulders. I should like to run my fingers through that hair. Her eyes, so black and sparkling. A man could be driven crazy with those eyes.'

Yashar recovered his wits enough to say quietly, in English, 'Have you gone off your head? She may understand what you are saying.'

'So what? How could any woman be offended by hearing an accurate description of her beauty?' I felt the separation of my two selves again and was able to watch myself acting the clown. 'Ah, those lips, so soft and red. Can't you imagine pressing your mouth against them, Yashar?'

By now he was scarlet-faced and agitated.

'But see how well she is dressed. How shapely are her legs. And those high-heeled shoes emphasise the curve in her ankles to perfection.' I began to imagine how she might respond to these compliments if she were English.

At that moment, to my discomfiture and Yashar's horror, the girl, who had ignored us without showing any signs of understanding what I was saying, turned to stare coldly at me and said in perfect English. 'Are you crazy or something?'

'My apologies,' I said at once, my two halves colliding with a crash that jarred my bones. 'I would not have spoken like that had I realised you understood English, but I could not help admiring you. I have just returned from a few months in England where I saw very beautiful girls every day, but compared with you they were thorns on a rose.'

She smiled a little and I heard Yashar sigh in relief. I thought I could enjoy this game but it was time to get off the ferry and the girl said goodbye pleasantly and hurried away. Yashar turned to me to say something but he was speechless and I roared with laughter at his expression. We tumbled off the boat with the crowd and were hurried along in the crush towards the bus stop. I caught a glimpse of the girl talking to a tall man with a beard. Then I heard someone calling behind us. We stopped and looked back. The man, several years older than we were, was hurrying towards us waving his arms. As he approached, he addressed me. 'Pardon sir. My sister says you insulted her on the ferryboat.'

'No,' I said. 'I did not insult her. I was praising her beauty to my friend. Besides, I did not know then that she could understand English.'

After listening politely to my explanation, he carefully took off my glasses and slapped me hard across each cheek. He handed me back my glasses and with as much dignity as I could muster, I said, 'Please accept my apologies. I meant no offence to your sister.'

He nodded curtly and disappeared back the way he had come. A few people glanced curiously at me as they hurried past, some looked sympathetic, others amused. As I stared after him, stupefied, I heard Yashar trying unsuccessfully to suppress a laugh. I looked at him and he patted me on the back and grinned. 'Welcome home Celik!'

The next few weeks were occupied with study for my final examinations. I passed all of them except statistics because I had found this subject boring and had not studied it thoroughly enough. The humiliation of failing this exam made me determined not to fail again so I studied far more about statistics than I needed to know to pass the exam. Consequently I learned more about related subjects such as modern mathematics, theory of probability and symbolic logic. I took another examination, this time passing and got my B.Sc. When I opened the letter that informed me of my results I sighed with relief and passed the letter to my father.

He read it, handed it back to me and said, 'Before you leave for Ankara I will give you a gift which is appropriate for this achievement,' and smiled at me as he walked out the room. I knew how proud he was feeling and I hugged myself with joy.

I was now ready for my military service. As I filled in my application form I remembered the small, skinny boy who was always a target for bullies at school and in the streets. I saw that weedy child, strutting in front of his friends in the splendid army coat and white captain's hat, as though the uniform gave him special powers and made him tall and strong. My friends had been very impressed and called me sir, but my father had laughed at me, telling me again and again that power lay in knowledge. Well, now I had acquired enough knowledge to graduate from university and to achieve my boyhood dream of becoming an officer in the army. In March I applied for it and in April, after I had bought a train ticket and a supply of food from the registration office, I prepared to travel to Ankara to join the school for communication officers.

As I stepped on the train my father handed me a small package wrapped in a green scarf. His face wore its usual calm expression and he said, 'It's yours now.'

I unwrapped the package and saw it was the Masnawi. I felt tears prick the back of my eyes and did not trust my voice to thank him for this gift. When I had recovered myself enough to look up he had already turned away and was striding across the platform to the exit.

I sat down on the seat and moved my hands over the worn, green leather surface. I held it to my cheek and inhaled the musty smell. It was like an old room where people have lived and loved for a long time. I opened my father's book at the place where the green silk bookmark lay between the thin, faded pages... 'I too have roamed, keening and crying, and passing through fair and foul. All smiled at me but none saw to my depths. The essence of my all is in this cry, but no-one hears and none perceives...' My eyes filled up with tears.

My first days at the school passed in a confusion of buying books, reading timetables, finding rooms and people I was meant to see. After I had settled in I began to enjoy my courses and took myself off to my room every evening to look over my notes and memorise the new points. My reward to myself was to spend the last hour of each day reading the Masnawi.

Mevlana Celaeddin Rumi was a religious scholar who founded the sect of Mevlevi, which later became known as Whirling Dervishes, in the thirteenth century. It was one of the Turkish-Islamic mystic movements which flourished during the spread of Islam throughout the Turkish world. For six hundred years of Ottoman rule until the founding of the Republic in 1923 it had occupied a very important place in Turkish society. Mevlana devoted his life to the composition of mystical poetry and ritual dance. The Masnawi is his most famous work. He saw death as something to be celebrated as a return to God. He referred to his death as a time of celebration saying that the day the soul leaves the body must be celebrated as a festival. Whenever I read this I remembered my father's angry reaction when I had cried at my brother's funeral and a hot flush of shame crept up my neck and ears.

I assumed everyone else was also working and reading in their rooms, until one evening, a few weeks into the course, a loud knock on my door made me jump. I opened it to see three of my fellow officers standing there laughing. They reeked of alcohol.

'Celik, we have some beer and we want to play cards. Come and join us.' They glanced into my room, at all my papers and books spread over my desk.

'What's this? You can't be serious!' and they doubled up laughing and fell against each other in the corridor.

I felt very annoyed at their intrusion but I didn't want to be thought unsociable so I said, 'Oh I was just finishing. I'm glad you came by. I need a break.'

They clapped me on the back and I accompanied them to their room.

This pattern was repeated every night over the next few weeks. At first

I enjoyed their light spirits and laughter, but soon their jokes began to seem silly and their conversations self-centred and juvenile. They mostly came from middle to upper-class backgrounds. Nothing in their lives had ever been a struggle for them. They had money, fashionable clothes, their own cars, summer houses, they had travelled widely in Europe and the USA. They just wanted to get this nuisance period out of the way so they could get on with their 'real lives.' I, on the other hand, did not know what my 'real life' was.

Eventually I began to make excuses not to join them in the evenings.

'What's wrong?' they asked, 'You surely don't want to stay in your room all alone reading those boring books?'

'Actually I don't find them boring. Besides I don't wish to get caught with beer.'

They laughed, 'But you don't even drink the stuff.'

Before I could control my tongue I said, 'It's against the rules.'

This caused whoops of mirth and one of them saluted me and called me 'lead soldier.'

This hurt me, but naturally I did not want them to see that it did so I immediately assumed the stance of a lead soldier and marched about the room. They screamed with laughter at my performance. After that, whenever I felt my privacy was in danger of being invaded I switched on a similar show. As always, my ability to joke and clown deflected attention from my real aims and ambitions. Eventually they accepted me as I was and left me alone.

I finished the course with an honours degree. I was selected to serve in the same garrison, as an instructor to corporals, for six months. After that I was transferred to the general headquarters of the armed forces as a translator. I enjoyed using my ability with language and here too I worked hard. I liked to relax in the evenings by reading on my bed. From time to time my colleagues dropped in to see me and on one occasion six of them burst in the door, drunk as usual, to persuade me to play cards. When they saw me reading they demanded to know what was so fascinating that it could keep me from a card game.

'Well,' I said, 'it's the most important text in Islamic literature after the Koran and the Hadith.'

'It is? Who wrote it?'

'Mevlana.'

'What's so wonderful about it?'

This was actually an opportunity I had been hoping for. I wanted to have a discussion about Mevlana's ideas for it was difficult struggling with them alone. I said, 'He believed that the love of mankind is equal to the love of God. This concept is so simple yet so powerful. The poems express his belief in the value of human existence and the importance of the individual and freedom of expression. His message is directed at the whole human race. Listen to this: *The rays of the sun shine fragmented a thousandfold into the courts of a thousand houses. But if you remove the walls between them you will see that these splinters of light are one and the same.*'

My companions blinked at me, then one of them said, 'Ah. The Dervishes. They plotted against the government.'

I replied, 'When Ataturk abolished the Caliphate the Dervishes tried to overthrow the government and restore the sultan, but did that mean they deserved to be hanged? Did it mean their rituals should be abolished? They were religious people who were devoted to peace and harmony.'

My companions shrugged. One said, 'I visited his tomb at Konya when I was a child and saw the dance. Weird!'

I realised my mistake in imagining these oafs could possibly comprehend the ideas expressed in this book. I decided not to bring up the subject again. Impatiently I waved them out of my room and returned to my reading.

I felt starved of intellectual companionship and the more books I read the more I realised how little I knew. I began to read more history to help me understand why Ataturk had been so determined to get rid of every trace of the Dervishes. I knew, of course, that the support for Ataturk had come about because of his success in the War of Independence which gave Turkey back its lands. Now I read that he might have become Caliph if he had wished to but that his ambitions were for Turkey, not for himself. I read those words with growing unease as I began to understand at what cost to the country he had achieved those ambitions. The more I read about the institutions of the republic the more my anxiety grew as I began to understand the nature of its roots.

One night I couldn't sleep. I tossed and turned and eventually lay on my back with my eyes staring up at the ceiling in the dark. Passing cars threw shadows onto my walls. I began to imagine they looked like the shadows of hanged men. I closed my eyes to shut out the image but they kept snapping open until I was forced to look at the wall over and over again. What sort of government would hang men whose sole purpose in life was to spread love and peace and understanding? I began to sweat. Why hadn't I thought about this before?

In the morning I was exhausted and feverish. Was I wrong in thinking about all this? Was the purpose of the republic's institutions disguised because of outside dangers and pressures? Maybe the people I had contact with were ignorant of it. I couldn't challenge my hypothesis by discussing it with anyone, so all I could do was spend my leisure time alone in my room, reading as much as possible. But the more I read, the more depressed I became.

I realised then, that despite all my acquaintances, I had no friends I could trust in this place, no one to whom I could speak about what I had learned. I started to get severe headaches and the pain was so great I couldn't sleep. Even medicine could not relieve my blurred vision and throbbing temples. I was driven in my desperation to soaking towels in cold water and lying them across my face. I didn't know what to do or where to go for help. One night, when the pain was at its worst, I drifted in and out of a feverish sleep and dreamed I was a child again standing with my father and Lale by a riverbank. The cool wind blew against my hot cheeks. When I woke up I struggled to remember where this place was. I saw the scene in my mother's kitchen when my father read the newspaper article about the discovery of King Midas and Lale telling me that one day we would go there. But we didn't, did we Lale? I tried to go back to sleep to see her face again and feel the coolness of the wind. Instead, my fever returned and I buried my head in the pillow to stop my crying.

I had a day's leave due in two weeks' time. The idea came to me that if I visited that place of my dream I might find relief. By now the pain of my headaches was with me day and night, sometimes slicing through my head like a cold, sharp knife, other times tightening bands of hot metal around my forehead. I swallowed pain killers every day to reduce the pain to a bearable level to enable me to carry on with my work.

On the day of my leave I took the train to Polatli. There I found an old battered taxi to take me thirty kilometres along the Eskisehir-Ankara road across the Anatolian plateau. For thousands of years this plateau had been a battlefield as waves of civilisations rose and fell. We came to the place where Ataturk halted the Greek advance in 1921, the last battle to be fought here, and took a side road to Gordion.

What a bleak, deserted sight! It was hard to believe that this had once been the key to Asia Minor and the cultural capital of the Phrygian state. The whole area was rich in history and legends. Now, there were only a few squat houses and only the noise of hens, goats and dogs broke the silence. A few peasant women sat cross-legged at their cooking in a communal cooking shed. Young men were working in the fields while the old ones smoked and played backgammon outside a tea-house in the pale sunshine. From a radio somewhere floated the mournful strains of a love song. The windswept flatness of the landscape was relieved only by a group of large grassy mounds which were the tombs of the Phrygian kings. I looked at this wasteland and wondered why I'd come. What was I hoping to find?

'Are you all right, sir?' The anxious voice of the taxi driver startled me. I looked up to see his big, red face looming close to mine. 'Can I help you? Take you to a doctor?'

The concern in his voice surprised and touched me and I felt close to tears but I would have died of humiliation if he had guessed it. I shook my head, 'No, no, thank you. I'm all right. Really, I'm fine.'

He looked unconvinced. 'Would you like me to come with you? Just in case?'

We were now at the ruins of the ancient city of Gordion. 'Thank you,' I said, 'but once I'm in the fresh air, I'll be okay. Please wait for me in the tea-house and I'll join you there for a glass of tea later.'

He ambled off, not at all happy. This made me smile. Why should he care about me, a stranger? I climbed to the top of the city mound past the temple of Cybele where the wagon of Gordius had stood, its yoke and shaft tied with its impossible knot. As I breathed deeply the cold, clean air I thought of Gordius's son, Midas, who was foolish enough to say publicly that Pan's music was superior to Apollo's and for his indiscretion was rewarded with the ears of an ass. Only his barber knew and was threatened with death if he ever told a living soul.

I looked at the dark waters of the River Sakarya flowing in front of me, the long rushes on its banks bending under the weight of ancient secrets. I stretched out my arms like wings and flew down the hill to the river, the cold wind slapping at my face, cooling my burning cheeks. Did the barber's secret swell inside him until he was driven half mad with the pain? I knelt on the riverbank and scratched at the hard earth with my fingers until I'd made a little shallow bowl. In the barber's shadow I lay down with my face so close to the earth I could smell its pungent darkness. Into the earth I whispered my secret. 'The republic's constitution is an ass's constitution.' The rushes caught my words on the wind and sighed, 'The republic's constitution is an ass's constitution.' And all the souls of the martyrs cried towards the heavens, 'The republic's constitution is an ass's constitution, the republic's constitution is an ass's constitution.'

I stood up, feeling all the tension and depression draining out of me at the accomplishment of this mission. I turned to go. There, standing on the hill, watching me, was the taxi driver. He couldn't have heard what I had said, but I suppose my actions must have looked extremely peculiar, judging by the alarmed expression on his face. I wanted to burst out laughing, but if I did, then he would surely have thought me mad. So I waved to him, to let him see I was unperturbed by his having just witnessed this strange ritual, and walked, slowly and casually, to where he was waiting.

CHAPTER
◆ SEVEN

The day after I had released my secret into the earth by the River Sakarya I woke up in the morning without the familiar throbbing in my temples. By the end of the week my headaches had still not returned. As I settled down on my bed that evening, I said aloud, 'So now what?'

And into my mind, as if in answer – develop a language to absorb the opposition.

Again I spoke out loud. 'What opposition?'

I picked up a pencil and paper and began writing down the types of people in the Translation Bureau, which I believed to be a true cross-section of the nation. Representatives of Turkish views based on Ataturk's reforms. Representatives of International Jewish views. Representatives of the man-in-the-street. One representative of Turkish views as an extension of its international historic roots based upon Moslem-Jewish-Christian practices in scriptures revealed by God through His Messengers.

I laughed with joy when I read what I had written. Now, all I had to do was try out my hypothesis.

The next evening after dinner, instead of going up to my room, I went into the games room to drink coffee with a dozen of my colleagues. There were cries of, 'Oho! Look who it is! So you have decided you want some intelligent company at last?'

'Come on, man,' I laughed, 'If that's what I wanted I would have looked in the mirror.'

There were hoots of laughter and someone threw a cushion at my head. Three people were playing cards, two were idly chatting. The others were either playing pool or smoking cigarettes while they watched a football game on television. I sat back in my chair, my feet raised on a stool, completely relaxed and looking forward to stirring them out of their torpor.

I put my coffee cup down and said casually to the three who were playing cards, 'Who were those guys who came together and formulated a constitution to shape the lives of millions? Who authorised them to do so? Do they represent a supreme power like God or USA or USSR? Are they Lords of Weaponry? Are they a gang emerged out of the relics of the Old Empire who want to rule under its image? Without that image they are nothing with their guns and ammunition and their system called Republic.'

Two glanced at me only briefly before continuing with their game. The third gaped like a fish. 'Eh?'

All I had to do was isolate that image of the Old from the Machinery, so I said, 'I follow the way of Abraham who was not an idolater and Alp Aslan who opened the gates of Anatolia to the Turks and Fatih who conquered Constantinople and rebuilt it and Yavuz who took the responsibility of the Moslem world on his shoulders.'

Now all three stared at me. Someone said, 'What have you been drinking?' and they laughed.

My relaxed feeling began to evaporate. But what else did I expect from these idiots? I took my feet off the stool and sat up straight. The couple talking about football were looking at me but they were not laughing. One said, 'You shouldn't say things like that, joke or no joke, it's against the Constitution.'

'Constitution?' Now it was my turn to laugh. 'I reject the Constitution!'

Three people wandered over to stub out their cigarettes in the ash tray on the table near where I was sitting. Two of them looked interested. The third, a man named Niyazi Onder, a political science graduate, scowled. 'How can you say that? On what basis?'

'On the basis that it contradicts and exploits the established beliefs of this nation,' I said loudly.

All conversation in the room stopped. Only the inane commentary from the television broke the silence. Someone called across the room over the pool table.

'The Constitution was written for the good of this nation, how can you say it exploits it?'

This was more like it! I chose my words carefully before I uttered them.

'Because it is inhumane and illegal. Why should a Moslem kill someone in Cyprus for the sake of the Constitution which is based upon Ataturk's ideology? Why should a Moslem pay half of his income in tax to keep the army and other constitutional institutions which are nothing to do with the workings of his way of life? Under Ottoman rule, religious minorities were not forced to fight for the Ottoman army nor to pay taxes to support it.'

From different corners of the room responses were fired at me like bullets from a machine gun but I caught them all in my language net, woven with words so strong that their bullets could not harm me.

'You're surely not suggesting our country was better off under the Ottomans?'

'Our country was a great empire for seven hundred years under the Ottomans.'

'And under Ottoman rule it degenerated into the sick man of Europe.'

'I'm not denying that some of the institutions had degenerated, because of aping the west and a lack of faith in Islam, though Abdul Hamid did his best to halt the decline.'

'Abdul the Damned? The Red Sultan? He was crazy! Everyone knows that!'

'Who knows anything? There was a lot of propaganda after he was deposed, to save the faces of the rabble who did it. How do you know what is truth?'

'Have you forgotten that if it hadn't been for Ataturk and 'his rabble' as you call them, we wouldn't have a country now?'

'It was Ataturk our great leader who led our country from the brink of extinction after the war.'

'Ataturk! Ataturk! Who was Ataturk? The son of a peasant!'

By now they were all gathered round me, some sitting on the floor, others standing with their hands in their pockets. Niyazi Onder stood slightly apart from the group, not participating but listening intently. Someone turned the television down. I felt elated that my language had the power to catch these people, who were products of a degenerate education system, like bees to a bright flower growing tall and strong in a field of weeds. An unhappy voice whispered in my ear: 'Celik, be careful, loose talk like this...'

But to stop now was impossible. A lifetime of words had been seeded in my head and fertilised with the thoughts of the great. They had crawled through my brain like larvae growing fat these long, lonely, painful months. Now, on this ordinary, sleepy evening their time had come to hatch. Nothing could prevent them taking flight. They spread their beautiful wings, delicate and strong and filled the dull room with colour.

'He was a drunk! A womaniser and a degenerate! Do you know what he died of?'

'What does his personal life matter, you can not deny he was a great man.'

'In any case, as far as his drinking and womanising goes, he was no different from your precious sultans!'

'...a brilliant military strategist.'

'...a man of vision.'

'...his reforms dragged our country out of the Middle Ages.'

'...it was Ataturk alone who set us on the path to civilisation and progress.'

My words flew about the room in flashes of bright light. Everyone was listening attentively now, their faces showing their astonishment.

'You all talk about progress, but we are a country without identity. Pseudo-Europeans, thanks to Ataturk's westernisation policies. When he banned the Arabic alphabet, he destroyed our cultural heritage. He forced changes on our country which were forbidden by the Koran, then stole money from the religious foundations to run his Mickey Mouse government of oppression.'

After I stopped speaking there was total silence. Nobody moved. After a few minutes, someone coughed and said quietly, 'There's something in what you say Celik. I have heard no one say those things before.'

That stirred the others up again. 'But you can't deny that the reforms... the Latin alphabet, for instance, meant that western literature was accessible to us. And look at our art galleries, you can't say we have no culture.'

'Western culture? Western art? Where is the calligraphy of the Ottomans? Was that not an art form worth preserving?'

'Well... but we have orchestras, operas, ballets.'

'How many of us enjoy Turkish music? Or even understand it? And why not? Because Ataturk said western music was better.'

'But look at the backwardness of our country compared to Europe – Ataturk was right in saying our archaic religious system was an obstacle to progress.'

'How can Islam be an obstacle to progress when Islam does not prevent the adoption of the technology of the west? But why should we copy the west in the areas of law and government when Islam is superior?'

Their arguments had no substance in the face of my counter-arguments, and finally their resistance was nothing more than the mouthing of the empty words that had been used to brainwash them as they were processed through the system.

'Well... most of the reforms... the industrialisation of the country, for example.'

'Means that hundreds of peasants swarm into the cities with no chance of finding work.'

'Well... the unveiling of our women... the replacement of Koranic Law with the Swiss Code which banned polygamy.'

'Go into any village and you'll see for yourself that these things haven't changed. Even fifty years of the republic have not been able to destroy some institutions.'

'But no one would want to see a return to the old days, apart from a minority of religious fanatics.'

'....so why make trouble? You aren't an ignorant peasant.'

'....besides, you can't change anything so why disturb yourself over what is past? We have to progress.'

I had said everything I intended to say. Sown the first seeds. Now I sat back in my chair and smiled. The group broke up, the talk turned to football, someone turned the television sound back up. I would leave them in peace now and give my words a chance to settle and grow. I glanced at Niyazi Onder who was still hovering at the back of the room, feeling uneasy about him, for by his silence he was showing himself to be feeling defenceless and unsafe and rootless. I raised my fist half-way in a salute and said, 'Peace. The only salvation is in Islam.' He looked back at me, expressionless, and slipped from the room. I shrugged. Well, that was his problem. I lay back in my chair and closed my eyes for I was feeling exhausted.

I thought over everything I had said that evening. Actually I was amazed at the effect my words had had on my colleagues, the way they had been forced to think for themselves, probably for the first time in their lives. As soon as that thought came into my mind it was followed by another: 'Who gave you this power over words?' I felt chastened then. I was no more than a vessel for whatever purpose God chose to use me.

I opened my eyes, stood up and stretched and wandered over to the window. The sky was saffron and the clouds around the sun were shot through with gold. I breathed deeply, feeling at peace. Two of my colleagues came over to stand behind me and watch the sun slide behind the rooftops. I heard more footsteps, then the voice of Niyazi Onder. 'What do you say to a walk Celik Ertas? I should like to listen to more of your talk.' He rested his hand lightly on my shoulder.

I was surprised but delighted. He had obviously thought over what I had said and, realising his mistake, had come back to learn more. Immediately I forgave him – after all I should have realised my discourse would come as a shock to most people. 'Sure! An excellent idea! We can enjoy this beautiful sunset together.'

He withdrew his hand and the room was suddenly silent. I was aware that a space had appeared around me. I turned and saw two military policemen. They stepped forward. 'Celik Ertas, you are under arrest.'

'On what charge? I asked, thinking this must be a joke.

'For violating the constitution by making propaganda to establish a theocratic state in place of the Republic of Turkey.'

'What!' I laughed and looked at the others in the room but they avoided my eyes. 'Whose idea of a joke is this? Come on it's late and I'm tired.'

They did not laugh however. I looked around for Onder but he had disappeared.

'For God's sake...' I said in exasperation.

'Come,' their voices were stony. 'We have to take you to the Head of Intelligence.'

As we walked towards the door everyone melted away, to play pool, read the newspaper, light their cigarettes. I picked up my jacket from the chair and put it on, then went with the policemen to the office of the Head of Intelligence.

I felt nothing but irritation at that idiot Onder. I did not know what kind of game he was playing but when I saw him tomorrow I would make a point of finding out and let him know what I thought of his stupidity.

At the office of the Head of Intelligence I was kept waiting for half an hour by the general who wanted to see me. Finally I was ushered into his presence and stood before his large mahogany desk. He continued shuffling papers on it for several minutes before looking up. His face was red and his white brows met over his bulbous nose. Behind him, Ataturk's piercing blue eyes glared at me from a huge gilt-framed portrait hanging on the wall.

The General couldn't endure me looking at Ataturk so coolly instead of cowering in fear, so he tried to intimidate me by barking, 'Ideology of Abraham, Alp Aslan and Fatih? What nonsense is that? We have no ideologies.' Then he realised his mistake and added quickly, 'Except, of course, Ataturk's ideology.'

I looked back at him calmly without replying and he continued. 'What are you trying to preach? Are we not Moslems?'

Still I didn't answer, nor could his glaring eyes force me to drop my gaze from his fat red face. To save his vanity he had to break the silence first, 'Did you not make an oath to protect the constitution?'

After I had finished the preparation school with an honours degree, I had been taken to give an oath to complete the ceremonies of becoming an officer. 'Yes I did,' I replied.

'Are you aware that it is an offence under Article 163 to distribute religious propaganda?'

'I am.'

His mouth twisted. He clicked his fingers at the two policemen who were standing impassively behind me.

'Take him to the court,' he said.

The court decided to arrest me. With the prosecutor and two officers, they took me back to my room with a search warrant.

I'm watching them fling open the doors of my cupboards and tear my clothes off hangers and go through my pockets. My mouth tastes as if it's full of ash but I won't ask their permission for a drink of water. I can't believe this is happening and I want to rewind the film to the frame where I am about to talk to my companions as they play cards. In my mind I replay the scene differently. I decide not to waste my words on their cloth ears and go for a walk instead to enjoy the gold and red clouds around the setting sun. But the slamming of drawers and doors and the thump of my possessions hitting the walls preclude any possibility that I might be caught up in the middle of a nightmare. I'm fully here in my room, watching my colleagues, with whom I trained, violate it, pulling my books out of their shelves and flinging them roughly to the floor. I want to order them to stop but my tongue is stuck to the roof of my mouth and I can't move my limbs. They are opening the top drawer of my desk where I keep my personal papers and letters. They flick through them and toss them on my bed. My heart is beating hard in my chest. I can not draw in enough air to breathe. I can not locate my legs and arms. One of the men looks like a gorilla and his huge hands close on Sarah's letters.

I force my cracked lips open. 'Please. These are private letters. They have no bearing on this whatsoever.'

'So you correspond with a foreigner?' the gorilla growls, looking at the writing on the envelope. 'This is in English, isn't it? What does it say?'

At least the ignorant bastard can't read English. He sniffs the envelope.

'A woman is it?' he leers, 'those foreign women like cock don't they? They can't get enough I heard. My brother's in Germany and he gets into a different cunt every day and he doesn't even have to pay for it, lucky sod.'

I want to snatch the letters from his hairy mitt and grind his ugly face into the wall. I want to tear off his nose and fingers and stuff them up his arsehole. The other officer is a man called Jemal who I have often played chess with. His parents are arranging a marriage for him and last week he showed me the photographs of his fiancée. He holds out his hand for the letters and speaks quietly. 'We have to follow orders but this is not our business.'

To my amazement the gorilla hands over the letters. Jemal replaces them in my desk and shuts the drawer. My relief at keeping my letters is so great I want to sink down on my knees and cover my face with my hands. But I have to keep standing here like a helpless animal watching this invasion of my privacy, knowing that not one single action or word from me can prevent it. I have absolutely no control over what happens to me now. My fate is in the hands of betrayers who will join the feeding frenzy rather than risk damaging their own reputations. Honour and decency have nothing to do with what happens now. One corner of my paralysed mind still functions enough to resolve to entrust my letters to Osman as soon as I can contact him.

After the search, I was taken directly to the military prison. During the revolution it had been used for political prisoners. Now it was a general prison for thieves, drug addicts, rapists, smugglers and murderers.

When we arrived it was getting dark. The building was flat and dingy, full of slow-moving miserable people. I felt frozen, like a gutted fish. There seemed to be no direct connection between my brain and my legs but somehow they carried me forward.

There was a section for officers so they put me in there. My room-mates were a drunkard sergeant from the air-force, another sergeant who had smuggled drugs and our servant was an invalid who had assaulted his step-sister. They questioned me.

'Why are you here? What have you done?'

'I have seen enough of outside,' I told them, ' I wondered what it was like inside.'

They laughed. I was amazed to find that I still retained enough presence of mind to act coolly. I must not be trapped into behaving recklessly or in any way that would jeopardise my safety.

Next morning was sunny. Through the windows I could see the courtyard. The first thing I noticed were people in groups of two, three or four, walking up and down on a certain route, each one arranged in such a way that would not cut across any other group's route. Then a black American joined us. He had been arrested for killing a child in a traffic accident. He kept his luxury even in there with his toilet paper, coca-cola and Playboy magazines. Soon, the leaders of the prisoners got a sniff of those magazines and spent hours of fantasy in their cells, coming out with popped eyes. After a few days, the American left and the magazines were dispersed in the vacuum.

Several days later, I was visited by the prosecutor. After I had repeated the conversations I had had in the Translation Bureau, he tried to encourage more confessions about my 'crime' by threatening my family.

'You miserable dog,' I said, 'you don't need to do that because I shall throw you all the bones you need without you even asking!'

He stared at me in the same way the General had. 'You are very arrogant.'

I retorted, 'If to believe in God like a human being and practise accordingly is a crime, then I am ready to be punished. What else is there left to defend?'

He was silent for a moment, then asked, 'How is it you have gone right through our education system and still have a mentality like this? I don't understand.'

I laughed at him. 'That means you have to revise your whole damn system!'

He glared at me and said, 'You realise that if I can prove you are connected with a political society you will be given five years? Minimum!'

I had not known that but in any case what did it have to do with me?

'Unfortunately for you then, you won't be able to prove anything of the sort because I don't have any relation with any such association.'

'Then why do you use their salute?' he snapped.

I didn't know what he was talking about, then I remembered. Of course! Niyazi Onder. I leaned towards the prosecutor, raised my fist and said, 'Peace. The only salvation is in Islam.'

He scowled. 'If you are not connected with a political group why do you make a gesture like that?'

'I sometimes use this form of salute to represent symbolically that my use of power will not exceed the limits of my knowledge and I will not impose anything using power as it is used by the Republic and other political groups. It also reflects my determination to fight back against oppressions of any sort for the freedom of humankind, using all my resources in a harmonious way.'

He shook his head slowly and said, 'You're either mad or fucking stupid.'

The next day I was taken to a small room which was divided in two by a wire mesh screen. 'Sit down,' commanded my guard, who remained standing. I sat behind the screen and waited, wondering who was coming to see me now. I looked up when I heard the door creak open and saw my father. I was shocked to see how lined and pale his face was.

'Are you ill?' I asked, jumping up.

He waved his hand at me to remain seated and sat down opposite me on the other side of the screen. 'No, I'm not ill, just tired after my bus journey. Eight hours is a long time at my age.' He looked around the dingy room and at the guard and back at me. He sounded exhausted. 'Why are you doing this?'

I had not expected this reaction from my father and I felt as if he had kicked me in the stomach. I couldn't speak for I was left winded. He held up the newspaper he was carrying. I read the headlines: MEMBER OF UNITY OF STRUGGLE ARRESTED. PLOT TO OVERTHROW THE GOVERNMENT DISCOVERED.

'What! Surely you don't believe...?'

'Don't insult my intelligence! Of course I don't believe it!' he cried, 'but others will, already do! Have you any idea what the future holds for you? Your friends will desert you. Not a single person will attempt to defend you or investigate the reality behind the scene set up by the prosecution and the newspapers. What are you fighting for?'

'I am fighting for the freedom of humankind.' My voice sounded unconvincing, even to my ears.

My father let out a long, low sigh and stood up. He quoted from the prologue of the Masnawi. 'For those without bread the days are long. The green fruit knows nothing of ripeness so to speak more would be fruitless. I will pray for you,' and walked towards the door.

When the door closed behind him I covered my face with my hands and wept. After a minute or so the guard placed his hand on my shoulder. I had forgotten he was there.

'Come on,' he said roughly, but I heard kindness in his voice.

I refused to defend myself in the frame of the constitution and the laws based on it. In my statements I ignored them altogether. Throughout the sessions of the court, I did not divert my denial of their constitutional tyranny which was contrary to human dignity.

To shake my determination, the court decided to send me to a madhouse to find out what made me believe in the tales of the ancients after coming through the education system of the Republic. I was put into a dilemma of choosing either sanity with punishment or insanity with release, certified invalid. I rejected the decision, crying, 'You always play the same game, don't you? First you accuse me of lying and when I insist, then you say I must be mad.'

If I could be proved insane by the machinery, everything would be settled for the safety of the Republic and its defenders, but for me, if it didn't help the dignity of humankind, what was the importance of a broken-assed Republic?

One of the military judges asked me, 'You are talking about Resurrection and the Day of Judgement. Do you really believe all this?'

'Yes I believe it. And other things written in the Koran. I am a Moslem.'

'Can you explain how?' he asked.

'I can not,' I replied. 'It is all written in the book. If you are really interested, you'd better read it.'

Then I asked my counter question, 'If something is the truth, wouldn't you believe it, just because it is written in the Koran?'

They looked at each other puzzled and they said to the record keeper, 'That last conversation should be kept out of the records. Those questions were asked for the sake of curiosity.'

During further sessions, they listened to the witnesses, except the one who had reported me – he never made an appearance. There were three witnesses. The most careful of them was a Jewish man called Metin. In that group of characters, he was the only one I had reached with a high level of interaction. He was aware that my talks had not been accidents but rather acts of a scene linked to other scenes in the past and extended to the future. So he was practising his stratagem cautiously, to avoid making disastrous mistakes which might attract lightning to his caste in the future.

I don't know anything about his background in the plot but I don't think he was responsible for anything in it. I believe that he played his role decently. He was conscious that one day this judgement would be repeated so that his testimony was out of context.

The judge said, 'Did he say...?'

The witnesses answered, 'Yes he did, besides that he said...'

At last they turned to me, 'What do you say?'

'Yes. I said all those things. If you count this as guilt, then I have nothing to add. You had better try me by throwing me to the lions... throwing me into the fire... killing my baby boys... keeping me in your dungeons. Or use your imagination to invent new methods to test me. You may refer to Caligula, Pharoh and the like. Ask your master, the Devil, who should show you the way and inspire you with novelty.'

'This is an interesting case,' another of the judges said. 'It will give us new experience.'

However, they didn't know how to handle the guinea-pig so they decided to apply every method. First I was sent to a mad-house for two weeks. It was full of mentally ill, aggressive people. Then I was set free on bail. After that I was sent to a more sophisticated asylum without keys and armed guards at the doors.

There was a man in the next room to mine who had strangled someone. All night I could hear him crying. He could not sleep. Even the strongest drugs could not make him sleep. He just lay there with his eyes open, staring and whimpering. One night as I was praying to God to give me strength this man wandered into my room.

'What are you doing in my bed?' he shouted.

God gave me the presence of mind to talk calmly and I said, 'Your room is next to mine. We are actually neighbours so you are welcome to come in and visit me anytime you like.'

The man mumbled something and left. I sat down on my bed, trembling. I was too afraid to sleep that night and the next morning I went to the superintendent and asked him to lock my door at night. Doctors came to question me and I was constantly under observation. After one interview by a psychiatrist and some students, I heard the doctor say as they moved out of the door, 'Those bloody courts. Why do they waste our time like this?'

The hospital reports were negative. I was not insane. So the military court decided I must be guilty. My lawyer applied to the higher court. They approved the verdict. The president signed the court decision to expel me from the army as an officer and my case was transferred to the civil court. Then I had to serve the rest of my punishment in a civil prison in Istanbul.

It was late at night when I arrived and I was kept in quarantine for three weeks in case I was diseased. Because there were not enough blankets in that prison, my brother brought some from home for me, but even so my finger joints were permanently swollen with the cold. After the quarantine period was over, I joined the other prisoners in a long narrow cell which had been a corridor.

There was a hierarchy amongst the prisoners and the newest inmate had to act as a servant, but they realised at once that I was different because I was educated and generally I was left in peace. I always talked to them with respect and treated them like human beings. However, the warder felt threatened by me and he did his best to make my life more miserable. When it was my turn to go in the shower he turned the water off. Because I was not clean, I could not pray. I started to write a letter of complaint to the prison governor. The warder saw me writing and wanted to know what I was doing. When I told him he became frightened and said, 'You have no right to do that. You should have complained to me first.'

After that, whenever he did something to annoy me I started writing, where he could see me. Eventually he left me alone but later he got his revenge when I started having very bad asthma attacks. I lay on my bed after a coughing fit and reached for the medicine that my brother had brought me that day. The warder snatched it out of my hand. 'Sorry. It's against the rules to have drugs in the prison.' I was too ill to argue. Deprived of any relief it was like trying to breathe through a broken straw. My lungs felt raw, as though they were bleeding. I knew if I allowed myself to panic the muscles in my throat would contract and I would suffocate. I tried to calm myself but while I lay there completely helpless and close to death I saw that warder grinning at me through the bars of the door.

There was a man sentenced for life for killing his wife with an axe and burning the body in a chimney. He had spent more than ten years in jail already. He sometimes attended prayers in the small prison mosque. One day, I was in that mosque for afternoon prayer. Towards the end of my prayer I heard unusual footsteps. I finished saluting right and left, then turned round to find out what was happening. That man was walking up and down behind me, muttering to himself. The prisoners never walked up and down in closed circles and I recognised immediately that he was out of his mind again, perhaps re-living the moment he had committed his crime. I was alarmed when I found myself alone with him and somehow managed to crawl towards the door silently – to the safety of the crowd of criminals!

One day as I was out in the courtyard exercising, a tall hairy man walked towards me. Before I could speak he asked, 'Where are you from?'

'Istanbul,' I replied. 'Why?'

'Have you ever been to the Black Sea area.'

'No, never.'

'Do you have any relatives in the Black Sea area?'

'None at all.'

He nodded and turned away.

'Wait a minute,' I said, 'why all the questions?' He hesitated then pulled out of his pocket a small bottle.

'Five years ago my brother was killed in our village by a man who looked exactly like you from the back. I was so sure you were that man that I was going to break this bottle and cut your throat. Just as I was taking it out of my pocket you turned round. Then I was doubtful. I couldn't be sure. So that's why I questioned you. Well, you are obviously not the one.'

He shrugged and walked away, leaving me staring at the back of his head trying to grasp the fact that at any moment my life could be snuffed out in this place by anyone who took it in his head to do so, and no one would lift a finger to help me. If I died who would continue the work I'd begun? 'Oh God, don't let me die for I have much to do and I've barely started.'

Immediately came the response. 'And what is so special about you? Who do you think you are? You who have suffered nothing in your life, how dare you suppose you have the strength to changes things for these miserable wretches around you, let alone the world?'

I cried aloud, 'Suffered nothing? What about my brother who died because of my jealousy? Lale, who died because I loved her and made my mother hate her? Sarah, who fell in love with someone else because I did not know the language I needed to keep her?' As soon as I uttered these words I was horrified. I looked around to see if anyone had heard. No, I was alone. Never had I thought these things before, let alone said them. But the voice showed no mercy.

'You call this suffering? Ha! You know nothing!'

A mentally retarded dwarf arrived early next morning. He couldn't speak properly and communicated in grunts. That night after the lights were turned off I heard him running down the corridor and the sound of feet running after him and coarse laughter. One of the voices was the warder's. When they caught the dwarf he squealed like a pig. I tried to cover my ears with my hands but I couldn't block out those squeals in the dark, nor the animal grunts that made it plain what they were doing to him. I felt sick because he was a human being and I couldn't help him. And I knew that if they could do that to such a person then they had no limits. I turned over in my bed and vomited on the floor.

The next morning I went to look for the dwarf. I found him crouching on the floor of his cell. When he saw me coming towards him he began to shake and moan. I sat beside him, talking softly. 'It's all right. I won't hurt you. Trust me. I'll protect you.'

He didn't understand what I was saying but my tone of voice must have soothed him for he stopped whimpering. I always carried the Masnawi in my pocket and I pulled it out and opened it. The dwarf was quiet now and I began reading to him:

'Like Joseph I had dreamed dreams.

He relied upon the true dream: in the
dungeon and prison he sought nothing but that.
Because of his reliance upon that, he cared naught for
servitude and reproach, whether more or less.
He had a great reliance upon his dream which was shining
in front of him like a candle...the heart recognised the speaker from the effect.
By means of that strength, he cheerfully endured every
affliction that came to him afterwards.'

The dwarf smiled at me. I put my arm around his shoulder and hugged him. I looked up to see the warder standing watching us.

'Reading bedtime stories are we?' He put out his filthy paw for my book.

I shook my head and with perfect calm in my heart I said, 'If you so much as lay a finger on this poor afflicted man again be sure that when I get out of this place I will make you pay for it.'

He stared at me with the corners of his lips about to curl but there was doubt in his eyes and I knew my words – and the confidence with which I had spoken them – had not come from within me but from a power without. I continued staring at him and he turned and skulked away. I took hold of the dwarf's hands and turned them palms out in front of him and prayed with him.

The fight to live through each day took all my energy. I spent my time reading the books my brother brought with him on his visits. The dwarf stayed with me each day and generally we were left alone by the other inmates. Occasionally someone stopped to listen to my reading but then usually got bored and wandered away. Whenever the warder saw me he turned and went in the opposite direction. This suited me very well. I continued to read to the dwarf in peace and prayed with him. He never spoke to me but his smile was enough reward.

After six months I went into his cell one morning as usual and he wasn't there. No one knew where he had gone. I had seen him only the night before so he must have been taken away during the night. I went in search of the warder. When he saw me coming he tried to hurry away but I caught up with him, demanding, 'Where is he? People don't usually get released in the middle of the night.'

'His case was special,' the warder shrugged. 'And it's none of your business.'

'But I'm making it my business. You'd better tell me or I'll report what you did to him.'

He avoided my eye and said, 'He was transferred to another prison. I don't know why and I don't know why it had to be at night. I just follow orders. That's all I know.' He scurried off leaving me unconvinced and cold with anxiety for my poor friend.

Over the following weeks I felt an ache in my chest with the frustration of not knowing what had happened to him. At night when I closed my eyes I saw the treatment that had been metered out to him here repeated in whatever place he had been taken to. Who would protect him? I also missed him for I had no one to talk to now. I couldn't endure the coarse conversations and laughter I heard around me and I stayed in my cell all day to avoid them. My poor, gentle friend. Who would care for him? Into my mind came the words, 'The same person who has always cared for him.' I lay down on the cold stone floor and wept with relief.

I spent the remaining months alone in my cell, reading and praying. I stopped marking off the days on the calendar on my wall and I lost any concept of time. It floated like wood smoke on the wind, drifting this way and that. When the warder appeared one morning to tell me this was the day of my release I was too numb to believe it or even to care.

My brother accompanied me out of the prison and we had to go straight to the police headquarters in Istanbul to complete the formalities of release. We arrived at nine o'clock in the morning and were kept waiting for twelve hours. During that time we were in a room full of other people, all waiting and miserable. From time to time a policeman came in and signalled to someone to go with him. The reaction of everyone else to this was to sit in silence, like frightened rabbits. My nerves were like elastic that had been stretched to its fullest extent. I began banging on the door and shouted. 'Even in Russia they don't treat dissidents like this, keeping us waiting more than twelve hours without food.'

The door opened and a policeman entered. 'I apologise for the delay. Unavoidable with so many people to see but please come with me now.'

He led us up three flights of stairs to a small, dirty room at the far end of a dark corridor. There, lounging on a desk, were six policemen. They watched in silence as we walked towards them. One of them stood up and without saying a word he drew back his fist and plunged it full force into my gut. I fell to the floor clutching my stomach, gasping for air. As I writhed like a worm the others jumped up and fell on me, including the one who had escorted us here. Someone kicked me in the head and I fell forward on my face, blood spurting into my eyes. Others threw punches at whatever part of my body did not have a boot already in it.

After enduring this for several minutes I raised my hands to the Merciful God. It was just naïveté to expect mercy out of that clutch, so determined to grind my flesh and blood to capture my soul and I cried, 'Burn me, as you did Abraham. I shall not obey your idols.'

They stepped with their high laced black boots between my raised hands to break my prayer.

I wept. 'How can the boots of the Republic break the unity of a prayer? The Roman Empire was stronger than you are and Caligula developed more refined means of torture to capture and freeze the spirit, squeezing it to the moment of life and death; and the Babylonians built towers to throw arrows to the Heavens to catch it; and the Pharoh killed every newly born baby boy to trace it; and the tyrants today try to corner it in their region of the state of being sane and insane.'

My brother was protesting but they ignored him. He tried to pull them off me and then they turned on him. When I saw them beating my brother, I ran to the door screaming, to bring their attention back to me. Then they rushed after me and dragged me to the floor.

My brother shouted, 'You ignorant pigs! Don't you know it's illegal to assault an officer of the army?'

They dropped me and stared at him. One of them sneered. 'He's no longer an officer. We can do what we like with him.'

My brother pulled his papers out of his pocket. 'I am an officer you bloody fool!'

They read his papers because at first they didn't believe him. Then they looked at each other in alarm and left the room.

After they had gone, my brother helped me up off the floor and wiped the blood from my face and hands with his handkerchief. I felt something gritty in my mouth and spat out pieces of a tooth. My hair was sticky and my vision blurred. My brother drew me to him and I felt his tears run down my neck. He wept bitterly. 'Those pigs! Those stupid, bloody, ignorant pigs!'

After a few minutes a different policeman entered. 'Please, the Chief of Police will see you now.'

I looked at my brother wondering what treats were in store for us, but we followed him to a room at the other end of the corridor.

The Chief of Police stood up when we entered. He was definitely worried. 'I apologise for that – er – unfortunate – er – incident. It was a mistake. I can assure you those officers will be dealt with. I have ordered tea and a hot meal for you and you can wash yourselves in my bathroom.'

I laughed at him. My brother tossed the release papers onto his desk.

'Just sign!'

I noticed the Chief's hand was shaking as he signed. He was still apologising as we left the room.

After they had shattered my prayer to pieces I made up my mind to dry their kind from their roots. I made a vow to God that I would direct the rest of my life to acquiring knowledge that their hands could not reach, that their kind could never use to oppress people. I would break the tyranny built by the bewitchment of language.

The tyrants would be remembered by future generations only by their black boots – which they used to break prayers. In the museums of the future, all that would be left of them would be a pair of black boots, hanging from the ceiling.

CHAPTER EIGHT

The taxi drew up in front of my parents' house. I climbed out and picked up my bags while Osman paid the driver. The night air was cold. Frost sparkled on the ground in the pool of light from the street lamp. I raised my face to the night sky, pricked with a million bright stars. The moon, hidden behind a streak of cloud, rolled out like a silver dish.

During my incarceration I had thought of little else but the day I would get out, stand in the open, and breathe as a free man. I had imagined myself leaping into the air, gulping great breaths of freedom into my lungs, cleansing away all the indignities and filth. But now my feelings were as frozen as the icicles hanging under the window of my mother's house. I stood under that star-filled sky, infinitesimally small and insignificant.

Osman was unlocking the front door. The warmth from the stove and the familiar smell of my mother's cooking greeted me as I stepped inside and took off my shoes. My parents came into the hall. I saw their worn faces and my father's white hair. I had never before thought of them as old and seeing it now made me want to weep. I took my mother's hand, kissed it and pressed it to my forehead. She held me to her and I felt her tears run into my neck.

For the rest of the week neighbours and relatives came to see me. My mother made tea and we drank it and talked about the weather, a funeral, someone's wedding, babies that had been born. But not one person mentioned my imprisonment. If anyone disapproved of my behaviour they did not show it. Only Osman knew anything about the circumstances I had been in and even he did not bring up the subject.

The day before he returned to Ankara he came to my room and asked me, 'Do you want to talk about anything?'

I shook my head.

He nodded and took a large, fat envelope out of his pocket and dropped it on my desk before he left the room. I picked it up and looked inside. A jolt of recognition when I realised what it contained caused me to catch my breath. Sarah's letters. I had almost forgotten I had given them to Osman to care for while I was in prison. I had forbidden myself to think of Sarah or my time in England for a whole year. If I had allowed those thoughts into my head in that place I would not have been able to endure it. I touched the letters with my fingertips but I did not want to look at the writing.

In the weeks that followed I stayed at home reading until late at night, getting up around noon. My mother cooked my favourite meals and served them to me on the dinner set that she reserved for special occasions. On the first day of spring I bought an old bicycle and each day I went for long rides by myself along the Bosphorus. I liked cycling out of the dirt and dust of the city to the rich residential areas of Arnavutkoy and Bebek. Here the air was clean and fresh and on warm days I swam and sometimes I took my fishing rod, or locked my bike up and walked for hours around the streets. I liked to walk in the ruins of Rumeli Hisar, built by Mehmet in ninety two days when he was planning to capture the city from the Byzantines.

The only thing preventing me from completing the task of recovery was the problem of my unfinished military service. Despite weeks of effort I was still unable to get the papers signed that confirmed I had completed it. The forms kept coming back and there would be a note telling me to send them to another office. I did so and the papers would lie around for weeks and no one was prepared to take the responsibility for signing them. Finally I wrote to Osman to ask him if he could find out what the situation was. A couple of weeks later his reply came. Though I was burning with impatience to open the letter I restrained myself until I had cycled out to Rumeli Hisar and climbed to the topmost tower so I could be entirely alone.

I leaned back on the wall and felt the wind in my face as I listened to the call to prayer from north, south, east and west. I thought of Lale and the stories she had told me about the conqueror. I smiled at the memory, but then other memories overlaid it like a dark shadow.

'What's your worst nightmare, Celik?'

'Having to do my military service as a private.'

I could almost hear her laughing.

I took Osman's letter out of my pocket, hardly daring to open it. My eyes scanned the paper until I saw the words I was looking for '...Military service has been reduced from two years to eighteen months and therefore it is highly unlikely that you will have to serve your remaining six months as a private...' I read this over and over again. It was scarcely believable. Almost immediately, however, my joy was extinguished by the fear that somehow a way might be found to make me do it as a further punishment. I put Osman's letter back in my pocket and crossed my arms over my chest and shoulders, hugging myself tightly. What could I do? Go on living in a state of constant fear and anxiety? Who could help me?

I saw a small boy running away from his mother in the street below. They were both laughing. As she chased him she called to him and the wind caught her words and whipped them up to where I was standing. 'Ali! Come back here!' As soon as I heard this I laughed too. Why was I so lacking in faith? Of course I was not alone! Even in my moments of deepest despair God was with me. And now He was reminding me that indeed there was someone who could help. Yashar's brother, Ali, was now an officer. I would go and talk to Yashar.

Yashar listened to my story in silence. When I had finished he said, 'I'll write to Ali. If anything at all can be done he'll find a way to do it.'

Three weeks later my papers arrived back in the post. I tore open the envelope expecting to read that I had to send them to yet another department. To my astonishment I saw Ali's signature. For a moment I stood there blinking at it. Then, slowly, I began to understand. Ali had found my papers and signed them himself. With that realisation, sweat seeped out of every pore in my body, soaking my skin and clothes. The odour was not the pungent stink of fear that had been my constant companion of late, but something else, which at the moment I could not identify.

There was too much feeling in my heart for me to contain. I needed someone to share it with. But there was no one. Not my parents, not Yashar, not even Osman would fully understand. As usual, I was completely alone. Except for God. I dropped down on my knees and gave thanks to Him for my deliverance.

CHAPTER
• NINE

My mother was getting impatient with me for not looking for a job.

'I'm in no hurry.' I explained. 'When I do get a job I will become so rich you will not believe it.'

'But you are not even trying,' she said in exasperation.

After enduring her nagging on this subject for several weeks, I locked myself in my room and went on a hunger strike for twenty four hours. She came up to knock on my door to persuade me to come down and eat but I would not. Then, late at night, when everyone was in bed, I crept silently downstairs and ate some food.

I stood in the darkness of the kitchen, looking at the shadows in the fields behind our garden wall and prayed aloud. 'May God grant that one day I shall have a full table. Then everyone shall eat from my table.'

The following morning I was up early and went out to buy a newspaper. Back home again I looked in the situations vacant column and saw that the Istanbul branch of an American computer company, ICS, was advertising for programmers. I decided to go along and present myself. I had been hoping to work for IBM as it was a bigger and more prestigious company, but still, I thought I could take a temporary job with ICS and later I could apply to IBM.

I went along to the offices of ICS and took a test and they said they would let me know the results within a week. After ten days had passed I had not heard from them so I went along again to see how I had done. I was shown into the manager's room.

'We were just about to contact you,' he said. 'You passed the test with a higher grade than anyone else and we would be pleased to offer you the job.

Would you be able to start tomorrow?'

I enjoyed the work and also the company of my colleagues. The only problem was that everyone smoked in that office and the air was always thick and stale. I made a fuss about this and to keep me quiet they found me the best place in the whole office, by the window. I kept opening it and leaning my head out to gulp in lungs-full of fresh air.

Soon I was a popular member of staff because I always treated everyone with courtesy and I joked and laughed when I felt the atmosphere was getting too serious. Once I asked two of the girls, Hatice and Zeynep, if I could take their photographs and produced my camera. Immediately there was a flurry of activity and protest. 'Not yet, Celik! We have not got our make-up on.'

They opened drawers and took out bags of cosmetics and started to apply lipstick, eyeshadow and powder. One of the electricians, sitting high up on a ladder stared in amazement at this scene and burst out laughing. Then Hatice smeared lipstick on her dress and with groans and sighs they disappeared to the ladies' cloakroom to repair the damage. They were gone for about twenty minutes and I exaggerated their actions of looking in their mirrors and checking every detail and saying, 'Oh not yet Celik, I am not looking beautiful yet.' Everyone left their desks and gathered around me, helpless with laughter.

When the girls finally emerged, Hatice had powder all over her dress. She moaned, 'That's because Zeynep said the best way to take out a lipstick stain was to throw talcum powder on it.'

We all laughed but those two looked really miserable by now. 'Why worry?' I said, 'I have a clothes brush in my drawer, I will brush you and you will look as good as new.'

I produced my brush and started brushing Hatice's shoulder. Zeynep was shocked. 'Give that to me, I'll do it, Celik.' But everyone laughed at her and this encouraged me to be bolder. Making sure no one could see my action I flicked the brush over Hatice's breast and smiled into her eyes.

'Now I will take the photographs.' She blushed deep pink but said nothing. I resolved to ask her to go out for a meal with me when I got a chance to speak to her alone.

The next day, however, I changed my mind. If I was seen going out with Hatice there would be never-ending speculation about when I would be marrying her. Worse, maybe I would be forced into marrying her. She was a pleasant girl but not intelligent and too short and fat for my tastes. By the time she was thirty she would be 'so beautiful she would have to go through the door sideways.'

After I had worked in that office for ten months, I began my training as a systems analyst. Over the next few years I worked hard and earned an increasingly good salary. I enjoyed spending it on smart, fashionable clothes. I started to grow my hair long and within a few weeks all the other men in the office had long hair too. I made a point of complimenting people on their appearance if I felt they had made an effort, and some of the girls came to me for advice if they were thinking of buying something new.

As my thirtieth birthday approached my mother started making hints that it was about time I had a wife. 'You are too old to be single. Rukiye, our neighbour's daughter has sent you a gift of this little embroidered tablecloth. See how pretty it is.'

I resisted all attempts to discuss the matter. To preserve my independence, I moved into a flat. My parents owned three flats which they rented out to provide them with an income since my father had retired three years ago. I rented one of these flats and lived by myself. Osman was offered a job with a civil engineering firm in London so he went to work there for a year. Mehmed was progressing well in his career as an officer in the army. Yashar had accepted a job as a systems analyst with IBM in Saudi Arabia and although I missed him very much we remained in contact by letter and continued our philosophical discussions that way.

Hulya was not particularly interested in her school work and though she passed all her exams she merely scraped through. One day I said to her, 'Hulya, I will be a very rich executive one day and you will be my cleaning lady, because that is the only work you will be fit to do.'

She was furious with me but after that she asked me to help her with her homework and studying. I spent a lot of time showing her how to do maths which she found extremely difficult.

'You must do this,' I insisted, though she was close to tears. 'You must go to university to further your education then you can choose your own career and live like an independent woman.'

My parents opposed this, especially my father. 'If she goes to university she will be spoiled. She has been to high school. That is enough education for a girl. At the university, girls no longer cover their heads. They are in constant contact with men. She will get ideas that oppose Islam.'

I leaned forward in my chair, struggling to keep the impatience out of my voice. 'Do you believe that Islam is the greatest, purest truth in the world?'

'Of course,' answered my father.

'Well then, why are you afraid to put it to the test?'

My father stood up and walked over to the window. 'I do not wish to continue this discussion any longer.' He thrust his hands deep into his pockets and peered into the street.

I saw my precious sister condemned to a lifetime of cooking and cleaning and bearing dead children, like my mother and all my female relatives. I walked over to my father and stood where he was forced to look at me. He scowled. I lowered my voice to stop it shaking for I had never before questioned my father's decisions.

'Baba,' I pleaded, 'if Islam is the total life system that we believe it to be, then all the western ideas Hulya will be exposed to will not change that. Will you at least think about this?'

He turned and strode out of the room. I sank back into my chair and covered my head with my hands. How could I have been so stupid as to talk to him like this? After all my reading and studying and praying had I learned nothing? I had to find a better way. Even if I angered my father I would not give up on this issue.

The next day, I got up early, after a restless night and went into the kitchen to make my breakfast. My father was already there. Judging by his tired face he had not slept either.

'Baba...' I began.

He held up his hand to silence me. 'You are right Celik. She may go to university.'

I stared at him unable to believe I had heard correctly. At last I found my voice. 'Thank you father. I will take full responsibility for her and I promise you won't regret this decision.'

He nodded. 'You are a good brother to your sister.' This was immense praise from my father and my pride in his words got mixed up with my relief at his decision so that my knees began to shake and I had to sit down before he noticed.

Hulya studied hard for the exams and I forced her to study when she didn't feel like it. Some days she was in tears at my criticism, but still I pushed her. She took the examination and passed. Everyone was amazed, especially Osman. He wrote to me from London. 'I can not believe that Hulya has done so well. She says it is because of you. What did you do to get her to pass this exam? I would not have thought she was capable of it.'

There was a great deal of opposition from our relatives to our decision, once it became known that Hulya was going to university. Even Mehmed, on one of his visits home, expressed his concern. One of my father's brothers had a very clever daughter, Zarah, but he would not let her continue her education past elementary school. The teachers had been so determined that she did not waste her talents, that they had finally persuaded him to let her continue her studies at home. They had supplied her with all the material and each time she sat an exam she passed it with the highest grades, even beating those who continued their education at school. Now she was doing a university course from home and still doing well. My uncle pointed this out to my parents with the advice that it was not necessary to expose Hulya to corrupt influences when she could do better at home.

My father was always anxious after these admonitions but I said, 'Hulya is not as clever as Zarah, who is exceptional. As you can see, for Hulya to succeed she needs all the help she can get.'

Finally, Hulya went to university. I met all her expenses and she worked very hard so she would not let me down. My father did not question her about her studies the way he had always interrogated me, but I knew this was not lack of interest in her but simply that he had put his trust in me to see that she came to no harm. In his own way he was proud of her. I was determined that she should not waste her life married to some Anatolian bear who would treat her like a slave and whenever I visited my parents' house I talked to her about how women in Europe had their own careers, their own money and could do what they liked with their lives. She listened with wide-open eyes but said she couldn't believe she could live like that because she would always have to care for my parents.

'Anything is possible,' I told her, 'if you want it enough.'

Osman came back to Istanbul after his year in England and he came to stay with me in my flat until he found one of his own. He asked my mother to help him find a wife. My mother was delighted and started negotiations with a family she had known for years who had a daughter, recently qualified as a teacher. This girl sent Osman an embroidered table mat as a gift and he met her once in her parents' house.

As he was examining it I said to him, 'Is this what you want? To be tied to a house and wife and children and no life to call your own?'

He said, 'Just because you don't like women it doesn't mean I feel the same.'

'Who says I don't like women?' I protested, but he just laughed.

Soon after this, he had a letter from a friend of his in London. This man was an Indian Moslem called Mustafa, who was engaged to an English woman called Francine. She had recently become a Moslem. This woman was coming to Istanbul for a holiday with a friend of hers, called Miriam. When Osman told my mother the news, she immediately offered to let the girls stay at her home and they accepted the invitation.

Osman spent a great deal of time taking them around the city. When they went back to London, he told me he had proposed to Miriam. I was very surprised because he had not revealed anything of this while they were here. My parents were surprised too but accepted his decision. He arranged to go back to London and apply for a job there.

I decided to go to England with him so I could attend his wedding, but also because I wanted to see the country again. Miriam was there to meet us at the airport. When she and Osman saw each other, they shook hands like strangers. It struck me as odd but I didn't take much notice for I was looking around, thinking, 'Here I am again,' and trying to remember what a green boy I had been the last time I had visited this country.

I loved seeing once again the clean streets and well-dressed people of my memory and I enjoyed listening to the soft flowing rhythms of the English language. Nothing harsh, or nasal, or guttural. As I looked at the tall, blonde, blue-eyed women striding along the footpaths I wondered what had become of Sarah. Had she followed her dream and become a journalist? Did she have children? Just for the briefest second I considered ringing her parents' number and asking for her address.

'Don't be a fucking idiot man!' I said aloud, horrified that I had even considered doing something so stupid.

The wedding had been arranged for the following week. In the meantime Osman found a flat and I stayed with Francine and Miriam in their flat and I met Francine's fiancé there, the Indian named Mustafa. In all that time I observed no signs of affection from Miriam towards Osman, but one night when I got up to go to the bathroom I saw Mustafa coming out of Miriam's room. I slipped into the shadows and stood there, heart pounding, my mouth dry. Osman! I had to tell him. Or should I confront Mustafa. But maybe there was a logical explanation for Mustafa's presence in Miriam's room. 'Don't be a fuckwit!' I whispered, 'what logic?' I resolved to talk to Osman in the morning and spent a sleepless night wondering what I should say and how to say it.

Osman came round next morning as I was in the kitchen making coffee.

'Hi, man, want some?'

He nodded. My heart started beating faster. I handed him the cup and began, 'This wedding... do you really...?' The door opened and Miriam walked in. Osman looked at her and his eyes brightened. She smiled at him. My words dissolved in my mouth. Maybe I was wrong. Maybe I even dreamed that scene last night. Osman turned back to me, 'Yes? What about the wedding?'

Miriam smiled at me expectantly. I said lamely, 'I was wondering what you would like for a present.'

The wedding took place in a registry office in London with twenty guests, mostly relatives and friends of Miriam. Osman had eyes for no one else during the ceremony. I observed Miriam closely but detected nothing in her face but maybe that was just modesty. How else should she have behaved? On the other hand, although she had become a Moslem, she was also English. English girls did not lower their eyes to the ground like this and keep such a solemn expression. I didn't know what to make of it. No one else seemed to notice anything amiss and people crowded round them to wish them well as they left for their honeymoon. Where they were going no one knew, for they wouldn't reveal the destination.

Hulya had arrived the day before and was also staying with us at Francine's house. After spending a few days showing Hulya around London, we travelled back to Turkey together. Though Hulya had been very impressed with the shops and architecture of London, she never mentioned the wedding or discussed Miriam. Normally I would have questioned her on this lack of interest but if I had then I would have had to open up my doubts. Best to leave it alone.

When we returned home my mother triumphantly informed me she had arranged a marriage for Mehmed with a cousin of ours. This girl came from a traditional family and had not continued her education past high school. She was nineteen and had lived at home without working for the past two years. The wedding was to take place at the Office for Marriages in Istanbul. I told Mehmed that I did not wish to attend. He was hurt.

'But you are my eldest brother. Of course you must come. People will think something is wrong between us.'

'I don't give a shit what people think. Never doubt that I wish you well in your marriage but I do not believe in any of the institutions of the Republic and I will not take part in any.'

He scowled and in a voice thick with frustration he said, 'Celik why do you have to make life so difficult for yourself and all of us? There's no point. What satisfaction do you get out of it?'

I was shocked at the passion in his voice but now he'd started he couldn't stop.

'You didn't care about the shame you brought on the family when you went to prison. You didn't see our mother's tears. You don't care about me either or you wouldn't put these so-called principles of yours before me. Just come to the bloody wedding for God's sake and be with our family.'

His head was thrust forward and he was clenching and unclenching his fists as if he could barely stop himself from hitting me. I couldn't believe what I was seeing and hearing. I snapped back, my voice tight with anger, 'How dare you talk to me like that? I should whip you for your insolence'

'Just try it!' he shouted, towering over me, his face red with fury, 'You care about nobody but your fucking self!'

Before I could stop myself I raised my hand and slapped him across the face. His eyes opened shock-wide and filled with tears. I wished with all my heart I could have re-wound that moment and I said, 'Forgive me. I didn't mean to do that.'

He stood there like an oversized puppet, his arms dangling by his sides. I pulled him to me and he threw his arms around my neck.

'I'm sorry for provoking you, Celik,' he cried. 'It was my fault.'

I swallowed to keep the tears back. 'No, don't blame yourself. But I will not, can not come to your wedding. If you think badly of me because of it then I am sorry, but I will not come.' I turned and left the room.

After he was married, my mother never lost an opportunity of letting me know I should be following the pattern of my brothers. I refused to be led into any discussion. One day, when she was feeling extremely frustrated with my silence on the subject, she said, 'I don't understand you! You are well educated. You have a good job. You could have your pick of the best girls here. Why are you so stubborn?'

How could I explain to her that my dreams at night were not of plump, black-haired, brown-eyed girls who could cook and clean and sew and averted their gaze from men, but of long-limbed, pale-skinned women who strode along streets with their heads held high and who stared at the men they desired with cool, blue eyes? Even if I had told her this she would ask why I did not look for a wife who fitted this description. I turned away so she could not see my face.

After six months, I received a brief letter from Osman to say his marriage had not worked out the way he had hoped and he and his wife had now separated. I wrote to him immediately and asked him to phone me at my flat and reverse the charges. A week later I was reading one evening when the phone rang. It was Osman.

'Hey, man,' I said, 'what's been happening.'

I scarcely recognised the flat, tired voice as my brother's. 'Even from the beginning Miriam was not prepared to support me financially while I was looking for a job. She went on holiday by herself because she did not want to use her own money to finance a holiday for me. Eventually I found a job with a firm of civil engineers and for a while I hoped the marriage would succeed...'

'And?' I prompted.

His voice began to shake. 'Mustafa became a regular visitor to our flat and often stayed until late at night. One night I asked him to leave because I had to get up for work early next morning but he replied that he was visiting Miriam and would leave only if she asked him to. I went to bed, leaving the two of them talking until early in the morning. After this had continued for several weeks more, I told Miriam that if she did not restrict his visits to normal hours, I would leave. She refused to do this. We had a row. I packed my bags. Went to stay with Francine until I found a flat. I have no money and no possessions, because I've left everything with Miriam. I want nothing from that marriage and all I want to do now is forget I ever met her.' He was close to tears so I did not push him for any more details.

'Look,' I said, 'I'll tell our parents. Leave that part to me. And don't worry about money, I'll send you some. If you need anything else let me know.'

I lay awake all night thinking about the things he had told me. I remembered Miriam's total lack of interest in him in London and I had no idea why she had married him in the first place. I blamed myself for letting him get involved with her. As I acknowledged that failing on my part I also saw clearly that actually I had very little idea of what constituted a normal relationship. That realisation shook me because I also knew that I had no context with which to judge any kind of relationship with a woman.

CHAPTER
◆ TEN

It was Osman's separation, or rather the subsequent revelation of the imbalance in my own life that propelled me towards change. I knew I had two choices. I could continue to follow my solitary path and end my life as a recluse or I could develop myself to the point where I would no longer feel vulnerable and exposed. I chose the latter course.

I decided to begin with a holiday and started collecting tourist brochures. I found out that Wittgenstein's house in Vienna was open to the public. For many years I had enjoyed reading Wittgenstein so I decided to go on holiday to Vienna to see the house where he had lived.

The following summer I arrived in Vienna and as soon as I had checked in at the hotel I took a taxi to the house. The place was crawling with workmen and they wouldn't let me in. I couldn't believe it.

'But I have travelled all this way for the sole purpose of seeing this house!' I said.

The foreman, a short, chunky man with a face like a bulldog said, 'Sorry, we have orders. It is being turned into a consulate. We can't have tourists traipsing all over the place.'

I was so frustrated and angry that I left before I made a fool of myself. I took a taxi straight back to my hotel and wrote to the Minister of Tourism, expressing my disappointment. Three days later, to my surprise, I received a reply from him by special dispatch, apologising for the inconvenience and even offering to take me on a guided tour of the place himself when it was finished. This courtesy soothed my temper and I decided that as I had another four days left I might as well make the most of my holiday.

I spent the rest of my time visiting art galleries and going to concerts. In that city I discovered the music of Mahler and the paintings of Gustav

Klimt. I decided to develop my knowledge in these areas and I also searched out shops where I could buy books – novels as well as philosophical works. I bought three Klimt prints, two Monets, and records of Mahler's symphonies.

In Istanbul, I spent a whole afternoon putting my prints into frames and hanging them on the bare white walls of my flat. I unpacked the books, holding them to my nose so I could enjoy the new smell, and filed them alphabetically by author in my bookcase. I placed the records in my cabinet. By the time I was finished the late afternoon sun was pouring into my living room, dappling light and shadow on my books and the rugs on the wooden floor. I felt deeply contented. I selected Mahler's symphony number two and put it on the stereo, then sat back in my chair, closed my eyes and let the beauty of the music fill my room. As long as I had music and paintings and books I would never be alone. I would build up a fine collection and wherever I went I would take them with me and I would always have a home.

I knew that people thought I had no interest in women. Perhaps they also thought that no woman could be attracted to someone like me for I was short and losing my hair now. I used to be conscious of my lack of height and wished that I was tall and strong, but not now. My best feature has always been my eyes, for they are dark and very striking. So I am not ugly. Anyway, now I didn't care what people thought. In the end, my greatest work would be myself and I would go on cutting and trimming and altering the pattern until I achieved perfection.

I became amusing company, I think, for I could make people laugh and forget their troubles, and I received many invitations to dinner parties. At these events people often asked me why I wasn't married. A beautiful woman would lean across the dinner table and purr, 'Why aren't you married, Celik?'

I would arch one eyebrow and reply, 'Why? Do you find me attractive?'

This made everyone laugh with delight.

Or curious colleagues, 'How come you never got married, Celik?' (meaning, you're not gay are you?).

I would reply, 'Are you kidding? How many systems analysts do you know who're not divorced or alcoholic? Or both!' And they would laugh and nod.

There were variations, according to the mood and scene.

'I'm married to my job... At least a computer will do as it's told!... I like the freedom of travelling to different countries... What woman would trust me in my way of life?' This last one was useful with my mother.

Then I met Gül.

I was giving a six week course on computer programming and there were thirty students in my class. Most of them were men in their early twenties and a handful of dowdy girls in grey or black, one or two with their heads covered by scarves. As I was introducing myself on the first day and giving an overview of the course there was a knock at the door and in walked a tall, slim girl in a red dress and high-heeled, black patent-leather shoes. Her hair was long and glossy and tied back from her face with a red silk ribbon. The class froze as she strode over to me and apologised in a loud voice for her lateness.

'A slight car accident!' She shrugged and walked past rows of staring eyes and open mouths to the back of the room to find an empty seat.

There was a moment's silence while the other students recovered from the effects of this dramatic entrance. They looked at me, half-smiling, to see my reaction. I made a pretence of turning the pages of my notes, aware that my mouth had gone dry. From the girl's accent and clothes she was obviously from Istanbul's high society. She was stunningly beautiful but appeared not to notice the heads that were swivelling round to stare at her. I swallowed and continued with my introduction, taking care not to look at her in case I forgot what I was going to say next.

She seemed interested in my talk and asked lots of questions. She was also usually the first to answer my questions and it soon became apparent – to the irritation of the other students – that she had more knowledge of the subject than anyone else there.

When it was time for the lunch break I noticed that no one was sitting beside her in the cafeteria. In fact some of the female students had their backs to her, though the males were glancing at her surreptitiously. I made a point of joining her at her table, determined to be friendly in the face of such rudeness from her fellow students. She told me she had just returned from studying maths for three years at Warwick University in England.

'Really?' I said, 'How I envy you. I had only three months in England when I was a student. If I'd had three years I would have regarded myself as the luckiest man alive. What was Warwick like?'

She shrugged. 'Working class.'

While I was thinking of a reply to this she went on to tell me that she'd been educated at private schools in Istanbul and she had wanted to spend time in England to improve her English pronunciation. Her father had insisted on Warwick because it would be useful for her to learn about another stratum of society at the same time. A group of students sitting at a nearby table listened to this conversation and looked at each other with raised eyebrows.

Over the next few weeks she always arrived late and created a stir in her bright European dresses. Sometimes her hair was piled high on top of her head, showing off her long, soft neck and perfect oval face; sometimes hanging loosely over her shoulders. She always wore dark red lipstick which accentuated her full lips and her creamy skin. The stares from the other students were hostile, but still envious or covetous, depending on the sex of the starer. Gül didn't care. She continued doing as she pleased and said exactly what she thought. I found this behaviour fascinating but I felt sorry that the others were making it so obvious that they disliked her. I made a point of including her in conversations in the breaks, or I thought of things to say to make her laugh. She appreciated it I think, and began to wait for me so we could go into the cafeteria together. She was always the last to leave at the end of the day and stayed behind to chat with me for a few minutes.

I wanted to invite her out to dinner. At the end of each day I was determined to do it, but at the last moment my courage always failed. If she refused me I knew I would not be able to face her again the next day. I decided to leave it till the last day of the course. If she rejected my invitation at least I would not have to bear the humiliation of seeing her again.

As the other students left the room and I was packing up my papers she walked up to my desk. My heart started racing and my mouth went dry. This was terrible! I couldn't do it. Keeping my head bent over my books I unstuck my tongue from the roof of my mouth and forced myself to say, as casually as possible, 'Are you free to have dinner with me next week?'

I could hardly believe my own boldness and almost shit myself with terror. Then, to my amazement, she said, as if my invitation were nothing remarkable, 'I'd love to. I was just about to ask you the same thing!'

My astonishment must have shown in my face for she burst out laughing. I started laughing too. That was how our relationship began.

Over the next few weeks we went out often. She always chose the most expensive restaurants, but I didn't mind. It felt exhilarating being seen in those places with such a woman, and I loved the way she drew attention to herself by her conversation and manner but seemed oblivious of the way people stared at her.

One day, a few weeks later, she came to my office and invited me to lunch. I felt my face grow red with pleasure and embarrassment as we walked out the door together and I saw everyone's eyes open wide. And afterwards: 'Celik Bey, we saw you go to lunch with a beautiful lady? Who is she? Is she European?'

'So?' I said, 'sometimes I have my lunch with a friend. And no, she's as Turkish as you are.' And that really drove them crazy!

One day as we were having lunch she asked, 'Can you cook?'

'Of course,' I answered, 'how else would I survive on my own?'

'Well then, you can cook dinner for me next week. I'll come to your flat.'

My mouth dropped open and she laughed and said, 'Have you got a wife hidden away in your flat?'

'Of course not,' I said.

'Well then there's no problem!'

I looked forward to the evening with great excitement and prepared for it carefully. First I visited a shop in Taksim which specialised in imported china and glassware from Europe. I chose a dinner service in eggshell blue, edged with gold, from England and several matching vases. I also bought a pale blue linen tablecloth and matching napkins and silver cutlery. I cleaned my flat till it gleamed. Next, I looked through an English recipe book and decided on steak and kidney pie with boiled potatoes and fresh carrots and green beans, followed by a custard tart. I wrote out the ingredients and bought them from the best markets so I could be sure of getting the finest produce. I also bought twelve red roses which I carefully arranged in the new vases. I put Mahler's symphony number six on the stereo and began my cooking preparations. Occasionally I took a break from chopping, stirring and simmering to walk into my living room and admire my table setting while I listened to the wonderful music. I found myself humming. I could not remember when I had last done that.

As I was patting aftershave on my chin and checking that my new blue silk tie was straight, the doorbell rang. I had to breathe deeply to calm myself before I opened the door. Gül stood there holding a bottle of wine. She was wearing a dark green dress with large gold hoops in her ears. Her hair was twisted on top of her head in a tight bun and the bones of her face looked exquisitely delicate.

She came in and said, 'That smells good, I didn't know you were a gourmet.' That pleased me enormously and I took the wine from her explaining that I couldn't drink any myself but I would pour some for her.

She walked around my living room, touching ornaments, bending to sniff the roses I'd arranged on the coffee tables, pulling books out from shelves and flicking through them. I watched her doing this while busying myself pouring the wine for her and some orange juice for myself, holding my breath as if she were doing some kind of inspection and I was worried that I might not pass. Then she sighed and said, 'You're so lucky, living here by yourself. No one to tell you what to do, who to see, where to go. This lovely place, all for you.'

Struggling to hide my pleasure I shrugged and murmured, 'It's not bad.'

She went on to complain about her parents who wanted her to marry the son of a business partner of her father. She said she didn't want that kind of life, she wanted to travel, learn more languages, see the world. I had never heard this kind of talk from a Turkish girl before.

During our meal she continued talking about her life and ambitions, frequently interrupting herself to compliment me on my cooking and to say how much she was enjoying being here with me. Despite my intense joy in her conversation and company I had to voice a niggling worry.

'What if someone finds out you've come here, alone, to my flat?'

She turned her mouth down at the corners and said, 'Oh stuff them, what the hell!'

I was shocked at this language, but thrilled at the same time. Then she said, 'You're the only person I can really talk to.'

This set the pattern of many such dinners over the next few months. We arranged to meet once a week and our meetings became the highlights of my life. Between meetings I would try to read or study but I found myself gazing at the same page for over an hour and the words would not sink into my brain. I went back to the Masnawi which had never failed to bring me inspiration before, but the same thing happened. The words were obscured by Gül's face. My brain could not work beyond thinking over our conversations and planning what I would say when next we met. Also I always worried that someone would find out that she was seeing me and I mentioned this to her often. Gül didn't care. After the meal she would lie on the sofa, her hands behind her head and her long black hair falling over the cushions. She would tell me about her ambitions for the future, her determination to go to France to learn the language, her current problems. I always listened sympathetically but never offered any advice unless she asked for it.

Generally she did not ask me questions, but once, she looked at me curiously and said, 'Celik, have you ever made love to a woman?'

My breath caught in my throat, I was so taken aback by such a direct question. No one had ever gone so far as to ask me that before. I was aware of her eyes on me and I stared back at her as coolly as I could manage.

'Well, I'm over thirty. What do you think?' And to cover my indirect lie I added quickly, 'have you ever slept with a man?'

Without the slightest hesitation she answered, 'Before I went to England I thought fucking was a vastly overrated activity. There were a few at Warwick who made me change my mind. But I get bored after a few weeks. I can't see me settling with this silly idiot my father wants me to marry.'

My heart was beating very fast during this conversation. I didn't actually want to know these things about Gül. On the other hand I could see that it could hardly have been otherwise. In comparison I felt like an ignorant boy.

A few days after this conversation she rang me to say she had finally persuaded her father to let her defer her marriage and go back to England for a year to study for her master's degree. She was leaving for England at the end of the week. She was sorry she couldn't see me before she went but she had a lot to do. She couldn't promise to write to me regularly as she was a poor correspondent but I must write to her. She gave me her address.

I missed her so much I developed pains in my arms and shoulders. People at the office kept asking me when we were going to get engaged.

This infuriated me but in my usual cool manner I said, 'Look! Just because I sometimes take a lady out for a meal, it doesn't mean I intend to marry her.' As I said that my chest was hurting and I felt very tired. No one noticed of course, they were too busy enjoying being shocked by my remarks.

Every evening when I got back to my flat after work, I walked around touching the pictures, the books, the blue and gold plates on the dresser.

After another week I emptied the dead roses from the vases into the rubbish bin in the kitchen. I heated some soup for my evening meal, though I didn't feel hungry. I sipped it standing by the window looking out onto the street. I saw a woman hanging out washing in her garden. A couple of hens ran in and out of her house. The sight irritated me and I turned away and put some Mahler on the stereo. This made me feel even more depressed.

I took out my long neglected books and determined to begin studying again. I opened Lawrence's Seven Pillars of Wisdom. Then I took out my notepad and wrote: 'How can we develop an inter-cultural language which humankind can use for meaningful communication? First we must develop a system for ridding language of ambiguity. Next we must clarify it to make it truly functional to express its purpose. Communication amongst nations....' My eyes closed and I saw Gül flicking her hair back over her shoulder. I covered my face with my hands. I scored through what I had written, tore the paper off the pad and screwed it into a ball, hurling it against the wall. I took a fresh sheet and began writing a letter to Gül. At once my words started to flow.

I thought I would bring her up to date with the news and include those comments from the people at the office, thinking she would enjoy the joke. I told her how much I missed her company and how I admired her beauty and personality. I expected a reply within a couple of weeks but there was nothing for two months. When she did reply she said she didn't quite know how to put this as she valued me very much as a friend, but those stupid people at the office who made such idiotic remarks... if it wasn't so embarrassingly annoying, it would be laughable...

After I read that letter I walked over to the mirror on the wall and stared at my reflection for a long time. When I could trust myself to speak I said, very quietly, 'Why should you expect otherwise?' Then I went over to the dresser and picked up the lovely dinner set I had bought. I carried each piece into the kitchen and dropped it onto the floor. I swept up the pieces and put them in the rubbish bin.

Nothing changed. I went to the office each day. I talked and joked with my colleagues. Occasionally I visited my family. I wrote letters to Yashar recommending books for him to read and I tried to read the books he recommended to me. I listened to my music. Sometimes I went for a walk in the evenings, looking in shop windows, buying some pickle juice to drink.

After several weeks I composed a letter. I wrote it many times before I was satisfied I had achieved the right degree of detachment... 'I have never asked you to marry me. I have never made any demands on you at all. I asked for nothing...'

I didn't hear from her until she came back to Istanbul at the end of her year's study. Then she rang me and said she had waited till we could speak together so that there would be no more misunderstandings. Her parents were away, she said and she wanted me to come to dinner.

I arrived at her house in Bebek the next evening. It was a white, three-storeyed house surrounded by high walls and there were bars over the windows. I opened the heavy iron gate and rang the bell on the large wooden door. The door opened and Gül stood there looking as if I had seen her only yesterday. No embarrassment or awkwardness. She hugged me and kissed me on both cheeks and drew me into the hall. It smelt of floor polish. I said jokingly, to hide my joy at seeing her, 'I see you've been busy today!' and pointed to the shining wooden floor covered by rich red and blue rugs.

'Don't be an idiot,' she laughed, 'why should my father pay a cleaning woman if I polished the bloody floors!'

I felt my neck go hot with embarrassment at my stupidity but Gül didn't notice and she pulled me into the dining room and made me sit at an enormous mahogany table decorated with silver candlesticks and a riot of fresh flowers.

I hardly tasted the meal she had cooked. All my concentration was focused on not appearing to stare at her while taking in every detail, from her red silk trousers and blouse to the small downy hairs on her cheekbones. I heard her say, '...and I didn't mean to hurt you and I'm sorry, will you please forgive me and promise you'll still be my friend?'

I looked at her shining dark eyes and I knew that whatever this woman did or said to me in the future I had no choice but to endure it. So I laughed and said, 'You're crazy! Maybe that's why I put up with you!' She laughed too and everything was all right again.

Three months later she invited me to her wedding. I refused her invitation.

'Of course, you know it won't last?' I said.

'What the hell?' she shrugged.

As I predicted, it didn't last. Her husband had no understanding of her personality. When she told him she wanted to go to France for a year to study the language, he said he wouldn't let her. Wouldn't let her! I roared with laughter when she told me this.

And once, when I was working in Ankara for six months and feeling lonely, I rang her at midnight as I'd sometimes done before her marriage. Her husband answered the phone and used the most abusive language to me. I didn't understand and I thought, 'You stupid bastard!' But I was courteous with him and controlled the situation.

She sent me a photograph of herself in a swimsuit on the beach. It was lovely and I kept it in a frame by my bed. However, she then wrote and said her husband had found out that she had sent it to me and insisted that I return it. She asked me, as a special favour to her to send it back, so I did.

She was fed up with him after that and said she was going to France whether he liked it or not. He said he would divorce her if she did. She said okay! He didn't expect that and was sorry. But Gül wouldn't change her mind.

Her father bought her an apartment in Rumeli, one of the best parts of the city, overlooking the Bosphorus, when she came back from France. Then she got a job teaching English in the university.

Shortly afterwards, I was promoted to World Headquarters in the USA with the Middle East/Africa Region. Gül and I kept in touch. She wasn't a good letter writer but she always remembered to send me a card on my birthday with a little gift.

I travelled all over the world on different assignments. My salary went straight into the bank and because I did not live more than a few months in each country, I didn't pay any tax. All my expenses were paid by the company and I stayed in the best hotels. In return of course, I was very useful to the company and was always willing to go where they wanted to send me at short notice. Some people called this selling your soul to the company, but it suited me.

Wherever I went, I chose beautiful, original gifts to take back home to my mother, sister and brothers, but the best ones were for Gül. She loved French perfumes, silk scarves and fine jewellery and I enjoyed her pleasure when I gave her these things. When she decided to go to London for a holiday I asked her how much money she had saved to take with her. When she told me she had saved three hundred pounds, I gave her an equivalent amount in addition.

While I was working in Zurich I wandered round the shops every weekend buying things for Gül. I bought her some Chanel 5 talcum powder and perfume, an ivory backed hairbrush, a silver bracelet set with sapphires and tiny seed pearls, but I wanted something very special. Then one morning I saw it. A magnificent white silk nightgown.

Inside the shop the assistant asked, 'For your wife?'

To hide my blushing cheeks I bent low over my cheque book, murmuring, 'Yes, indeed.'

She laughed softly, 'Ah, I see you have not been married long. I can always tell.'

Beads of sweat began to form on my forehead. I found I had filled in the wrong amount and had to start again. The girl continued, 'How long have you been married?'

'Er... six months.'

'Is she very beautiful?'

'Yes, very.'

'What a lucky lady, to receive this beautiful nightgown,' she laughed again, 'I hope it brings you luck too and some beautiful babies.'

By now my entire body was about to burst into flame. I handed her the cheque, snatched the parcel from her hand and bolted from the shop.

When I got it back to the hotel I spread it out carefully on my bed and gazed at it in admiration. The material was so fine that it was almost transparent. I sat in a chair, looking at it for a long time. No. I couldn't give it to Gül. It would be most inappropriate. How could I have thought otherwise? I felt embarrassed and foolish. I folded it carefully in tissue paper and put it back in its box, thankful that, this time, I did not have a witness to my red face.

That night I lay in bed thinking about the beautiful garment and about the shop assistant's teasing. My heart started beating very fast. I got out of bed, took the lid off the box and lifted the nightgown out of its wrappings. Oh it was exquisite. I carefully laid it on the pillow next to mine. I went into the bathroom and picked the Chanel 5 talcum powder off the shelf, carried it over to the bed and sprinkled it lightly over the nightgown. Then I got back into bed, laid my head on my pillow and stroked the silky material with my fingertips, breathing in its cleanness and coolness.

After an absence of two years I visited Istanbul on my way to Libya, where I was going to work on an eight-month contract. I had negotiated an excellent salary because the company could not find anyone else who was prepared to work there. It was early summer and the city was alive with flowers. The first thing I did when I arrived at the hotel was to ring Gül and arrange to meet her in Yildiz Park next day. It had always been one of my favourite places in summer, the gardens being full of roses and the outdoor café serving the best tea and chocolate cake in Istanbul. I could hardly sleep that night. I left the presents I had brought Gül at the hotel because I was going to ask her to come back with me.

When I got to the park next afternoon, she was already there. I saw her sitting at a table sipping tea. I waved and she saw me. She jumped up and ran to meet me. I stretched out my hand to shake hers and she laughed out loud.

'So you've gone European at last have you?' And brushing away my hand, she threw her arms around my neck and kissed me on both cheeks. Trying to ignore the stares from people sitting nearby, I led her back to the table.

We ordered tea and chocolate cake. I gazed at her face to discover whether there had been any changes in my absence. There was a little scar on her right cheek. I reached forward and touched it. She brushed my hand away impatiently.

'What happened?' I persisted.

She shrugged, 'This time it was my fault. I was driving too fast.'

'And the other times?'

'Not worth mentioning.'

I didn't pursue the matter but kissed my fingertips and stroked her scarred cheek. She relaxed and smiled at me. Without any need for adjustment we were completely in tune again.

Then, in that direct way of hers, she said, 'Celik, I'm getting married again.'

After only a moment's pause I said, 'So?'

She laughed. 'He's a Christian. Greek.'

I raised my eyebrows. 'So that's why you've taken to sending Christmas cards? What does your family say?'

She didn't answer. Then she said, 'He's very old. To remind him how old he is I tease him by pinching his wrinkled arm and he can see how smooth my skin is in comparison.'

She waited for my reaction but my expression didn't change. She went on.

'I met him on holiday in Bodrum last year. He picked me up in a bar. He's excessively rich and he knows how to treat women. Sometimes the wrinkles bother me, but...' She shrugged.

Still I didn't comment and after glancing at my face several times, she changed the subject. We talked for a while longer, about her job, about my job. Then she had to leave. I said I would contact her next time I was in Istanbul. She kissed me again. Then she was gone.

I finished drinking my tea. A warm breeze carried the scent of roses and stirred some crumpled papers on the marble floor near my table. Waiters moved silently through the murmurs of the other groups. Birds sang in the trees. In the distance, the faint rumbling of the city.

A white cat jumped up on the empty chair beside me and started to lick the remains of my chocolate cake.

'Hey,' I said, 'cats do not eat chocolate cake.'

In reply it leaped onto the table and started rubbing itself against me, purring loudly.

'Look,' I said, 'I don't like cats.'

It continued licking the cake, purring all the time.

I said, 'Okay. Let me cut a piece off for myself, then I will leave the rest to you.' I looked up to see a waiter glancing at me.

I said to him, 'This cat thinks it's a palace cat. Perhaps its ancestors belonged to the Sultans.'

He laughed and nodded and repeated what I said to another waiter. People at the nearby tables heard him and enjoyed the joke too. I ordered a taxi to take me back to my hotel. Then when it came, I dismissed it and started walking.

CHAPTER
◆ ELEVEN

I stayed in Libya for only five months. It was the most depressing country I had ever been in. Nothing worth looking at in the shops and Colonel Gadaffi occupying most of the television programmes. I thought I would go mad with boredom and I told the company I was leaving and going to London where I would wait until they found me another assignment. They tried to persuade me to stay, even offering a substantial rise in salary but I was not interested. I left and flew to London.

For the next three months I stayed at Francine's house waiting for another assignment. In the meantime I bought a bicycle and enjoyed myself cycling around London, walking through the parks and wandering around the shops spending a lot of money on books and beautiful clothes, which gave me a lot of pleasure to wear. I went to theatres and cinemas with Osman and ate at expensive restaurants with Francine and Mustafa.

Osman was, of course, no longer friends with Mustafa and even after all this time since the divorce he couldn't bear to meet him. We discussed Wittgenstein's philosophy and he told me about his own intensive study and that he and Ali and Yashar were corresponding on the subject.

'How is your study going?' he asked.

'I can't concentrate on it at present,' I said.

He glanced at me, 'Why don't we make a start together then?'

I shook my head.

'Why not?'

Again I just shook my head.

After a moment's silence Osman said, 'Why don't you enrol at a university and begin a doctoral thesis in philosophy? That way you'll have deadlines and guidance.'

'So now you throw my own words back at me! Well, I don't want to do that kind of work at university. What would be the point? I have more knowledge than the people teaching there.'

'Then use it,' he persisted, 'otherwise it's useless.'

When I left him that night my heart was heavy. He was right. I was wasting the knowledge I had worked so hard to gain. What else would I do with my life if I didn't put this knowledge to use? Before I slept that night I prayed for forgiveness and vowed to begin again.

Next morning I found Francine in the garden. She was a thin, energetic person in her mid-forties. After working in a bank during the week, she liked to spend her weekends weeding and digging. She looked up from a flower bed and said, without any greeting, 'Osman's looking a lot happier these days.'

'I think so,' I nodded.

'He was talking a while back about asking his mother to arrange a marriage for him. Did anything come of it?'

'He met some girls while he was visiting Istanbul but he said all they were interested in was travelling to London and how much money he had. He's decided against it for now I think.'

'Pity,' she sighed. 'He isn't the sort to live alone. He needs someone to love him.'

'He's perfectly happy,' I laughed. 'With his work and his reading he hasn't time to be lonely. He's a busy person.'

'Busy, sure. Not the same as happy. Haven't you noticed how much weight he's put on lately?'

'So?'

She snorted and sat back on her heels, taking her glasses off to give them a vigorous polish with the cuff of her sleeve. She put them on again and stared at me.

'You know Celik, for all your intelligence you are amazingly dim at times!'

'Why?' I asked, surprised. 'I have never heard you express this kind of concern over my living alone. Or yourself for that matter.'

She picked up her trowel again and began stabbing at the earth with it.

'You're alone by choice. It hasn't been forced on you. You're not the marrying type. You need to be independent to function the way you do. Like a computer! Sometimes I wonder if that's the reason Mustafa and I never got married.' She picked up a weed and studied it closely at the roots. 'Anyway, financially, I'd be worse off if I did marry him.'

'Why don't you just live with him then?'

She hesitated, 'His family, you know.'

Francine was the only relative in a large family of elderly spinster aunts and she had inherited a lot of money as each of them had died. She used the money to travel and had stayed with me for two weeks when I was working in Cairo. She mentioned this now, to change the subject, I suspect.

'Do you remember when you were showing me a mosque and you found one of the attendants smoking?'

I laughed loudly at the memory. 'That idiot! He was sticking his head out of the door and blowing the smoke outside.' I imitated his gestures.

'That's when I saw a completely different side to you. I had never seen you so angry! The way you ordered him to put it out. He couldn't believe it! I guess no one had ever spoken to him like that before.'

'And then the idiot asked me if I was a Haj! "What is it to you whether I am or not?" I said! "This is a sacred place and you are polluting it with your filth!"'

'It might have been easier for you if you had admitted to him that you were a Haj. Then he wouldn't have argued.'

'It was none of his business whether I had made a pilgrimage or not.'

She grinned and poked me in the chest with the trowel.

'Celik, you just like a fight, don't you?'

I laughed with her, 'You know something? You talk too much! Let's get this bloody awful weeding finished and then we can go out and have a nice lunch!'

This conversation had cheered me immensely. I felt God was reminding me, through her words, of the kind of person I was and his purpose for me. Well, now it was time to leave my old life behind and live again, though Him. A feeling of elation rippled through my body. The first I had felt in a long time.

Next morning, the telephone rang. It was Cyril Clyde, the manager of ICS Zimbabwe. He was in the city and wanted to have an interview with me about my next assignment in Salisbury. Delighted, I arranged to meet him that afternoon at the ICS office on Marylebone Rd. Two weeks later, I was on my way to Salisbury from Gatwick airport, leaving behind all the happy, sad memories and overcast days of autumn for spring and sunshine. I was feeling refreshed and ready to start working hard again.

When I arrived in Salisbury airport it was late spring in November 1980, an unearthly brilliant day. To my surprise, Mr Clyde was at the airport to meet me. We drove through a boulevard of purple, pink, blue and white blossom, on trees I hadn't seen before. It was exciting and unbelievable after the greyness of London and I felt that the city was welcoming me in full decoration. The pavements were covered for miles with fallen flowers, resembling the richness in colour of a Turkish carpet. A carpet for me to walk on to enter my palace after returning from a victorious campaign to put things in order in barbarous Europe. I began to realise why Englishmen didn't want to leave this paradise so easily.

My first talk with Cyril Clyde spoiled my pleasure. He said that when he'd agreed in London on the figure of $1500 per month, he'd meant gross. That meant I had to pay thirty percent income tax and the transfer of money outside was restricted to thirty percent. I argued that all the figures I had supplied him with were nett, in dollars, and how could I know how much tax I would be paying here to be able to talk in gross? Besides I had been promised by the SSD director, Mr Branars, when I was in Cairo, a figure of $1500 per month and that couldn't be gross for I was already getting $1200 nett per month, plus $24 a day allowance.

'Oh,' he said, 'they were looking after you well.'

'They got value for their money,' I retorted.

He stood up. 'Well I'm sorry, but it isn't possible for me to accept your conditions. It would upset the salary structure of the company.'

I stood up too and faced him across his desk. 'That is not my problem, for I won't accept anything but a promotion.'

He closed my file with a snap. 'Then I'm sorry, but in that case, I have no other choice but to send you back to London.'

'If that is your decision, I can't help you.' I turned to leave.

Then he changed his tone and said quickly, 'I will have to report this situation to headquarters.'

'Yes, you will.'

He picked up the phone and began dialling as I walked out the door.

During his phone call to the USA he had instructions, I imagine, that he shouldn't push me too hard and they would need time to go through my personal file to evaluate the situation. Next afternoon I was back in his office and when the USA called him again, Mr Branars was on the phone and wanted to talk to me. He said he didn't remember how much he had promised me in Cairo but if I said $1500, then it must be right. He also said they were preparing something better for me. Perhaps they would send me to Blantyre for a short assignment. I thanked him and hung up. Cyril was not looking too happy now.

'If more than one person interferes with one business then it ends in a mess,' he said.

I didn't comment for I was busy thinking. Blantyre? Where was that? What was waiting for me there? Well it didn't matter. For a couple of months I could live anywhere.

Later on I talked to my friends. They said, 'Blantyre? It's an excellent holiday resort for Middle Africa by the lake of Malawi.' Malawi? Till then I didn't even know that such a country existed.

After spending ten lovely warm days in Salisbury, I started off for Blantyre. Salisbury was one of the most beautiful cities I had ever seen. It was naturally air-conditioned and the climate was so regulated that almost every afternoon around 4.00 pm it rained for half an hour to get the city clean and cool. The air was crisp, clear and unpolluted. On the plane I felt certain that I would be coming back to stay there for a longer time. For that reason I left half my baggage behind.

I had been instructed by Headquarters that I would be joining a team in Blantyre to install a banking package system called WBIS (World Banking Information System) at the Commercial Bank of Malawi as a pilot site. A system working on ASC I8250 under IMOSCTME supporting 279 teller terminals online. The team would consist of a project leader and a support person from Dayton, a support person from South Africa, two Bank of America consultants and myself as a site representative. I would be reporting to the SSD director and to Cyril Clyde and Bob Harris, SSD manager in Johannesburg. Everything sounded under control.

Although I lacked knowledge of the package, I was enthusiastic about joining a team developing such a modern online banking system. However it was odd that they had chosen a bank in Blantyre as a CVT (customer verification test.) site for such a package. I had heard last year, in Cairo, that it used to be called IBIS and remembered how two of my colleagues, Amr and Edward, were working day and night to translate it into Arabic and were having waves of modifications from the USA now and then which was pushing them to the brink of frustration. And how Amr was feeling happy and high when he received his invitation from Canada for emigration, that at last he was getting rid of that monster called IBIS.

When I arrived at Blantyre airport, the field engineer, Mark Rider met me there. He told me that he was a South African from Durban where he had left a son and daughter with his divorced wife. While he drove me towards the hotel, he admitted he drank a lot and was always homesick. He explained to me that Rob Stokes left yesterday, leaving behind all his clothes and laundry.

'But I was expecting him to hand over the system to me and orientate me with the bank!'

He shrugged. 'I think he had malaria.'

I was surprised and alarmed, thinking, what a strange site, people running away leaving behind their clothes!

As we approached the city, the road became crowded with black people walking on both sides of it. The city was situated on a hill with an altitude of around a thousand metres. The hotel, Mount Soche, was opposite the bank, fifty metres away. The test site was at a garage behind the bank. The bank's computer site was in the branch where they were running General Ledger Module of the system which we would be testing, the current accounts and savings modules.

Mark introduced me to BA consultants Tom and Alice Moore. Later, I learnt that Tom was a Vietnam veteran, an unpredictable New Yorker who believed, and was proud of the fact, that he was from the centre of the universe. I had been thinking that the centre of the universe was Istanbul!

He told me the history of the site, how it started with the installation of the G/L system. Then he complained that ICS had promised to finish the installation last April and changed the date to November and now to another date. Typical, I thought!

Before we had arrived, there had been another team consisting of Frank, Betty and Laurelie. Now they had appointed Julia Somers as project manager for C/A tests, for she was in charge of the development of the module in USA. He said Rob left yesterday in haste because of his suspected malaria, but Laurelie would be back next week to help me by explaining the system till Julia arrived from the USA in two weeks. He told me how charming Betty, the American, was.

I asked, 'What does Laurelie, the South African look like?'

'You'll see. But she is fat and dull,' he replied.

There was also a dim character, Gary Turnbull, the programming manager of the live system, from England, and the DP manager of the bank, Mike Sanders, a kind English gentleman.

Mark helped to familiarise me. Everything was so different that it was like discovering the world anew. Mark and I were staying in the same hotel. He had found a flat to move into but it wasn't ready yet. He had arrived a month ago so he had a few friends but he was feeling desperate to find a European girlfriend, for the Malawian girls were not attractive in general, with small breasts and plain facial features, although their legs were not bad at all. Mark referred to every white girl he had been intimate with as Fred. I recommended that he call the beautiful black girls Tambala Kings after the peanuts commercial name in Malawi. Then we started cutting it short, calling them Tambalas.

One day, a South African coloured prostitute settled at the hotel and she was after Mark. She was a small, well-endowed, sticky creature. I started calling her Booby Trap. When Mark saw her he didn't know where to hide. He was so disgusted with her that he decided to find himself a decent girl by randomly calling numbers from the local telephone directory. He made a date with one, inviting her to dinner, saying, 'This is your lucky day, you are invited to dinner.'

It turned out to be his lucky day for the person he contacted was a pleasant, attractive teacher from England, who had also been to Istanbul with her parents when she was a child. Her father worked for Foreign Affairs at the Consulate. Her name was Liz.

It was in Malawi that I discovered the concepts of white, black and coloured, which were alien concepts to my cultural background. In this masquerade I fell into the category of white.

After one week Laurelie arrived. She was in the bank when I walked in one morning. Mark introduced us and she shook my hand and smiled warmly. I thought, what did that idiot mean, fat and dull? She's beautiful. She was about twenty three with long wavy blonde hair and soft creamy skin and light blue eyes. A little plump, but well-proportioned. An enchanting person. I thought, ICS have sent her to keep me happy here so I won't run away too! She had that air of sincerity and friendliness that I later discovered to be common to most South Africans.

While we worked together we discussed – apart from business – art, politics, science and philosophy. We were staying at the same hotel, and having breakfast, lunch and dinner together most of the time. I became very easy and high-spirited with her. Apart from Gül she was the only woman I had felt comfortable with. As the day of her departure drew closer, I realised that once again I was going to be on my own.

One evening, over dinner, I asked her to join our team and stay with us.

'I'd like to,' she said, 'but I have a job waiting for me in Jo'burg.'

'Well, I wouldn't mind if you didn't work at all,' I said jokingly. 'I could work for both of us. All you would have to do would be to keep the atmosphere happy with your charm.'

'I'd be bored out of my mind!' she laughed. 'Besides, I'm involved in so many things at home that I can't leave the place for more than a few days.'

'That's a big disappointment to me Laurelie, for I would really love you to join our team here.'

'And I've enjoyed working with you, Celik. I'll be back when I'm needed.'

After a moment I said, 'When this project is finished, I'll be taking a month's leave. I was thinking about spending it in Europe. Would you come with me?'

'Well, for one thing I couldn't afford it!' she laughed.

'I'm inviting you as my guest,' I said. 'Of course I wasn't thinking you would be paying for yourself.'

She stared at me. 'You can't be serious?'

'Of course I'm serious. It isn't fun always travelling alone.'

She shook her head. 'I couldn't possibly accept.'

Because she did not react spontaneously to my proposal, I didn't repeat it and after a week she left. That is how our friendship started and we kept it warm by exchanging letters. The following May when I went to visit South Africa she came to meet me at my hotel in Johannesburg for dinner.

I had very little free time but occasionally I would go mountain climbing with Mark at weekends. The other people on the team frequently held parties and I was always invited. Mark began seeing Liz regularly and soon he moved into a flat. After a couple of months it became obvious that this assignment was going to take longer than I'd expected, so, fed up with staying in the hotel, I found a house to rent.

The house was furnished and came supplied with a housekeeper and a gardener. I went out and bought linen and china and made myself really comfortable. Life there was very easy and luxurious. But I grew bored after six months because the only people I saw in my leisure were the people I worked with, and although they were very kind and hospitable there was no one with whom I could discuss things that mattered to me. Most of them were married with small children and the few bachelors there liked to spend their evenings going to dirty Malawian pubs and picking up prostitutes.

Once, out of curiosity, I allowed myself to be persuaded to go with them. We visited a succession of these pubs, each one seeming to me to be darker and dirtier than the last. Of course my companions didn't care because by now they were drunk but I got more and more depressed. The women were ugly and they stank. In the last pub, one of them wound her arms around me and danced very close so that I could feel her enormous breasts pushing into my shoulders. It was like being trapped in a nightmare. When I finally escaped, I went straight home and took a long hot shower to rid myself of the smell of those women. After that, nothing would induce me to go to those places again.

Over the next two months I occupied myself by taking driving lessons and when I passed my test I bought a car. Then I began to enjoy the freedom of driving through the countryside on my own at weekends and stopping to look at the wild flowers growing in the fields. Some I picked and pressed immediately to preserve their colour and freshness.

One day, while I was talking to one of the black technicians at work, a small, beautiful woman came up to him and said something quietly. He introduced her to me as his cousin and then excused himself and went outside with her. After a few minutes she came back in and asked politely how I liked being in the country. I answered that I was enjoying it very much now that I was staying in a house and had my own car to give me more freedom. I asked her where she lived and if she had any family. She said she was working as a waitress because her husband had deserted her three months ago and she had no children so she got lonely. All the time we talked she was looking at me with such dark, shining eyes. As she was about to leave

I invited her to come and have dinner with me at my house the next evening. She looked surprised and pleased and immediately accepted the invitation.

The next evening, my housekeeper finished preparing the meal and then left so I was alone when the doorbell rang. I opened the door and the small black woman stood there, smiling at me. She was wearing a yellow dress which showed off her small waist and firm breasts.

We ate the meal and I played some Mahler on the stereo. And all the time she gazed at me with those huge, glowing eyes, so black the pupils were not distinguishable from the irises. No woman had ever looked at me like that before. I could see desire and frustration in her eyes. In these hot countries it must be difficult for a woman without a husband, I thought. I would be helping her.

I looked at her and asked, 'Why me?'

'Because you are a good man,' she answered.

I leaned over and kissed her on the mouth and she started circling her tongue around mine, triggering sensations I hadn't known existed. She put her arms around me and held me close. It was the first time I had ever been held in that way. Normally I did not like physical contact. I pulled away in a sweat.

'I'm a good game,' she said, gasping.

I didn't understand till she repeated it. Then I felt cheated, but it was too late. She took my hand and put it on her breast and as soon as I felt the softness there I began to tremble violently. She took this for excitement and she unfastened her dress and slipped it down over her shoulders. Her exposed breasts were small and shapely with huge black nipples. I buried my face in them and began kissing them frantically, pulling at the nipples with my lips.

She was a very passionate woman but although I was sweating with excitement now, I also felt disgusted. Sour and salty is how I thought of it afterwards. She pulled me to the floor and sat on top of me. I immediately came. I made an excuse about not being well and got rid of her.

She visited me twice more and the same scene was repeated. Each time I felt more disgusted and I wanted to end the affair. Fortunately it was Ramadan the following week and I made this the excuse. So ended my first experience of sex. Now I too knew the act that drove men mad with obsessive desire. The curiosity that had tormented my youth, the subject of poetry and literature through the ages, magazines and movies and jokes, was no longer a mystery to me. But without love it was as unappealing as touching dead flesh.

In that moment of realisation I knew that there was no longer any barrier to my completing the work for which God had destined me. I returned to my books as joyfully as most men return to their homes and families after a long illness. I filled notebook after notebook with my writing.

After I had been in Malawi a year I was asked to go to Dayton in the USA for a month and then return for three months before taking up an assignment in Dayton. I felt very happy about this for it was my ambition to work for World Headquarters, though of course I had not told this to anyone. I started packing my bags and giving away the crockery and household utensils I had bought to Mark and Liz who were going to be married soon. They came to my house to say goodbye because they were leaving the following afternoon for a week's holiday.

I decided to go for a drive next morning, which was Saturday. I was leaving on Monday so this was my last chance to go out and have a picnic in the country. The morning was bright and I felt at peace as the road unwound in front of me with the blue mountains as a backdrop and flowers growing by the roadside. There was some Mozart on the car radio which I was enjoying. Then the radio went crackly and I lost the station. I fiddled with the knobs but I couldn't find the right station so I glanced down to see what I was doing. When I looked up again I saw an enormous boulder on the road directly in front of me.

My God, who put that rock there?

An explosion in my head. And then blackness.

I don't know how long I was unconscious but when my eyes opened again the car was on its side and there was blood all over my face and arms. My head throbbed. I tried to unfasten the seat belt but my arm wouldn't work. I heard someone shouting. I looked up to see half a dozen natives all crowded round the car staring at me. They started to lift it and suddenly flames leapt out of the engine. The natives ran away immediately. I saw the back of their heels disappearing in the dust.

I thought, what! Will you leave me here to fry? I couldn't move at all and the flames were creeping nearer. I prayed to God and He soothed my heart. He gave me the strength to pull my trapped arm free and unfasten my belt. The natives came running back and with a lot of shouting and jabbering they were able to open the door and pull me out and carefully laid me by the side of the road. They threw earth over the fire and extinguished it. I kept drifting in and out of consciousness and was only hazily aware of a car pulling up. The next time I awoke, I was lying in bed in hospital without any recollection of how I had got there.

'You were very lucky. I hope you realise that,' the doctor said.

'How soon can I leave?' was my response.

He laughed. 'You have a broken arm, two broken legs and a fractured rib. You'll be out of commission for a few weeks I'm afraid.'

'Weeks? But I'm leaving for the States on Monday.'

He shook his head. 'You won't be leaving for anywhere.'

I sank back on the pillow and groaned.

Before I could remain in that hospital I had to be examined by another doctor to ascertain whether or not I could be classified as white. When he had finished all his measuring and examining he said to me, 'You are a perfect specimen. Everything is in perfect proportion.'

'Am I white then?' I asked, not really convinced I could be classified as such.

'You are definitely white,' he said reassuringly.

I burst out laughing. Later that day, the door to my room opened and Liz and Mark walked in. Their faces were pale and shocked.

'Oh Celik!' Liz sat on the edge of the bed and put her cheek on mine. There were tears in her eyes.

'Hey! I'm alive you know. No tears please.'

Mark shook his head and said, 'You look like a bloody mummy!'

Only my eyes were visible so I must have presented quite a sight. Mark told me they had been driving along the road to start their holiday when they passed my car lying upside down. They had turned back at once and phoned the hospital to find out if I was there, convinced I must be dead. I was touched by their concern and they said they were going to cancel their holiday so they could stay with me and visit me every day. I protested at this but they were adamant. Soon, word got around about what had happened and each day, to my surprise, there was always someone to visit me.

After a month all the bandages came off and I was healing quite well. Still the doctor would not commit himself as to the length of my stay. I asked the nurse to bring me a mirror and to my great relief I saw that there were no scars on my face. I had grown a beard and when Liz came in that evening with Mark she said, 'Hey! Very nice!'

'Do you think so?' I asked, surprised.

'You must definitely keep it,' she said, 'It makes you look sexy!'

I couldn't believe this. 'What! You must be kidding!'

'Sexy?' snorted Mark, 'it makes him look like bloody Castro!'

'Nonsense,' said Liz, 'it makes him look all intense. And mysterious.'

I began to laugh and then my ribs hurt so I said, 'Please! No more comments!'

Her verdict was repeated by all the ladies who came to visit me over the next few days so I decided that the beard must stay. After two months of lying on my back I was ready to scream with frustration. I could not even read for long without great discomfort. I constantly rang my bell to bring the attention of the nurses to me, but they were so busy they just got irritated.

Then one night I had a very strange dream. In the dream I was talking to a woman. Her face kept changing. Sometimes it was oval with olive skin surrounded by glossy, black hair, then round and plump with black curls, creamy with blonde wavy hair, then sometimes it was a face I thought I knew better than all the others though I couldn't recognise who it was. This dream was so vivid that I couldn't get it out of my mind for days.

Next time Liz came to see me I asked her to phone Laurelie and tell her I was in hospital and longed to see her. She came back next day and I looked at her hopefully but she shook her head.

'She was very surprised to hear from me. Sounded a bit put out actually. Anyway, she said she couldn't come as she was far too busy but she sends her regards and hopes you'll soon recover.'

I didn't react to this news in front of Liz, simply saying, 'Ah well, you win some, you lose some,' but as soon as she left, I turned my face into my pillow and wept. After that I was awkward with the nurses, demanding that they talk to me and complaining constantly until eventually they all lost their patience, snapping, 'You are not our only patient. We have other patients to see to, more seriously ill than you are!'

I shouted, 'What am I supposed to do, lying here on my back all day long, miserable and bored with no one to talk to and all you can say is you're busy!' Tears of frustration streamed down my face.

They scurried out of the room and a few minutes later the doctor appeared and sat down beside my bed and asked me what was wrong. I told him that I had invited a friend to come and see me and she had refused so I was upset. Also I was going mad with boredom. He stayed and listened and talked for half an hour. Before he left he took a small book out of his pocket.

'This is called Ring of Bright Water, by a guy name of Gavin Maxwell. I've just finished it and you're welcome to borrow it.'

I realised how busy he must have been and I appreciated his kindness. I wrote a letter to Laurelie telling her how lonely I was and pleaded with her to come and see me, just to talk. I felt certain that she would respond to my letter once she understood the terrible situation I was in. I enclosed a cheque to cover her air fare. One of the nurses posted it for me, and to help me endure the rest of the week until I got her reply I opened the book the doctor had given me and began to read. Soon I was engrossed in this tale of one man's connection with a wild animal in the solitude of a Scottish island. I was very impressed with the beauty of his language. One phrase stayed in my head and I liked saying it out aloud to hear how it sounded: 'Thank you for the times of contact.' I enjoyed the feel of those words on my tongue.

On the morning I finished the book a nurse breezed into my room and threw a letter on my bed, 'Something to cheer you up,' She said. I recognised Laurelie's handwriting on the envelope and eagerly tore it open. Out fell the cheque. I looked at it, puzzled, and opened the single sheet of paper that accompanied it.

Dear Celik,

I have to return your cheque because I really can not spare the time to come to Malawi. I have a boyfriend here and it would cause problems. I am truly sorry about your accident and I wish you a speedy recovery.

Love,

Laurelie.

I closed my eyes and wrapped my arms tightly around my shoulders. I stroked my neck and ran the back of my hand slowly across my cheeks and mouth. I rocked myself back and forth from the waist. Then I crumpled the letter up and threw it in the rubbish bin. That was the end of Laurelie.

That night I had a very bright dream. I was bringing a woman to meet my parents but I did not know how to introduce her. She was more than a friend but she was not my wife. I did not see her face but I was filled with happiness and warmth. When I woke up I had the feeling that something wonderful had happened if only I could remember it. Within seconds I realised it was only a dream and the euphoria vanished, to be replaced with aching loneliness.

I lay there thinking about that and wondering why this was my habitual state. I went over the scenes of my life as if I were rewinding a film, from Hulya's birth, Ahmet's death, walking over Galata Bridge with Lale, writing to Sarah, my time in England, my trial and imprisonment, Osman's wedding and divorce, Gül, my escalating career and travels all over the world, meeting Laurelie, my first sexual encounter with the black woman, my accident. And what of the future? I would travel more, get a bit richer, read more books, listen to more music, visit countries I hadn't yet seen, meet a few more women who sometimes wanted to be friends but more often didn't. And then? And then? Grow old and die. And who would remember my life and grieve for my death? Who would be changed by knowing me? What difference did the fact of my existence make to society or to any single person within it? What was the point of my existing at all?

I had heard that when people are drowning they experience scenes from their life flashing in front of their eyes as if on a fast moving film. The feeling I had was like that. I lay back in my white sheets and looked at the white ceiling and the white walls. Silence. Only the sound of my own breathing. I lay there counting the beats of my heart. I had never in my entire life felt so completely abandoned and alone. I felt as though I had been lying in that bare white room all my life.

I struggled onto my side and leaned over the bed to open my locker door. I pulled out my bag and hauled it up on to the bed and frantically searched for my address book. Finding it, I turned the pages of familiar names. Francine, Yashar, Osman, Gül. Colleagues I had worked with in various countries. The names of all the people I had connected with at some point in my life were there. I started at the beginning again and read the names aloud. Then I looked at the pages and pages with no names. As I was about to close the book I saw one more name on the last page. Weston – Sarah. I stared at the name and said it out loud a few times.

Soon I would be forty years old. Sarah would be about thrity seven. I wondered if she had children. I looked at the address again and told myself, 'You're crazy!' but still I reached for pen and paper. My hand wouldn't write anything. It hovered above the paper. Into my head came the line from Ring of Bright Water. 'Thank you for the times of contact.' Before I could change my mind I wrote the line, signed my name and put the paper in an envelope, sealed it and wrote Sarah's name and address. Then I called a nurse and asked her to post it for me. I didn't write my address for I did not expect an answer to this note and I had no idea why I had written it.

After I had rotted in that place for three months I was allowed to leave. I was able to walk on crutches but it was awkward for me to move about. My relief at getting out was so immense however that I didn't care about any difficulties that I might encounter. I asked the wife of one of my colleagues, who was a registered nurse, if she would look after me at home during the day and as I offered her a good wage she was pleased to do it. Over the next eight weeks she helped me to exercise and she massaged my legs so that gradually the strength returned to them. At last I was fit enough to travel to the USA via London.

At Gatwick, I looked up from my wheelchair to see Osman's astonished face staring at me from the groups of people waiting in the arrivals lounge. He sprinted forward, his mouth and eyes open wide so that I couldn't help laughing.

'What on earth...?'

'Someone planted a rock in front of my car while I was driving.'

'Why didn't you write and tell me?'

'What would have been the point? What could you have done except worry?'

He shook his head in disbelief and embraced me right there in the middle of that crowd of people, something he did not usually do in England.

I ruffled his hair. 'Come on. Let's go man! I'll tell you all about it when we get to your flat.'

CHAPTER TWELVE

After I left my brother in London I flew on to Dayton. My assignment was for two months so the company provided me with a flat near World Headquarters. I couldn't believe the facilities in that place. There was a gymnasium and swimming pool, squash court, pleasant cafés. I saw a different film each night. People called this place Fantasy Island. It was, in fact, like a small self-contained city and it was easy to insulate myself in such an environment. For now, this suited me very well. I kept meeting several of my colleagues from Egypt, Turkey and Libya. And Julia was back from Malawi.

Later in the week she invited me to her place for dinner. Her apartment was furnished with dark, elaborate mock-colonial furniture, lots of heavy table lamps and paintings in big gilt frames on the walls. As we sat in front of her fake log fire drinking coffee I thought about the last time a woman had invited me to dinner. Gül's silky olive skin and long black hair glowing in the candlelight. A muscle contracted in my throat. I looked closely at the crêpey, yellow skin around Julia's eyes and neck, the streaks of grey in her coarse red hair, the brown age-spots on the backs of her hands, the heavy thighs and drooping breasts. No. She had no appeal for me sexually. Fortunately! The last thing I needed now was to be distracted by a woman.

She started telling me how she had got married at twenty and began her career as a maths teacher but had got fed up with the poor salary so had trained as a programmer and later a systems analyst. '...and I divorced the bastard ten years ago because he didn't like me earning more money than he did, can you believe it?'

Privately I thought that this was a normal reaction but I nodded sympathetically.

'...and I was often away on assignments overseas while he was stuck at home looking after the kid. When he gave me the ultimatum of giving up my job and staying home or he'd divorce me, I said, "Well go screw yourself because I sure as hell am not giving up what I've worked so hard for just to play mommy to you". Yeah, the work is pretty addictive. I guess that's why we all end up divorced or alcoholic.'

I shook my head. 'For me, my work is just fun and games. Outside working hours I don't give it a thought.'

She considered this for a moment then said, 'But to survive in this job you can't be anchored. I have a great salary, I go where I like, fuck who I want, and move on. No commitments. Suits me just fine.'

I was shocked to hear this kind of talk from a woman but I kept my expression under control. Of course I had heard such remarks countless times from the men I worked with. But that was different. From a woman it sounded vulgar and coarse. Even Gül had never expressed herself so bluntly.

'Where is your son then?' I said, to change the subject.

She got up and took a photograph of a handsome, dark-haired youth off the mantelpiece. 'Sammy. He was a great kid.'

'Was?'

'Killed in a car crash three years ago.'

I closed my eyes. 'Oh no! Oh my God.'

She stroked the silver frame. 'Only thing that saved me from jumping off the roof was my job.'

I looked at her. Her eyes were too bright. She put the photograph back.

'Worked twenty hours a day so I didn't have any time to think or feel. Company couldn't believe their luck. Agreed to any conditions I asked for. Still do.'

'Oh Julia, I'm so...'

She held her hand up to stop me. 'Got my own ways of coping. Don't need anyone's sympathy. Don't need anything. Only way to survive. Change of subject. When are you going back to Malawi?'

That night, as I lay in bed, I thought over my conversation with Julia. I had glimpsed a side of her I hadn't realised existed. I felt confused and dissatisfied, but I didn't know why. Was it what she said? Was it my response? I switched on my bedside light and reached for my notepad. I wrote... 'how can we develop a functional language which will facilitate closer interactions between human beings, forcing artificial layers to crack so that we may express our identities as we are?' I fell back on my pillow and slept a restless sleep. My dreams were filled with running after a woman I thought was Gül, but when she turned around her face was lined and tired, her breasts sagging to her waist. As I turned away from her in disgust she stretched out her arms towards me, crying. At this point I woke up gasping for breath, only to fall asleep almost immediately and repeat the cycle. When I woke up next morning I was exhausted. I resolved not to see Julia again. I could not endure to go on another emotional roller-coaster ride with a woman. After work each day I made sure I arranged to go out with colleagues – a squash game, a bar, a movie, a barbecue. Eventually Julia got fed up with my excuses and stopped inviting me to visit her.

The weeks passed quickly and I enjoyed myself so much there, mixing with different kinds of people and going out every night that I was not looking forward to my return to Malawi. I flew back to London and stayed with Osman overnight before continuing on to Malawi next day. We discussed philosophy most of the evening and he outlined his plans about writing a book.

'Don't think about it, man, do it!' I said.

'And what about your plans?' he asked. 'Did you study much in Dayton?'

I shook my head. 'No. It wasn't possible because of the distractions of the social life. As soon as I'm back in Malawi I will begin again.'

'I seem to have heard this before, Celik,' he said reprovingly.

This annoyed me because I was perfectly well aware of it and I said, 'Cool it, man! I have my own rhythms.' But I felt disturbed and promised myself that I would not allow any more distractions when I got back to Malawi.

Next morning Osman came to the airport with me and as I turned to leave him, he said, 'There's a letter for you. Hulya sent it on from Istanbul, knowing you would stop here on your way back to Malwai.' I took the envelope from him and put it in my pocket without looking at it.

When I had settled in my seat on the plane I took the letter out of my pocket. It had already been opened. At first I did not recognise the writing. Then when I saw the name at the end of the letter I had to close my eyes and lean back in my seat to regain my composure. After a minute or so I opened my eyes and began reading.

Dear Celik,

I was astonished when my mother sent on your postcard. It was an amazing coincidence that you thought of me after such a long time. I say coincidence because at about the time you must have written the card I had just returned from New Zealand and was in the process of moving things from my mother's house to the one I've bought in Reading. While I was at my mother's I found all your old letters and photographs. I sat on the floor in my old bedroom and read them. I remembered your phone call when you were in England. We were cut off and I waited for you to ring back but you didn't. I wrote to you a couple of times repeating my invitation to you to come up and visit me but as you didn't reply I assumed you weren't interested or you were too busy. As I read the letters I was very curious about how your life had turned out.

The few days in my mother's house was the strangest thing for me. I felt eighteen again, when the whole world was new and prickling with possibilities and just waiting for me to choose a door to step through. And there were so many doors!

The one I chose all those years ago took me along the same route my mother had taken. I can't believe now that I repeated it so exactly, that is, to live on a farm in New Zealand, end my marriage, leave New Zealand and return to England to begin again. But I do know that I married Dave to return to a life that I felt my mother had unravelled which had left me feeling like an uprooted plant. So I had to go back to where it all began – New Zealand – and live the life I thought she should have lived with my father. In a way it was also punishing her for burning my father's letters and cutting off all contact with him, though I didn't think that at the time, not consciously. My mother never once criticised my father to me and so I never knew what her life had been like with him. All I remembered was what a kind, funny, sweet man he had been. Just like Dave, in fact. Now that I have been through the same situation I understand exactly what led my mother to leaving my father and for the first time ever she has opened up to me about it. We've both shed a lot of tears. And now, here I am, where I left off twenty years ago, looking at a row of doors again.

Dave is still in New Zealand and I have custody of our two boys, Nathan (5) and Jeremiah (7). I was working as a journalist before I left England for New Zealand and now, thanks to some old connections, I'm working part-time on a local newspaper. It isn't much, but it's a start, and I'm excited by the possibilities for the future. I have my house, my children and the beginnings of a career. At present that's enough.

My best wishes,

Sarah.

I wondered why Osman had waited until the last moment before giving it to me. He had looked after Sarah's letters while I was in prison and it was possible he had read them and knew something of our former friendship. He had obviously read this letter before passing it on to me and, I judged, had not been able to make up his mind about giving to me. Why?

I couldn't believe she had replied to my card. I read the letter several times to convince myself it was true, then I drafted a reply. I also looked for a nice photograph of myself which I could include.

Dear Sarah,

Thank you so much for taking the trouble to write to me. Your letter gave me more pleasure than you can imagine. I'm also very happy to hear you have children because I have always imagined you with children. It's great that you are able to work as a journalist. I remember very well that that was your dream.

Well, my life didn't turn out quite the way I expected it to either. After the phone call in 1966 I returned to Turkey to finish my degree and then went into the army as an officer to do my military service. Because of my religious beliefs I was imprisoned for one year. After my release I found a job with ICS Turkey as a computer programmer and later as a systems analyst.

In recent years I have travelled all over the world on different assignments for the company and at present I am based in Malawi. In July last year I had an accident when the car I was driving crashed into a rock and I spent three months in hospital. While I was in the hospital I grew a beard, though my face wasn't scarred, thanks to God! All the ladies who visited me there said I looked better with a beard. What do you say?

I have just returned from an assignment in the USA and will go back there again in three months' time.

Well, I have not been married and I have no children. I think I am too independent to be a husband or father. In my spare time I direct all my energies to studying the Koran. I would love you to continue writing to me.
Celik.

I posted this as soon as I arrived in the airport. Feeling slightly light-headed I went to buy a newspaper and while I was waiting to pay for it my attention was caught by a row of little glass bottles on the counter inside the shop. Each bottle had an ornament in it. I picked one up to look at it more closely. Inside was a tiny blue duck. On impulse I bought it.

Three weeks later another short letter arrived from Sarah, this time with a photograph of herself and her two children. She looked just the same with her warm smile though her hair was short now. The boys were both beautiful blonde children.

Our correspondence continued over the next couple of months. Her letters were full of descriptions about the house she was decorating, her daily life, and questions about mine. She recommended me to read books she had enjoyed. My letters were short, containing the replies to her questions. I recommended that she read the novels of John Fowles, especially The Magus, which had left a deep impression on me. I also sent her a book list of my favourite philosophical works. Then I had to start making plans to go back to the USA. I wrote to tell her this and added, '...if you wish, if God wills, perhaps we might meet?'

And I prayed. 'My God, will you let me meet her at least once before I die? Please let me see her holding her children in her arms.'

She replied saying she would like to meet me and I would be welcome to stay in her home. She had a spare room.

I read her letter, listened to some Mahler, read some poetry from the Masnawi, looked out of my window at the purple mountains. I found some of my pressed wild flowers and put them in an envelope to send to her.

A few weeks after I'd sent the letter there was a party at Mark and Liz's house. They were now married. We had a barbecue around their swimming pool and there was a good deal of laughter and banter. Someone asked me the usual question. 'Celik, why did you never marry?'

I put my arm around Liz and said, 'Soon.'

They were all surprised and didn't believe me of course and Gary asked if I had a photograph of the lady.

'No comment,' I said.

'Is that what she said, "No comment"?' he replied.

Everyone laughed and I joined in but we were laughing at different things and only I could see the joy and beauty encompassing the present and extending to the future. To redirect their attention I lifted Liz in my arms and carried her squealing to the edge of the pool.

'You wouldn't dare!' she yelled.

By now everyone was gathering around the pool and egging me on to throw her in.

'You see my difficulty?' I said to her, 'I can't disappoint all these people,' and dropped her over the edge with a big splash.

Everyone roared with laughter and then some people jumped in the pool themselves, fully clothed. Liz swam to the side and scrambled out, 'I'll kill you Celik! Look at my dress!'

'Don't worry about your dress,' I said, 'when I go to London I promise I will buy you a dress so beautiful you won't believe your eyes!'

'I'll keep you to that!' she called over her shoulder as she stormed off to change. I joined in the laughter and felt more carefree and lighthearted than I had done in years.

Next morning came Sarah's reply. I found myself smiling with anticipated pleasure as I turned the letter in my hands. I made myself a cup of coffee. Before I opened it I thought about the teasing I had got at the pool, and my response. I thought about Gül and her rejection of me as a sexual partner, although she hung onto me as a friend whenever her life didn't go the way she wanted it to. The woman I had fucked in Malawi. Even at this moment, when I thought about that I felt like throwing up. And Laurelie. Well, she was pretty, but in a few years her soft creaminess would turn to fat. Julia? Had she wanted me to fuck her? It would have been doing her favour if I had, I was sure of that, though her body was not attractive to me at all. In any case, there was my resolve to concentrate on my work and stay away from emotional entanglements, which were, I was sure now, just forms of bewitchment Satan liked to tempt me with to deflect me from my study. Then why had I written to Sarah? Just on a random impulse because I was bored out of my brain at being incarcerated in that hospital? And why had she replied? Was Satan tempting me again or was this a gift from God to end my solitary life? I opened the letter.

Dear Celik,

After reading your last letter I feel I should warn you that I'm still recovering from the consequences of a disastrous marriage and I don't want any emotional involvement with anyone at present. But friendship I definitely need. It may be that I've misinterpreted your letter or you misinterpreted mine, but I should makes things clear before we meet to avoid any misunderstandings.

Regards,
Sarah.

I didn't realise I had closed my eyes until the scalding liquid from my cup pouring on to my leg made me yell and jump out of the chair. I hurled the cup against the wall where it smashed into a dozen pieces. I shouted, 'Why do they all want to be friends with me? I am a man. My body functions like a man.' Then I cried bitter tears. I was ashamed to be seen next morning with my red, popped eyes and I wore dark glasses for the rest of the day.

That evening I sat at my desk to write a reply to Sarah's letter but after more than an hour I still couldn't summon up adequate words to express my feelings. And then I saw the little duck in the bottle on the shelf above my desk. I went to the cupboard to take out my polaroid camera and took a photograph of the ornament. I sat at my desk again with the photo in my hand watching the colours and shapes take form. When the duck had completely materialised I wrote on the back. 'This is Celik. He wishes you every joy and success in your life. And may God forgive you for you have hurt a human being.' I put it in an envelope and wrote Sarah's address. I posted it then flew to London to stay with Osman before travelling on to the USA. I kept the duck in my pocket so I could take it out and look at it whenever I felt I was in danger of forgetting what I had just learned.

When I arrived in Dayton I invited Julia over to my apartment for dinner the same evening. If she wanted me to fuck her, then I would, what the hell? I was quite looking forward to seeing her by the time she rang the doorbell. But when I opened it I saw she was wearing jeans and an old beige sweater and her hair looked as if it hadn't been combed. I was annoyed that she hadn't gone to at least a little trouble to attract me. She didn't seem to notice my disappointment and swept past me with a 'Hi stranger!'

I had prepared a simple salad and grilled steak as I hadn't wanted to go to a lot of trouble over this meal. For dessert I took some ice-cream out of the freezer. As we ate she told me what she had been doing. I had to clench the muscles in my throat several times to stop myself from yawning. God, I was tired. I just wanted to go to sleep. Then I heard her say, 'Screw anyone interesting while you were in Malawi?' Normally I had no trouble producing a witty response to this kind of comment but now my mouth went dry. After a few seconds of embarrassing silence I took the duck in the bottle from my pocket and handed it to her. She raised her eyebrows.

'This is my life in Malawi,' I said. 'Or anywhere else for that matter.' And to my horror, I burst into tears I could not control.

She sat rigidly in her chair and stared at me, white-faced. It was the first time I had ever cried in front of a woman. When I finished she was still sitting there, looking at me in amazement. Then she handed the duck back to me and in a soft voice that did not sound at all like her she said, 'Keep it Celik. Perhaps you can break the bottle?'

During the next few weeks I took Julia's advice and worked every day from seven in the morning till midnight so that I had no time to think or feel. I was so tired at night I fell straight into bed and into a dreamless sleep. Then a letter arrived from Sarah. It had been redirected from Malawi to Dayton. I wanted very much to send it straight back but, despising myself for my weakness, I opened the letter.

Dear Celik,

I am so sorry to have hurt you. Please do come to visit me. I would love to see you. I have to send this to Malawi for I don't know where you are now.

Sarah.

Always I had been able to protect myself from becoming enslaved by any person. That was why I had the ability to make friends easily and enjoy them but when it was time to leave I could do so without any regrets, without missing them at all. I saw myself as an international citizen with no concept of home and friends. Sarah had once told me she was descended from a witch. Well, I had no intention of being bewitched by her or anyone else. I had devoted my life to fighting against bewitchment which enslaved people to become victims of tyranny. And yet now I was beginning to lose faith in my own ability. My reason told me that after all my years of study I couldn't possibly be wrong. If I was, then I would have to go back to the beginning and start again. For that reason alone I decided to continue writing to her. That way I could put to practical use the language I was developing. I could clarify it and make it functional so that I could identify myself to her. If I couldn't do this with one individual then how could I ever hope to create a functional inter-cultural language that could be used between nations?

Three months later, completely unexpectedly, I was told by the manager to go to Zurich. I wrote to Sarah to tell her the arrangement and asked if I might stay overnight with her, then added if it was not convenient I could stay in a hotel. She replied at once to say that she would love to see me but she was planning to fly back to New Zealand at the end of July for one month to settle custody arrangements with her husband. I asked the secretary to book a hotel for me and then I rang Sarah.

The phone rang for a long time before she picked it up.

'Hello. Sarah Dawson speaking.'

My mouth went dry and the palms of my hands started sweating. I managed to say, as if speaking to her was no big deal for me, 'Hi. It's Celik.'

'Hello!' She sounded so cheerful.

I swallowed. 'I'll be in England on the 28th of July, flying to Zurich on the 31st. Could we meet?'

There was a pause. 'Celik, I'm flying to New Zealand on the 30th and my house is in absolute chaos at the moment.'

'It's okay. I've reserved a hotel.'

'Which one?'

'The Regency.'

'Great, that's close to the airport so I'll make a reservation for the same one then we can spend a little time together, but we're flying out so early in the morning a little time is all it's going to be.'

I laughed. 'Well, shall we meet for an early dinner at the hotel on the 29th?'

'Fine.' A pause, then, 'Look why don't you come here on the 28th anyway and have dinner with us and never mind the mess?'

'Thank you very much. I'd like that.'

When I put the phone down I was sweating so much I had to go and take a shower. Then I lay down on my bed and rehearsed the moment of our meeting, over and over in my mind. I got up and stood in front of the mirror in the bathroom. 'How do you do Sarah?' No, too formal. 'Hi. Nice to see you at last.' No. Too familiar. 'Well, fancy us meeting at last!' God, how pathetic.

I arrived at Heathrow on the morning of the 28th. I went straight to my hotel and took a bath and went to bed so that I might be in a fit state to present myself that evening. When I woke up I showered again and then prayed to God to give me the power to behave gracefully.

I took a taxi and then realised I had forgotten to write down her address. Relying on my memory of it I directed the driver to what I hoped was the right place. The taxi pulled up outside a yellow, brick terraced house in a quiet, tree-lined street. I paid the driver and asked him to wait until I had confirmed it was the correct place. I walked up to the front door and rang the bell, breathing deeply to calm myself.

The door opened and Sarah was standing there holding out her hand and saying, 'Welcome Celik.'

I had thought of everything she was likely to say so that nothing would cause me to behave stupidly or disgrace myself. Now here she was, no longer a name on the end of a letter, a two-dimensional photograph, but a warm, breathing person, who was shaking my hand and talking. I went through what I had practised in the taxi.

'Hello Sarah. I'm glad I found the address all right. I wasn't sure.' I turned and signalled to the driver and he drove away. Then a small boy appeared at her side and stared unsmilingly at me.

'Celik, this is Jeremiah.'

I held out my hand, 'Hello Jeremiah, I'm pleased to meet you.'

He solemnly shook my hand and I experienced an unexpected thrill of pleasure at the feel of his small, warm fingers. Sarah led the way into her sitting room, which was at the front of the house, and motioned me to sit down. The room was small and furnished in an old-fashioned Edwardian style. Green was the predominant colour.

The door opened and in ran a smaller version of Jeremiah. He glanced at me without speaking and climbed onto his mother's knee and put his thumb in his mouth. She cuddled him and kissed the top of his head. I couldn't believe this scene was actually happening. For months I had tried to imagine it and now that it was actually taking place I felt I must still be dreaming. While Sarah was busy with the child I watched her. She was wearing a rose pink dress with long sleeves. She had a silver chain around her neck and small silver earrings. She sat there, self-possessed, in complete control of her environment, like a diamond in ashes of roses. I noticed for the first time that her nose was pointed, yes like a witch's! I had not known she had such a nose. And her blonde shoulder-length hair – I had not known it looked so soft. I wanted to reach out and touch it. I was so much engaged with her nose and hair that I hardly noticed the rest of her. She looked up then and saw me staring at her. To cover my embarrassment I said, 'I have presents for these beautiful children.'

She protested, 'You shouldn't have!'

I brought them out of my bag and handed them to the boys. The children opened them eagerly and Jeremiah took out a little mechanical plane and Nathan a picture book.

'What do you say to Celik?' Sarah said quietly.

The boys turned their big blue eyes on me and chorused, 'Thank you Celik.'

'You're very clever knowing what children their age like,' said Sarah.

I shrugged. 'Well, I was a child once.'

After a moment she excused herself to check the dinner and I got down onto the floor to show Jeremiah how to wind up his plane. Nathan edged nearer to watch and lowered himself onto my knee. I had not expected such acceptance from the children and wondered if Sarah had told them how to behave, though it seemed natural to them.

She had prepared a meal of chicken and salad, followed by strawberries and cream. As we ate she asked me about the countries I had lived in. She listened carefully, her eyes shining with interest. Our conversation was easy and natural, but I did not ask her any questions about herself.

Afterwards I said, 'That was delicious Sarah. I do not often get the chance to sample home cooking.'

'Yes,' she laughed. 'It must be agony for you having to suffer all that room service!'

'No really, it's terrible. After a while all hotel food tastes the same. Sometimes I get so desperate I go out to buy a fresh lettuce and some bread and butter so I can eat something that doesn't taste of plastic.'

Then it was time for the children to go to bed. She disappeared for twenty minutes while she got them ready and I looked around the room. It was furnished with an old wooden rocking chair, chaise longue in green velvet and green velvet curtains hanging from heavy wooden poles. An open fireplace was stacked with logs and pine cones, though not lit as it was summer. A bookcase filled one wall from floor to ceiling. There was a small round oak dining table in the bay window which is where we had eaten. Photographs of the children and a water colour painting of an old church hung on the white painted walls. The room looked freshly decorated and when she came back into the room with a tray of coffee I asked her how she had got it organised so quickly.

'I chose the colour scheme and fabrics and the interior decorators did the rest. The other rooms are still in the process of being done.'

Despite my initial resolve to ask her no personal questions, I was very curious. 'So why did you decide to come back to England? Why not another country?'

She poured out the coffee into two green mugs. 'Roots, I suppose.'

'But you were born in New Zealand. Why aren't your roots there?'

Before she could answer me, the children, now in pyjamas, ran into the room. They both came forward and kissed me goodnight.

'Help yourself to milk and sugar while I see these rascals off the premises,' said Sarah.

When they left the room I touched the place on my cheek where the children had kissed me. I thought how lucky Sarah was to have them and I wondered how she could bear to leave these precious kids each day and go out to work in a nondescript job? It didn't make sense. When she reappeared I said, 'They're marvellous kids. How did you train them like that?'

She laughed and replied, 'They have their moments.'

I could see she was pleased by my comment. I asked her to continue what she'd been saying about leaving New Zealand. She sipped her coffee before replying. 'When we got married Dave wanted to go to New Zealand and buy a small dairy farm. I was excited about it because I'd been very happy there as a child. I suppose I also wanted to relive my mother's life and see if I could do it better. But don't ask me to explain all that!' She shrugged her shoulders. 'Anyway, I learned that you can't live someone else's life. You can't be someone else. You can't reclaim the past.'

She was silent for a moment and I prompted, heart beating fast, 'And your husband?'

'In the end he agreed to me taking the boys back to England for an extended holiday and said that in six months I'd be clamouring to get back to New Zealand.'

I watched her closely. 'And are you?'

She shook her head. 'No. My mother could so easily have said "told you so!" but she didn't.'

She looked so sad then I wanted to cover her hands with my own but I didn't dare. She looked up and saw my expression and smiled. 'It's in the past. I'm starting to get my life together again and I feel good about it.'

I had to ask her the question I'd rehearsed but I was so afraid that my jaw was stiff and I blurted, 'Why did you reply to my card?'

She shrugged. 'I guess I wanted to know if we were really cut off or if you had just put the phone down.' She stared at me smiling.

I found myself blushing and said, 'It's a long time ago now, I can't remember.'

Her grin got wider. We both laughed, and suddenly we were completely in tune with each other. We spent the rest of the evening talking about books, music, plays we had seen, the different countries I had visited. Conversation flowed easily and at ten o'clock I took my leave. We arranged to meet for dinner at the hotel the following evening.

Back at the hotel, I lay awake trying to absorb what had happened. The things we had talked about, the surroundings I had seen her in for the first time, her children. I felt lightheaded from the effect of our meeting. Eventually I drifted off to sleep and my dreams were not of Sarah but of children climbing onto my knee.

Next evening I was waiting in the hotel lobby when I saw Sarah and the children come in with their suitcases. She gave brief instructions to a porter and then saw me and walked over. I stood up and we shook hands and the children greeted me.

'Give me a few minutes to get organised and I'll join you.' she said.

When she came down again with the children we went into the restaurant and ordered dinner. She did not eat very much and conversation was stilted. She put the children to bed after the meal and then sat in the hotel lobby talking to me for a little while. She kept looking at her watch and finally she said she had to go to bed as they would be leaving on the five o'clock flight.

I nodded and asked the question I had been dreading. 'Is it a reconciliation?'

She laughed. 'Oh no. He has a girlfriend.'

I raised my eyebrows but she shrugged. 'I'm glad for him. Truly. My father didn't have anybody after my mother left.'

We said goodnight and I walked down the corridor to my own room. I lay awake, half hoping there'd be a knock at my door. It didn't come of course, and eventually I fell into an uneasy sleep.

When I met her again next morning she was preoccupied with the children's breakfast. I ate with them and then accompanied them to the airport.

Jeremiah put his hand in mine. 'Celik, will you come and see us again?'

'I hope so,' I replied, looking at Sarah, but she was searching for something in her handbag.

Then it was time for them to leave. Sarah leaned forward and kissed me. I smelt her perfume. I felt her lips lightly touch my cheek. I watched her walk away from me. It was as if my soul were drifting away from my body. She turned once to wave and then they were gone.

CHAPTER ◆ THIRTEEN

I flew back to Dayton and didn't hear from Sarah for two months, then I received a letter to tell me she was back in England and working full time at the newspaper. She made little mention of her visit to New Zealand.

...Dave has installed his new woman in his house. She's exactly what he needs. She weaves and spins and knits and bakes and preserves etc, and as well as having three children of her own from a previous marriage, she's already pregnant with Dave's child. At first Dave was insisting I leave Jeremiah and Nathan with him and we had some ugly scenes, but after a couple of weeks of all the children arguing and fighting he began to weaken! The end result is he will not contest custody, in return for my relinquishing my half of the matrimonial property.

She went on to say that the editor of the newspaper she worked for was planning a series of articles about unusual holiday destinations.

...and I suggested one about Istanbul and told him I had a friend there who could act as an interpreter! He thought it was a great idea and he's sending me there in November. At long last I'll get to see it! Any chance of you being there at the same time? If not, does anyone in your family speak English? I've started a crash course in Turkish but I doubt it'll get me very far.

When I read this piece of news I felt that God was arranging my life perfectly. I went to the personnel director in Dayton and asked if an assignment to Istanbul could be arranged. He said it was not possible as I was needed at headquarters, though an assignment to Istanbul was likely sometime in the next year. Bristling with disappointment I had to stay in the USA while Sarah went to Turkey.

In November I received a letter from my sister Hulya.

...I met Sarah at the airport and went with her in a taxi to the Sheraton Hotel. I stayed for a cup of coffee with her and then took my leave, inviting her to come for dinner the following evening. She was very interested in learning about Turkish customs, what you were like as a child, how I felt as a modern woman in Turkey!

The next evening she came to our house. Mother had spent all day cleaning and washing the curtains. I let Sarah in. She kissed me and I gave her some slippers to put on and then mother came out to greet her. Sarah shook her hand and we went into the living room. Mother asked her about her children and Sarah brought out photographs of her two sons. Then we went into the kitchen for dinner. I gave her some soup and she said it was delicious and to our amazement she turned to mother and said the same to her in Turkish! 'Ayesha Hanim, coc guzelle corbah.'

Father of course did not want to eat with us but he came down later to meet Sarah. When he came into the room she stood up and shook his hand. She asked him how he was, in Turkish, and he said to me, 'How can she speak Turkish when she has been in the country one day and you have been learning English for two years and still cannot speak it?'

'What!' I laughed, 'just you listen to me!' and I started asking Sarah, in English, what her impressions were of the city. Father was amazed I think and then he started talking to her himself and I translated. She asked him questions about his childhood and he began talking so animatedly that mother and I could not believe it. He had intended to stay downstairs for just a short while but he stayed till it was time for Sarah to go.

She came back again a few days later and this time father ate with us! His eyes were shining and he was so eager to talk and answer her questions about Islam, with me doing all the work of translating. Father hates visitors and his reaction to my friends is often embarrassing! He starts coughing loudly and says he has to go and lie down. Yet with Sarah – all smiles and charm and shining eyes!

One day I took her to meet our aunt and uncle. The house was full of relatives. Uncle asked her if she had any questions and he would do his best to answer them. He then took off his jacket and settled himself more comfortably on the chair and started talking without a break for half an hour. Aunt was embarrassed that she did not have any cake in the house and was going to send Gonu out to buy some. Sarah wouldn't hear of it so aunt cut up some apples and oranges and handed the largest selection on a plate to Sarah with a fork. Sarah picked up a piece of apple with her fingers and began to eat it. Everyone laughed and uncle said, 'If I had done that she would have said I was a barbarian.'

Fortunately she didn't understand him. But he forgave her bad manners when she started asking questions about Islam. Everyone asked how you knew her and if she was married.

Osman came for a week's holiday. When I told him about Sarah he did not want to meet her. He said he wouldn't be able to think of anything to say.

I said, 'Oh but she isn't difficult to talk to. She is so eager to know about everything.'

In the end he was curious! After he had met her he said, 'She isn't like any other woman I have known.'

When she left us to fly back to London she said she hoped to come back to Turkey so we would all meet again. I hope so too...

When I finished reading this letter I realised my eyes had filled with tears and I was smiling. So Sarah had made a good impression on my family? I went outside to my car to drive to work, then I noticed how blue the sky was. I stood and stared at it in amazement for a few minutes. For the rest of that day I caught myself singing sometimes as I worked at my desk.

When Sarah's letter eventually arrived it included her article on Istanbul. In my haste to open the article I tore it in two and had to spend a frustrating five minutes hunting for tape and scissors to stick it together again. At last I sat down in my chair and with a sigh of happiness began to read.

...What a muddle of noise and confusion. Traffic, pedestrians, donkeys and dancing bears negotiating the labyrinthine streets. Shoeshiners with gleaming brass stands, street pedlars shouting in raucous voices, exquisitely coiffured women shopping in Taksim, taking afternoon tea at the Hilton, ragged children in the gutters with their hands outstretched. Women with covered heads and long drab coats buying wedding presents in the bazaars. Men strolling hand in hand through the streets, swinging prayer beads and gossiping in coffee shops, the air thick with smoke and Turkish music.

Coolness and richness in the ancient carpets and tiles in the mosques. The polished cleanliness of one's body after a Turkish bath. Red and gold tulips in the parks, giant plane trees lining the roads, fresh fruit and crusty bread in roadside stalls. A beggar displaying the oozing green hole in his leg. Men peeing behind crumbling Byzantine columns in reeking streets.

Topkapi palace: Behind its threatening grey walls, diamonds and rubies and golden thrones are displayed in rooms where once no stranger dared to enter. Triumphal gateways from which sultans rode to bring victory and glory to the Empire. A hidden stone by a fountain where those out of favour lost their heads. Small barred windows in the harem overlooking flower-filled gardens. A small gate where the pregnant concubines of dead sultans were taken in their weighted sacks to be thrown into the Bosphorus. The shuttered rooms where small princes were strangled on the accession of each new sultan in accordance with the fratricide law of Mehmet II. The tour guides speak of his military brilliance, his courage in bringing 'glory to the empire.' But while Mehmet was being congratulated on his accession to the throne by his stepmother, her baby son was being drowned in his bath on Mehmet's orders...

I read those last lines several times before I realised I had stopped breathing. I took a deep shuddering gasp of air and read them again to make sure I hadn't misunderstood. The trembling in my hands spread to my arms and legs. I felt icy cold and sick to my stomach. Then wave after wave of heat washed over my body, and sweat from my temples and neck trickled into my collar. I tore Sarah's letter, article and envelope into tiny pieces then tossed them into the kitchen sink where I set light to them with a match. The words flared and blackened and crumbled into dust. I extinguished the flames with my hands, welcoming the pain as my fingers burned.

CHAPTER ◆ FOURTEEN

After I had bandaged my hands I prayed to God for guidance and asked Him what I should do. I felt no peace during my prayer and at first I thought God did not want to communicate with me. Then I was angry with myself for such an arrogant assumption. At that point, I knew beyond any doubt that the Devil was working in me now and oh how happy he must be at the confusion he was causing. God sent me the strength I wanted to be still until I had the language I needed: If you leave her now the Devil will win this fight.

Weak with exhaustion I found pen and paper and wrote to Sarah.

Dear Sarah,

After reading ... 'the pregnant concubines of the dead sultans were sown into sacks and thrown in the Bosphorus...' I could easily say that if you still judge like that then, 'This is the parting between thee and me.' (Koran 1819.)

But I am compelled to be patient with you and offer ten constructions for each destruction. This is the leading edge of our relationship. What I see with the above sentence of yours and similar sentences you quoted, is confusion of history with fiction, or rather, with horror fiction.

What do you want me to do with them? Do you want me to spend all my time trying to prove or disprove them till you invent something else? Or do you want me to change my image of the Ottoman Empire and its institutions, based on a broader and more reliable source of history in favour of individual alien sources who don't even understand the basics of the Ottoman way of life, and interpret events in distortion of their own cultural point of view?

Celik.

As I expected of course she wrote to tell me not to order her what to think and that what she had written was not her own invention but recorded history. So, after more prayer to keep the Devil at bay, I wrote to her to try to put the whole topic in perspective.

Dear Sarah,

Please do not misunderstand my criticism of your writing about the harem. I didn't mean to tell you what to think or what to write except that I am not an accomplice to your literary crime for which I believe you will one day be judged by God. If you are that much in favour of freedom of thought and writing you should be able to tolerate my criticism by the side of your writing. Now that you have published it then you should erase your error by publishing a correction in the same columns.

Supposing you had been a Sir who visited Istanbul during the reign of Murat III and Mehmet III and reported, '...the pregnant concubines of the dead sultans were sewn into sacks and thrown in the Bosphorus...' based on rumours, (for definitely you wouldn't be invited to the bizarre ceremonies) should this be called recorded history? What if I say perhaps they reported what they did for the same reason as you?

Today the Ottomans cannot defend themselves against your accusations. But they were human beings like you and me and what if there is a Day of Judgement as they believed? Your being sorry then wouldn't help you. Not even God Almighty Himself would help you for it was a violation of the rights of individual souls. Are you rich enough to afford to restore the dignity of the Ottoman sultans who might be found innocent? Think about it with justice and love, remembering that one day you yourself will be dead like those sultans.

Celik.

PS. I'm sorry about telling you what to think. I can't help it. If I were an angel I should indeed choose the parting of thee and me... but I am a human being and I have been recommended in the Koran... 'O ye who believe! Endure. Outdo all others in endurance. Be ready and observe your duty to Allah in order that ye may succeed.'

I thought about Sarah's letter every day and every night, frustrated beyond endurance at her inability to grasp the implications of what she had done. But never for a single moment did I waver in my belief that my language was stronger than hers because mine was directed by God and hers by the Devil. Whatever happened I must not give up and hand this victory over to the Devil.

Dear Sarah,

Here is my criticism of your writing about the harem, which, by the way, I take as a product of your pseudo-personality, therefore it is non-significant, an idle talk. I pray your real personality takes command in the whole extent of your existence, otherwise, what a waste!

What you wrote doesn't reflect anything about the spirit of the institution of an ancient culture, except a superficial material account of it which would be written by any petty western intellectual who is under the curse of, 'west is west and east is east,' to flatter the vanity of the working class women and housewives of their culture. It brings no understanding to anyone. It is just self-satisfaction for the justification of your institutions. An unconscious culture-centric-self-defence. It is all your opinion in relation to your culture so I have no counter or alternative opinion for it, for I am not a member of that culture. The difference between you and me on that issue is not a difference of opinion but in belonging to different ways of life.

Now just imagine that the Ottoman scientists, by the order of the sultan and his council, developed the A-bomb and the army used it to kill Greeks on Crete, children and women, old and young, to wipe out the population from the island. What would you call the victorious Ottomans and their accomplices, say Arabs and Iranians for Ages?

Never forget Hiroshima and the Japanese infant burned by the A-bomb, crying, 'What was my crime?'

The Ottomans paid for their injustice by being erased from existence. So if you are really serious in your hunt for an active criminal, knock at next door and don't waste your precious time and energy against phantoms like the Ottomans, because that wouldn't help to save your children from the destiny around the corner waiting from U.S. and S.U. which are determined to destroy themselves with the product of their own hands. Certainly their partners in victory will have a share in that destruction. Where were you when they were killing the whole population of Hiroshima? Clapping your hands for the victorious?

My dear friend, ask me how it feels to pay for an injustice committed by one's ancestors – suffering in defeat and despised by all.

I am a son of an Ottoman and of a Roman but I am not an Ottoman or a Roman. I am emerging free from their errors through my suffering and being despised. S.U. and U.S. are my stillborn brothers. I am the one who is alive and shall inherit the Empire.

With love,

Celik.

Sarah's reply to this was to send me a sheaf of pages photocopied from various history books with sentences underlined which detailed the 'atrocities' of the sultans, including some pages by Turkish professors of history. She had scribbled on the top page that she had researched the topic very well before writing anything about it. I immediately responded:

...You are not sorry to write a loose sentence like, 'the pregnant concubines of the dead sultans were sown into sacks and thrown in the Bosphorus.' And you say... 'it was thoroughly researched.'(???)

See it yourself with my grammatical analysis.

If a sultan was dead and he had a pregnant concubine then she was sewn into a sack and thrown in the Bosphorus.

Let us apply it to Mehmet I (Celebi)

Mehmet was a sultan. Mehmet was dead and... if Mehmet had a pregnant concubine (which is most likely otherwise he was unlucky) then she was sewn into a sack and thrown in the Bosphorus. So, don't eat fish from the Bosphorus! Or better change your editors!

Here is another question.

Would Elizabeth II, Queen of U.K. let her youngest son be strangled by decree if she and her Council were convinced that the civil war between Catholics and Protestants in Northern Ireland, which causes hundreds of brothers, sons, husbands, wives and daughters to be killed, would be stopped? If not, then she wouldn't cry but every other day a poor non-royal mother in Northern Ireland would cry. What is the difference between a non-royal Christian mother in Northern Ireland and the Queen, mother, Elizabeth II? Nobility! That is why she would be generous enough to sacrifice her sons or daughters to keep peace in her kingdom. That is why people recognise her as Queen.

In the historic environment of their age, the Ottomans executed their sons and brothers under the regulations of law to prevent massive and further killings in civil wars which were causing thousands of brothers to kill each other. Therefore they were sacrifices of the family of Ottoman for the safety and well-being of the Empire in its struggle with injustice and disorder in the way of God. That is how they managed to bring together more than thirty different nations and religions to live together in peace. To achieve this, they preferred to kill their brothers and sons rather than killing millions of Vietnamese or Jews or Christians or the inhabitants of Hiroshima. They didn't cook other families' babies in ovens with A-bombs. So leave them in peace and say, 'May God forgive their sins.'

For a second, just assume that there will be a Judgement Day and you and the human beings and sultans you accuse will be brought together and then definitely you would be questioned.

Which sultans? Which pregnant concubines? Where? When? Which pasha?

And then the babies will be called.

My friend, better prepare answers to those questions. Or ask forgiveness from God while you can. You are hurting the human rights of dead sultans and pashas.

Think about it with love,

Celik.

While I waited for a response to this letter lack of sleep made it difficult for me to concentrate on my work and I had no appetite for food. I knew from the way they looked at me and raised their eyebrows at each other that I was snappy with my colleagues and they began to avoid my company. I didn't care. My only relief came from the times I could spend in prayer. One night, after weeks of silence from Sarah I could not sleep at all. My sheets were tangled up in a hot, sweaty knot so I threw them off the bed and got up and looked out of the window. The sky was black and filled with stars. Nothing moved in the streets. The whole city was asleep except me. Words formed in my mind: 'Dark waters run through you.' I felt so terrified by this message that I hugged myself tight moaning over and over again, 'Poor boy, poor boy.' I knew I had to protect myself quickly for in my agitation I was in serious danger. I prepared myself for prayer. As soon as I began praying God soothed my heart.

At the end of my prayer I was completely calm. In my state of calmness many things became crystal clear to me. It was as if I were looking into a clear blue lake and seeing in the reflections all the truths of my life. I understood that God had directed me along this path not for the purpose of destroying me but to strengthen my faith. Every time I stumbled and hurt myself He would be there to remind me He had given me a precious gift, the power of language. It was my duty to develop my knowledge so I would know how to use this gift, not just for myself, but for the benefit of all humankind. My pain in the past had given me the will to fight the Devil. Every humiliation had been a signpost to guide me along the road that was my kismet. My present pain was the fire in which my tools were being forged to fight the work of the Devil and his reign of oppression. If I refused this gift and walked along another road the Devil would seize a glorious victory.

After this revelation I felt so joyful that for the first time in many months I actually began to laugh – at first softly, then in wonderful billows of sound that echoed off the walls of my room and shook my body, leaving me weak and helpless on the floor, and there, finally, I fell into a deep, dreamless sleep.

Next morning I awoke early, charged with new energy. I sang in the shower and whistled as I ate my breakfast. I was even able to send jokes to the Devil to confound him in his rage at losing this battle. When I arrived at my office I continued joking, saying aloud, 'Well, you see Devil, I am more powerful than you for I have been created Human!' and I doubled over in delighted laughter. I heard a cough behind me and looked around to see one of the young office girls who had come in early to make tea. She was staring at me with big eyes. This increased the power of the joke and I had to sit down in a nearby chair.

'Come on,' I invited her, between paroxysms, 'we all need to laugh more in this world!' She smiled and nodded as she backed quickly out of the door. I shrugged and still chuckling, went over to my desk in search of pen and paper.

Sarah...

Watch closely how your idols judge about the future of your children.

Hand in hand with the BIG BANG GANG.

You may say, what has this to do with the Ottoman oppression? But trust my experience that this sickness starts like that.

I have burned those photocopies you sent me. If you call this 'recorded history,' I have nothing to say, except you had better read some books in methodology in history and proof in history. I have no time to spend to prove or disprove that sort of garbage. All it proves is that those authors invented what you have quoted!

I think the problem with me is that I don't believe in professors of the Republic, as I don't believe in its constitution or any of its institutions. Of course I have thousands of good and bad reasons not to and it is all shown with my way of life in the context of human history, but not for people whom... 'Allah hath sealed their hearing and their hearts and on their eyes is a covering.'

Those people interpret history with an Ataturk bias, like the communists interpret it according to dialectical materialism. They criticise the Ottomans to rationalise and to cover their theft of Ottoman foundations laid by believers, (Moslems, Christians and Jews).

I take information coming from heathens with pepper and salt, for I have no reason to trust them. What I mean is this. As you trust in the institutions of your way of life, your professors at your universities, I also trust mine, even though most of them are dissolved, banned, buried in history, or hidden by heathens. I rediscover them to carry the light on.

Celik.

This brought no response either but by now I knew what I had to do. If I could make Sarah trust me I could teach her my language. If she could be made to see that her language was useless and outmoded and that mine contained the key to the secret of the universe, surely she would beg me to teach her? I was prepared to be very patient. I slept only a couple of hours each night but I was so filled with energy that I got through my work without any problems and I had started re-reading my books and making notes to arm myself with the truth. So I determined to keep on writing. I would not give up no matter how long it took. Now, I could see that God had brought me to this point, not to judge Sarah harshly – for in her ignorance how could she know she was ignorant – but to provide me with the best reason to complete the work he had been preparing me for all these years. I no longer had to wrestle with my guilty conscience for all the distractions that had kept me from my work. Everything that had happened – all those devil temptations – was part of the Plan. How arrogant of me to have thought otherwise. What lack of trust I had placed in Him who so carefully had designed my life. I fell to my knees in humility and prayed for forgiveness before I wrote to Sarah.

Sarah

Present day tyranny runs by the threat of nuclear holocaust and is based on the mosaics of nations which do not depict the real division of the way of life of the people. This error will become more distinct by further development in the means of communication which will facilitate and accelerate the means of communication to provide closer interactions among people who share the same way of life and values. These practices will cause the emergence of the hidden nations in healthier forms, forcing the artificial layers of shell of the tyranny to crack. The clarification and the development of language utilising this ease of communication will allow those nations and cultures to express their identities as they are, which will then be the foundation of a further development for meaningful interactions among nations and cultures towards the achievement of giving birth to a new civilisation.

I see the struggles of our relationship as a model to such emergence. You and I have developed a functional language by which we achieve meaningful interactions, but the tyranny still resists on our way with its artificial laws, regulations, conventions, customs and institutions, fabricating glamorous images of the future about itself. But our relationship is real, so that none of the ghosts or ghost stories can stop its emergence. The shell is doomed to be cracked, to give birth to a new empire. We are a new nation!

Read Wittgenstein. And relate his philosophy to art, music, literature. Then perhaps you will be able to understand the background behind Islam and its relation to the emergence of the new empire.

Celik.

After another month had passed Sarah sent a letter. I opened it with relief that finally I had triggered a response, no matter what kind of response.

...I underestimated the effect my article would have on you. I'm sorry, because I should have remembered how you responded to some of my letters on Islam years ago. That used to really blow me away because I could never imagine myself feeling that passionate about an institution. And you're absolutely right when you point out acts of western barbarism like Hiroshima. But I wouldn't even attempt to defend those acts so I don't understand why you should try to defend the barbarism of the Ottomans. Okay, so you can say all those sources I quoted just invented it but that's a bit far-fetched isn't it? I wasn't trying to slander your religious beliefs, I was just writing about a piece of your country's recorded history...

...and I have no idea what you mean by the new empire. You say you're trying to develop a new language? What language?...

At last I detected a glimmer of hope. I felt as though I were climbing the vertical slope of a very high mountain and the effort was exhausting but I never doubted reaching the top. I gave thanks to God and wrote back at once.

Sarah

I will try to answer your question 'what do you mean by the new empire' in the simplest way I can, but please realise it is not a matter of just writing or reading but of training and practising. I can't train you from this distance. You would have to work with me for at least a couple of years. Understand it like this: communication regenerates the culture's functional part of the language. A nation is formed in order to accomplish a purpose which can not be achieved by an individual working alone but instead requires the joint efforts of a group of people.

In the same way an empire is formed in order to accomplish a human purpose in the form of a civilisation which can not be achieved by an individual nation working alone, but instead requires the joint efforts of a group of nations directed to accomplish respective purposes in the form of respective cultures.

Don't you sense the magnetism and importance of this? Leave everything aside and listen with your soul which is created human-woman. I implore your human-woman, the core of your core, tell me what else a free man can offer a free woman? I see Satan's utter destruction in the creation of the new empire.

'...as unstable as water and like water would perhaps finally prevail. Since the dawn of life in successive waves. Each wave was broken but like the sea wore away ever so little of the granite on which it failed and some day, ages yet, might roll unchecked over the place where the material world had been and God would move upon the face of those waters...'(T.E.Lawrence, Seven Pillars of Wisdom, p21). '...I meant to make a new nation...'(p23).

You see, Lawrence was my brother! Our subject matter is the same but our methods and aims are contrary.

I suggest you re-read all my letters to you starting from the beginning because they contain excellent original material in contrast to Satan's bewitchment of language. Like all other women, including my mother, you don't believe me but I think your Kismet is in my hands. As mine is in yours. And there is only one way to attain it. And I believe we'll find that way, leaving Satan amazed at the superiority of humankind. You need extensive reading in certain subjects. And you need my direct supervision. And you have to work hard and you have no time to lose. Think about it with love.

Celik.

I felt very satisfied with this letter. My language was working in the best way it could. I could barely contain my excitement while I waited for Sarah's response. After three weeks a letter arrived. In my impatience I tore the letter so that I had to piece it together like a jigsaw puzzle before I could read it. I scanned it quickly for the key words.

.... forming a coalition of nations which work in peace and harmony towards a common goal via knowledge of a philosophical language might some day exist in Utopia... what you're really saying is a version of 'one person can make a difference'. I'm afraid I'm too cynical to believe that, but if you believe it then I wish you luck in your endeavours...

After I read those lines I had the worst asthma attack of my life. All the tortures and loneliness of my confinement in the prisons of the Republic were nothing compared to what I suffered now. I prayed to God to let me die. When he didn't, I cried, 'Why me? Why must I always be the one to suffer?'

As I trailed into the office next morning, empty and without hope, the manager telephoned me to come and see him. He told me that the assignment to Istanbul had come through and I was to go there next month.

'And when that assignment has finished we want you to stay in Turkey on a permanent basis.'

I raised my eyebrows, 'On what salary?'

'Turkish of course. Or it will cause trouble with the other employees.'

I stood up and pushed my chair back, 'No way man! I've been through all this before!'

He stood up too. 'If you won't accept the conditions there are others who will. You are not irreplaceable.'

I couldn't be bothered to argue and I turned and strode out of his office, slamming the door behind me.

CHAPTER ◆ FIFTEEN

I couldn't breathe properly for a week after I had read that letter. Every time I tried to take a deep breath I would double over in a spasm of coughing and wheezing. The muscles in my neck and shoulders became as stiff as rope, so that even in bed it was impossible to rest. By the end of the week there was no place in my body free from pain and I was exhausted and weakened.

Finally, in desperation, I went to see the doctor and got pain-killers and sleeping tablets. That night I swallowed some and for the first time all week I was able to find a comfortable place to lay my head in bed. Greatly relieved I drifted off to sleep, only to dream of drowning babies. I awoke crying and found my sheet was soaked. At first, horrified, I thought I'd wet myself, then I realised my body was drenched in sweat. I changed the sheets and dried my skin with a towel before lying down again.

Immediately I was standing inside a circle of fire. Sarah stood on the outside looking at me but not seeing me. I couldn't reach her for the flames were hot and scorched my outstretched hands. As the heat became unbearable she turned and walked away. I called her name but all that escaped from my mouth was a whimper. Again I woke up crying and wet.

The sheets were twisted around my body and I had to stand up to untangle them. I couldn't stop crying. I threw the window open and hung out my head so I could breath some cool air. The street was in darkness and there was no sound except an animal panting somewhere below my window. I saw the movement of shadows in a doorway. I strained my eyes to make out the shapes. Then I saw a woman with her skirt up around her waist and her legs wrapped round the waist of a man with his trousers down by his ankles.

Sickened, I shut the window to block out those sounds and stumbled into the bathroom to take a shower. I turned on the light and saw my sleeping tablets on the shelf near the basin. I filled a glass with water, unscrewed the lid on the bottle, poured the contents into the palm of my hand in what seemed all one movement. I shoved my hand against my lips and with a backward flick of my head I had all the tablets in my mouth.

In the mirror I saw a face I barely recognised. Appalled, I lowered my hand, bent over and opened my mouth. All the tablets fell into the basin with a clatter, leaving a bitter taste on my tongue. I turned on the cold water tap and rinsed out my mouth.

My skin began to prickle with the sensation of someone standing behind me. I forced my head up to the mirror again. Nothing. Only my own reflection, wild-eyed and spiky-haired. But the presence of Satan was so strong I could smell Him. The smell was foul, like rotting meat, and I started to retch. Satan was grinning with glee at his triumph. I spun round and round in that small enclosed space, waving my arms and shouting, 'You will not win!' The sound of my own voice echoed off the white-tiled walls. Though I was weak with misery I shouted again, with all the strength I could gather, 'I... am... stronger... than... you!'

I must have passed out at that point for when I came to I was lying on the floor looking at a small trickle of red on the white tiles. I raised myself slowly, dabbing at my forehead with a towel, and sat back on my heels. Behind the throbbing in my temples, three thoughts formed in my head as pure as the water running from the tap over my basin. 'You must build an Empire. You must begin immediately. You must find a mate capable of building an Empire.'

When I went to buy my plane ticket to London I picked up a copy of Time Out to find out about theatre shows in the city. I returned to my flat and lay on my bed flicking through the magazine. At the back I saw that people were advertising for companions. At first I laughed with scorn at such an absurd way of finding a mate, but then the idea grew that if I took this initiative God would certainly not send me someone unsuitable. The more I thought about this the less absurd it became and I began to understand that this signpost had not been revealed to me without reason. I picked up a pen and a sheet of paper and began to write my advertisement. It enquired simply: Are you a woman capable of building an empire? Reply Box G 264.

The next morning I faxed it through to the magazine's London office. After it had gone I celebrated my liberation from Sarah's bewitchment with a wonderful lunch of smoked salmon at a little French restaurant. Because of this I was half an hour late arriving back at the office. That stupid idiot of a manager was standing in the doorway pointedly looking at his watch. I ignored him and started whistling.

While I waited out those weeks before the replies to my advertisement started arriving I didn't know what my moods would be like from day to day. Some days I would be up early and amaze everybody at the office by working non-stop all day without saying a word to anyone. Other days I walked in when I felt like it and sang and whistled until they told me to shut up so they could concentrate on their work. I didn't care.

Then the letters began to arrive. Twelve of them altogether. Some I tore up because the writers sounded like perverts or homosexuals, but five seemed promising.

Hello,

I'm Megan. I'm in my early thirties with long red hair, blue eyes, eight stone and 5ft 10ins tall. I don't know if I have the characteristics you require but I do have a wide range of interests. At the moment I'm working as a nurse aid. If you care to contact me drop a line at the above address with your telephone number. If you contact, a snap would be appreciated. I was born in Wales.

Best wishes,

Megan Jones.

Dear Box G 264,

I am a young mid-thirties art historian – attractive, quirky, with a wicked sense of humour when I resonate with the right person. I am successful and enjoy successful men who have an interest in theatre, art, music, antiques, travel, and weekends in Paris or Rome.

I mix hard work with hedonism. So why don't you phone me at 773265?

Pamela.

Dear Box G 264,

I am but with whom?

Expecting further information....
Victoria.

Dear Box G 264,
Your ad. suggests you have a strong sense of purpose, a clear vision of the future, with the financial resources to achieve your goals. A touch of megalomania? But a necessary quality for the founder of an empire. I believe that the hand that rocks the cradle rules the world but I won't market myself without more information.
In anticipation,
Kate.

Dear Box G 264,
Yes I am! Lets talk about it.
Regards, Kitty Stone.

Then it was time to leave. Singing in my heart I flew to London. Osman met me at Heathrow and commented on how well I looked as we took a taxi to his flat. I replied joyfully, 'Because I am directed by God, man!'

The flat was in a small, terraced house owned by a Pakistani couple who let one room to Osman and he shared kitchen and bathroom facilities with them. I had offered several times to help him buy a decent place but he'd always said that his flat had the advantage of being cheap and he preferred spending his money on books.

As we talked in his cramped room we could hear the wailing of a baby and feet running up and down stairs and doors banging and people shouting. He noticed my irritated expression. 'They have a baby now and they're expecting another one soon. The noise disturbs my work so I've started looking for another place. Actually, I'm thinking about buying a house.'

'Great!' I said. 'That's the best news I've heard for a long time! I'll arrange to transfer some money to your bank. How much do you need?'

He shook his head. 'You've given me too much already. I'm grateful for your offer but I have enough.'

'Well let me know if you need anything,' I said and added, 'actually I'm thinking about settling in England myself. What do you think about that?'

His eyes opened wide. 'What on earth for?'

I told him how the company kept insisting that I stay in Turkey after the end of my contract, despite my repeated objections. I told him how unpleasant it had become working in those conditions.

He considered this for a while and then explained how difficult it would be for me to find a job in England without a visa and I couldn't get a visa until I had a job.

'But what if I were to marry an English woman? Wouldn't that automatically entitle me to a visa?'

'Do you have anyone in mind?' he laughed.

I shrugged off the question and he didn't pursue it. Then he said that if I wanted to settle in another country, the USA would be the best place for me.

'You'd be accepted there and I have a friend in California who would be able to help you. In England, even if you lived here twenty years, to the English you would always be a foreigner. For me it's different, but you wouldn't like it in this country. Also the climate would be bad for your health.'

What he said made sense. I said I would think about his recommendations and then asked him if he had had any reaction to his book which had now been published.

He smiled widely. 'It's aroused considerable interest in philosophical Moslem circles in England and Turkey.'

I leaped out of my chair and hugged him. 'Of course it has! There is no book like it in Turkey. Look, even if you have to wait ten years, one day it will be recognised as an important work. I have no doubt about it.'

He clapped me on the back. 'Thank you for having faith in me Celik. And for pushing me! If it hadn't been for you the book would never have been written.'

I hugged him again, 'Faith in you? I tell you man, you are going to be very famous!'

'I don't like the idea but it seems you may be right. Anyway, to quote President Reagan – "You ain't seen nothin' yet".'

I laughed, feeling more light-hearted than I had for a long time, 'I like that! I like it! We'll adopt it as our new motto!'

He looked at me and said carefully, 'It was because of you that I pushed myself into finishing the book. Your belief in my ability prevented me from giving up even when, at times, my doubts overwhelmed me. Now that my book exists, where previously there was a vacuum, I realise how little I know, how much more there is to learn, so I am thinking about enrolling at London University to begin a Ph.D But your philosophical knowledge and your understanding of the Koran is far greater than mine, yet you do nothing with it. You could write a book more influential than mine will ever be. A doctorate would bring all your years of study to fruition. At the risk of offending you, brother, I must ask, what keeps you from doing this?'

I did not want to get into this discussion again so I said, 'Well, Satan has been very busy keeping me from my task. That's why in my heart I know he must be very frightened of me, for he knows that when my work is completed it will be the end of him.'

Osman leaned forward. 'Completed? So you do have a plan?'

'I do, but I can't tell you what it is yet. Be patient man. And let's eat! I'm starving.'

He served the chicken and rice that he had prepared for us and while we ate I said, 'No one would understand my work unless they spent years in my presence and studied the concepts I have studied. Therefore it would be meaningless to write a book or do a doctorate as you suggest.'

He thought for a minute. 'I have all your letters and the notes I have taken during our discussions together. Already there is the basis for a book on how we are using concepts from the Koran in the wrong way. Perhaps not everybody would understand it but if even a few people did...'

I interrupted, 'You have my permission and wholehearted approval to use those notes to write another book. The key concept is inter-cultural language as the means of communication. See it in the context of the nuclear arms race and the lack of communication among nations – the tyranny of the broken integrals!'

We discussed this for an hour more then I was anxious to get back to my hotel so I could make some phone calls. After arranging to meet my brother in two days' time I said goodbye and left.

In my hotel room I unpacked my case and sat on the bed with the letters I'd brought with me. I glanced at my watch. Ten o'clock. Still time to phone. Now I was so close to actually doing it I hesitated, feeling shy and embarrassed. With a shaking hand I dialled the first number. A woman answered.

'Hi. Pamela speaking.'

I took a deep breath. 'Hello. This is Celik Ertas. You answered my advertisement in Time Out.'

There was a pause. Then – 'Oh! Right! It's nice to hear from you.' The accent was faintly American.

'Thank you,' I began to feel a little more confident, 'It's nice to hear you too. I'll be in London for a few days before I fly to Istanbul. I wondered if perhaps we might meet?'

Another pause. Then she said, 'You're Turkish? Oh... Can you tell me something about yourself – why you placed the ad?'

I'd expected this and had an answer ready. 'Certainly. I'm working for an American computer company as a systems analyst and because of disagreements over my contract I'm thinking of changing my job and settling in England near my brother. I've travelled a great deal in my work so it has not been easy for me to form a permanent relationship with a woman.'

I wondered whether I ought to tell her about Sarah, but decided against it. 'Besides, the kind of woman I have in mind has to be a very special person.'

'In what way?'

I tried to express myself clearly to avoid any confusion over my intentions.

'My concept of Woman has been given to me by God and I have a very clear picture of her. First, she must be strong and independent enough to shed the conventions which have been artificially imposed by her culture. She must not be a slave to the rules of her society. If she is prepared to join me as a free woman then I will stand with her and together we will create the foundations for a new kind of civilisation – a civilisation based on meaningful interaction and communication.'

Excited, I waited for her reaction. There was a long pause. I didn't speak for I realised that my statements would take some time to be absorbed and understood. Then she coughed. 'Mmmhmm. Well... your idea sounds fascinating. And I would like to meet you to find out more. The only thing is, Celik, I'm about to take a vacation. In fact you were lucky to find me here at all, I should have left already. But listen, if you're ever over here again, give me a call and maybe we can get together some time.'

I tried not to feel too disappointed because naturally I knew that most people would not understand the significance of what I was offering. Even

Osman had pointed that out to me. I must be patient for when I made contact with the right woman she would know... she would feel... the truth of my words. So I thanked Pamela, said I would be in touch and wished her well.

The second one was Megan. I decided to cut short my speech and just give a hint of what I was offering her so she would be intrigued enough to want to know more. She sounded interested and agreed to meet me so we arranged the time and place. I felt better.

The third one, Kate, was not at home so I rang Victoria. She was polite but told me quite plainly that she was interested only in Englishmen and that there was no point in wasting my time taking her out to dinner.

Finally I called Kitty Stone. The phone rang for a long time and I was about to put it down when she answered. She sounded out of breath. When I identified myself she was surprised but her voice was warm and friendly. She said she would meet me at my hotel tomorrow evening. When I asked how I would recognise her, she thought for a moment then said she would be in green.

I spent the following day shopping, buying books I could not obtain in Turkey and some presents for my mother and sister. I went back to the hotel in a state of excitement and anxiety and started to prepare myself for the evening ahead. I showered carefully and trimmed my beard. Then I put on a pale blue shirt and matching silk tie that I'd bought that morning at Liberty's. I splashed cologne on my face and neck. When I had attended to every detail and was satisfied that I was looking my best, I went downstairs to the restaurant to wait.

After ten minutes the door opened and a tall, slim woman came in. She paused to look around the room and I noticed at once how plain she was. Not ugly. Just ordinary. I was surprised because I'd formed certain expectations based on the type of woman I imagined would answer ads in Time Out. She was in her early thirties with frizzy brown hair and dressed in a lumpy green wool suit. To my disgust I saw she was carrying a brown vinyl handbag. I stood up and she saw me. I must have looked unfriendly because she seemed a little uncertain so I smiled and introduced myself in what I hoped was a warm voice.

She relaxed and shook my hand. 'I'm pleased to meet you Celik.'

I pulled out a chair for her opposite mine and she sat down. The first thing she said was, 'Who do I remind you of?'

The question surprised me and I didn't know what I was expected to say.

'There must be someone you know that I resemble?' she repeated.

I considered, then said, 'Well... now you mention it, you remind me of a woman I used to know in Malawi. My friend's wife.'

'What's her name?'

'Liz Rider.'

'What is it about me that resembles her?'

I looked at her closely. 'You have the same brown hair. And hers is curly too. Your height is about the same. Also the build. And she has the same fine facial structure.'

'Anything else?'

I studied her carefully. 'No. I don't think so.'

'In what ways are Liz and I different?'

'Well... although you're both English you have different accents. She has brown eyes, they're rather bigger. Yours are blue. She laughs a lot and then her expression is altogether different to yours. You look like a more serious kind of person I should say.'

'Do I still look like Liz?'

I laughed. 'No, you don't look much like her now.'

'Liz Rider is a brown-haired, brown-eyed, lively woman who lives in Malawi. I am a blue-eyed, brown-haired, rather serious English woman who lives in London. She is Liz. I am Kitty. Despite a superficial likeness, we are two completely different individuals.'

I was amazed. That was the first time anyone had spoken to me like that.

'How did you learn that language?' I asked.

She told me she worked as a physiotherapist with physically handicapped children and it was a technique she used to help them identify themselves. I was intrigued and asked her to tell me about her work. She said she had married when she was very young but her husband was a gambler and she had eventually divorced him. She had one daughter age twelve. She had worked at various jobs to support herself and her daughter, including massage work and two years ago she had qualified as a physiotherapist. She had been in her present job for a year.

From her appearance, I guessed she did not have much money and I said it must be difficult supporting herself and a child on a single salary. She said the work was interesting and she had found her direction at last but she didn't have the opportunity to meet people. She had seen a copy of Time Out in the staff room and flicked through it during a coffee break. When she saw my ad. she felt curious and decided, on an impulse, to reply. She hadn't really expected to hear any more from me so when I phoned she was very surprised.

After we'd ordered dinner she asked me about myself. I started telling her a little about my background, my present difficulties with the company, my thoughts on finding somewhere else to live and work. She suggested America as a better place for me than England. She said I would find a job there if I paid five thousand dollars to a job consultant agency. They would use a computer system to find exactly what I wanted. I knew that already but I thanked her for the information all the same. Then she asked me if I had had a serious relationship with a woman.

I hesitated, then slowly found myself telling her about Sarah. I had not spoken about Sarah to anyone before, so at first I found it difficult to gather together the right words, but after the first few sentences the whole story rushed forward, like a river breaking through its dam.

She listened quietly till I finished speaking.

'But why should she accept your ideology? It's yours, not hers.'

I immediately regretted mentioning Sarah's role in this. Kitty's comments annoyed me so I said, 'Then what ideology does she have? Am I exploiting her for my ideology while I can't understand hers? It is difficult to interact with someone when you don't know what they believe in. And I am not sure whether she is a Christian or a Buddhist! Why can't people identify themselves clearly? Why do they muddle? How confused they must be if they don't know what they believe in, like drunkards wandering about without any sense of direction!'

'Just because you believe in a particular philosophy there is no reason for her to believe it. Why should she accept your ideas as though they were the only correct ones that existed?'

I couldn't believe this. After I had clarified my language to identify myself and instigate a meaningful interaction this woman was saying ... I pushed my chair back in irritation.

'It is finished now. Over. I will never accept a relationship on that basis.'

I looked at her, expecting to see that she was alarmed by my outburst, but she was watching me with an expression I could not identify. I decided it was probably sympathy, after what I had just said. This encouraged me to continue.

'You see, I have all the material necessary. After years of study I have developed a very powerful language... as one of my Jewish friends commented three years ago, I am establishing such a knowledge that nobody will be able to use it for the benefit of tyranny, destruction or injustice.'

Kitty smiled, 'How much of the ocean can a sponge drink?'

I asked if she'd read T.E.Lawrence. She said she hadn't.

'Lawrence said, "I meant to make a new nation." Our subject matter is the same.'

I think Kitty was amazed. And although she did not have a background in philosophy, she was able to follow some of my ideas because I simplified the language for her. I told her that I felt deep in my heart that Lawrence was my twin brother. 'We have the same determination and endurance but he was an empire destructor whereas I am an empire constructor. I spread and sow love and clarity and harvest civilisation!'

'How will you go about it?' she asked.

'To use Lawrence as an analogy, I may say that he was practising near Babel – "Come let us go down and there confuse their language that they may not understand one another." Have you read that in Genesis?'

She shook her head.

'My mission in this life is to bring clarity and functionality to their languages that they may understand one another's way of life, to interact in such richness in order to achieve a new civilisation. My urging for the development of inter-cultural languages is based on the work of Wittgenstein and is radically different from the search for a unified-pseudo-functional international language which would never help to express the differences among various cultures. What I see as the most important thing for the understanding of those cultures is the development of meaningful interactions among them to create the new empire and the new civilisation.'

'And how do you think this can come about?' Kitty repeated.

'The course of action to take is this – to clarify the languages to make them functional; to identify the cultures as they are and describe their activities in their way of life, in their own terms; to develop functional inter-cultural languages to realise meaningful interactions. And do you know what the result will be, Kitty?'

She shook her head.

'The result will be a civilisation composed of all the richness of colour and sound imaginable.'

I do not enjoy philosophising. It is like suffering and struggling with the bewitchment of language. I looked at Kitty expecting to see amazement on her face. Instead she was smiling. 'This all sounds very complicated. Why are you bothering? What's in it for you?'

I thought about her question for a minute or two before replying.

'It's not a question of what's in it for me. It's a question of responding to the demands God has made upon me. He creates everyone for a specific purpose. In our vanity that purpose may not be to our liking. We may have to suffer greatly even before we become aware of the purpose, but once we do then we can not run away or we lose our very souls.'

Kitty looked at her watch and said she had to go. I asked her if she would like to come to my room as I had a present for her.

'I do not want to have intercourse with you,' she said

I was shocked and embarrassed. 'Intercourse? What do you mean intercourse? Did I ask you?'

She answered, with a slightly mocking smile, 'I am clarifying my language to identify myself. Isn't that what your philosophy is all about?'

I ignored her question which I felt was posed deliberately to provoke me. Then I felt insulted. 'Why not? What's wrong with me.'

'Do you think something is wrong with you?' she asked.

'No I do not. But still...'

'There is nothing wrong with you Celik. But I don't want to.'

'Of course not,' I answered. 'It is a matter of harmony reached to a peak to have intercourse with someone. And it is so interwoven with the rest of the state of affairs that one can not escape from doing it. So I think it is meaningless to say, "I want it" or "I don't want it." I think it is more related to the concept will, which is related to, "You do not will unless God wills".'

She didn't reply and after a pause I said, 'But I would like to give you the present all the same.'

She came up to my room and I gave her a box. She unwrapped it and took out a bottle of perfume. She smiled and kissed me on the cheek.

'Thank you very much. It was a lovely thought. I did not expect a present.' After inviting me to meet her daughter the next evening, she left.

The room was suddenly silent. I lay back in a chair and thought over all that had happened that evening. Everything we had talked about. There was a sense of unreality, like being in a dream where one wanders around lost in a foreign country and even the signposts do not make any sense. She had taken my own words and used them to reject me. Was my language still not clear enough? Must I work more? I suddenly felt weary through to my bones. Why did I complicate my life like this? It would be so simple if I asked my mother to arrange a marriage for me and settle down to become a husband and father. Even as these thoughts passed through my mind I received a warning. 'Satan is tempting you.' Though I longed for rest I quickly prepared myself for prayer to strengthen myself against Satan.

Next day I walked round the shops again as it was raining. I bought some books and as I was about to pay for them I noticed a row of Penthouse magazines. On impulse I picked one up. When the shop assistant took it from me to wrap it up I found myself going red. I avoided looking at her face and hurried from the shop. From there I went to the National Gallery where I could forget my embarrassment. While I was looking at the magnificent paintings words formed in my head, 'Don't feel ashamed. You must read everything from philosophy to pornography. How else will you fully understand the cultures which produce such literature?' I felt an enormous sense of relief.

I met Osman for a meal in a Chinese restaurant. We continued our discussions from the first evening but I could not concentrate and kept glancing at my watch. I had already told him that I had to leave early as I was meeting a friend. He seemed surprised but didn't say anything and I arranged to meet him the following day which was Saturday. We would spend the whole day together.

I took a taxi to the hamburger bar where Kitty had said she would meet me. I assumed she would invite me to her house later where she would prepare a delicious meal for me. It was a depressing place – Formica, chrome, worn green linoleum. It reeked of onions. There was only one vacant window table so I took it and ordered a coca-cola. After a few minutes, the couple at the next table lit cigarettes.

'Oh shit!' I thought and moved my chair out of range, up against the window. The rain made little rivers on the steamed-up glass. I cleared a space with my hand so I could look out for Kitty. Big red buses squelched past, honking black taxis with squealing brakes, a sea of pale faces under dripping umbrellas. Street lights quivering in black oily pools. The door continually squeaked open and shut, letting in the cold damp air as customers came and went. It was almost three quarters of an hour before Kitty appeared.

She was wearing a long, grey raincoat and her hair was wet and straggly. Behind her was a tall, thin, fair girl. Kitty saw me at once and hurried over, apologising for her lateness. The bus hadn't arrived and they'd had to walk two blocks to catch another one. I said it was okay and she introduced her daughter. 'Celik, this is Jane. Jane – Mr Ertas.'

The girl nodded shyly.

'Hello Jane,' I said, 'I've brought something for you.'

She took the packet from me, blushing, and unwrapped it. It was an embroidered Turkish bag and she seemed very pleased with it. They took off their wet coats and draped them over the back of the chairs. We sat down and Kitty picked up the menu. Apparently we were not going to her house. Perhaps she was ashamed to let me see her home. Or maybe she didn't want the neighbours to see she was with a foreigner. In any case I didn't feel like eating another meal, having just finished one with Osman. Nor did I want to eat in such a place. But I ordered a hamburger and Kitty and Jane had the same, with chips.

The ease of the previous night was missing. The conversation was stilted and trivial with long uncomfortable pauses. Possibly because of the presence of Jane, though she was a pleasant enough child. I asked her about her school and her hobbies and she answered me in a quiet, friendly way, but I was bored and restless. I looked at Kitty. She wore no make-up and had not gone to any effort to make herself attractive. I felt annoyed and I think she must have sensed it because she kept glancing at me uneasily.

I was relieved when the evening ended. Perhaps Kitty felt the same. Anyway, we shook hands, wished each other well and went our separate ways without arranging another meeting. I paid for a taxi to take them home. At first Kitty protested but when I said that Jane would catch a chill she accepted. I went back to my hotel feeling very depressed.

By the next evening I was better because I had spent a whole day with my brother. Also I was anticipating an interesting night ahead with Megan. I tried to imagine what she might be like, while I got dressed. Having already gone through such a meeting with Kitty, I did not feel nervous this time. In fact I was looking forward to it and feeling the adventure. I was brushing my hair when the phone rang. It was Megan. She could not meet me tonight she said, as her child was sick. She was very sorry. What about the next night, I asked. A pause – then, no she didn't feel that she could leave her son with a sitter till he was well. He had a virus infection and it would be at least a week till he was better. I said I was sorry but thanked her for ringing, and put the phone down.

I sank into the chair, heavy with disappointment and frustration. All my senses had been preparing for the evening ahead and now – nothing. There was an ache in my stomach which increased till it reached my throat. This whole trip had been a waste of time. I had accomplished nothing. I tore the wrapping off the Penthouse and flicked through the pages. Page after page of tits and pussies. So what? I hurled the magazine against the wall.

A creeping anger circled around my heart. Anger with the Megan woman for letting me down. Anger with Kitty for her dowdiness. Anger with the stupid English women who thought they were so superior to 'foreigners.'

And Sarah? At the thought of her my anger intensified to white hot rage. If it hadn't been for her I wouldn't be in this situation now. I doubled over till my head was on my knees and I folded my arms across the back of my head. I clenched my teeth, squeezed my eyes shut, refusing the tears that pushed against my eyelids. They slid through anyway, soaking my face.

After twenty minutes of weeping there were no more tears left. The passion was spent and I was cold and drained. I made myself a cup of coffee and while I drank it I picked up a copy of Time Out from the bedside table. Flicking through it I saw ads for massage parlours.

'Why not?' I thought bitterly. 'What else are women good for?' And before I could change my mind I picked a number at random and dialled. The woman who answered the phone told me it would be twenty pounds for a massage in my hotel room and I could negotiate the tips when the girl arrived. She said she was not allowed by law to negotiate on the phone. I told her to send me a blonde. Then I lay on my bed and waited.

About fifteen minutes later the door bell rang and I got up to answer it. A small woman with long blonde hair and a brown leather skirt and jacket stood there. She looked very young.

'Hi, I'm Sharon,' she announced, wiggling into the room.

I introduced myself and she smiled and asked sweetly, 'Did the agency explain the terms to you? Is there anything that isn't clear?' She sat down on the edge of the bed and waited for my reply. It was like discussing a business deal. After a few minutes of bargaining we agreed the payment should be one hundred and fifty pounds. She asked for the money in advance. I gave it to her and she counted it and put it into her handbag. Then she stood up and took off her suit. She was naked underneath.

'Hey! What's this?' I asked in disbelief. 'Is this all you wear?'

She said she did not wear underclothes when she was working because of the time involved in putting them on and taking them off and besides it was difficult to take care of them. She started to remove my clothes and I asked her if she was going to give me a massage. She laughed and said she had never learned how to. I felt cheated because I had been expecting – what? Still, I wanted to talk to her and treat her like a human being.

'Why are you doing this?' I asked.

'For adventure. And I meet such interesting people.'

We sat on the bed and she began kissing me but I was too shocked and disorientated to respond. So she took my hand and moved it over her breasts. They were small and hard and very beautiful. I took her nipple in my mouth and began sucking.

She moaned quietly, saying, 'Easy, easy.'

This excited me and I began to caress her body. Her pussy was golden and I wanted to kiss it. When I did, she squeezed my penis in her hand and asked if I wanted her to take it in her mouth. Disgusted, I said no. She lay on top of me and moved her breasts over my penis. Still it wouldn't harden. So she sat astride my legs and rotated her hips till I came.

She got up immediately afterwards and asked where the bathroom was.

The whole episode lasted no more than fifteen minutes from the time she'd rung the doorbell.

'Are you going already?' I asked. 'I thought you would stay the night.'

'Then you should have told that to the agency,' she said briskly. 'I have another appointment.'

I pulled on my trousers. When she came out of the bathroom, fully dressed, she said, 'You've had your orgasm and I've had mine. Now I have to leave.'

When she'd gone, I turned off the lights and lay shivering face down on the bed. It stank of sweat, cheap perfume and semen.

After a few minutes I got up and switched on the lights and opened the window wide. I pulled off the bedspread and stuffed it in the wardrobe. Then I turned on the hot shower and took off my clothes and stood in the steam for a long time before I picked up the soap.

By the time I'd finished, I could not even recall her face.

CHAPTER
◆ SIXTEEN

I came out of that shower with a clean body, but all the hot water in the world would not cleanse my soul. The knowledge of my degradation was almost beyond endurance. I knelt naked on the floor, my arms crossed over my chest, and cried aloud, 'Why me? Why have I travelled this far only to be crushed like an insect?' I was on the edge of an abyss so black and so deep that, if I fell into it, I would never find my way out. To survive this I must fight harder than I had ever done in my life.

I must pray alone in that room for four days, without food, without sleep, drinking only water. After telephoning instructions to the hotel reception that on no account was I to be disturbed I began my preparations.

I lost track of time and did not know how long I had been sitting there when the smell of evil filled that room. I saw scenes of past humiliations long-forgotten... the little blonde girl who lived in our street throwing a glass at my head after my song, my grandmother telling Lale that I should have been the one who died, my trial and imprisonment, Lale's contempt when I returned her bowl of blood and mucus, Gül's rejection of my letter, Laurelie... Sarah... every hurt that had ever been inflicted on me was replayed like the sound and light shows I had loved to watch at Sultan Ahmed as a child. I exhausted myself weeping. And then Satan picked that moment to creep up behind me and bend low over my ear whispering in a voice so honey-soft that I fell back in his arms in gratitude. He wiped away my tears and told me to look again.

I opened my eyes and saw two gates wrought in intricate patterns of flowers and fruit. They parted to reveal a garden filled with flowers so bright I had to shade my eyes. Beautiful women wandered naked amongst the flowers holding trays of fruit and cooked fish on their heads. Spicy aromas filled the air and mingled with the delicate scent of an almond tree under which one of the women lay. She was smoothing oil over her shoulders. Her breasts looked as though they were filled with cream. She leaned over a wicker basket at her side and from it lifted a tiny infant. It fastened its rosebud mouth on her nipple and sucked until her milk flowed and bubbled around its lips. I stretched out my hand to touch the child and Satan whispered, 'I show you the tree of immortality and an everlasting kingdom. Your Lord has forbidden you to approach this tree only to prevent you from becoming immortal.'

Though I longed to touch the infant's silky skin I snatched back my hand and closed my eyes, forcing the words from my mouth: 'Satan is your enemy, therefore treat him as an enemy. Satan makes promises to deceive you. Satan leads you far astray. Satan stirs up in you vain desires. Satan uses you to tamper with Allah's creation. Satan makes your foolish acts seem fair to you. Satan seduces. Satan tempts. Satan sees you whence you can not see him. Satan says, "No man shall conquer you this day. I shall be at hand to help you". Satan whispers, "Shall I show you the tree of immortality and an everlasting kingdom?".'

Satan threw me out of his arms, raging, 'I am done with you for I can see what you cannot!' I hit the ground as the gates slammed shut in my face.

I lay for a long time in the dark with my knees curled up to my chin and my arms pressed into my sides with my hands over my ears and my eyes squeezed shut. Listening to the sound of my own breathing. Telling myself I was still alive. Not daring to believe that my ordeal was over.

I awoke from a long, dreamless sleep. For every step I took towards the Empire Satan would set ever more cunning traps to destroy me. Because Satan was afraid of my strength! And I had the knowledge to confound him! I had temporarily lost sight of this truth and had blundered about hopelessly, like a free man seeking shelter in a camp for slaves. Why? Because I had allowed myself to be bewitched. My punishment for this was the degradation of my body and soul. With God's help I was now free and ready to begin the task before me.

I ordered a meal to be sent to my room and took a hot shower to relieve my cold, aching joints. Then, refreshed and renewed, I sat at the table with pen and paper to write through the night.

SYSTEM EMPIRE

1 A group of parts
Nations-Cultures

2 Integrated parts
Intercultural languages

3 Common purpose of achieving some objectives
Civilisation
What is the common purpose of human-kind?
What are the common objectives of cultures?
How can we discover those common purposes and objectives?
Through cultural interactions
Cultural interactions help to develop inter-cultural languages
How can we develop inter-cultural languages?
Identifying our cultures in clear terms by expressing the ground sentences in inter-cultural terms...

At the dawning of the new day I drew back the curtains and opened the window wide to breathe clean air. I did not know what the future held for me but with God's help I would survive.

CHAPTER
• SEVENTEEN

After I arrived in Istanbul I had to look for a flat as it seemed that I would be there for at least six months. I found a spacious one in Bebek overlooking the Bosphorus. A few days after I had settled in I rang Gül. Squealing with delight at the sound of my voice she invited me over for dinner.

Gül's flat was in Rumeli, close to Bebek. She opened the door and flung her arms around my neck. 'It's so good to see you. Welcome, welcome! Why haven't you written? I have so much to tell you! What have you been up to? Come in come in!'

I was taken aback by this display and even more surprised when I noticed the fresh flowers in the hallway and living room. Gül had put on some weight and she had cut her hair short but she still looked as beautiful as ever. She was wearing tight jeans and a blouse of green silk and I realised she had gone to some trouble to make herself and her home attractive for me. As she herded me into the dining room she told me she had cooked my favourite meal of groper and tomatoes. I felt myself smiling with appreciation.

Gül pushed me into a chair and disappeared into the kitchen to bring out the serving dishes. 'This has to be eaten the minute it's cooked or it loses its flavour,' she called over her shoulder.

'Since when did you get domesticated?' I teased.

'I'm a woman of many talents,' she yelled from the kitchen, 'quite apart from my amazing ability to stuff up relationships.'

'Then why don't you learn?'

She laughed. 'Easy for you to say! Every time I think, right, this time I'll quit. No more entanglements. Just me and my cat, like peace and harmony. The problem is I don't like my own company.' I had no answer to that so I just looked at her quizzically as she put the dishes on the table. 'This sounds as if you have something to tell me?'

She waited till she'd sat down and I'd begun to help myself to the fish and rice and salad.

'I've got a new man,' she began, obviously bursting to tell me the news. 'Well, if you can call an eighteen year old a man.' She laughed, running her hand through her hair. I noticed that it had a few streaks of grey at the crown. I wondered why she hadn't dyed it. Perhaps she hadn't noticed?

'Eighteen!' I said, 'My god! Are you in the baby snatching business now? I thought you liked old men.'

She picked up a piece of rice from her plate and flicked it at me.

'Didn't you know that women in their thirties and young boys...'

'I get the idea!' I protested. 'So he's tall and handsome?'

'All of that. But he has no money. He's a fisherman from the Black Sea. Of course he doesn't like me to pay when we go out, but sod that, it's so archaic, don't you think? I have more money than I know what to do with so why shouldn't I spend it on him if I want?' She laughed. 'Besides it's worth it just to see people's faces when I walk in with him.'

'Do your parents know about this... baby boy?' I asked.

'Don't be an idiot!' and in a dismissive voice she said, 'Oh and my other news is that I'm going to Cambridge to do a Ph.D in medieval French.'

I looked up to see if she was joking, but by the way she refused to look at me I knew she wasn't.

'Gül, that's tremendous news! Congratulations. I'll take you out to dinner at the Hilton to celebrate. When do you go?' She bent her head low over her plate to hide her pleasure at my reaction.

'Beginning of next year. I'm going to be one of the most over-educated old maids in Istanbul. So, for this year I'm entitled to play a little, don't you think? So don't be so stuffy over this baby boy as you call him.'

'Me? Stuffy?' I said, 'Come on man!'

She laughed, showing her beautiful white teeth. Then she tapped her plate with her fork. 'With you I've never had to pretend.'

I shrugged, 'If people are repelled by your honesty then that's their problem, not yours.'

She looked up at me, smiling, and just for a brief second I saw something else in her eyes. An invitation? Then it was gone so quickly I didn't know whether or not I'd imagined it. She started moving dishes around the table and piling salad onto my plate. Avoiding eye contact she said, 'So what state is your love life in then?'

'Non-existent!' I said. 'I'm not attractive to women.'

She stopped what she was doing and looked at me with raised eyebrows. 'You're a man aren't you?'

'I think so,' I laughed.

'Have you got any bits missing?'

I threw a piece of rice at her, "No!"

'Then you don't have a problem!' She looked at me, and again there was that expression in her eyes. I wasn't mistaken. But all I could say to her now was, 'My dearest friend, tell me about your Ph.D plans.'

The merest flicker of a shadow crossed her face, then she leaped up to clear away the dishes and bring in dessert. We filled up the evening with conversation and food and coffee until it was time for me to go. At her front door, as we were saying goodnight she suddenly leaned forward and kissed me on both cheeks, then she took a step back and stood looking at me with her hands clasped together behind her back. She looked small and vulnerable and afraid, like a little girl who had broken my best toy and wanted my forgiveness. I wanted to ruffle her hair and tell her everything was okay, but instead I said, 'It was a great evening. Let's do it again soon,' and walked out into the night, hating myself for my ineptitude.

In the early hours of the morning, unable to sleep, I went over the events of the evening in my mind. Why had she looked at me like that? Years ago I would have given half of my life away for the gift of such a look. Now, all I could do was throw it back in her face. It made no sense. I looked at the scenes of our times together from our first meeting. It was like watching a fast-moving film. I listened to our conversations, which were always dominated by Gül's latest crisis. In all the years I had known her I had never discussed with her the intimate details of my life. I tried to imagine what her reaction would be if I told her about my imprisonment, Sarah, my discussions with my brother, my thoughts about the Empire, those women I had advertised for, the prostitute. I had no idea what she might say. None whatever. I realised with a shock that she didn't know me at all.

Eventually I must have fallen into a fitful sleep because I awoke next morning with the knowledge that I had been unable to respond to Gül because of Sarah. The solution was clear. I must say cut away the last sticky strands that bound me to Sarah. I owed Gül that much. I thought a long time about the best way to do this and after a few weeks I decided to send a single red rose with a note thanking her for the friendship she had given me. After I left the florist's I expected to feel liberated from a great burden of responsibility, but instead, I felt as if the sap had been scraped from my insides as though from a living tree, leaving me hollow and dry, like an old log.

I filled all my spare time reading and making notes about the Empire, trying not to wonder if Sarah would reply to my letter. Probably she would realise my intention was to say goodbye and leave it at that. On the other hand she might reply with a similar message. I told myself endlessly that it didn't matter whether she wrote or not as the outcome would be the same. I tried hard to concentrate on my work and studies. I read the Koran and the Masnawi. I went for long walks by myself. I visited my family. I developed my thesis:

...Identify other cultures the same way, eg trade, war, culture, commerce, travel, sports, music, art, literature. (tuning the instrument up.)

Cultural interactions – help develop intercultural languages...

- help to tune the cultures to harmonise with other cultures
- establish common objectives and purpose
- help achieve civilisation (orchestral music)

For now I wanted to keep my thoughts of empire to myself until I had properly established a coherent philosophy, so I wrote to my brother only about the concepts in the Koran which we had spent so many years studying together. He wrote back with suggestions and modifications '...my biggest concern is not the concept but the language. It is so complex most people wouldn't understand it, therefore you should make it more accessible. I suggest, for example...'

I was fully occupied with these modifications and sometimes I couldn't sleep, so I worked through the nights after my days in the office. The lack of sleep seemed to have no effect on my work, fortunately.

Several weeks after I had sent my letter to Sarah, I came home hungry and cold in the dark and the rain one evening, as I had been working late to finish a project. No stars were visible in the murky sky and the sea was a sheet of dull grey metal. A clinging drizzle settled over my head and neck as I searched my pockets for my key, found it, pushed it in the lock and opened the door. I was glad to feel the rush of warm air on my face as I went inside. I picked up a letter from the floor. Sarah's writing. A jolt tore through my chest like an electric shock. I dropped my briefcase on my foot and ignoring the pain, tore at the envelope. My hands shook so much I could hardly read the words on the thin airmail paper.

...surprised and touched by your beautiful rose. The day before it arrived I realised I hadn't heard from you for ages and I was about to write to you to let you know my good news... a return trip to Istanbul... end of the year... series of articles about Anatolia... please be my interpreter...

I pressed the letter to my face and closed my eyes, sliding my back down against the wall until I was sitting on the floor. Huge tears welled up and rolled down my cheeks. I opened my eyes and looked straight into the mirror on the opposite wall. 'How foolish you look, Celik,' I told my reflection, 'sitting on the floor blubbing like a baby! How undignified. And now look at you, your face like a split melon with that idiot grin!' I sprang up, took off my jacket and threw it on the sofa and jumped as high as I could into the air then twirled round and round like a Dervish, holding my arms high, singing at the top of my voice like a demented bullfrog. At last, dizzy, I staggered over to my desk, laughing and gasping for breath, to search for pen and paper.

My reply to Sarah's letter took the whole night and twenty three drafts because my words kept leaping off the page. Just before dawn I had them under control.

...so naturally I am pleased that you will be in Istanbul at the same time as myself and I would regard it as a privilege to be your guide during your stay, if you wish...

CHAPTER ◆ EIGHTEEN

One cold grey morning in November, I waited at the recently opened Yesilkoy airport in my new black leather coat, black and white striped suit and black shoes. I had spent the previous night at my mother's house as it was nearer the airport. When Hulya saw me dressed ready to go she laughed and said, 'You look like Charlie Chaplin!'

'What! Don't you know this is very fashionable just now? Anyway, look at how you are dressed this morning! Oriental upstairs and American downstairs!'

'You are right!' my father laughed. 'She shouldn't be wearing those horrible jeans.'

Hulya threw a cushion at me. 'American eh? And what are you – Londoner?'

My mother glanced at me curiously.

The automatic doors kept opening and shutting to reveal brief glimpses of arriving passengers. My frustration was so great that I almost hurled myself through the doors, screaming. But suddenly Sarah was there. Bending over the luggage carousel. Wearing a pale grey suit with a pink scarf at the neck and high-heeled black shoes. Her hair was longer than the last time I had seen her and fell over her shoulders in soft waves. I had to clench my teeth to prevent myself from calling out when the doors shut again. Then she was looking at me and waving. I waved back smiling from ear to ear just as the doors closed again. Then she emerged with her case and my carefully rehearsed speech evaporated in my head as she leaned forward to kiss my cheek and I smelt the warmth of her skin.

Unable to speak I took her case and led her to the taxi, aware of the curious stares of the groups of waiting people. She didn't seem to notice I had been struck dumb and chatted on about her flight. In the taxi she stared out of the window, exclaiming her pleasure at being back in Turkey.

'It's unique, Celik. A country with one foot in Asia and one in Europe, one in the past and one in the present.'

I smiled at her enthusiasm though I couldn't suppress a rising irritation at her language. 'Yes, well... I'm afraid I don't have the glaze of the tourist over my eyes,' I said lightly, hoping I didn't sound too sour. Nothing was going to spoil this visit, I was absolutely determined about that.

We reached my flat and as I carried her suitcase in she walked around my living room, touching furniture, picking up ornaments and books, looking at my paintings. I took her case into her bedroom and when I came out she was standing by the window gazing out over the Bosphorus. For just a second or two before she turned round I stood in the doorway watching her, hardly daring to breathe in case she disappeared. When she saw me she smiled and to hide my pleasure I said, 'While you unpack and freshen up I'll book us a table at the Hilton for lunch.'

During our lunch she talked about her work and how much she was enjoying it.

'It's really important that I make a good job of these articles. That's why I asked you to help me. There's a position as travel editor coming up soon and I want it.'

The way she stated this so bluntly took me by surprise. I had never heard anyone say such a thing so directly. Even Gül never disclosed the extent of her ambitions. I noticed the tilt of her chin and the gleam in her eye and laughed. 'Sarah, if you look at your boss like that you will get exactly what you want.'

She didn't laugh, in fact she frowned a little.

'What?' I said, puzzled.

'Journalism is a highly competitive field and ability is what counts.'

I had thought she would be flattered by my compliment and I was upset to find she was annoyed, so I apologised, though I still didn't understand. Then she began telling me how interested she had become in Turkey and how she had spent a lot of time reading Turkish history. I listened, watching her, and then she laughed.

'Someone asked how I'd picked up so much information about the harem and I said perhaps in a previous incarnation I'd been an inhabitant!'

I laughed with her, avoiding any discussion on the subject of the harem but allowed a fleeting image of myself as Sultan, surrounded by the most beautiful women in the world and the most beautiful of all – First Kadin – was Sarah.

'Oh it feels so good to be back here,' she said breaking through my daydream. 'But I must admit, nice though it is to be in the Hilton, I prefer eating in Turkish restaurants. This is just a bit of America transferred to an exotic setting.'

'In that case I'll take you to the Konak next time. It's a new hotel just opened in Sultan Ahmed,' I said, delighted I had a chance to please her. 'I stayed there for a few days because the Sheraton was over-booked with the Islamic conference.'

'Oh, right! I remember it being built last time I was here.'

'Not built. Restored. It used to be a Pasha's mansion and was just about falling down when the Ministry of Tourism bought it and started renovating it for use as a hotel.'

Our conversation continued like this in a light, pleasant manner until we had finished our meal. Then I sprang my surprise.

'Last time you were here you did not see the tomb of Eyub. I would like to take you there now.'

'Mohammed's flag bearer?' she asked

I nodded, pleased by her happy expression, and asked the waiter to order us a taxi. We got out of the taxi at Eyub and looked around at the quiet grey courtyards, tottering tombstones and narrow cobbled lanes. A drizzling white mist draped the buildings like a bridal veil. The only sound was the ubiquitous cooing of pigeons. As we approached the tomb we saw a newly married couple go up to the window to pray, followed by a crowd of relatives.

'It's the holiest shrine in Istanbul,' I explained. 'Newly-weds, circumcision boys and anyone who wants a special blessing come here. All the Ottoman Sultans came here to be girded with the sword of Osman upon their accession.'

It was Friday, so the courtyard of the mosque was more crowded than usual and as Sarah moved through the throng of head-scarved, long-coated women, they turned to stare at her. I was pleased to see she behaved discreetly and did not attempt to take photographs of the men sitting praying outside the mosque. We stood in front of the window of the tomb and I turned my palms upwards to offer a prayer. Sarah glanced at me and moved away.

'Ottoman architecture is not beautiful but it's very satisfying,' she remarked as we walked out of the courtyard and down a side-street.

My previous anxiety and irritation evaporated and I allowed myself to feel relaxed. But just then we saw a large pool of blood on the pavement. Sarah asked if there had been an accident. I was embarrassed.

'Some of these people come from the villages. They do not know how to behave in a city. They sacrifice a chicken on the pavement instead of going to the correct places.'

She turned to say something but just then a family emerged from a nearby building. They all had a spot of blood on their foreheads and one of the small girls was holding a baby, also with a spot of blood. They gathered around the baby and joked about the blood on it. Sarah asked me to request their permission to take a photograph.

I said to the woman who appeared to be the mother of the child, 'This lady is a journalist from England and she is interested in taking photographs of Turkish families. She would like your permission to take your photograph.'

She looked doubtful and turned to her husband to repeat my request. He glanced at Sarah. 'Better tell her to take photographs of another family. I'm sorry.'

As they walked away from us one of the men in the group turned apologetically to me and said, 'Good cheer.'

'Never mind,' Sarah said. 'The café of Pierre Loti is somewhere in this vicinity and I would like to take photographs of that. Can we?'

'Pierre Loti?' I replied. 'I've heard of it, but I haven't been there. We shall have to ask directions. But first, I have another surprise for you.'

She smiled expectantly as I led her into a nearby café and gave my order to the waiter. In less than a minute, two cups of steaming hot salep were brought to the table. Sarah laughed with pleasure and held the cup to her nose so she could inhale the wonderful cinnamon-scented aroma. After she took the first sip she had a creamy moustache on her top lip. Without stopping to think I automatically reached over and drew my finger-tip across to wipe it off. Instantly I realised the intimacy of this gesture far exceeded the terms of our friendship and my face began to redden. Sarah didn't appear to notice my embarrassment, though she smiled widely.

'Thank you. There's no elegant way to drink this, is there? But it doesn't matter because it's the most divine drink in the world!'

We asked directions from the waiter to Pierre Loti's café and after we'd finished our salep we started off up a steep hill past peeling wooden houses leaning into each other like drunken old men on each side of the street. Half way up I asked directions from an old man coming down the hill. He immediately offered to take us there and despite my protests he led us to the top of the hill and gave us directions through the cemetery, '...and you'll see the café when you come out the other side.' We followed his instructions till we found it.

Inside the café a waiter in a costume of baggy black pants with a wide red sash, a black waistcoat embroidered in gold, and a white turban, brought us glasses of tea on a tray. We sat at a low brass table by the window, looking out over the Golden Horn.

Photographs of the French writer adorned the walls. After examining them closely Sarah said, 'Alexandra was right. It must have been a lovely view when Pierre Loti saw it.'

'Alexandra?'

'Ah yes. I haven't told you yet. Years ago, when I was a student, I had a classics tutor, Simon. I was good friends with him and his wife, Alexandra. She was a photographer.'

I nodded. 'I remember.'

She raised her eyebrows, 'You do? Well, they went to live in Italy, I got married and went to New Zealand, so we lost touch. A couple of months ago I read about a photographic exhibition in London. I saw the name and wondered if it was the same Alexandra, so I went to the exhibition. The pictures were all taken at an orphanage in India for abandoned babies. There were a hundred and sixty babies and only six staff to care for them. The babies were fed and changed by the clock. They were fed with their bottles propped up on a pillow beside them. No one ever held them. Can you imagine that?'

I nodded, but didn't comment.

'The babies cried a lot and the staff were driven mad by the crying for the first few days, but then they didn't even hear it. It ceased to disturb them. Some of the babies gave up and died, though they were well cared for physically. The others...'

'And Alexandra?' I prompted.

'Ah yes. As I was absorbed in the photographs – in that section their faces were completely blank, they didn't react to any stimulus – I completely forgot the reason I was there, to see if the photographer was the Alexandra I'd known. Then someone tapped my shoulder and said, "Sarah?" I turned round and she was there!' Her face broke into a wide smile. 'I couldn't believe it! If anything, she looked even more beautiful in her fifties than she did in her thirties, though her hair is completely white now. She invited me to lunch.'

'So what does she have to do with Pierre Loti?' I asked, wondering why Sarah hadn't written about meeting up with this woman.

'She was here five years ago – she's visited just about every country in the world. She knows such a lot.'

'And Simon? What happened to him?'

Sarah looked out the window. 'She left him, oh, about ten years ago.'

Now it was my turn to raise my eyebrows. 'Because...?'

'It's pretty complex. Well... things hadn't been good for a long time, apparently. They'd been living their own lives. Then she met someone else.'

'Someone even more handsome than the perfect Simon?' I laughed, thinking how predictable this story was.

She blinked at me. 'You do have a long memory.' Then she smiled, 'But it's not what you think. She left him for an Indian woman she met in Canada. Shanti. After Shanti qualified as a doctor they went to live in Calcutta. It was through Shanti she got the connections to visit the orphanage. After they exhibited the photographs in Calcutta the orphanage was deluged with offers from volunteers to come in each day just to hold the babies.'

My jaw dropped. 'A woman?'

She nodded, as if this news was nothing out of the ordinary. 'Shanti died a year ago. Leukaemia. Alexandra nursed her at home. She says that's when her hair turned white. She decided to come back to England to try to get her life together.' She smiled ironically. 'We had a lot to talk about.'

I wanted to ask what they had talked about but I decided not to.

'She gets on very well with the boys,' she said.

'Oh? So she's met them?' As soon as I'd uttered those words I regretted it for now the conversation would be prolonged when I wanted to change the subject entirely.

Sarah nodded. 'Well actually she moved into my house last month. The lease on her flat ran out and she didn't want to renew it because she's thinking about going to Israel to work on a project about kibbutzim.'

I scrutinised her face but she looked completely neutral. It was difficult to read the faces of English women, I knew that, so I had to ask. 'Is she... involved with anyone at present?'

'No. She's still grieving over Shanti.'

I glanced over the warehouses now littering the waterside like a pack of tattered cards about to come tumbling down, and the shitty brown murk of the Golden Horn.

Sarah murmured, 'I read somewhere recently that life is what happens when we have other plans. That's so true, isn't it? And we can never really know what the life of another person is like, even when we think we understand. That's what I've discovered about my mother. I don't know why it took me so long to realise.'

I did not want to get involved in this kind of discussion now. There would be a time and place when I would introduce the topic in its proper context. To change the subject I suggested we take a taxi to my mother's house. Sarah protested that my parents should have more notice, but I assured her they would be delighted.

As I knocked on my mother's door, I wondered how she would react for this was the first time I had brought a woman home. The door was opened by Hulya, her hair in curlers. She shrieked when she saw Sarah and fled upstairs. I took Sarah through to the living room. She was protesting, 'I knew we shouldn't have come without notice, poor Hulya is so embarrassed now!'

Then my mother came in. As soon as she saw Sarah, she held out both her arms and said, 'Sarah! Sarah! Salems, salems!'

Sarah rushed forward to embrace her. They were clearly delighted to see each other. My father appeared next, smiling and nodding affably. It was like a reunion of old friends. I was amazed. When Hulya came into the room she apologised for her greeting and Sarah apologised for coming without notice. Soon we were all talking and laughing. I had not expected this scene and I had a strange sensation in my throat.

My mother insisted we stay for dinner and Hulya cooked some chicken in a tomato sauce and made a salad. She and Sarah and my mother discussed at length the correct way to make yoghurt, then my mother kept up a non-stop monologue – which I had to translate – on the superiority of home-cooked Turkish food over hotel food, with Sarah listening intently and asking questions about recipes. At last we left with many pleas from my parents that we should come and stay with them so that Sarah would be able to sample my mother's cooking every day.

My parents didn't have a phone in yet for there was a long waiting list, so we had to walk a little way through Kocamustaphapasha to find a taxi. It was dark and I had to hold Sarah's elbow to stop her tripping over the holes in the road.

Delicious smells of freshly baked bread and roasting chestnuts filled the frosty air as we squeezed our way through the throngs of people doing their shopping, or just standing around gossiping. Everyone turned to stare at Sarah as we passed. She noticed it too and laughed, 'I feel like an alien.'

'It is because you are so beautiful,' I dared to say.

She shook her head and said, 'No, it's only because I look foreign.'

As we drove back to my flat in the taxi she told me how happy and welcomed she felt here.

'Your family are so kind. You'd think they'd known me for years instead of just a few weeks.'

'Of course. They know you are my friend, so naturally they would behave like that,' I replied. 'Before you came I had concerns that you might not like it here. It is not so convenient as it is in your own country. I thought, I felt, that perhaps... what I mean is, I could never, for instance, introduce Gül to my parents.'

She glanced at me but didn't reply.

When we reached my flat I showed Sarah where everything was kept and brought out the records and books I had bought for her to make her feel at home.

'There is a selection of Turkish music here, from folk to classical. Also some French songs in case you don't like the Turkish.'

She looked surprised and said, 'That was very thoughtful of you, you didn't have to go to all that trouble.'

'It's my pleasure,' I shrugged, 'and here is a three volume translation of the Masnawi by Luzac. I ordered it for you in London. It was written by Rumi who founded the sect of whirling dervishes in the thirteenth century.'

She picked up the heavy volumes, 'I'll look forward to reading them. I was planning to visit Konya to see his tomb.'

'Excellent!' I exclaimed, 'We'll go there together. In fact we can watch the rituals if we go in December. They are performed for one week only, to commemorate Mevlana's death. But we'll have to book a hotel soon. People come from all over the world to watch the dance. It's a very famous event.'

'Why just one week?'

'When Ataturk established his secular government and banished the caliphate the dervishes were involved in plots to overthrow him and restore the sultan. He was afraid of their influence so he seized their properties, banned the rituals and publicly hanged some of the leaders. Later, for tourists, the rituals were allowed to be performed for one week each year.'

'Then I'll definitely have to go and see them. I'll take these to bed with me to begin reading.'

'It's mostly an allegorical work. So you may find parts of it a little difficult to understand, or relate to,' I explained, adding, 'Osman and I used to enjoy reading it very much.'

'Good night then. And Celik – thank you for welcoming me so warmly.' She kissed me on the cheek and was gone.

That night I lay awake staring out of the window at the night sky. I could hardly believe that Sarah was separated from me by only a wall. I could still feel the warmth on my cheek where her lips had touched my skin. I kept drifting in and out of sleep with a feeling of amazement and not knowing why until I remembered and then I felt almost unable to contain the joy. I planned to take her to all the places she wanted to visit and amaze her with my organisational ability. I would allow nothing to upset her or spoil her pleasure in any way.

The next day we walked around Bebek and explored the shops and sat by the Bosphorus watching the fishing boats, breathing in the cool salty air. Then we walked to Rumeli Castle and climbed to the highest tower and listened to the call to prayer coming from every direction.

We went to the Grand Bazaar and I took her to a small dusty shop specialising in amber jewellery. I used to go there with Lale sometimes on our expeditions to the bazaar. I remembered that Lale had got some ear-rings made out of old prayer beads while I had sat and watched, fascinated with the jeweller's delicacy in crafting the ear-rings with fingers like giant sausages. I wanted Sarah to see the process and I told her to choose two beads and I would have them made into ear-rings as a gift for her. The jeweller cleared a space for her on a seat and sent out for some tea while she chose the beads.

In the meantime people wandered into the shop to look over her shoulder to see what she was doing or made transactions with the shop-keeper. There were arms crossing over her head and under it as money was exchanged and more people pressed into the tiny space. I watched anxiously in case she was disturbed by the crush but she appeared unruffled. At last she picked two beads and as we watched them being turned into ear-rings, a boy arrived balancing a tray of tea glasses on his head. He set one down in front of Sarah and handed one to me. Sarah did not immediately pick hers up as she was so interested in what the jeweller was doing and he unthinkingly reached out and drank the tea himself. When he realised what he had done he was overcome with embarrassment and offered profuse apologies and insisted on ordering another cup for Sarah. So we had no option but to wait a further ten minutes until the tea arrived.

In the meantime she asked him questions about his craft and I directed the questions to him in Turkish. He told me he had been working at it for twenty-five years. He poked around on dusty shelves for little boxes containing minute bits of silver and twisted them onto the beads. At the finish, with a little bow, he presented her with an exquisite pair of ear-rings. She was very happy with them and as she tried them on, more people came into the shop to admire them. She laughed with amusement at this.

'English people would never dream of doing anything so uninhibited as admiring someone else's purchase.'

I knew exactly what she meant and I burst out laughing.

That night I lay in bed, going over each detail of our day together. I lay very still to see if I could hear her breathing in the next room, but of course I couldn't. I drifted off to sleep only to jerk awake several times during the night, disorientated and anxious. I actually pinched the skin on my arms to wake myself up so I would know whether or not I was dreaming.

In the morning I got up early to prepare breakfast as usual and I smelt the slightest hint of Sarah's perfume in the air. I closed my eyes, breathing it in, whispering, 'She's here, in my home.' But when she actually came into the kitchen and stood behind me to sniff the tomatoes I was frying I was overwhelmed by her closeness and I moved away on the pretext of getting the salt.

We went to Topkapi Palace and joined a tour group there. There were too many people so the tour was rushed and at the end Sarah asked the guide if he would take us back and show us some of the rooms not normally open to the public and she would pay him to do so. He replied regretfully that he could not, she would have to get special permission from the administration office and directed us to it.

We crossed the courtyard and entered the building and knocked on the manager's door. A woman emerged and said she was in charge of the harem. Using all my charm and my most refined Turkish I explained that Sarah was a journalist from London and she wanted to write about the harem. Would it be possible to arrange a private tour? She shook her head reluctantly and said that permission was sometimes given but it took a long time and had to go through the Ministry of Tourism in Ankara. Again I cajoled and persuaded, pleased at the opportunity to show Sarah the power of my language. At last the woman agreed to get permission from the manager and said she would take the responsibility of showing us around herself. And if she wasn't there then she would leave instructions for her friend. She told us to come back on Monday after telephoning first to confirm it. Sarah, delighted by our success thanked her and as we left she said, 'Celik! What an amazing man you are!' I had to turn my head away to hide my pleasure.

Next day we took a boat trip to Scutari and saw the barracks where Florence Nightingale had worked. We tried to see her room and were taken to the officer in charge but he sadly informed us that it was under construction at present as a museum so we were not allowed to enter. I was sad too that on this occasion my language had failed but we walked around the cemeteries instead and I was able to show her the graves of those soldiers who had died in the Crimean war.

'There are so many cemeteries in Istanbul,' she commented, 'and so many close to the living quarters of people.'

'Well, as Moslems we do not cremate our dead. It is forbidden. And there are many people in Istanbul! Also we do not fear death so why should we not have our cemeteries built close to where we live?'

'But it's so depressing.'

'No. It serves as a reminder that we are here on this earth only a short time.'

On Monday morning I phoned the manager of the harem to confirm our visit. She was not there but her friend, Neriman, with whom she had left instructions, informed me that she would take us around and we could come straight through the gates without paying. The guards would be informed of our arrival.

I was delighted at our success so far. When we entered the palace offices again I knocked on the same door and asked for Neriman Hanim. A large woman in black asked, 'Why do you want to see her?'

I explained that she was going to take us around the harem.

The woman snapped, 'You have no right to be looking around the harem. Neriman Hanim has not the authority to show you. You should have applied to the manager. Wait outside.' She angrily snatched up the phone.

I went back to Sarah in the hall and said quietly, 'I think we've blown it. She did not know of our visit. I think I've blown it!'

A short while later the woman bustled out of the office and abruptly directed us to Neriman's office upstairs. Neriman opened the door, full of apologies and said that her friend had been going to show us the rooms as a special favour, but now the woman downstairs, who was the secretary to the manager of the museum had found out, it looked as though we would not be able to see them. She herself had been trying to get hold of the manager all morning to get his permission but he was busy. She was very embarrassed and I was upset to see the look of disappointment on Sarah's face. I thought quickly about how I might recover the situation. Neriman said she had to leave us for ten minutes and she would send us a glass of tea. In a few minutes the tea arrived and we drank it dejectedly. Three quarters of an hour later she came back and said she had arranged for us to go to the manager of the museum to ask his permission in person.

We were shown into a huge room with elaborate dark furniture edged in gilt and enormous portraits of Ataturk on the walls. The manager sat in his throne talking to another man who was trying to get permission to take some photographs inside the palace for advertising purposes. The manager replied that it was not allowed. There was a special directive from Ankara which specifically stated that it was not allowed, but he could take photographs outside which would be more interesting anyway. This interchange went on for twenty minutes while Neriman sat still and quiet and the manager completely ignored us.

After the advertising man had gone he turned to me and asked abruptly, 'How can I help you?'

Again I explained how my friend was a journalist and would like to see the rooms of the harem not normally shown to the public so she could write about them for her newspaper.

He said, 'But why? They are no different from the public rooms. When you have seen those you know what the rest looks like.'

At this Sarah asked him if he spoke English.

'Of course,' he replied.

'I would like to feel the atmosphere of the whole harem complex, which is not possible by viewing only a few selected rooms,' she said.

He replied that he could not understand her, she talked too quickly. So I had to translate. He told her again that all the rooms were the same. She would not gain any more understanding by seeing any others. And in any case, some were not in a good state of repair. And he would not like the public to see rooms which had not been properly restored.

Then to me he said, 'I do not trust journalists. Not seventy percent of them, not ninety percent of them, but one hundred percent of them write bad things about the harem.'

'This lady would not write anything bad,' I said.

'Even if they think they are writing something good, it is bad,' he replied. 'It gives the wrong impression. And some of these rooms are very dirty and she will say we are not taking care of them properly.'

I turned to Sarah to translate all this and he interrupted hastily, 'No, no! If you tell her that it will be as if she has seen them for herself. She will print it.'

In the end, as if he were granting us a special favour, he agreed to let us see a few extra rooms and gave Neriman careful instructions about which rooms to avoid. Sarah shook his hand and smiled at him as we left his office and thanked him for his cooperation. I thought, stupid Ataturk idiot!

As we walked to the harem, Neriman said, 'You see what it is like? It is not easy working here. So much bureaucracy. But there is no point in getting upset. That does not help.'

I thanked her for all her efforts and added, in English, 'This woman is driving me crazy. Ever since she came here all she wants to see are harems. All she wants to talk about is harems!'

We all laughed and in good humour she proceeded to show us the rooms.

She led us through secluded courtyards and dusty rooms and through grand rooms overlooking high-walled gardens, and small dark cells at the top of narrow winding stairs, telling us the history of each room we entered. In one small room, fairly well-preserved except for the dust, she said it had belonged to Mirimah.

'Sulieman's favourite daughter?' Sarah asked.

Neriman nodded in surprise. 'She knows?'

'How did you know that?' I laughed. 'I myself do not know the names of the sultans' children.'

'I told you, I've been doing a lot of reading.'

We continued our tour and Neriman showed us rooms which I had heard the manager specifically tell her to avoid. She said, 'These are on me!' and smiled at me.

Standing for a moment in one of the upstairs rooms staring out over a forlorn weed-tangled garden, Sarah said, 'Just think. We are standing in what was once the most forbidden place on earth. No outsider had even entered this place until early this century. Imagine the scheming and plotting that must have gone on in this very spot. The fears and hopes. I wonder what they were like, those women.'

Neriman glanced at me and smiled. I shook my head.

Finally, we thanked Neriman for her time and trouble and as we walked away from Topkapi, Sarah said, 'I am so grateful you were able to do that for me Celik.'

I was still smarting from the way that manager had treated us so that my pleasure at Sarah's words was diminished. 'I'm sorry you were subjected to all that nonsense from that idiot.'

'He was only doing his job.'

'He was an Ataturk idiot! Believe me I know how to recognise those people. That was the type I had to deal with during my trial. Do you know why he was so superior with me? Because he knew I am a Moslem. Always I have to endure that kind of treatment from those people.'

'How could he possibly know that?'

'Because I wear a beard. And by my manner.'

'But I thought all Turks were Moslems.'

'The statistics may say ninety nine percent of Turks are Moslems but in reality the percentage is much smaller than that. Those people, they are not Moslems. They are Ataturk men.' I felt my good mood disintegrating but continued, 'I will never get managerial status in my own country because I am a practising Moslem. The élite of this country are not practising Moslems and they despise those who are.'

'But why?'

I frowned, not wanting to continue this discussion but I decided to explain. 'While I was working in Ankara, I had to entertain an important American customer, a responsibility I shared with three colleagues. One of them, a man named Talat, suggested we carry on our business discussions over lunch and drinks. I told him I could not, for as a Moslem I do not drink alcohol anyway, and as it was Ramadan I was fasting. He got very annoyed and told me I should just go with them and not eat or drink anything if I was so set on sticking to my principles.

'I told him that would be intolerable for me, to stand around watching others eating and drinking while I was fasting. And besides it would be embarrassing to the customer. At this, he got really angry and left me. So I went back to the office on my own, intending to rejoin the discussions after lunch. Two hours later he stormed in and shouted at me in front of everyone. "You miserable creature. How could you leave us like that? You have a stingy soul!"

'I got up and walked out of the office and refused to speak to him for several days after that. At last he came to me and apologised. I accepted his apology because we had to continue working together, but I did not forgive him. And soon afterwards I requested a transfer to the Istanbul office where I knew and liked the people I worked with.'

Sarah looked at me in amazement. I felt my throat tightening.

'Now, please! No more questions. Especially about harems. I do not want to even think about harems!'

We walked to Suleiman's mosque in silence. The air was warm and soft and the leaves glowed red and golden on the trees. I took her arm to help her through the crowds of people, past the shoe-shiners and braziers of roasting chestnuts and letter writers sitting with their old battered typewriters writing documents for the illiterate peasants who swarmed daily into the city, and felt myself grow calmer.

We stood outside the tomb of Roxelana, the favourite wife of Sulieman and I said, 'They are very famous for their love, these two. Many poems and stories were written about them.'

'I know,' Sarah replied, 'but it isn't known whether she really loved him or whether, to make the best of the awful situation she was in, she just used him for her own purposes.'

'What do you mean?'

'She may have been his favourite but like all other favourites she had to live with the fear that her sons would end up strangled by the bowstring on their father's death.'

'No, no, no! You don't know anything about it!' I protested.

'To remove this danger she plotted against Mustapha, Sulieman's heir and falsely implicated him in a plot against his father. Sulieman had him strangled.'

I looked at her in astonishment. 'How did you know that? I have never heard that.'

'It's in all the history books.'

'You can't believe everything you read. Some of those books were written with an Ataturk bias to discredit the Ottomans. I have read enough and what you say is not true. Those Ottoman sultans, they were not like ordinary people. Besides which, they were accountable for their actions. There was no divine right of kings in the Turkish tradition as there was in Europe. They could not just go around slaughtering their sons as they chose.'

She didn't answer but plainly she was thinking over what I had said and I knew that the topic I had been so anxious to avoid would not be put off for much longer. As we climbed the steps to the mosque, a man in front of me threw down a cigarette butt. All my frustration boiled over at the sight of this careless act and I said sharply, 'Excuse me, you should not throw down your used cigarettes in this place.'

He looked at me and then stared at the crumpled cigarette as if he were seeing it for the first time. 'You are right,' he replied. 'I should not have done that.' He picked it up and put it in his pocket. 'With God's help I will not do it again.'

'May Allah go with you,' I said as he went on his way.

To Sarah I said, 'If you wish to go inside the mosque you must cover your head.'

She looked surprised. 'But I went in and out of mosques on my first visit here and no one seemed to worry about that.'

'I wish to pray in this mosque,' I answered sharply. 'I can not pray here if you go in without covering your head. However, if you do not want to, then go in and I shall remain outside until you come out.'

'That won't be necessary,' she said a little coolly, and she pulled the blue silk scarf off her neck and tied it over her head.

I was angry at my boorishness but by now it was too late to recover the situation. There was a notice up at the main entrance informing tourists to go through the side entrance. As we walked to the door, one of the doorkeepers ran after her, 'Lady, lady, please use the other entrance.'

'The lady is with me,' I shouted at him. 'This is my mosque and I shall use any entrance I choose. Who are you to tell me which entrance to use?'

'Sir, I'm sorry,' he cringed. 'I didn't realise she was with you.'

'You had no right to speak to her! You should have spoken to me first!'

'You are right, but some of these foreigners don't know how to behave. See! She has not removed her shoes.'

I gestured to Sarah to step off the canvas and as she did so she adjusted the scarf around her head.

The doorkeeper tried to placate me, 'Oh, she is covering her head, that is very respectful.'

Ignoring him I took Sarah's arm and walked in with her.

The vast silent coolness of the mosque soothed my agitated heart and I knelt to pray as Sarah walked away to look at the tiles on the walls. She is embarrassed by my praying, I thought. She mustn't be. I'll teach her, but I must be patient.

CHAPTER ◆ NINETEEN

Next morning over breakfast I felt stiff and awkward. The previous day had stirred up feelings in me that I didn't want to acknowledge. I wished I could erase that day and start again. If Sarah noticed my embarrassment she didn't comment. We had olives and white cheese and tomatoes and cold meats and fresh bread, and I had bought lots of different types of jams.

'Celik, your breakfasts are out of this world!' she said. 'Do you eat like this every day?'

'Something like it – at weekends anyway. During the week I have no time so I wait till I get to the office and order food there. Try this jam please. The flavour is very delicate. It is made from rosepetals.'

When we finished she began to clear the table. Before I could open my mouth she said, 'This time I will do it and I won't listen to any more of your protests that I am a guest. It makes me feel lazy just sitting here while you do all the work.'

I laughed for I had anticipated this. 'I thought that if there was an argument you would win! So I have taken precautions.' I pulled out a pair of rubber gloves from a drawer in the kitchen. 'If I cannot prevent you from washing up at least I can protect your hands!'

She grinned and put on the gloves. 'I'm not used to being pampered. I was a farmer's daughter and a farmer's wife, you know.'

'But you are neither of those now,' I said.

'True, but a single mother doesn't get much pampering either.'

'But being a single mother is not the sum total of who you are,' I countered. 'Besides, you do not have to play that role here. Here, you are just Sarah.'

She turned to face me, her smile widening. 'What a delicious thought.'

We spent the morning exploring Yedicule (the castle of the seven towers) which forms part of the walls of Istanbul.

'Emperor Theodosious II built walls on either side of the victory arch – which had been erected by the Byzantine Emperor, Theodosious I – thus joining it to the city walls, and had four towers built. After the Conquest, Mehmet II added three more towers, bringing the number to seven. I spent a great deal of my childhood roaming this place, Sarah.'

The guide who took us around was well-informed though he told me he had left school when he was only twelve so he had not had a chance to learn much history, but he had picked up a lot of information from the historians who came to the museum. He told us that in Culieman's time each tower had been filled with treasure. It had also been used as a prison. He pointed out a field where the soldiers had at one time used prisoners as their target practice. He took us to one of the towers and led us through a dark, dank-smelling passage to an equally dismal hole, where the young sultan Osman had been kept prisoner. The only light available was when he struck a match. Then he took us to a larger room with wooden cages around the top of the walls and a wooden post in the middle of the floor. He showed us where it was pitted with holes.

'This is where they used to tie up the prisoners and shoot them with arrows,' he said, glancing at Sarah. 'And there,' pointing to the cages, 'the other prisoners watched what was happening. And here...' showing us a hole in the ground, 'is where Osman's head was chopped off and the blood drained away down this hole into the sea.'

'Oh my God, oh my God!' I whispered.

I did not translate the guide's last sentence to Sarah but from his explicit actions she knew what he had said and murmured, 'His head was sent back to his step-mother, Kosem. His ears had been sent to her earlier but she wasn't convinced he was dead until she had his head.'

The guide was about to launch off on another gory explanation but Sarah said in a quiet voice, 'I've had enough of this place. Let's go.'

When we emerged into the daylight I saw she was very pale. I touched her arm. 'Are you okay?'

She shivered. 'No! I almost passed out in there. The air positively reeks with evil.'

The guide, looking anxious, asked me what was wrong. Reluctantly, I repeated what Sarah said.

He shook his head emphatically. 'No! If we felt like that, we would not stay here! These are just stories. Nothing to do with the present.'

My mother's house was close to this place so we set off in that direction but after a few minutes of walking in silence Sarah stopped and leaned against a wall. Concerned, I touched her face. It was clammy and cold. I helped her to sit down on a stone.

'Hey! This is terrible. Even I felt something in that place but I did not expect you to react like this. It's my fault for taking you in there. I'm sorry.' I took her cold hands between my own and rubbed them to get her circulation going.

She shook her head, 'No, no. It's not your fault. I'm not squeamish, it's not that. When I was a child in England I used to go out in the fields with my grandfather looking for rabbits that were dying of myxomatosis. He showed me how to whack them on the head with a stone to put them out of their misery. And on the farm with Dave I sometimes had to slit a sick calf's throat.' She took a deep breath. 'It's the cruelty. The air in there was thick with it. It's the thought of what human beings are capable of doing to each other. And for what? A bit of extra land, a little more power. Look what happened to my ancestor simply because another woman's husband fell in love with her. She was lucky she drowned. The fire was her next destination.' She covered her face with her hands and to my astonishment I saw tears running between her fingers. 'I wonder if we really learn anything from history?'

I put my arm around her and drew her head onto my shoulder. 'No, I don't think so. But I believe another way of living is possible, and with God's help I'll find that way.'

I could feel the warmth of her neck through my shirt and the softness of her hands in mine. I did not want this moment to end, but she lifted her head, took a tissue out of her bag and wiped her eyes.

'I don't know what brought that on,' she said. 'I'm sorry.'

'There's nothing to apologise for,' I answered. 'We can stay here till you feel better. My mother is preparing a nice lunch for us but there's no hurry.'

She looked at me and smiled. Her face at least had some colour in it now. 'Thank you for being so sweet to me,' she said. 'You're a very sweet person,' and she leaned forward and kissed me on the cheek.

'Hey, man, I've been called a lot of things in my life, but never sweet,' I joked, to hide my pleasure. I helped her up and held her hand as we walked to my mother's house. 'In case you trip,' I said, 'this road is very rough.'

At my mother's house she made no mention of our visit to that prison and confined her questions to food and recipes.

I had asked Gül to meet us that evening for dinner at Rejan's, a popular Russian restaurant. She was going to bring her friend Kay who was staying with her and also taught at the same university. Sarah and I were first to arrive and sat at a table to wait. Sarah talked about the recipes my mother had given her and I nodded and tried to be interested, but I kept glancing at the door, feeling more and more nervous. Finally, more than half an hour late, Gül and Kay arrived. Gül was looking spectacular, as usual, in a short, tight, black leather skirt and red, low-cut blouse. Her thick, black hair was pulled back from her face and fastened with a tortoiseshell clip. Her beautiful red lips curved in a smile when she saw me and she waved her hand in greeting. She squeezed past the crammed-together tables, occasionally murmuring 'Excuse me', oblivious to the heads swivelling in her direction, and introduced herself and Kay to Sarah before I had a chance to open my mouth.

'And what have you been up to today?' she asked in a loud voice.

'Sightseeing,' replied Sarah, after a pause so minute that maybe I imagined it. 'It amazes me that so many of the ancient buildings are not even marked with a plaque. I suppose because they are still part of everyday life and people don't treat them with awe.'

I pulled out chairs for Gül and Kay and, ignoring Sarah's comment, Gül began to tell us about a party they had attended the previous weekend. With much laughter she added, 'They told me that I opened the window, stuck my head outside and threw up. I can't remember doing such a thing but I know I was definitely very drunk!'

I glanced at Sarah but her face betrayed nothing beyond polite interest. She was wearing a grey silk dress with a pale pink scarf tying back her blonde hair and beside her, Gül, who had looked so wonderfully dramatic on her entrance, suddenly looked tawdry and vulgar. I had never thought this about her before and a jolt of shock jarred through me. I had expected her to be very interested in Sarah and besiege her with questions, but, to my surprise and disappointment, she barely glanced at her. Sarah, on the other hand, was watching Gül intently. It seemed strange to hear Gül talk in English and I wondered if this was contributing to my feeling of disorientation. Her accent was good but Sarah commented that Kay's was perfect, though with an American accent. Kay explained that her father was a diplomat and she had spent nearly all her childhood in the USA coming back to Istanbul only six months ago. Sarah asked her if both her parents were Turkish because Kay's hair colouring was so light and she had blue eyes.

'Oh, yes, pure Turkish stock,' Kay replied. 'Turks are a mixture of bloodlines you see.'

'Or a bunch of mongrels, depending on how you look at it,' added Gül, quite unnecessarily, I thought.

Two men sitting at a nearby table gestured towards Gül and Kay and commented, 'Americans.' This made both women laugh uproariously.

Sarah didn't talk much during the meal and when she did she addressed her comments to Kay who seemed interested in her impressions of the city. To my relief she did not introduce harems or executions into the conversation. Gül almost completely ignored her but after dinner, inexplicably, she invited us back to her flat for coffee. I looked at Sarah uncertainly before I accepted the invitation but she said to Gül, 'Thank you. I would love to visit your house.'

Gül drove very fast and honked her horn continually. When someone honked back at her, both she and Kay held up two fingers. At this, I protested, 'Oh no, you shouldn't do that!' But they laughed. I cursed my stupidity in accepting this invitation.

As we entered Gül's flat, Gül disappeared leaving Kay to invite us in and show us where to leave our shoes. We went downstairs into what had been a basement but Gül had had it converted into a sitting room. She showed us the video recorder which her brother had bought her and asked me some questions about how to operate it. Then she disappeared to make coffee.

Over coffee Sarah started questioning Gül about her childhood, and Gül, delighted at any opportunity to talk about herself, told us how she had learnt to swim when her uncle took her out into the Bosphorus in a boat and dropped her into the water on the end of a rope.

'Do you still swim? After such an experience?' Sarah asked.

'Oh yes. Of course one can not swim in the Bosphorus now,' Gül laughed, 'it is too disgusting. I do not like tomatoes and banana skins floating beside me when I swim. Now I go to the Hilton to use their pool.'

The phone rang and Gül leapt up to answer it. She reappeared seconds later and mumbled something in Turkish to Kay. Kay excused herself saying she would take the call on the upstairs extension. She did not reappear during the remainder of our visit. Sarah admired the polished wooden floors with beautiful Turkish rugs scattered on them and asked Gül how she kept the floors so shiny.

'Oh I don't clean them!' laughed Gül. 'I have a woman to do that. How she manages it I don't know, for I have never watched her!'

'I like the effect,' Sarah replied. 'It's very welcoming. But with my two children I would never be able to keep the floor looking so clean.'

Gül looked surprised. 'You do your own cleaning?'

Sarah nodded. Gül glanced at me and rolled her eyes.

Without Kay the conversation limped along for another twenty minutes. As I was wondering how to terminate this visit without offending Gül, Sarah suddenly stood up saying she was tired and we must leave. She thanked Gül for the coffee but I noticed she did not say how nice it had been meeting her. I stood up feeling my neck flush red with embarrassment. Gül showed us to the door and called a brief goodnight before immediately shutting it.

In the taxi I realised I was holding my breath waiting for Sarah to comment. When she didn't, I said, trying to force a lightness into my voice, 'Well, what did you think of her?'

She gave a wry smile. 'Do you really want to hear?'

'That bad?' I laughed, though my stomach plummeted. I'd expected her to at least pretend to like Gül for my sake.

'She's the centre of her own universe. What else can I say? Best to leave it at that seeing she's your friend.'

I thought about this for a few minutes and answered, 'You are quite right. That describes her exactly.' I decided that when we got back to the flat I would tell Sarah about the history of my relationship with Gül.

I made us a cup of tea and while we sipped it I began at the beginning. Sarah listened without interruption to the whole, long saga. I ended with, 'I was very much in love with her once.'

Sarah looked at me. 'What a sad story. Was she the only person you've loved?'

I hesitated for a long time. She didn't urge me to speak but I found myself telling her about Lale. Again she listened without saying a word. When I finished, I saw, to my surprise, that there were tears in her eyes.

'Hey man!' I tried to joke away the tears. 'That was a long time ago.' And to change the subject I said, 'And what about you? How many times have you been in love?'

'I don't think I've ever been in love!' she said.

I raised my eyebrows. 'Come on, man!'

'When we moved back to England I went to a private girl's school. The main topic of conversation was boys and I wondered why the girls found them so fascinating. For me the end-of-year dances we had with the boys' school were absolute torture. The boys never asked me to dance and I saw that they liked girls who wore a lot of make-up, giggled a lot and agreed with everything they said. Those boys were never anything like the heroes in the books I read, people like Heathcliffe and Rochester! One year I tried putting make-up on to see what I looked like. I hated the greasy feel of it on my skin. I went to the dance and this skinny, spotty boy asked me to dance and trod all over my feet. Then, without any warning he leaned forward and kissed me and stuck his tongue in my mouth. I was so horrified I bit it.'

I looked at her in disbelief then roared with laughter.

'And what did he do?'

'He squealed then ran off holding his hanky to his mouth.' She wrinkled her nose. 'I could taste his blood on my teeth. I ran to the bathroom, washed my mouth out with cold water then went home. I decided if that was romance I wasn't interested! At university it wasn't any better so I preferred reading and listening to music on my own to going out. The boys my own age all seemed so juvenile. Then I met Simon and Alexandra. My friends kept asking which one I was in love with! That really used to annoy me because I didn't know how to explain that we just seemed to be on the same wavelength. One night I dreamed I was making love with Simon on a tropical beach but he kept turning into Alexandra! The next time I saw them I felt so guilty, but I dismissed the dream as being the result of all the teasing I got about them.'

Now we had started on this topic I could ask the question I had not yet dared to ask. 'And Dave?'

'After Simon and Alexandra left for Italy I was all on my own again, but for the first time in my life I felt lonely. Then Dave came along. He told me we had great conversations. At the time I was grateful that he didn't stop talking long enough to notice that I didn't actually say anything. He was very popular. Everywhere we went we were surrounded by people, all laughing at his jokes. Girls turned to stare at him every time we went anywhere. He was very tall, broad-shouldered and handsome and I reasoned that as I had to lose my virginity some time it may as well be to him.'

My heart skipped a beat when she said this but she didn't seem at all embarrassed by such an admission.

'The first time with Dave wasn't at all the way my friends had described it. In fact it was such a non-event I assumed it must be my fault, that I must be dysfunctional in some way. I didn't want to hurt his feelings so I pretended it was as fantastic for me as it seemed to be for him. After that, whenever we made love I pretended it was with Simon and that improved things a little. As they were out of the country by then it didn't seem quite as treacherous.'

By now my mouth was so dry I couldn't swallow and my tongue had stuck to the roof of my mouth but I managed to say, 'Then why did you marry him?'

'I don't ever remember agreeing to marry him. Dave and everybody else just assumed that this is what would happen. He had this way of taking over decisions and I, who could never make up my mind about anything, found opting out of responsibility very seductive. Everybody thought he was a great catch, everybody except my mother, that is.

'The fact that she didn't want me to marry him had an added attraction. I had never stopped blaming her for leaving dad. I thought she had put her own career ahead of her marriage. While I was growing up she pushed me to excel academically but I never felt I could reach her expectations. Now, of course, I know that she wanted to equip me to live my own life without ever having to depend on anyone, but she tried too hard to protect me from making the same mistakes she had. The result was I could never make a decision without first filtering it through her. In effect she chose my friends, my clothes, the books I read, the university I went to. Marrying Dave was the first time I made a decision on my own. The irony was that I didn't! I simply went along with what Dave wanted.'

She stood up and walked over to the window and looked out for so long that I wondered if she was crying. However, when she turned round again her eyes were dry, though sad.

'In New Zealand we bought a small dairy farm in the South Island, close to Dunedin. Dave worked very hard. I spent my days cooking enormous stews for the workers, and later, looking after our two babies. I visited the farm where I grew up. It had been subdivided and the old farmhouse no longer existed. I didn't recognise anything.

'Dave wanted four children. Even after I had three miscarriages he insisted we keep trying. His parents were killed in a car crash when he was very small and he spent his childhood being parcelled around to various relatives. He was desperate to create his own family.

'One day, I was chopping up meat for the workers' stew, one child in a sling on my back, the other on my nipple. I stared at the blood on my hands. Out of the window I could see the morning's washing flapping on the line. I saw my whole life stretching out in front of me like a long straight road with an unchanging landscape of washing lines and stews. At the end of the road was the setting sun, nothing else. I started taking the pill again and didn't tell Dave. My highlight was a fortnightly trip to the city library where I took out books on ancient Rome and Greece. Dave once asked me what I was reading so I started to tell him and read out an extract. When I finished I looked up to ask him his opinion. He was asleep in his chair!

'When the boys were old enough to go to kindergarten, I enrolled for a master's degree in ancient history and moved into a flat in the city, near the university, going home about once a term. After his initial objections about ancient history being the most useless qualification he could imagine for a farmer's wife, Dave accepted the situation on the grounds that he worked such long hours he hardly ever saw us anyway.'

This was the first time I had heard this part of Sarah's history and I listened to it incredulously. I began to form some idea of what kind of man her husband was that he would allow his wife and children to live away from him. As soon as I thought this I remembered that Gül had divorced her husband because of his attempts to control her. As I was struggling to accommodate these two points of view Sarah continued.

'For the second time in my life I was with people I felt compatible with – people who wanted to learn for the sheer joy of learning. I also found out something I'd never known before. That I wasn't shy at all, but I'd always accepted other people's judgements of me without questioning why they were making those judgements.

'Then I teamed up with three other women postgraduates who had small children and we rented a large house together. In the evenings we drank a lot of wine, listened to music, sang songs, discussed and argued about every subject under the sun. We shared the cooking, the cleaning, and looked after each other's children when someone was sick or wanted to go out. We kept each other going when we wanted to pull out of university because the workload was killing us and we said how wonderful it would be if marriage could be like this! When we completed our theses, we threw a huge party to celebrate and asked all our friends to bring a delicious dish. We decorated the house with enormous bunches of flowers and balloons and invited a magician to entertain us. We laughed so much we cried!

'When I arrived at the farm with my suitcases and my books and a few balloons I found a note from Dave in the kitchen to apologise for not being there to meet us but he'd be back after milking. There was also a large parcel wrapped up in brown paper with "welcome home" written in black felt pen. I opened it to find a new frying pan and a set of kitchen knives.

'After a month Dave said now that I had all that out of my system we should have another baby. I told him I wanted to go to England to see my mother. When she met me at the airport I fell into her arms and cried. That was when I knew I wasn't going back. And when I understood why she had left my father.'

All the time she stood there relating this story I watched her hands clasping and unclasping in front of her. The light from the window framed her face and made it difficult to see her features. I didn't know what to say to let her know that I completely understood. I searched for language that was beautiful and appropriate.

Before I could speak she walked away from the window and sat down beside me on the sofa. 'So, as you see, the sexual revolution of the sixties completely passed me by,' she laughed, though I detected no humour in the sound. 'While I was doing my master's degree I had a lot of time to make up. Sex without attachments.'

While I was trying to digest this new piece of information, tossed in so casually as if it were of no significance she asked, 'And what about you?'

Taken off guard by her directness I said, ambiguously, 'In my way of life it hasn't been possible to form attachments. Of any sort.'

CHAPTER • TWENTY

The lights from the ships glittered on the black water as the taxi hurtled across the Bosphorus Bridge to Scutari. I was in a relaxed mood and looking forward immensely to the play we were going to see. We had spent that day shopping and I had taught Sarah the art of bargaining. She had successfully bought a pair of silver sugar tongs for a third of the price the shopkeeper was asking so she was feeling very pleased with herself too. Now I heard her draw her breath in sharply and her hands gripped the edge of her seat.

I leaned forward and said to the driver, 'We would like to get there on time, but would prefer it to be in one piece.'

'No problem, no problem.' he grinned.

I touched Sarah's hand lightly, 'It's okay. These people know how to drive,' but I noticed she didn't breathe easily until the taxi screamed to a halt in a puddle in front of the theatre, scattering pigeons and splashing passers-by with oily water.

In the theatre I asked for the best seats in the house and we were shown to the front row. Sarah protested. 'If we stay here we'll get a crick in our necks. Let's move back.'

'But these are the best seats,' I said. 'They gave us the best seats because you are a beautiful European woman!'

'Rubbish,' she laughed, 'We can see only their feet here!'

I was embarrassed by my stupidity, for of course she was right. She found seats in the middle row and the usher told me he might have to move us if someone else claimed the seats. Soon afterwards another group did. The usher asked if we would mind moving and I saw an opportunity to recover the situation by using my most charming language.

'Well you see, we like it here,' I said. 'We don't want to move.'

The usher scratched his head and stared at our tickets as if they might give him inspiration, while the group patiently waited. At last he said, 'Okay, just shove on down a bit.'

We did and the other group happily fitted in on the end of the row. The second usher called to him. 'What if these seats are claimed too?'

'Then we'll move them back a bit,' his friend replied.

To my delight Sarah was doubled up with laughter by this time, 'I don't believe this!'

'Actually there is some kind of order,' I explained. 'I can see that you think our system here is unstructured and random but in fact there is a system operating which may not be apparent to you.'

She wiped tears of laughter from her eyes as we settled down to watch the play.

I leaned towards her so that I could whisper the translation. I was close enough to smell her skin and feel the warmth emanating from it. The play concerned the problems of a contemporary Turkish family which was about to be evicted from their apartment because the landlord was selling the property. The mother was trying to find her daughter a husband by advertising in the paper. The entanglements that followed as all the stereotypes of modern Turkish society were portrayed left us aching with laughter.

We left the theatre smiling and relaxed and I enjoyed the curious glances that were directed towards us, though Sarah didn't appear to notice. In the taxi she asked me to clarify some points of the play and I was happy to explain these elements of Turkish society. This led on to a discussion about the role of women in Turkey in the context of the play.

'It seems then,' said Sarah, 'that the mentality of the harem still lingers. I suppose it's easy enough to change laws but to change the mentality of a nation is something else again.'

'In Islam there is no harem mentality,' I responded. 'Women have equal opportunities here. They were admitted to the courts as judges long before it happened in England, for example!'

'Well of course a few gifted women were able to get themselves represented in the professions,' she replied, 'but that doesn't change things for the majority of women.'

'Women have always held a great deal of power in the home here, Sarah.

Women were never slaves. They owned their own property when in England a woman's property automatically became her husband's upon marriage. They had the right to divorce.'

'I don't dispute that. But under Islamic law husbands were able to divorce their wives without any reason – just cast them off. The wives on the other hand had to take the men to court and prove there were grounds for divorce.'

'That law was to protect the woman. If a woman was dragged through the court then she would lose her reputation. But it was considered necessary to expose the behaviour of the man publicly so that no one else would want to marry him.'

'The point I'm making is that this is still a male-dominated society and half the population is kept in subjugation.'

'It might seem like that to you but you are judging from the viewpoint of a middle-class English woman. It doesn't automatically make you right. There are other ways of life equally valid. You have to look at them within the context of their own culture. In Islam there is no concept of oppressed women. Moslem women would say you are oppressed!'

She was quiet for a few minutes and I added, 'As for this... this harem mentality, you seem to have the idea that the sultans captured and imprisoned hundreds of helpless women and kept them in prison for their own pleasure.'

She raised her eyebrows. 'And didn't they?'

'No! Those sultans, they were not like ordinary human beings. They were God's shadow on earth – holy men. They had only one wife in most cases. If they had more than one there was a good reason for it. For instance, if the woman was infertile the law allowed a man to have children by another woman.'

'And the same applied if a husband was infertile? The wife could take a second husband?' There was a sarcastic edge to her voice.

'Look,' I said in exasperation, 'you don't understand. Please don't presume to tell me the customs of my own country.'

'I thought we were having a discussion,' she said, indignantly, 'so that I could learn from it.'

She had a point there so I breathed deeply and said, 'I've already explained that many of those books you read were written by Europeans who were judging another culture from their own biased viewpoint. And some were written by Turks with an Ataturk bias.'

'Is that how you explain all those children put to death by the heir to the throne when their father died?'

'Children were not put to death Sarah! Occasionally it happened that a brother who was causing civil war would be put to death – to prevent more bloodshed.'

'Let's go to Selim's tomb then, in the garden of St Sophia, and count the little graves there. There were nineteen siblings put to death by Mehmet III. He listened to them being strangled in another room and saw them laid out in their coffins afterwards. It's recorded that he wept. Even the population of Istanbul, who were used to violence, did not sanction the murder of innocent children. It's recorded by one of the writers of the day that "the angels in heaven heard the mourning cries of the people for the deaths of those children".'

I was feeling horribly upset now. Although I still tried to speak slowly and calmly my voice shook. 'What would those graves prove? In those days lots of children died from plagues.'

'Yes, but those murders are recorded in every single book I read on the topic. Would you believe it if you were convinced of the authenticity of the source?'

'It doesn't matter whether or not I believe it. It wouldn't change anything. If the source is biased then all the historians who've taken their so-called facts from that source are biased.'

I was so dismayed I couldn't continue. What more could I possibly say to refute such an accusation?

'You say the sultans were holy,' she went on, 'and I saw you were praying at the tomb of Mehmet the Conqueror, yet he was hardly holy!'

'What is that supposed to mean?' I managed to say.

'In the books I read he was portrayed as being quite depraved. He had a couple of boys beheaded for refusing his bed. I'll give you the source if you want to check it.'

'I don't want to check it! It wouldn't change anything if I did! Why are you doing this Sarah?' I could not now control my rapidly rising voice and I saw the taxi driver glancing nervously at us in his rear view mirror. But I couldn't help myself.

'How do you imagine that a sultan could behave in a degenerate way without everyone around him knowing? Do you think he would be able to get away with it? Do you think he was not answerable to God for what he did?'

She threw up her hands. 'I don't understand why you should feel so personally involved with events that happened centuries ago. I don't feel it necessary to vindicate Henry VIII!'

She was staring at me but I turned away to look out of the window.

'There is really no point in continuing this discussion.'

'Well, no. Not if you insist on keeping a closed mind!'

Now I turned to her and shouted, 'What would satisfy you then? That I should change my beliefs? That I should change my religion?'

'Don't be ridiculous!'

I laughed bitterly. 'You are not the first person to say that to me. It does not hurt me that you have said that.'

She folded her arms and looked out of the window for the rest of the journey. When the taxi stopped outside my apartment the driver looked relieved but he gave me a sympathetic glance. I threw the money on to the seat beside him and slammed the door as I got out.

Inside the apartment Sarah sat down on the sofa and, keeping her back to me, read the programme we had brought from the theatre. I asked her if she would like a cup of salep. She shook her head. I went into the kitchen and made some anyway, cursing under my breath. I went back in and set a cup beside her and sat down in the chair opposite with my own cup.

I looked at her for a minute and said quietly, 'I am Celik. I am a Moslem, and a Turk. You are Sarah, and English, and have no religion. We are two people from two different cultures. Different tribes if you like, with a totally different outlook on life. But still we are human beings. We both must eat and laugh and love and go to the toilet.'

I saw a smile creep over her mouth. She looked up at me. 'I'm sorry I said you were ridiculous. That was very rude of me. I'm your guest here. I had no right to speak to you like that. It was a terrible abuse of your hospitality and kindness.'

'Don't be sorry. Maybe you're right. And you are not just a guest here so there is no need for you to be on your best behaviour.'

She stared at me, looking troubled. 'Well, maybe I have got it all wrong. This is your culture, not mine, but I don't understand the way you think.'

I sighed. 'For years my brother and I have been studying key concepts in the Koran. Using my work in that area as a basis I have been trying to develop a functional language that one day can be used by all human beings to identify themselves as they are, in their cultures, to promote understanding, love and tolerance amongst nations. That is what I meant when we sat outside Yedicule and I told you I believed we did not learn from history's mistakes but that I also believed it was possible to live in another way. Try to understand my outburst tonight in that context.'

'Can we start again then?'

I nodded. 'Of course.'

'But now I'm pretty exhausted, so I'll say goodnight.' She stood up and touched my arm as she passed by my chair. 'Sweet dreams. And thank you for a lovely day.'

'My pleasure.'

I sat still and listened to her door click shut, then covered my face with my hands.

I couldn't sleep. Every time I shut my eyes I saw the blackness of Yedicule. Smelled blood. In the darkness I was crawling beneath the sheer walls of a high building with lighted windows. A sickness rose in my heart. Then I heard a scream. The sound went on and on and I knew it was coming from my own throat but I couldn't stop it. Then I heard another voice and someone was shaking me, 'It's all right. It's all right.'

I struggled to sit up, disorientated and sweating, tears streaming from my eyes. 'You were having a nightmare.' Sarah's voice, closer this time.

'Did I wake you?' My voice sounded loud in my ears while the echoes of those other horrors faded away.

'You were crying.'

I held my head. 'I was dreaming of those murdered children.'

'What?'

'I feel responsible. You were blaming me for those deaths.'

She put her hand on my arm. 'But that's nonsense! How could I blame you for something that happened centuries ago? Why should you feel responsible?'

'I don't understand it myself,' I wept. 'I felt responsible about the Armenian massacres when I read about them too. When I hear a news report about soldiers anywhere in the world killing and maiming people then I feel guilty. I am a human being and a crime committed by another human being is my crime also.'

Her grip on my arm tightened. 'I'm sorry, I'm sorry, I'm so sorry.'

I smelt talcum powder on her skin and felt the warmth and softness of her against my cold body. But the sweetness was mixed up with anger and horror and fear. Without stopping to think I touched her face with my hand and kissed her eyes, her nose, her cheeks. I stroked her hair. She leaned against me and my hand touched her breast and I felt the warmth and softness there. I pulled her down beside me and wrapped the blankets around her and held her close. 'Your warmth,' I said, 'everything about you is warmth and softness and sweetness.'

She didn't reply but kissed me on the lips so that I felt dizzy with pleasure.

'No woman has ever held me like this, Sarah. Not one.' I smelt her skin and felt the smoothness of its texture and my mouth moved over her neck and shoulders and I traced her collar bones with my tongue. 'Look at this beauty! Oh look at this beauty!' My hand covered her whole breast and my fingers touched her nipple. I could hardly endure the emotions that were breaking over me. I fastened my lips around her nipple and sucked gently. She moaned and this gave me feelings of excitement that I had not known existed. I pulled her nightdress off her shoulders and gazed at her breasts. 'You even taste sweet,' I said, and I sucked her nipples again trying to draw sweet milk out of them. My hand caressed her arms, her back, her shoulders, and moved under her nightdress to the creamy skin of her belly and down to the soft hair beneath. She opened her thighs and I slipped my hand between them and felt the warm folds of flesh, tracing every secret crevice with the lightest touch of my fingertips. She felt slippery wet and warm as I started to enter her. Her thighs moved rhythmically beneath me and her breath sounded urgent in my ear. I was overcome with so many unaccustomed emotions that at the moment I was inside her my seed spurted into her womb.

I lay on top of her until the trembling in my limbs stopped and I murmured, 'Don't leave me or I will die.' Then I fell asleep, still clinging to her body.

CHAPTER
◆ TWENTY ONE

For the next three days we stayed in the flat making love. We got out of bed from time to time to take a shower together and cook a meal. We walked naked around the flat for there seemed to be no point in getting dressed. By the end of three days we were satiated with love. I would have happily stayed there forever but Sarah wanted to go to Bursa, the old capital of the Ottomans and from there take a bus to Ankara. From Ankara we could explore Central Anatolia and see the whirling rituals of the Mevlevi in December.

After a boat trip to Yalova, we found a dolmus to take us to the hotel in Bursa. I had picked that particular hotel because of its beautiful Roman baths.

As soon as we had settled in our room I booked half an hour in the baths. Towelling robes were sent up and we put these on and made our way along the landing to the lift. This took us down directly to the baths. The floor and walls of the foyer were covered in blue and white tiles and a little fountain played in the centre. The attendant unlocked the door to our bath and we entered the cool room where he laid out towels on the couch. From there we went into the domed room of the bath itself.

I showed Sarah how to cleanse herself before entering by scrubbing herself all over with a rough linen cloth.

'In the old days this was made of horse hair,' I explained. 'Then you rinse yourself with that little metal dish attached to the fountain in the side of the wall.' I finished first and slid into the steaming hot water. 'Hurry up, this is heaven!' I called.

She stood up and walked towards the water smiling with anticipation. She tested the water with her toe, wincing at the unexpected hotness. To stop my mocking she quickly slid in. I caught her in my arms. We separated and turned and floated away and came back together again. When we started to feel too hot we climbed out and began the second cleansing and we scrubbed each other till our skin was red and glowing and then sluiced more water over each other from the metal bowls. Into the water for a second time and we splashed and turned and twisted, abandoning ourselves to the pleasure of the heat, the privacy. Our laughter echoed around the dome. I wondered how all my colleagues would react if they could see me now. I said to Sarah, 'Can you believe that some people think I don't like women? That I must be gay or something.'

She laughed.

'Maybe I should take some pictures and pass them around,' I joked.

'To prove what to whom?' she said. 'And for what purpose? You are who you are. If people like to speculate about you it shows the lack of substance in their own lives, not yours.'

'Lale said something of the sort once,' I told her. 'She was born into the wrong society, I think.'

'Oh? So are you admitting...?'

'Pax!' I said at once. 'No arguments please. Not in this place.'

She inclined her head in agreement.

'But I sometimes wonder what her life would have been like if she'd lived,' I said. 'She didn't want to get married again. I could never understand why.'

'Perhaps she just wanted to live alone,' said Sarah, 'or maybe she preferred women.'

I looked at her, astonished. 'What! Oh come on! She was beautiful.'

'What's that got to do with it? Alexandra is beautiful too.'

With a shock I realised I had put Alexandra right out of my mind and I did not welcome her re-introduction. However, as Sarah had brought up the subject I decided to pursue it.

'How is it she left her husband? You said he was very handsome.'

She dived under the water and came up shaking her wet hair to get rid of the drops running into her eyes. 'So was Dave.'

'But you didn't leave him for a woman?' I joked.

She shrugged, 'Well, she left him for lots of reasons.'

'Such as?' I persisted.

'He wanted children, she didn't.'

'She doesn't like children? I can't believe this!'

'Oh she loves children, but she wanted to continue with her career, and children and travelling the way she did weren't compatible.'

I struggled to understand this concept.

'He wanted her to make a home for him. Bake cakes. Entertain his colleagues.' She laughed, 'Simon was more like Dave than I could possibly have imagined during all those intense conversations we had on the meaning of life. It seems that Simon resented that she earned more than he did and was better known than he was. Some of her photographs gave him nightmares, he said, so he asked her to stop taking them. She diminished herself to become the kind of wife he wanted. She said she felt like a tree that had been pruned so much its shape had become unrecognisable.' She smiled again, but there was no reflecting smile in her eyes.

'Then she found out he was having an affair with one of his students. So she left him in Italy and went to work in Vancouver. A year later, at her first exhibition in years, she met Shanti. While they were together her work production increased. She said even the sex was better.'

I decided not to comment on this but privately I felt disgusted. Sarah, on the other hand, seemed to think there was nothing unusual in what she had just said. Well, I reminded myself, she came from a degenerate culture.

'My mother, on the other hand, never got involved with anyone after my father.'

'So did she prefer women too?' I smiled, to hide my distaste.

'No. She told me she loved my father too much to want to end up hating him. That's why she left, because as long as she lived with him she felt she was wearing someone else's skin.'

I shook my head. 'That makes no sense to me, that she should leave him because she loved him.'

'No? Well, that's because you don't know my mother.'

'True. There's an analogy in there somewhere about why Islam makes no sense to you,' I said.

She grinned. 'Touché.'

I climbed out of the water. 'Come on, it's time for the third cleansing. At this stage your skin begins to feel like silk because all the impurities have been steamed out and scrubbed away. Lie down and I'll give you a massage.'

She lay down on her stomach on the hot wet floor while I massaged her neck and shoulders and slowly moved down to her ankles. Then she turned over and I started again from her neck. I leaned over her and licked the water off her breasts and belly.

'How could a woman prefer this from another woman?' I asked. 'Does it make any sense to you?'

She paused for a minute, then said, 'Well, my first affair was with a woman.'

At first I thought she was joking, then when I saw she was not I sat bolt upright. 'You what?'

'Don't look so shocked! It was just a part of the process of liberating myself.'

I felt winded by this revelation and said, appalled, 'Why on earth are you telling me this now, in this place and at this time?'

'Because I don't want any false assumptions between us. To use your own expression, I'm identifying myself as I am. If you can't accept that between individuals, then how on earth can you hope to promote tolerance among nations through your functional language?'

I searched her face to see if she was mocking me but her eyes betrayed nothing of the sort. I could not argue with her logic but I wished I had not had to hear this. I didn't even want to think about it. I knew I should have been sick with disgust, but in fact my throat was aching with longing, and all I felt was, inexplicably, mounting excitement. I lowered my head to her belly and nuzzled with my lips until I found the silky flesh I was searching for. She tasted sweet here too and I licked her sweetness with my tongue until I could take the swelling tip into my mouth. She began moaning and dug her fingernails into my head. Her excitement aroused me so much that it needed all my self-control to stop biting her. She arched her back and cried out. She pulled me up till I was lying on her and in her. My body moved in slow rhythm over hers because I wanted this sensation to last forever. Then the lights flickered on and off reminding us it was time to go.

'First we'll come before we go,' she laughed and rolled over till she was on top of me. The tension drained out of my body with my jet of semen and left only warmth and softness. I reached out to hold her close but she leapt off me and threw me a towel. I stood up, groaning, 'Too soon, too soon!'

As we left the room the bath attendant inclined his head and said, smiling, 'Sihhatler olsun.'

I said to Sarah, 'He says may it be health to you.'

She laughed, 'What 'it' is he referring to?'

I remembered the echoing dome and the cries of our lovemaking.

'Oh my God!' I said.

The three days we spent in Bursa will remain in my memory as the sweetest in my life. Each new morning we began with a Turkish bath then went into the hotel restaurant for a delicious breakfast of goat's cheese, olives and fresh bread. Hours of walking round Bursa in the pale winter sunshine, eating roasted chestnuts from smoking braziers, drinking cinnamon scented salep from street stalls, stopping in kebab houses for lunch, travelling up the pine-covered slopes of Mount Olympus by cable car with Sarah wanting to know how the snow was transported from there to Istanbul for the sultans' sherbets without melting. And all the time laughing, and talking, talking, talking.

We visited all the main mosques in the city and the tombs of the early Ottomans. When we asked a man for directions to the tomb of Osman he took us there himself in his car. We entered the tomb of Mustafa, son of Suleiman, and read on a plaque the story of how he had been tricked by Roxelana and strangled by his father as a result. I translated it reluctantly for Sarah but she just nodded. However I was upset and told her, 'That story should not have been written here in this sacred place. It is very wrong to speak so of the dead. That woman can not defend herself now.' Sarah squeezed my hand and laid her head on my shoulder. The tightness around my mouth softened and I kissed the top of her head.

We were sad to leave Bursa, but anticipated with excitement our journey to Ankara. The bus station was crowded with the usual touts, loudly trying to sell us tickets for the bus company they represented. I reserved seats at the front of the bus as I knew we would have problems with the smoke and these were the only windows that opened.

As the bus started, only half an hour late, we settled back in our seats and prepared to enjoy the journey. Apart from two peasant women in the back all the other passengers were men. They all stared at Sarah as they entered the bus, then stared at me with envy in their eyes. I felt my chest swell with pride. Within minutes however everyone on the bus had lit their cigarettes. Sarah opened the window a few inches. The man in the seat opposite us immediately leaned over and said, 'Please would you mind closing the window. It is cold.'

'I know,' I replied, 'but we do not like the smoke.'

He hesitated then said, 'I myself do not smoke but it is the custom in this country.'

'I'm sorry,' I said, 'I can not help you. In Britain hardly anyone smokes and this lady is not used to it.'

He was silent for a while then the bus stopped at a café so we could all get out and have a glass of tea. When we got back in, the window was closed. Sarah opened it again. Within minutes the steward, on the pretext of adjusting the outside mirror, leaned over and closed it.

Sarah smiled sweetly and said, 'Hier, hier!' and opened it. The poor steward could do nothing except disguise his misery by sprinkling cologne on our hands. The man opposite now leaned over and asked me to tell Sarah to close the window. I told him to tell her himself and in English he said, 'Excuse me madam but would you please close the window.'

She replied apologetically that she could not because of the smoke. He then appealed to the bus driver to ask her to close the window and when the driver repeated his request to me I said, 'Sure, we will close the window if you ask all these people to stop smoking.'

He glanced at all the passengers puffing away at their cigarettes and shrugged. The two men immediately behind us said, 'We'll put out our cigarettes. We do not want to cause a fight.'

Sarah closed the window a fraction. But still the man opposite was not satisfied and he launched into a bitter tirade.

'What sort of man are you to let a woman get away with that! You call yourself a man? What kind of a man would let himself be dictated to by a woman? A spoiled European at that! You should beat some sense into her head!'

I clenched my teeth to control my temper for I did not want to make a scene in front of Sarah. 'If you are so cold,' I said, 'then you should put your coat on. I think we have clearly established we have no intention of breathing this filth all the way to Ankara.'

The bus driver turned round at this point.

'How do you know he has a coat?'

'Because I saw him take it off and put it up on the rack. Besides everybody has a coat in winter.' I really wanted to laugh now at the absurdity of this conversation. I could not imagine this scene being repeated in any other civilised country that I had lived in. 'What is this, Disneyland?' I said to the man opposite, now crouching in his seat.

The man complained again, 'I myself do not smoke but still I don't wish to freeze to death.'

He then sprang out of his seat and leaning across Sarah pulled the window shut. The arrogance of this act pushed my temper beyond the limits of my control and I leaped up out of my seat shouting, 'How dare you behave so rudely to this lady? She is with me. You had no right to do that.' He stepped towards me, his eyes flashing. The men around us leaned forward with interest at the prospect of a fight but Sarah touched me on the sleeve and said, 'Celik, ignore him. The man is behaving like a child and not worth losing your dignity over.'

I saw immediately that she was right and I sat down, wiped the sweat off my brow with my handkerchief and whispered, 'I'm glad you said that, otherwise I would have had no option but to kill him.'

'You're not serious?' she looked at me in disbelief.

'These people are Anatolian bears,' I said, still shaking, 'if a man insults the woman of another man then the punishment is death. It would be dishonourable not to kill him.'

She opened her eyes wide. 'The woman of... what century are we in?'

'Are you not my woman after what we have been doing the last few days?' I joked.

Sarah scowled and whispered, 'If you think that then you are no better than these... Anatolian bears as you call them!' Her voice was low but angry and I was so mortified I wanted to go down on my knees to beg her forgiveness. But a few men around us had heard the tone of her voice and seen the expression on her face and they were nudging each other and looking at me with great interest and amusement. I could hardly believe what I did but I leaned across Sarah and closed the window with a bang. The men nodded approvingly and murmured to each other. Sarah did not look at me but calmly opened the window again, then looking directly at all those men and ignoring me completely, she said, very slowly, in a voice as cold as an ice-pick, 'The window stays open!'

No one moved after that. Not one in that whole bus load of men. I sat absolutely still while wave after wave of emotion hit me. First fury at my public humiliation, then astonishment that she had dared to behave like that, then disgust at my own idiot behaviour and pride in Sarah's cool control of the situation, and finally horror at the image of myself as an uncouth bear in her eyes. As I felt myself surfacing from this maelstrom I became intensely aware of Sarah sitting close beside me, her face slightly flushed, the faint musky scent of her skin. I recalled the scene in the baths at Bursa, saw again her creamy breasts and my tongue circling her nipples. These roughnecks would never in their wildest dreams believe what we had been doing. At whatever cost to my pride and dignity I could not endure making her angry with me. I leaned towards her ear and whispered. 'I'm sorry. Please forgive me.'

After a minute she looked sideways at me and said, 'It's okay.'

I breathed out in relief and took her hand in mine. I closed my eyes and occupied myself with mental images of her naked body until we arrived in Ankara, promising myself that as soon as we got to the flat and locked the door behind us I would put into practice everything I was imagining now.

I had arranged accommodation in an ICS flat and we used this as our base. We spent all next day in Ankara, shopping and getting train tickets for Polatli. We visited the museum of Anatolian civilisations and wandered round the higgledy-piggledy lanes in the old part of the city. Children played here, flying their kites, and old veiled women carried large bundles on their heads up the steep slopes of ancient cobbled streets. It was hard to believe we were in the twentieth century.

We went to Ataturk's mausoleum at Sarah's request. As it came into view I said, 'It's a blot on the landscape. No person should have such wealth and glory dedicated to his corpse.'

'No,' she said, 'it's right that it should dominate the capital he created.'

I stopped and put my hands on her shoulders. 'Do you know what he was? An illiterate peasant.'

She took her guidebook out of her bag and opened it. 'It says here that when he was born, Turkey was already known throughout the world as the sick man of Europe. The final collapse under Abdul Hamid was already on its way.'

I snatched the book out of her hand, tore it in two and dropped the pieces into a rubbish bin.

'Bullshit! Abdul Hamid tried to restore the greatness of the Ottomans but there were too many western influences by then.'

Sarah strode over to the bin, retrieved the torn book and, glaring at me, said, 'How dare you be so bloody arrogant as to make arbitrary decisions over what I read for Christ's sake!'

'I'm sorry,' I said.

'Ataturk didn't rise to power as an illiterate peasant, did he?' she reasoned, calming a little.

I sat on a low wall, watching a couple of elderly tourists taking pictures of the mausoleum. 'Okay. So he graduated from the War College in Istanbul.'

Sarah came and sat beside me fitting together the pages I had ripped and trying to read them. I turned away, irritated, but she ignored me and continued, 'It says here that Abdul Hamid was known as the Great Assassin because of his part in ordering the Armenian massacres.'

I turned to her and said in a raised voice, 'Propaganda! Ataturk became a member of a revolutionary society and he took part in the Young Turks military coup in 1908. When Abdul Hamid was deposed there was a lot of propaganda put out by the revolutionaries to justify what they had done.'

I realised the tone of my voice had attracted the attention of the tourists. They looked American with their expensive clothes and cameras. I lowered my voice. 'The ironic thing was that the leader of the Young Turks, Enver Bey – who, by the way, was the son of a woman who washed corpses – was far worse than Abdul Hamid. When World War I started he joined forces with Germany, an act which ended in the virtual destruction of our country...'

Sarah, oblivious of the curious gaze of the Americans, interrupted and said, 'But it was Ataturk who saved the country.'

I jumped off the wall and turned my back to the tourists, and put my arms around Sarah's waist. She was wearing jeans and a soft turquoise sweater. I wanted to run my hands over her breasts and bury my face in them and I felt the now ever-present hardening in my loins.

'Why did we waste time coming here,' I asked, 'let's go home. I can think of much more interesting places to explore.'

'Listen,' she persisted and read aloud, '...if Ataturk had not been able to persuade the Turks to fight the War of Independence, Turkey would not be here today. The Treaty of Sevres would have seen to that. It was because of Ataturk's efforts that the Treaty of Lausanne replaced it and Turkey got back its independence.'

I groaned and walked a few paces away from her. 'Ataturk! Ataturk! Why are you so interested in Ataturk?'

She slid off the wall and ran to catch up with me. 'But when you think about the public support he had he might have become Caliph, or even Sultan.'

'Rubbish!'

'Why not? It's happened in other Moslem countries!'

I quickened my pace for I did not want to hear any more but she wouldn't shut up, 'You have to at least credit the man for putting his energies into dragging Turkey out of the middle ages.'

I stopped pacing and faced her again, 'You have accused me of being arrogant, but you are displaying the height of arrogance by equating civilisation with westernisation...'

'Think about the old ways Celik!' she sighed in exasperation. 'Does a civilised country educate only fifty percent of its population? Does it keep the other half veiled and secluded and subject to the laws of polygamy?'

I was so angry now I couldn't keep my voice down and I shouted, 'Are you saying it was civilised to abolish Koranic Law and replace it with codes of law taken from the Swiss Civil Code, ignoring the fact that the most sacred part of Islam is the law? Was it civilised that the new constitution eliminated every reference to Islam? Was it civilised to order soldiers to tear the veils off women until there were so many deaths when their husbands intervened that even Ataturk himself had to stop trying to enforce that one. Was it civilised to purify the language by replacing words which had been assimilated from other languages throughout centuries with those from Turkey's pre-Islamic past?' I stood still, red-faced, and almost crying.

'Can you imagine what would happen in your country if Latin was eliminated from the English language and replaced with Anglo-Saxon?'

She began, "Well if...'

I held up my hand, 'Please. No more,' and I put my arm around her shoulders and walked with her towards the entrance of the mausoleum breathing deeply to calm myself before I could continue.

'He abolished religious education in schools and closed the Dervish sects. He told the country that western music was better than Turkish music. He encouraged painting and sculpture which is forbidden by the Koran and replaced Friday as the day of rest with Sunday.' Again I stopped and faced her, 'Can't you see now that his reforms tore the heart out of this country.'

She didn't reply and I said quietly, 'I do not wish to go inside. Please go in yourself and I'll wait for you out here.'

She opened her mouth to say something, then changed her mind and walked away. I leaned back on one of the statues and waited for her, watching other groups come and go, posing with the guards for their photographs. I could not understand her refusal to listen to my counter-arguments to the propaganda she accepted as truth. I searched my memory for information I had picked up about New Zealand society from National Geographic magazines.

After ten minutes or so Sarah came out again. I noticed one of the guards watching her as she walked towards me. She noticed too and smiled at him. He was delighted and smiled back.

As she reached me I pointed to the statues, 'Do you know what these symbolise? Liberty and peace.' I laughed bitterly. 'Liberty and peace? If that smirking moron in uniform understood English, I would be sent back to prison for what I have just said in this place.'

She touched my arm. 'I'm sorry. Of course you're right. It was arrogance on my part to assume a position on something that has affected your whole life. We should drop the whole subject.'

I couldn't believe what I was hearing and immediately I felt like a child having a tantrum because a toy had been withheld and, suddenly realising that the desired object was actually being proffered, felt foolish and guilty.

'It's just that I thought you would have understood my feelings after what I had told you about my imprisonment,' I tailed off.

'I know that you suffered in a way I can barely even imagine, but I thought that wouldn't preclude us from discussing the issues. I was absolutely wrong about that. I was trying to understand how this society works. Obviously I'm never going to and it was presumptuous of me to try.'

Now my anger and frustration were completely swept away and I took both her hands in mine, explaining, 'Your perspective comes from the fact that you are a descendent from colonists who believed the indigenous people of your country were savages who would benefit by being assimilated into western culture. And what happened? You now have a displaced native population who have lost their language. If you have no language how can you have a culture? When is your government going to admit its crime and give back to those people what it stole from them?'

'It's not as simple as that,' she said. 'There are other considerations...'

'What other considerations?' I interrupted. 'The matter of theft is simple enough, isn't it?'

'Oh come on!' She snatched her hands out of mine and stood back a few paces. 'There are houses, schools and hospitals on land that originally belonged to the Maori. It can't simply be handed back to them. How many countries can you name that don't possess land that was originally stolen from someone else? How far back in history is it permissible to go? What's magical about a hundred and fifty years? Why not three hundred? A thousand? You know absolutely nothing about the situation in New Zealand. You've never even been there!'

'Exactly,' I said softly.

She frowned, 'What?'

'Let's look at what you've just said in the context that your opinions on Turkey are formed by what you have read from the outside of a civilisation that has no common roots with your own. Mine have been formed from the inside, and through living in hell for a time.'

She opened her mouth as though she was going to continue arguing, then suddenly, she looked unsure of herself. 'Well... maybe you're right. Maybe I'm not the right person to do these articles.'

I closed my eyes in relief. For the first time I detected a glimmer of hope that I might be able to persuade her to leave the past where it belonged. I put my arm around her shoulders, 'Let's go home.'

Later that evening while Sarah was taking a shower I started preparing a salad in the kitchen. The juicy aroma of the steak in the grill made me feel very hungry. We would have a delicious meal then spend the rest of the evening making love. I thought of Sarah's face when she expressed doubt about her ability to do the articles. Did this mean she would really withdraw? Did I have the right to persuade or even insist that she withdraw? Would she hate me if I did? I was going over all these implications when the phone rang. A woman's voice asked for Sarah, in English. I called her and she came out of the shower draped in towels and smelling so sweet I wanted to pull off the towels and hold her close and breathe her into my body. I gave her the phone, however, and went back to the kitchen.

I heard her give an excited shriek. 'Alexandra!...'

I rolled my eyes. Sarah had given this woman our phone number? What on earth for? I chopped the lettuce with greater vigour. The fact that I was contemplating persuading Sarah to give up working on the articles caused me some guilt. I knew how much it meant to her to do them and also how much her future prospects depended on them, but on the other hand she should definitely consider my feelings first. If we were to have a future together she would not be able to travel much in any case, because she would have other responsibilities, especially when we had children, although naturally, I would take her with me, whenever possible, on any interesting assignments I went on. This would satisfy her curiosity about other cultures and she could use her experience as a journalist to write freelance, thus freeing her from the stress of a high-pressure job. I was feeling more relieved now that I had worked this out and I started arranging in my head the correct language for explaining it all to Sarah. I heard the click of the phone. I expected her to come straight into the kitchen to report on the conversation but she went back into the shower and didn't reappear until she was dressed.

I set the table and poured some coca-cola in my glass. I went to get the bottle of wine that Sarah had bought to pour some for her, but then I decided to give her coca-cola instead. Actually I did not like her drinking alcohol, even though she limited it to the occasional glass of wine at dinner, but this was something she would have to give up in the future anyway. In respect to my feelings she would not regard it as a great sacrifice. I was pouring the coke in her glass when she appeared at the door.

'Not for me thanks,' she said, and picked up the wine bottle and a clean glass from the dresser.

'Think of the brain cells you are destroying,' I joked, trying to hide my annoyance.

'Maybe, but what do you think you're destroying with that junk?'

There was a sharp edge in her voice so I said lightly, 'Okay, whatever you like. I hope you enjoy the steak I've cooked.'

'That was Alexandra,' she said, pouring out some wine and sipping it.

'She's made her decision about accepting the kibbutzim project.'

I nodded, though I wasn't in the slightest bit interested in this woman's plans.

'The writer they had lined up to go with her has changed her mind.' She paused, 'and so she's going to suggest me as a substitute. She wanted to check it out with me first.'

'And...?' I said cautiously.

She sighed, 'Well, it's all up in the air at present. A lot depends on how well I complete this project.'

I stared at her. I had been very hungry a minute ago, but now my appetite completely vanished.

She sat down at the table with her hands cupping her chin. 'I am really very scared about doing these articles. It was a big act of faith that I was asked to take on this project. There are other people on the staff with far more experience than me. In some ways it would be easier to find an excuse to back out than to risk failing, and just continue at the level I'm at now.'

I closed my eyes. Of all the times that woman had to choose to phone! I wanted to reassure Sarah that none of these fears of hers were of the slightest importance. I sensed, however, that, in light of what she had just said, this would be disastrous. I stretched out my hand and stroked her arm.

'Do whatever you want,' I said.

CHAPTER ◆ TWENTY TWO

Next morning we took the 8.00 am train to Polatli and from there we made our way by taxi to Gordion.

I told Sarah, 'When I was a child my father told me so many stories about this place, about King Midas and Alexander the Great.'

'Alexandra's parents met at Gordion,' she said, 'when they were archaeological assistants working on excavations there. She was conceived during a night of passion in the ruins of the temple of Cybele. That's why they called her Alexandra.' She grinned, 'Isn't that lovely?'

I had to admit it was.

We found the museum locked and wandered around to see if we could see anyone. The caretaker was tending his vegetable garden and hurried across when he saw us and unlocked the museum. It contained only a few pieces taken from the excavations of the tumuli. He told me the best pieces had gone to the Museum of Anatolian Civilisations in Ankara. He said it used to have more interesting pieces but some gypsies had stolen them to sell to tourists. After that, all the most valuable relics were moved to Ankara. He led the way across the road and along a tunnel into the largest tumulus. Inside, the tomb was empty.

'When it was excavated in the 1950s,' he said, 'The skeleton of a short man about sixty years old – believed to be King Midas – was found lying on a table. I was just a child then but I remember the excitement when the American archaeologists came.'

I told him we had seen the decorated wooden screens and bronze grave offerings in the museum in Ankara.

'You were so lucky to have actually seen the excavations,' said Sarah. 'You saw history uncovered.'

I translated this for him and he smiled at her enthusiasm. 'We came every day to watch. The Americans gave us sweets. When the skeleton was brought out one of them who could speak Turkish said to me, "Imagine the scenes of mourning and ceremony when the king's body was brought here to be buried." I tried to imagine it. I used to play games here with my friends about the battle.'

Outside in the sunshine again Sarah said, 'It's hard to believe, looking at this bare landscape, that this was once a flourishing empire, the origin of all those stories about Midas turning everything into gold.'

After I translated this for the guide he shrugged. 'Empires have risen and fallen here for centuries. Now, thanks to Ataturk we have finished with such foolishness called Empire.'

'What did he say?' Sarah asked.

'He said he was glad to have the opportunity to show us around,' I said.

We said goodbye to our guide and got back in the taxi and drove to the city mound. As we climbed up the hill to the ruins of ancient Gordion I said, 'It was funny listening to him telling us about his make-believe games. It reminded me that when I was a child I used to pretend to be Sultan Mehmet riding on his white horse, bringing victory and glory to the Empire.'

Sarah laughed. 'I wonder if the village children acted out the oracle predicting that a man would come to this place in a donkey and cart to rule over the Phrygians? Can't you just see a little ragamuffin Gordius dedicating his wagon to Cybele? What a wonderful drama for children. And they'd know it was real and they were standing on the very soil where those events took place.'

'When I was a child,' I said, 'I auditioned for a part in a school play about the arrival of Alexander the Great to untie the knot that bound the yoke and shaft of Gordius's wagon together. I wasn't chosen and I was very envious of those children who were. It was my dream to play the part of such a great conqueror. Then the teacher told us that actually he hadn't untied the knot at all, he'd just sliced through the rope with his sword. When I heard that I felt he had cheated. That the prophesy hadn't in fact been fulfilled. Then I was glad I hadn't been picked for the play.'

Sarah looked at me and laughed again.

We wandered around looking at the piles of stones on the desolate mound and tried to identify them through the map in the guide book. We found the Temple of Cybele but the guide book informed us that the exact location of the wagon wasn't known, so we enjoyed ourselves speculating where it might have been. I picked a place and mimicked the actions of Alexander the Great drawing out his sword and slicing through the knot that bound the yoke and shaft.

Sarah sat down in the long grass in the temple ruins, laughing at my antics till the tears ran down her cheeks. The wind blew in my hair and the sun warmed my face as I ran about. I felt as free and happy as a child. I suddenly had to throw my arms in the air and sing at the top of my voice with the sheer joy of being alive at this moment and in this place with Sarah. I flung myself down on the grass behind her with my legs on either side of hers.

She wiped her eyes. 'I haven't laughed like this since the night of the magician! This is a kind of magic too! I still have to pinch myself from time to time to believe I'm really here.' She leaned her head back till her cheek was on my cheek. I leaned forward till I could see her face. She was gazing down the hill at the River Sakarya, just smiling and smiling.

'I should have done this when I was young, instead of getting married. But back then girls just didn't take themselves off to exotic lands the way they do now, with nothing but their backpacks and a sense of adventure. Alexandra was such an exception. I was so attracted to her bravery. I wish I could go back to being twenty, but with all the knowledge I have now. What a pity it all comes when we're getting old!'

'Old?' I protested.

'But I mean that by the time we have a head stuffed full of experience, adventure and wisdom, it's time to die, so what good does it do us? I wasted so many years trying to make myself into someone I'm not.'

'And who are you?' I joked.

'When I find out I'll let you know!' she laughed. 'But, on the other hand, if I hadn't married Dave, I wouldn't have my children, and I have no regrets about that.'

'No. They are beautiful boys,' I agreed.

'I just don't know why it took me so long to leave. At first I thought it was because I had never failed at anything in my life before. But of course it was much more than that. By leaving Dave I would have been doing exactly what I had always blamed my mother for doing and I couldn't admit that to myself let alone to her, because then I would have had to face a whole lot of other truths.'

'How did your parents meet?' I asked curiously.

'Dad was doing his master's degree in law in London and he met my mother at a university party. She had just begun her master's in literature. They fell in love, got married and continued studying together. Dad wanted mum to have children but she wanted to begin her Ph.D. Then dad got word from New Zealand that his father had seriously injured himself falling under his tractor wheel. They decided to go to New Zealand until he recovered and dad ran the farm with his younger brother Pat. The diagnosis was that grandad would be in a wheelchair for the rest of his life, but Pat could take over the farm. It's what he'd always wanted to do anyway. Two weeks before my parents were due to fly back to England Pat went to Timaru for the weekend with a few of his friends. They'd been drinking, went for a swim. Pat drowned.'

'Oh my God!' I murmured.

'Grandad was devastated. So dad decided he couldn't leave. At the same time mum found she was pregnant. So dad ran the farm, mum did the accounts. Grandad sat on the verandah all day in his wheelchair. As I grew up he found a new lease of life telling me stories.' She smiled and shook her head at the memory.

'I can just imagine you listening with wide open eyes and mouth, asking questions, questions, questions!'

'That's right,' she nodded. 'After school I used to make a pot of tea and carry it out with a plate of biscuits to where grandad was sitting. It was a ritual that went on until he died of a stroke, when I was about twelve. My mother assumed that dad would then sell the farm and we'd all go back to England. He refused on the grounds that his father would turn in his grave if he thought his precious farm was going to strangers. He thought mum would stay if he did. She thought I was growing up wild and she also felt her life had been put on hold long enough and that dad had reneged on his promise to return to England when his father died. She packed our bags and booked our plane tickets and we left. I didn't mind too much at the time because I couldn't bear seeing that empty wheelchair. And mum kept telling me that dad would join us when he came to his senses.'

'And did he?' I asked, privately thinking that surely no man would lower his pride to the point of running after a wife who'd so clearly deserted him. In fact, how was it possible for a man to have so little authority over his wife that he would allow her to humiliate him in this way? Naturally I did not voice these feelings to Sarah.

She shook her head. 'We went to live with her parents in Northumberland, the same house that she had grown up in. She stayed on in the house after they died and that's where she still lives. Even though she finally got the Ph.D she'd always wanted most of her relatives thought of her as a failure because she was divorced. They couldn't understand why she didn't want to get married again. She said they were just jealous because she had control of her life and they didn't.'

'That's how my relatives view my sister now,' I said. 'They don't care about her master's degree, her work as a lawyer. However, I was the one who encouraged her to remain single so she could have a good life. If she married a Turk she would just be a slave and all her education would count for nothing.'

'But you're a Turk!' Sarah laughed.

'I don't think of myself as a Turk,' I protested. 'I'm a citizen of the earth! But tell me what happened to your father.'

'A couple of years after we left he had a heart attack and died sitting in grandpa's wheelchair on the verandah. A neighbour found him a week later. I thought that was about the worst thing I had ever heard. I wondered why he had gone to sit in that chair. Had he been thinking of us? I had nightmares for weeks afterwards – thinking about him dying there all alone. When mum got the news she didn't cry, just went to her room and stayed there all day. I took a tray of food up to her in the evening. I opened her door and she was asleep on the bed. I put the tray on her bedside table and saw her wedding photos scattered on the bed. We found out later that dad had left instructions for the farm to be sold on his death and all the money to go to mum. She wouldn't touch it. She put it all in a trust account for me. When I returned to England after leaving Dave I asked her why she had burned my father's letters. She said she could not forgive him for choosing New Zealand over her.'

I stroked her neck. 'Well, the truth is painful. When I had to face the truth about my country it was the worst ordeal of my life. But it was also the catalyst for changing my life.'

'What do you mean?' she asked.

'I came here once before,' I answered, 'when I was a young officer. Listen to the wind, Sarah. Tell me what you hear.'

She put her head on one side, listening intently. She smiled, 'Midas has ass's ears?'

I shook my head and brought my lips close to her ear, 'The Republic's constitution is an ass's constitution.'

She laughed and whacked my shoulder so hard that I overbalanced and fell backwards. I lay there laughing and saw, by the side of my head, a tiny piece of pottery. The discovery thrilled me though I knew it had probably been tossed aside by the archaeologists because it was of no value. I picked it up and put it into my pocket as a memento of this day.

'From my father,' I said, 'I learned about a tribe of Turks, the Ottomans, who captured Constantinople in 1453 and founded an empire which ended only with the First World War. Now, as you can see for yourself, we have the shambles that we call the Republic.'

'The fate of empires, Celik?' Sarah murmured.

I shrugged, 'Perhaps. But I believe a more enduring kind of empire is possible.'

'That's probably what Alexander thought too,' said Sarah and lay back on the grass with her arms behind her head. She laughed. 'I wonder if we're lying in the same spot where Alexandra was conceived.'

The idea excited me. 'It's a good place to make a child, don't you think?'

'The best,' she answered dreamily.

Her eyes were closed so I couldn't read her expression. I lay on top of her. 'Is that a hint?' I asked, keeping my voice light so she could take it as a joke.

'No it isn't,' she laughed and pushed me off.

With our arms around each other's waists we left that ruined city with its ghosts and walked in the sunshine to the little tea house in the village. The owner of the tea house clapped his hand over his heart in greeting and brought us a glass of tea each. He proudly introduced us to the oldest man in the village who was ninety eight and sitting on a chair in the sun outside. This man tried to rise to greet Sarah but she protested that he remain seated and asked him questions about the excavations of the tumuli which I translated into Turkish. The men playing backgammon left their game and wandered over to listen. Some of them remembered the time the Americans came and described the scenes in the village. One of them laughed and said his mother had made him wear a blue bead around his neck while the

Americans were present but even so she was very nervous. Sarah wanted to know what this meant.

'Blue eyes are thought to be evil,' I said. 'Children wear a blue bead to protect them. It works on the basis that parts of a whole remain in contact so that the evil from blue eyes goes into the bead – like lightning into a conductor.' She was very interested in this and began to ask more questions but I noticed some of the men were staring at her in a way I didn't like and I started to lead her away.

CHAPTER
◆ TWENTY THREE

Next day we were picked up by the tour bus which was to take us into Cappadocia in Central Anatolia. The other members of the group were an elderly American couple and two middle-aged Italian couples. Our young Turkish guide eyed Sarah with interest as soon as we seated ourselves. I took her hand in mine and delighted in the look of amazement on the guide's face. I closed my eyes and thought over the magic of these last few weeks with a feeling of disbelief.

This was to be the final stage of our journey, culminating in the highlight of our time together, the witnessing of the Dervish rituals in Konya. After that, Sarah would fly back to England. I had pushed all thoughts of her departure out of my mind but now it registered like a dull ache in my gut. I searched for ways it might be possible to delay our separation. Suddenly, an idea occurred to me. It was so obvious I wondered why I hadn't thought of it before.

'Sarah,' I said, 'when you fly back to England I will go with you.'

She turned to me, surprised.

'I have to renew my passport sometime soon anyway and it cannot be done in Turkey without endless bureaucratic tangles, so I'll travel to London with you and renew it there, though I'll only be able to stay a few days.'

'Great!' she said. 'I wasn't looking forward to saying goodbye. I've been thinking how much I'm going to miss you.'

'Really?' I said, delighted.

'Of course! It's been a wonderful time for me. I'll never forget it. Maybe we should plan to spend a couple of weeks every year in some far-flung country. Would you like that?' She was smiling at me, her eyes bright and shining.

'Just a couple of weeks?' I said. 'I'm sure we can do better than that.

When I've worked it out I'll tell you.'

'Sounds intriguing!' she grinned.

I had not yet discussed the future with Sarah, partly because what we were sharing now was so incredible I wanted to preserve the illusion that it would never end. To discuss the future meant having to admit that for some time, at least, I would not see Sarah and that thought was unendurable. After we had seen the Dervishes – that would be the most appropriate time to discuss a future together.

As I pondered this it dawned on me that I should give Sarah a gift to mark that momentous occasion. It should be the most beautiful and significant gift imaginable to celebrate what we had shared and discovered together as well as the merging of our two lives for the future. But what kind of gift? As soon as I asked myself this question I knew the answer. The force with which this idea hit me was so powerful I almost cried out. Sarah herself had hinted at it when we lay together in the Temple of Cybele. Tears welled up in my eyes and I had to keep them tightly shut to conceal the evidence of my happiness. I longed to tell Sarah about this now and see the look of pure joy in her face, and it took enormous self-control not to. I contented myself thinking about the new heights our love-making would reach which would result in my seed fertilising Sarah's womb and creating our daughter. I did not know why I thought our child would be a girl but I knew, without a shadow of doubt, that this would be so. Our union would mark the formation of the New Empire and our child would be its inheritor.

I opened my eyes and stole a look at Sarah's face. I would tease her with a secret smile that I knew would torment her till she discovered its cause. I would keep on teasing her until her curiosity had become unbearable and thus heighten the intensity of her pleasure when I informed her of my decision. But she was not looking at me, she was smiling at the guide.

As we passed through the bleak, bare countryside on our way to Kayseri, I felt my happiness dissipating. The dun colour of the fields and squat houses was relieved only by a light scattering of snow and the occasional peasant riding on a donkey and cart along the muddy roads. A leaden sky leached through the bare branches of the straggly trees. This landscape oppressed me and I squeezed Sarah's hand so I could feel her warmth, and remind her I was there.

The Americans kept up a non-stop commentary, beginning by

introducing themselves and eliciting everyone's name. I couldn't remember the names for I was not interested. I hoped they were not going to hang around us at every stage of this trip. Sarah didn't seem to mind their intrusiveness, however, and joined in the general chatter until we arrived at the primitive little town which was our destination.

'A bit incongruous surely?' she laughed as we pulled up in front of a large modern hotel on the dirt road.

'So tourists can experience the real Turkey,' I replied, sarcastically, then immediately regretted it. Fortunately she didn't seem to notice.

After we had unpacked and settled ourselves in we gathered in the dining room for our evening meal of soup, cracked wheat, mutton and yoghurt. It was served to us by a waiter in a black and gold embroidered waistcoat.

The American woman said, 'It's real interesting trying the authentic food, isn't it? We always eat the local food wherever we go, don't we hon?'

'Sure do,' said her husband, 'only way to experience the real McCoy. 'Cept for the coffee. We always carry our own coffee-maker with us 'cos we can't stand the way other countries make coffee.'

I met Sarah's eyes and she struggled to keep a straight face. The American, a tiny man, even smaller than me, went on to tell us he had been an opera singer before he retired. His wife had been married to his best friend and when the friend lay dying he recommended his wife to the opera singer. Sarah was delighted with this story but I thought privately that I would not have disclosed such intimate information to strangers.

One of the Italian couples could speak no English and they kept to themselves. The other two appeared on edge with each other. The woman looked downcast during the American's conversation though her husband joined in the laughter, so I made a point of drawing her out. She told me they had been living in South Africa where she had been very happy, teaching in a school there and enjoying a high standard of living. Her husband had accepted a promotion which transferred him to Ankara and she had had to leave their daughter behind in Italy with her parents until they made a home. She did not like travelling, she said. She did not speak Turkish and she was lonely and homesick. I suggested ways in which she could help herself.

'For a start, you could learn Turkish and if you are unable to get a job you could spend some of your time learning the history and culture of our society.' I joked with her and spoke kindly and after a while she started to smile.

It occurred to me that Sarah might be resenting the length of time I had spent talking with this woman and I looked around anxiously. However, she was engrossed in the bare arm of the American who had rolled up his sleeve to show her a tattooed number. He was explaining that he had been imprisoned in Dachau in the war. Sarah asked him why he hadn't had the tattoo surgically removed after the war.

'It's not something I'm ashamed of,' he said. He went on to tell us in a matter-of-fact voice that he had been part of a team that decided each morning which prisoners were unfit to work and had to be killed.

I looked at the lump of mutton on the end of my fork and put it back on my plate. I heard Sarah say, 'Oh you poor man! That must have been an impossible task!'

He shook his head. 'Nope! I knew if I didn't do it I would die too. In that situation all you care about is surviving.'

Sarah asked him to tell her about his life in the camp. I couldn't believe this! The Italian couple who spoke no English excused themselves and left us. I didn't want to hear any more so I excused myself too. The others were so absorbed in the story that they didn't notice me leave the table. I waited for Sarah for two hours in our room then eventually went to bed and fell asleep, feeling irritated and depressed.

When I woke her the next morning with a breakfast tray of water-buffalo milk, cheese, bread and white butter, the first thing I said was, 'I don't want you to tell me what he said, okay?'

She blinked at me and yawned but to my relief she said, 'I wasn't going to. You haven't the stomach for that kind of thing.'

This was true but I thought it was a strange way of putting it and it sounded like a criticism. I decided not to say anything but my nerves were on edge as we prepared ourselves for our journey. This was probably because the decision I had made about our future was so momentous and I was carrying all the responsibility for it myself. Once I had shared it with Sarah, everything would be different. This thought consoled me a little.

The first stop was a Seljuk caravanserai. There were some local celebrations going on and children in traditional costume were performing a dance, watched by a crowd of on-lookers. Sarah moved closer to take photographs. Soon she was surrounded by a group of men directing her where to point her camera. One of them put his arm around her shoulders and they were saying, 'Address? Address?'

The women, huddled with the children away from the men looked on disapprovingly. I moved in to guide her away. 'They are being too familiar,' I said sharply.

'Nonsense, they were just being friendly.'

'Well, there is a fine line between friendly and familiar and they need no encouragement. These people are not sophisticated and they are not used to European women. They all think European women have no morals anyway so you have to be careful how you behave.'

Her lips tightened and with a sinking feeling in my stomach I thought we were going to have another argument, but to my surprise she just said, 'Okay,' and followed me back to the bus. I was still annoyed with her for putting herself in the situation that encouraged those men to touch her. My flesh crept at the thought. On the other hand, I reasoned, trying to be fair, as far as Sarah was concerned she was still a single woman. If I had told her what was going to happen at the end of this journey then definitely she would not have done such a thing. Therefore, even if she had behaved with indiscretion, the fault was mine. I breathed more freely, actually quite pleased with myself for taking this approach. I resolved to tell this to Sarah later, just as evidence that in fact I was more liberal in my attitudes than she sometimes gave me credit for.

As the bus approached Goreme Valley, a wonderful moonscape of eroded rocks in shades of amber, rose and slate came into view. Everyone on the bus exclaimed their pleasure at such a sight and Sarah leaned forward, her nose pressed up against the window. 'Oh look at that! Those witches' hats must be people's homes. They've even got vegetable gardens.'

In some places the erosion had formed pointed hat shapes, in others towering pillars with a cap of lava, looking like giant toadstools. 'The landscape looks like an artist's impression of fairyland,' said Sarah. I smiled, enjoying her excitement.

The guide, a handsome, lean man – I hated to admit this – in his early thirties, also noticed Sarah's enthusiasm and as we were stepping off the bus he told her unnecessarily, 'They're often called the Fairy Chimneys.' I felt irritated at his familiarity in talking to Sarah like this but I wandered away pretending to take photographs as I did not want Sarah to see my annoyance.

I could hear his voice droning on, '...in the first century the early

Christians searched for remote areas where they could be safe from the persecutions of the Romans. In Cappadocia they found the soft volcanic rock easy to carve into shelters and churches. Some, as you see, stand alone on high cliffs, others are grouped together.'

'Oh boy, did ya hear that, hon?' asked the American woman, behind me.

'So howdya get into them?' asked her husband.

'Only through a system of secret tunnels,' said the guide. 'Better keep in mind though that they were designed to trap intruders. Light and shadow create clever optical effects and the walls have hidden shafts. This entire region of five thousand square kilometres is honeycombed with cave churches, rock tombs and secret subterranean cities.'

Sarah of course was immensely interested in this information and asked question after question. The guide was delighted at the opportunity to show off his knowledge. After enduring his boastful meanderings for several minutes I put a stop to it by asking him to show us inside the cave churches.

While we examined the murals on the walls and ceilings I made sure I stood between Sarah and him so that his comments would have to be directed to me. 'Most of the murals, as you see, madame, have retained their vivid colours,' he said in my ear. The rest of the group came up behind us.

'Say, why have the eyes of the saints been gouged like that?'

'Yeah and the frescoes blackened and all?'

The guide somehow manoeuvred his way through this group and touched Sarah on the shoulder. He began in an anxious voice, 'Islam has a history of tolerance towards minority religions, madame, and I hope you don't think this appalling vandalism had been caused by religious prejudice.'

My annoyance was held in check by his words and I listened as he went on.

'It was the fault of uneducated villagers of the past – probably children – who did not realise the value of what they were destroying.' He shook his head sadly, 'Perhaps all this beautiful art will be lost to future generations.'

As I was thinking about that we heard the sound of buses pulling up and hoards of noisy children leaping out and running about, shouting. The guide said, 'They are from Tarsus. Today is a holiday for them.'

'Tarsus? You mean like in St Paul an' all? Ain't that something, hon?'

'Oh look at them,' laughed Sarah, 'they're so happy.'

As we made our way back to our bus the children surrounded us and begged us to dance with them. No one was willing but then a teenage boy pulled at Sarah's hands, 'Please madame. It is one of our customs.'

Before I could stop her she was part of their rapidly forming circle and singing and clapping and dancing with them. The rest of our group gathered to watch and started to clap too. The guide leaned back against the bus and lit a cigarette, watching Sarah with narrowed eyes. I felt physically sick to see her making such an exhibition of herself. It took all my self-control to prevent myself from going into the circle and pulling her away. All I could do was stand helplessly and watch. The guide looked at her legs as her dress flared above her knees and ran his tongue over his lips. I wanted to smash my fists into his eyes. My heart was thumping so hard against my ribs I thought my chest would burst. Then the dance was over. The children were thanking Sarah and waving to her as they ran off to explore the caves.

'Gee honey you looked great with those kids,' said the American. 'That sure was a nice thing to do. You made their day.' And everyone was laughing and agreeing.

Sarah was smiling broadly, face flushed, eyes sparkling. 'This would never have happened in England or New Zealand. Those children weren't in the least bit inhibited,' she said, slightly out of breath.

'Well, there must be times when even the English are uninhibited,' the guide said. The American burst out laughing. This was beyond endurance. I climbed into the bus so I could not hear their rude jokes. I busied myself with taking off my coat and folding it up and putting it into the rack so that no one would see the tears of anger in my eyes.

I sat back in my seat and looked out of the window. Sarah was too busy chatting to the others to notice anything amiss and to save my dignity I pretended to doze. By the time we reached Derinkuyu, a little village on the edge of Goreme, I had at least recovered enough to make a pretence of grace.

The American announced to everyone in a loud, delighted voice, 'All these villages have their mud houses, their peasants in floral baggies and headscarves, their donkeys wandering along the roads. Rustic simplicity, huh? But have ya'll noticed that every house has got a television aerial?'

The others murmured in surprise as if they hadn't noticed but were glad he had pointed it out. I gritted my teeth wondering how much longer I was going to be able to stand this. As we clambered off the bus, the guide reached out his hand to Sarah's elbow to steady her, then helped the elderly American woman off. She leaned across to Sarah and said in a loud whisper, 'Bit of a hunk, huh?' To my immense annoyance, Sarah laughed. Why? She should have either refuted this lascivious remark or ignored it altogether. Of course I realised she was a westerner, but still she should have adapted by now to the customs of this country, and particularly to my own feelings. I should have to discuss this very seriously with her when I had an opportunity.

The guide was telling everyone with an air of satisfaction, 'You are all thinking this is just another Turkish village, eh?' He beamed. 'But you are wrong! In 1963 an underground city was found here.'

'So how come it took ya'll so long to find it?' guffawed the American.

The guide smiled politely. 'The Anatolian villages were very isolated until recent times and that is why the existence of these cities was not generally known, although there are old men here who say they have walked from one city to the other through subterranean tunnels. The villagers have always known about them.'

He stood back to let us climb down the concrete steps which led to the entrance of the city. A labyrinth of corridors branched off in every direction.

'Each city covers an area of four kilometres and they were capable of sheltering twenty thousand people for up to a year. They belong to a network of over four hundred such settlements in the area which form a circle around Derinkuyu, all of which were at one time connected by long tunnels,' he informed us. 'In each unit there were living rooms, with niches for oil candles, bedrooms, storage areas. There were places for pressing grapes, channels for collecting the juices and vats for wine making...'

To get to each of the twelve levels we had to creep doubled up through narrow twisting tunnels. I made sure I was right behind Sarah the whole time. There was no room for more than one person and it was impossible to turn back, as the American woman found out when she complained of claustrophobia and tried to retrace her steps.

Her husband called out, 'Just keep right on going hon. No one's going to stab you through these slits in the walls, like those poor bastards who had to live here!'

His remark struck me as tasteless, but Sarah heard him and laughed. I could not understand why she found him so amusing. Then she said to that American woman, 'Look, I'm right behind you. Don't worry, there's plenty of room to move forward. You won't get stuck. See, I can move my hands over the walls on either side of you.'

The woman gave a few muffled snorts. She was not too happy, but at least she continued moving forward now. We came to a section shaped like a cross and the guide explained that it had probably been used as a church by the Christians. Next to it was a large room which he said had been used as a prison and he pointed out the three pillars supporting the roof and the chain holds in each of them. Sarah shivered. The guide noticed this and he added, in a reassuring voice, 'However, they pre-date the Christian era – possibly they're of Hittite origin.'

I whispered to her sarcastically, 'Why are you shivering? You love this stuff. You would have reserved a front seat by the guillotine if you'd been there, just so you could write about it.' As soon as these words were out of my mouth I was appalled that I had said them.

But Sarah just laughed and said, 'You're probably right!'

I felt dizzy with confusion. Walking through that labyrinth of passages I began to feel increasingly disorientated.

To my immense relief we finally emerged into sunlight, Sarah asked me, 'But why would people in the second millennium, need to build a network of secret subterranean cities?'

I shrugged, still annoyed with her and angry with myself. The guide, who had managed to get himself right behind us again, replied, 'No one knows, madame. They were used by different people for different purposes over the centuries. Their identity and purpose will remain one of life's great mysteries.'

I walked away, leaving Sarah to talk to him if that was what she wanted, for I had run out of patience. I should, of course, have slapped her face right there but that was not my nature. Nonetheless, she was pushing me very close to the limit of my endurance. She thanked him for giving her so much of his time and then she came over to where I was standing examining my camera.

She slipped her hand into mine. 'I knew what you were thinking and feeling in that place,' she said.

I closed my eyes in embarrassment but she was saying, 'You like to pretend that you are aloof from all this but I could see from your face that you were as awed as I was.'

I couldn't believe I was hearing this and I struggled for a moment about whether or not to disillusion her. Then, from the corner of my eyes I saw the guide watching us. I bent forward and kissed Sarah on the lips. I saw his eyes widen. Encouraged by this I put my arm around her waist and as we walked past him I slid my hand over her buttocks. Let him be in no doubt!

That evening as we walked into the hotel restaurant for dinner, the American, who was already seated at the table, looked up at Sarah and said, 'You know, honey, you and Julie Andrews have a lot in common. You both look as if you'd just stepped out of the shower.'

I felt the muscles in my jaw tighten, but Sarah smiled at him and said, 'Why thank you. What a nice compliment.'

Nice compliment! I shook my head in disbelief. Well, he was old, but if he had been a younger man I would have smacked him across the face. We sat down and the waiter brought our meal which was fish tonight. I poked at it with my fork but, though it smelt delicious in its sauce of garlic and tomatoes, I did not feel hungry. The American leaned across the table to me.

'You're a lucky guy! How long have you two been married?'

I was too stunned to reply. Then I heard Sarah say, 'We aren't married, we are just travelling together.'

The American flushed and his mouth dropped open. 'Oh! I see! I'm sorry, you must excuse me. But you... you look kinda married.' He winced sharply as his wife gave him a kick under the table and she said quickly, 'You know, since I've been in Turkey I feel like I've been travelling through some kind of open-air museum. Do y'all feel the same? Did you know that St John wrote his gospels in Ephesus, which is the last home of the Virgin Mary? Father Christmas was born near the Taurus mountains. St Peter founded the first Christian church in Antioch. Abraham lived in east Anatolia before he went to Canaan. St Paul was born in Tarsus and it's where Anthony and Cleopatra met for the first time.' She sat back looking triumphant.

Her husband was still red-faced and rubbing his sore leg. I felt the colour rise in my own face. How could Sarah have made such a remark? Not married! When they obviously thought we were! How could she have done that? Did she have no sense of propriety? And what did she mean by 'just travelling together'?

'You're absolutely right,' I heard her reply. 'I don't ever want to forget this trip. I've learned so much. I can't wait to begin writing my articles.'

Then they all began talking over what they had seen and felt at the various places we had visited. Even the Italians were laughing and relaxed. I didn't belong here. After a few more minutes I could no longer stand being in the same room and I politely excused myself and left the table. As I went out the door I turned to see Sarah doubled up at some stupid joke. She didn't even notice me leaving. I sat in our dark room looking out the window at the snow falling onto the silent street. I covered my face with my hands and wept.

We woke early next day and showered and dressed quickly, for after breakfast we were to leave for Konya. I wanted to set the atmosphere for our visit there so I forced myself to joke and talk lightly with Sarah, never alluding to the previous evening. She didn't say much in reply but I told myself that she was never very lively first thing in the morning.

On the bus she was still quiet and preoccupied and did not join in the loud conversation of the others. I was glad about this, of course, but she gave only desultory answers to me too when I talked to her. I put up with this for a while and then I said in exasperation, 'Why don't you smile?'

'What?' She frowned.

'Are you upset with me?' I asked.

She looked surprised. 'No, of course not, why would I be?'

'You haven't smiled once this morning,' and to cheer her up I joked, 'a woman always looks more beautiful when she smiles.'

'Oh is that right?' she responded.

I ignored the totally unnecessary sarcasm in her voice and said, 'I wondered if you were annoyed with me for leaving you so early last night.'

She blinked at me and said, 'Not at all. You weren't interested in the conversation so why should you have stayed?'

'Well, what's wrong then? Why are you so quiet?'

'I'm just a bit tired, that's all. I got to bed late last night. Tell me about Konya.'

I wasn't convinced by this sudden change of topic but I decided not to pursue the matter. In any case I was happy to focus her attention on Konya. I began, 'When it became the capital it developed into one of the most important centres of culture in Anatolia. Under Sultan Alaedin Keykubat, it attracted scientists, scholars and philosophers, including Mevlana Celaeddin Rumi, whose book I gave you.' I realised the conversation of the others had ceased and they were all listening to me.

I stopped, disconcerted, but the American said, 'No, please go on. It's real interesting.'

I didn't especially want an audience but if they wanted to listen to this I couldn't actually stop them so I continued. They all interrupted me from time to time to ask questions and the journey passed quite quickly. Sarah, for once, did not ask any questions and I knew she was barely listening. I felt hurt and puzzled. As we entered the city of Konya I turned to look at her and saw her attention was caught by something outside the bus. I followed the direction of her gaze to where a woman was walking on the pavement with two small, blond-haired boys. They looked about the same age as Sarah's own children and that was obviously what she was thinking too. As we got off the bus I saw the woman point to the conical green-tiled dome of the tomb and say something to her boys in German.

We followed the family through the outer courtyard garden and past the fountain where pilgrims stood washing their feet. We paused at the entrance to the mausoleum and I read aloud the inscription over it. 'This tomb, this station, is the goal of the Dervish's pilgrimage. He who enters lacking leaves whole.'

A guide at the door politely asked us to remove our shoes. I explained to Sarah, 'Although it is no longer used as a mosque the mausoleum has priceless carpets covering the floors.'

As soon as we entered I sensed the change of atmosphere. Soft, haunting music from a reed flute filled the air. No one could fail to be moved by the melody. All my irritation and disappointment dissolved and I felt my heart lift in response. Pilgrims filed slowly passed the sarcophagi, the palms of their hands turned upward in prayer. The biggest sarcophagus was Mevlana's, covered with an embroidered green and gold cloth, with two enormous turbans on top. I whispered to Sarah, 'The sarcophagi are symbolic. According to Moslem burial tradition the body must be in direct contact with the earth.'

The German woman whispered to her sons and they nodded and stared. The smallest of them looked up to see Sarah watching him and he smiled at her. She smiled back.

As we examined the convent where the disciples of Mevlana used to perform their whirling dances and admired the musical instruments used by the sect and the beautifully illustrated copies of Mevlana's poems, I explained. 'The Mevlevi was one of the Turkish-Islamic mystic movements founded during the spread of Islam throughout the Turkish world. During six hundred years of Ottoman rule it was prominent in Turkish society. Mevlana devoted his life to the composition of poetry and ritual dance. The most important of his works is the Masnawi, which gave me such comfort when I was in prison.'

Sarah nodded, but in such a lack-lustre way that I whispered anxiously, 'Are you all right? You look pale.'

'A bit queasy. Probably the fish last night.' She squeezed my hand.

Of course! This explanation solved the mystery of her strange mood. I felt enormously relieved and at the same time annoyed with myself for my stupidity in not realising she was unwell. I determined to make it up to her later, as soon as I could talk to her in private.

On our way to the hall where we would see the dance we were almost crushed by the crowds of tourists all trying to cram past us. The German woman lifted the youngest of her sons in her arms. The older one started whimpering as he was squeezed in the crush of bodies. Sarah held out her arms to him. He hesitated for a moment then shyly reached out his arms to her. She lifted him up and his mother smiled her gratitude. I was touched by this gesture of Sarah's and patted her on the shoulder to let her know I approved, but she was too preoccupied with the child to notice. We found a seat and settled ourselves to wait. I touched Sarah's hand to let her know how much it meant to me to be watching this ritual with her. She didn't respond and I saw she was smiling at the little German boy on her knee. She sang a song to him, in German, with hand actions. He was delighted. Yes, I thought, deeply moved, she is a mother and she is missing her children.

The Dervishes filed barefooted into the room their arms crossed over their chests. They wore tall camel wool caps which symbolised their tombstones and black cloaks representing their graves. They stood with the toes of their right foot over the left and their heads to one side. Then the elders of the order entered and lastly the Sheyh.

Someone recited from the Koran and then music was played on the reed flute. They paraded around the hall three times. This, together with the four periods of turning during the dance, represented the seven stages of effort in a dervish's life.

The dervishes taking part in the dance, took off their black cloaks, symbolising their emergence from their tombs. Then they began turning to the rhythm of the music. They spun full circle and as they turned slowly around the hall, they spread out their arms with the palm of the right hand opened upwards and the palm of the left hand downwards – a bridge between the earthly and heavenly spheres.

The ceremony ended with a communal prayer and they all filed out of the hall leaving an awed silence behind.

As we emerged into the pale sunshine once more my heart was full. All my petty jealousies and anxieties had been washed away by the purity of the music and the sacred ritual. Sarah was still carrying the little boy. When she put him down his mother thanked her in German. Sarah replied in the same language. She bent down and gave the child a kiss on the cheek. He put his small arms around her neck and kissed her back. The family walked away, waving and smiling.

The spiritual importance of what we had witnessed together in the hall was the climax of our visit. This is what I had been waiting for since Sarah had arrived in Turkey. It was absolutely fitting that she had been involved with a child during the ritual. I believed that she felt so, too. I wanted to seal this day of celebration with words so profound neither of us would ever forget them.

I bought some roasted chestnuts from a street vendor and we sat under a shady tree to eat them. After a few minutes I asked her, 'Well, what do you think?'

'It was one of the most beautiful things I have ever seen,' she said.

Thrilled by her response I said softly, 'I saw your face when you were carrying the child. You were thinking of your sons, weren't you?'

She nodded. 'I've never been away from them for this length of time,'

I touched her cheek with my finger. 'Of course, it's only natural that you should feel that way. You love your children. You are a mother.'

She smiled and kissed my finger but didn't say anything. All my senses directed me that this was the moment to tell her. I should not put it off any longer. My heart beat fast as I put my hand under her chin and lifted her face so I could look directly into her eyes.

'Sarah, I have a lovely child. Let me give her to you.'

CHAPTER
• TWENTY FOUR

She took my hand off her chin and looked away, 'I think you already have.'

Her words fell like drops of spring rain on parched earth. I absorbed them through my skin, into my bloodstream, into my heartbeat. I opened my mouth, but I knew no language that was adequate. After a few attempts all I could manage was the most prosaic of clichés. 'You mean...?'

She nodded.

I grasped her hands. 'But that's wonderful! It's the most perfect thing that could have happened. It's what I want.'

She looked at me for a moment, then said quietly, 'But it's not what I want. Another child is the very last thing I want.'

Then, for the first time, I saw that she was not smiling. Her face was pale and tired and her lips had a blue tinge as though she were very cold. I took her face between my hands.

'No, no. You don't know what you're saying. You are shocked, that's all. Of course you will welcome this child. You are a woman. It's only natural that you should want this baby.'

'Why don't you listen to what I'm saying?' She stood up. 'I already have two children. I'm thirty six. I stayed in a bad marriage for years longer than I needed to because of my children.'

I stood up too and put my arm around her waist.

'Nothing you say will ever convince me that you don't want my child. You'll get used to the idea. For me it's not strange at all because that's what I wanted to happen. In any case it is not a question of whether you or I want or don't want it. It's God's will. Look on it as a gift from God.'

Her face flushed a dark red. 'I shouldn't have told you. I wasn't going to.

There's still a possibility that I'm mistaken.'

'What mistake?' I laughed. 'You either know or you don't know, surely?'

'My cycle has always been irregular so a late period is not especially unusual. But I was sick this morning. I thought it could have been the fish.'

'Fish? Nonsense!' I shook my head. 'If it was the fish the others in the group would have been sick too. You are going to bear my child, Sarah. This news couldn't have come at a better time for me.'

She started to say something but then we heard a shout, 'Hey c'mon hon, we're waitin' for y'all.' I looked around and there was the little American, hanging out of the bus window, waving at us.

Sarah started walking quickly towards the bus. The guide leaped onto the pavement and took her elbow to help her on. Even this action did not upset me now. I smiled at him, wanting to say, 'Yes, it's kind of you to help my pregnant wife on to the bus. Thank you.' A surprised expression flitted across his face as I nodded at him.

The rest of our group was already seated and talking over excitedly what they had seen. I gathered they were all impressed with the rituals and normally I would have joined in this conversation but now I wished we had the bus to ourselves. There were many things I needed to say to Sarah.

When we had settled ourselves she closed her eyes, saying she had a headache and wanted to sleep. I glanced around at the other passengers and saw the guide had positioned himself where he could watch Sarah. Yes, watch her all you wish, I thought. Imagine my lips on hers, my tongue in her mouth, my hands on her soft breasts, her legs clasped around my waist. Imagine my penis thrusting deep, deep, as she cries out in her passion, my seed spurting into her body. Imagine the sweet bud forming in her womb, growing in the warmth and darkness. Imagine Sarah's thighs wide apart as she pushes our child out of her body into the world. And I, not you, will be there to witness that day. The poor man caught my eye and looked quickly away. I closed my eyes still smiling widely.

On the journey back to Ankara a small bubble of joy began to swell in my soul until I could barely contain it. Sarah was going to have a child. My child. Our child. To my utter astonishment tears began to roll down my cheeks. I opened my eyes to look at Sarah, hoping she would see, but her eyes remained shut. I wiped my tears with my hand then settled back in my seat to dream. This child of ours, would it be a boy or a girl? A girl, yes, that's what I had decided. This girl would be the inheritor of an empire so unique, so perfect, that it was almost beyond imagining. At that moment I felt a sense of profound humility that I had been chosen by God to be the vehicle for bringing this child into the world. I thought over my whole life, all my past sufferings. Unworthy though I was, everything that had happened to me had been for this purpose. There was nothing random in the experiences that had been given to me to endure.

A baby. I tried to imagine what she would look like. Tiny, with golden hair and blue eyes. I saw myself holding her, stroking her soft cheek with one finger. This was too much. Too much! If I didn't tell the entire bus this news I would surely die of happiness.

I looked at Sarah again. Maybe she would not forgive me if I announced such a private matter in public. Okay, I could be patient. Soon we would tell the whole world.

We were the first to leave the tour bus which dropped us off at the door of our flat in Ankara. The Americans gave us their address and made us promise to visit them if we were ever in the USA. The two Italian couples wished us health and happiness. If only they knew, I thought! The guide brought our cases round to the front of the bus. Sarah thanked him for his kindness in answering her many questions.

'It was a wonderful trip and you were a wonderful guide,' she added, unnecessarily. I didn't mind. When we were married I would teach her the correct way to behave in my presence.

He bowed, 'Madame, it was a pleasure to be of assistance to such a beautiful, intelligent lady.' He avoided my eyes and got back on the bus. It accelerated away, everyone waving and calling goodbye. Then we were alone, standing on the pavement in the fading light. Our breath gathered in puffs in front of our mouths. The first pale stars blinked in a violet sky.

My hands shook as I unlocked the door and brought in our cases. The rush of warm air felt welcoming. I said, 'Do you want to go to a restaurant or shall we eat at home? I can quickly defrost a couple of steaks.'

'I'm not hungry. I've eaten too much on this trip already. A cup of coffee is all I need. But what about you?'

We were being polite with each other. This created a strained atmosphere and I didn't know what to do to relax it.

'Well,' I said, 'a cup of coffee will be enough for me too after that bus journey. I'll make it while you unpack your things and have a shower.'

As I carried the coffee into the living room she came out of the shower, wrapped in a red towelling robe that she had bought at the Bazaar but hadn't yet worn. She was winding a towel around her hair. I put the tray on the table in front of the sofa and poured the coffee into two cups. She sat down and I stirred sugar into her cup and handed it to her. She took a few sips. I sat next to her, breathing in her scented softness.

'I tell you I am completely renewed,' I said quietly. 'Completely in command of my dreams and hopes. Many things are worrying me but I know that I am under treatment by God and I shall emerge shining if I manage to be patient enough. None of your objections are valid in view of the importance of the Empire. Together we will lay the foundation stone for its emergence.'

'Celik...'

I reached out and touched her arm. 'I am not a fanatic. Nor a megalomaniac. Nor a fool. But I have a dream and it is shining. I will realise that dream. I was born for that. And you will eventually realise it is what you were born for too.'

She didn't speak for a long time. I listened to the clock ticking on the wall. I had never before noticed how loud it was. Then she said, quietly, 'When we were in the temple of Cybele I told you about my life with Dave. I thought you were listening. I thought you understood.'

'Of course I understood,' I answered. 'But what has that got to do with our life now?' I stood up and walked over to the window. The street lamps were glowing red. A woman was hurrying home laden with shopping bags. I felt the blood rush into my face and throb in my temples. I waited till I could trust myself to speak calmly then I turned to Sarah.

'We're talking about our child, my darling. Already I have made so many compromises for you. This is one issue I will not compromise on.'

She didn't answer but unwound the towel from her head. She picked up her brush from the table and began to untangle her wet hair.

'One more won't make any difference to you,' I pleaded. 'You are a natural mother. You can't say you are not interested in children.'

She brushed slowly and rhythmically.

'Of course I realise that it will cause complications in your life, but you are a woman and you should know how to deal with these things.'

She stared at me, her hand frozen in mid-air. I stared back at her. She was looking at me as though she didn't know who I was. I had never seen this expression on her face before and it frightened me. In desperation I said, 'Let's discuss names.' This was the kind of thing women loved, I knew that from my reading. 'We should discuss...'

She stood up. 'No Celik. I'm very tired. I don't want to discuss anything tonight.' She left the room.

I stared stupidly at the space she had vacated. The smell of her shampoo and soap still floated in the air. The clock ticked louder than ever. Slowly I walked over to the sofa and sat down. It was still warm. I leaned my head back till it rested in the place her head had lain. A blonde hair had fallen on the arm of the sofa. I picked it up and held it to the light. It shone brightly. I ran my finger down it, feeling its softness.

I awoke cold and stiff in the grey light of the morning. At first, I didn't know what I was doing there on the sofa. An unpleasant something hovered about at the edges of my mind and I didn't want to remember what it was. Then it crashed into my consciousness, forcing full awareness through my befuddled brain. I jumped up and threw back the curtains as if movement would ward off the pain in my chest. I rushed into the bathroom, turned on the shower and tore off my clothes. I let the steaming water run over my frozen limbs till I felt my blood flowing again.

When I walked into the kitchen Sarah was already there in her bathrobe, making breakfast. She had dark circles under her eyes and I guessed she hadn't slept. She looked up from the pan where she was frying tomatoes.

'It's nearly ready, make some coffee will you, while I get the plates out?'

'Sure,' I said and started clattering cups and spoons out of cupboards onto the bench.

We moved through our morning routine with excessive politeness. She offered to make me some toast, though she herself ate nothing. I refilled her cup. She mentioned it had been snowing during the night. I said that was usual for the time of year. She asked if I would wash up while she took a shower. I said of course.

I paid special attention to wiping down the benches and putting the crockery and cutlery away tidily. I was still putting things away when she came back into the kitchen. She said, 'How about a walk?'

'Great idea!' I said. 'We'll go round the walls of Topkapi.'

She stood in the doorway looking at me. I glanced at her.

'Right then' she said, 'I'll get my coat and scarf. It's been snowing during the night.'

I nodded. 'Yes, so you said.'

She gave a nervous laugh. 'Yes I did, didn't I.'

I said nothing. She went to get her coat.

From where we stood we could see over the Bosphorus to Scutari. A sharp wind bit my ears and Sarah saw me rub them. She pulled my scarf out of my coat and wrapped it around my head and over my ears. She left her warm hand on my cheek. 'Now you look like a Pasha,' she smiled.

I turned away quickly so she could not see my face. Then, without looking at her I said, 'I advertised in Time Out for a woman to have my child, but none were suitable.' I waited but she didn't say anything. 'So I hired a prostitute.'

I heard her sharp intake of breath. 'A prostitute?'

'Yes!' I turned round and looked her in the face. She was staring at me with wide eyes.

'You of all people, who have even had sex with a woman, have no right to judge me on that. No one has the right to judge me except God!'

Her face paled. 'I'm not judging you,' she said. 'It's none of my business. It's just so bloody sordid, that's all! You might have caught a disease.'

'Don't use that kind of language!' I shouted. 'It's demeaning for a woman to swear. I do not like to hear a woman swear.'

Her jaw dropped for a second, then she said very quietly, 'Well, that's just too fucking bad, isn't it?'

We glared at each other then I pushed my hands deep into my coat pockets and walked away from her, biting my tongue till I felt the salty rush of blood in my mouth. With my back to her I cried, 'Yes, it was bloody sordid! And it was your fault!'

'Mine?'

'Yes!' I turned round. 'If it hadn't been for you I would never have done it. You have only yourself to blame!'

She walked away from me now then suddenly stopped and turned back. 'You're responsible for your own behaviour, didn't anyone ever tell you that?'

'I am responsible to God!' I yelled, 'no one has the right to judge otherwise. If any number of unbelievers came up to me right now and accused me, I would spit in their faces!'

She walked right up to where I was standing. Her eyes were no longer blue. I had time only to register the impression of black ice. Before I knew what she was going to do she spat in my face. I drew back my hand and with all the force I could gather I hit her across the side of the head.

In the seconds that followed I don't know which of us was the more shocked. Her hand flew to her cheek and tears sprang into her eyes. I stopped breathing. If I could be allowed enough breath to beg her forgiveness I would have gladly died at that moment. But we just stood there, looking helplessly at each other, because there was no language left in the world to cover what we had done.

The call to prayer broke the silence. ALLAAHHH!!

We slept in separate beds on our last night together and the next day she helped me tidy the flat and throw out the remains of the food we had shared. We didn't speak much but this was not because we were especially tense, it was just that there was nothing left to say. That evening we flew to London.

After we buckled our seat belts up I told her where she could contact me if she missed her connection at Birmingham. She was going straight to Northumberland to stay with her mother who had been looking after the children. I was going to stay with my brother.

'Are you sure you do not want me to travel at least as far as Birmingham with you?' I asked. 'It's no trouble for me. And I would know you were safe.'

She shook her head.

'Ring me at Osman's then, as soon as you get to your mother's house?'

She hesitated.

'Please?'

'Okay.'

Then the plane was lifting in the air and Turkey was soon a miniature relief map. I turned to her and whispered, 'Don't kill my child.'

She looked out of the window.

We didn't speak again until we arrived at Heathrow and got caught up with reclaiming baggage and going through customs and catching a taxi to the station.

Sarah couldn't find an empty seat so we ran in opposite directions alongside the train to look for one. The porter threw her cases onto the train as it was about to leave. I turned to look for her but she had gone. Then her head appeared out of a window and she waved. I started to run towards her but the train was already moving off. I stood on the platform waving till it disappeared.

She phoned me, as she had promised, to say she had arrived safely.

I said, 'Please don't kill my child.'

She put the phone down.

A week later I wrote her a letter.

... I had a dream once. You were running away from me, in a line like this ______________. And then you disappeared, leaving only three pebbles, with a message, 'Say goodbye by phone.' I caught them in the air.

One night I couldn't sleep. I tossed and turned because I was so cold I thought I was back in Cappadocia. I put my arm out to reach Sarah's warm body and touched only a cold, empty sheet. I got up and found a pen and paper and began writing through the rest of the night.

The Empire is emerging.
An advanced communication network will make available the knowledge base to the user and inter-cultural communication and resource management will help the emergence of new cultures and the development of existing ones. The emergence of sharply defined cultures will create the foundation of meaningful interactions among cultures through the help of hi-tech communications which will reduce the functionality of the simple generalist universalist political institutions. Over-developed sub-structures communication, transportation and accommodation facilities, will release the boundaries of the individual's given location and environment. He will then have the mobility to identify himself in small cultural units within the safety of cultural interactions, without the paranoia of losing his identity.

The above is meaningless unless it is based on the difference in the creation of the devil, angels and human beings, and the distinction between the differentiation of human beings into nations and the confusion in their languages, starting in Babel.

CHAPTER
TWENTY FIVE

In February I left Turkey after more rows with the management who wanted me to stay there permanently. I went to London and lived with Osman while I tried unsuccessfully to find a job. Sarah had not contacted me since December after she had rung to say she was safely home, though I sent frequent letters to her house in Reading. Whenever I rang her home the answerphone took my calls and she did not return them. Then, at the end of March a letter arrived.

Dearest dearest Celik,

I'm leaving tomorrow for Israel with Alexandra and the boys. We'll be there for a year.

I'm sorry, I have no words to say goodbye.

Celik – it was the fish.

Sarah

As I read those lines the traffic and street noises receded and my ears filled with the sound of my heartbeat. It echoed like a clock in a deserted room. I stared at those words till they merged and blurred and the blank page I was gazing at was the emptiness in my soul. I was as cold as stone. I moved my lips to say, 'No child, no child, no child.' The sound was dull and heavy, like a hammer beating out the memory of Sarah's pale face as we sat eating chestnuts in the winter sunshine in Konya. But no one else suffered after eating the fish.

I drove myself half mad by going over these questions endlessly. I longed to confide in Osman but though I dearly loved and trusted my brother this was a subject I could never have brought up with him. He noticed of course and expressed his concern about the black shadows under my eyes. I told him it was through worry about my job situation.

'I think the best solution for you is to begin writing a book about the concepts we have been studying in the Koran. It's a project that has been too long delayed. Now you have no reason not to do it. I am earning enough to support us both while you write. Forget about looking for a job until you have finished the book.'

When he put it like that I could see that he was right. 'Thank you,' I said, 'that is what I shall do.'

Over the next few months I read and wrote every day. In the evenings Osman and I discussed the progress of the project. Those months were a time of great hardship for me but I survived by concentrating all my energy on my work so that at night I fell asleep exhausted. Osman cooked my meals and from time to time insisted we see a movie together or go to a concert. By the end of August the initial part was finished and I had used up the limited energy and resources at my disposal.

'To complete this project,' I said to Osman, 'I need at least five post-graduate students working for a year, mini-computers and half a million dollar funds.'

Osman smiled widely at this and suggested I write a paper based on my work so far and send a copy to the Islamic Centre of North America at Indianapolis. 'If they are interested they will be able to arrange university contacts for you.' He was hoping this would finally push me into beginning a Ph.D but as far as I was concerned it was the first step forward in the emergence of the Empire. We therefore, for different reasons, awaited the Indianapolis response in a state of excited anxiety.

At the end of September the Islamic Centre sent back my report with a thank-you note attached. They did not even comment on it. I couldn't believe this and said to Osman, 'What's wrong with those idiots? Are they blind that they can not see for themselves the importance of this work?'

'It's a setback,' Osman shrugged, 'but we can try another route. I have a friend in Los Angeles called Abdullah. He and his wife, Zubaida, are Americans who lived in England for seven years and converted to Islam. I will write to them and ask if they can help you. Abdullah is very involved in the Moslem Association there. If anyone can help you with contacts he is the one.'

I didn't particularly want to go to Los Angeles but when I received a letter from ICS a few days later, terminating my employment with them because I refused to accept another assignment in Turkey, I knew I had little choice.

CHAPTER
TWENTY SIX

At the end of October I was driving back to my apartment after posting hundreds of copies of my résumé. The car radio was on and Crystal Gayle was singing '...here I go once again with my suitcase in my hand...' I laughed and started humming the tune.

That night I dreamed I was standing in front of a huge building which was flying the flag of every nation in the world. I looked for the Turkish flag and found it was at half mast and torn. My suitcase felt very heavy and I moved my hand to adjust it. Then I saw it was not my suitcase I was carrying. It was my coffin. I awoke to the sound of the telephone bell.

'Celik? It's Abdul Siddiq here. My secretary gave me your message. I'm sorry for the delay in contacting you. I have been very busy this week.'

'Yes I understand. Alhamdulillah. I wanted to know did you receive my letter and report?'

'Yes Brother and I've already shown it to Khalid.'

'Did he like it?'

'Yes he did. He's very excited about it.'

'Really! Well, I am ready to discuss about it!'

'And someone is going to make an arrangement for one of the Sunday meetings of the computer society at the South Bay Mosque and you can present it then.'

'Really I would like to do it! I have prepared documents for a presentation...'

'All right. Now what I'm suggesting is that you come to one of the... either this Sunday or the next... and then we can discuss... I'll introduce you to Khizar. In fact I'll be introducing you to all kinds of people – other people who are on the Board. Do you know how to get to the Centre?'

'Yes, I have been once with Abdullah. Just give me the time and I will make the arrangements.'

'Right. I also believe your paper is worth publishing.'

'Is it? I am very happy to hear you say that, because you know this business – I mean the computer business and you know the Koran.'

'Yes indeed, and by the way, I think I know why they declined it at Indianapolis. I think if we correct that you'll reach a wider audience. It's not the subject matter you understand, it's the way it looks.'

'Yes I know. I just wanted to – strike – something! But I can do without it, definitely. Actually I have a programme already worked out.'

'If you come on Sunday you can get to know our speakers and programmes... how things are arranged. And you'll meet people and they'll get to know you. And if you attend a few Sundays, you can get the feel of things. We usually have a speaker from twenty to thirty minutes and ten minutes for questions. You are mainly doing research on the Koran, right?'

'Yes. I initiated it with my brother and we started with certain concepts, for example, millet. With our mini-computer we wanted to figure out the internal relation between those concepts. And we wanted to know if today Moslems are using some of those concepts in a similar way they are used in the Koran.'

'As you know millet means nation.'

'Well, when I explain it you'll see it doesn't mean nation.'

'Oh really?'

'We ourselves were shocked with our own ignorance – how we are using most of these concepts in the wrong way.'

'Oh... I see.'

'So it's a very important subject you see. I mean, my work is based on just a few concepts in the Koran. There are hundreds – thousands of others. But it is very helpful to work on that line. It gives us an object of comparison in our use of these concepts and it tells us if we are in harmony with the Koran or not. Then we are able to judge our use of language.'

'Celik, could you give this talk during Ramadan, Insha'allah?'

'But you see my visa expires in two months. I am looking for a job here and people are very interested in employing, me but as soon as they realise I am not an American citizen then they lose interest.'

'Oh, I see! I think it'll be a great shame not to see you stay here and get involved in our organisation. We need people like you. Look... can you make a point of giving your talk this Sunday? There will be many people there who may be able to help you. And bring copies of your résumé. I will introduce you to all those people and Insha'allah, something will be done.'

After this conversation I could hardly contain my impatience till the evening I was to give my talk. At last it came and I was introduced to the forty odd people in the hall by Abdul Siddiq. He told everyone I was looking for a job and if they had any vacancies in their companies they should see me afterwards. He handed out copies of my résumé to several people.

I talked for thirty minutes. Originally ten minutes had been allotted for questions at the end but I was worried that this would not be enough time to cover all the inquiries in sufficient detail so I had asked for an extra five minutes. This was the first time I had spoken in public about my work and although my voice shook a little at the beginning, my nervousness soon evaporated and I spoke enthusiastically and authoritatively. When I finished I closed my notes, stepped back from the lectern and waited. And waited. Then someone coughed, a chair scraped, feet shuffled. Abdul stood up and thanked me for my time and everyone clapped politely. Then there was a general scuffling of chairs and coughing and a buzz of conversation as people got up and moved around, greeting their friends. I passed my hand over my forehead to wipe off the perspiration, and, sick with frustration, I began to make my way towards the door.

I heard a voice call my name. I turned and saw Abdul with a tall middle-aged man walking towards me.

'Celik, this is Fikri Nassef. He comes from Egypt and owns a small computer company in Los Angeles with a branch in Saudi Arabia. I have explained to him something about your situation.'

Nassef stretched out his big hand to shake mine and said, 'Please don't be despondent about the lack of questions. What you are doing is incomprehensible to the man-in-the-street. That is why I myself did not ask you to explain the background to your research in front of those people.'

The conviction with which he said this took the edge off my despair.

'I know that,' I replied, 'and it does not matter because the man-in-the-street is not responsible for government and change in society. Even if I reach just a few people who are in a position to effect change, then my work will have been worthwhile.'

He nodded vigorously and threw his hands in the air. 'Here in America we have the most educated group of Moslems in the world. We lack nothing except faith. Instead of using our wealth and talent to establish an Islamic society we live in a way in which we compromise our main duty – to lead the world and rule by Islam. We need skilled and dedicated people like you to help us develop an Islamic movement. That was the purpose in establishing our computer society – to serve Allah and all of humanity according to the principles of Islam. Our immediate goal is to establish a bulletin board system to facilitate communication among Moslem communities in the United States.'

My mind started buzzing. A bulletin board... electronic catacombs...

'You should be directing this work to the universities,' Fikri was saying.

Despite my agitation I couldn't help smiling. 'So my brother keeps telling me.'

He continued. 'I have contacts who will be able to help you get it published and fund further research.'

'But if no one will offer him a job, then what can he do? Can you not do something yourself?'

Fikri glanced at my résumé. 'Come and see me in my office tomorrow. Ten o'clock?'

Abdul grinned widely and clapped me on the back. I thanked them both and left the meeting.

As soon as I closed the door and stepped out into the night, my knees gave way under me. I leaned against the wall for support, my eyes closed, listening to the roar of the traffic. I hardly dared let myself breathe. I looked at the stars in the sky and said aloud, 'And He it is who hath set for you the stars that ye may guide your course by them amid the darkness of the land and sea. We have detailed our revelations for a nation which has knowledge.'

I slowly headed towards my car, my footsteps echoing on the tarmac. I crossed the strip of grass and flower beds along the side of the car park fumbling for my keys. As soon as I pulled them out of my pocket they fell from my hands into a bush. I knelt down, scrabbling amongst the leaves, the pungent odour of damp vegetation in my nostrils. My fingers closed on cold metal and I dug a shallow bowl in the soil. I lowered my head and whispered into the hole, 'I mean to make a new nation.'

The words wrapped themselves around my ears like a warm scarf that kept out the cold, dark night. Tomorrow, the wind would carry them to every corner of the earth.